AUTHOR'S NOTE

All the Little Truths is a full-length standalone enemies-to-lovers high school romance intended for **MATURE** readers. Be aware that it contains triggers that some readers may find bothersome. I tried my very hardest to keep the characters as authentic as possible, as well as their feelings towards certain traumas. Please keep in mind while reading that everyone deals with trauma differently—and these characters are no different.

All the Little Truths is the third and final book in the English Prep series. Although it is a standalone with its own HEA, following Eric and Madeline, it is **highly** recommended to read book one, All the Little Lies, and book two, All the Little Secrets, before this one!

ALL THE
LITTLE TRUTHS

PROLOGUE

ERIC

The second I pulled myself from sleep, I knew something was off. Call it intuition, or maybe it was something else entirely, but I knew something wasn't right. My father's Rover was in the driveway, but he wasn't in the house. I continued to stare at my mom from their ajar bedroom door. She was curled up on her side as her chest rose and fell gracefully, a blanket draped over her body, with the sun barely making daybreak through the far window. My stomach clenched even tighter as I continued to stand there. I was fuming.

Fuck.

I'd already searched the house, high and low. My father was nowhere to be found. His phone was still laying on the bedside table, and the sheets were still crumpled on his side of the bed. I swallowed back a harsh growl as my knuckles almost popped from the grip I had on the door jamb.

I gave my mom one last look before I quickly jolted around and rushed down the steps.

I was finished with this shit.

My father was mistaken if he thought I was going to let this go. He was a cheating son of a bitch.

"It was a mistake. One your mother doesn't need to know about."

Yeah, fuck you, Dad.

Once you admit you've made a mistake, you usually stop making it.

Our front door flew open with my rage. My gaze skimmed over our driveway and the freshly cut green grass that stood between our house and the neighbor's. I recognized both cars parked out front, which only increased my anger. My heart thumped like a ticking time bomb. My hands shook with fury as I stomped my way over the dewy yard in my bare feet. Who needed shoes at a time like this? Fuck shoes. Goose-bumps clung to my bare chest. Who needed a shirt at a time like this? Fuck clothes.

I tried to take a steady breath to reel in my temper as I twisted the doorknob and pulled the door open. I was sure it was just my head fucking with me, but I swore I could smell the sex from where I was standing.

It had been forever since I'd stepped foot in this house. The smallest ache in my chest made itself known with forgotten memories—memories that I'd consistently pushed away for the last several years in order to stay sane. I shook my head as I rounded the steps and climbed them in sets of three. My eyes went directly to Madeline's bedroom door, but I quickly skimmed past it, annoyed that her face was floating around my brain so early in the morning. I tilted my head, the strands of my dark hair flinging down in my eyes as I began to listen.

The sour taste of vomit caused a rough swallow to bob down my throat.

It took no more than three seconds to get to the door that held sounds of skin against skin and high-pitched whimpers behind it. But from the second I tore open the door, everything went into slow-motion.

My heart banged against my ribcage so hard it hurt. It was the only sound I could hear. With every thrust of my father's bare fucking ass plowing into Madeline's mom's pussy, I felt my rage intensify to a scary high. I saw red. The entire room tinted to a hellish color as I barked out the words.

"Get. The. Fuck. Home."

"Eric!" My father paused, still plunged inside Madeline's mom. "What the hell? Get out of here!"

"I will rip you out of her fucking pussy myself if you don't do it yourself. You're disgusting."

"Brett." Madeline's mom wiggled underneath my father, and my head sliced to the left as I peeled my eyes away. I felt sick. And angry. Really fucking angry.

My poor mom.

The rustling of blankets and loud, exasperated sighs from my father had my voice climbing.

"I'm not hiding this shit anymore. This is taking it too far. Fucking the neighborhood slut—*again*—before crawling back in bed with your loving wife?" I met his dark stare head on, which was infuriating because I was certain my expression mirrored his: dark, furrowed brows; sharp, taut jawline; inky hair rustled at the top; steel-blue eyes armed and ready to attack. I was a carbon copy of him.

"I hate you. I hate you so *fucking* much. Mom deserves so much better than you."

I hadn't always hated my father. Up until recently, he was my idol: hard worker, charismatic in the way that others moved out of his way without even being asked, made my mother blush on occasion, intimidated those that needed to be put in their place. But then, I grew the fuck up and started putting two and two together.

My father looked away for a moment as Madeline's mom pulled the satin sheets up to her chest. I glared at her. She was just as much at fault as my father. It takes two to fuck. They were both fucking assholes.

"We will talk about this outside."

I scoffed, my sarcastic, dramatic laugh cutting through the air. "There's nothing to talk about. You're going to walk your sorry, pitiful ass home and tell Mom what a piece of shit you are."

My anger was still there, boiling underneath my skin, but I'd have been lying if I said there wasn't a moment of hesitation on my part as I saw my father's brow line deepen. Amongst the other attributes that I'd listed, he was also arrogant. My father didn't like to be embarrassed in front of others. I'd watched, in full disclosure, how intimidating he could get when threatened.

"You don't get to talk to me like that." He paused, zipping up his pants as I stood with my arms crossed over my chest. My jaw ticked as I held back a snarl. "I'm not telling your mother anything. This will only hurt her."

"I'll fucking tell her myself then, *pussy.*" The word spit out with so much distaste and raw anger that I caught the slight startle from Madeline's mom. I turned around, my arms hastily falling to my sides, ready to tear a path down the hallway on an unfortunate mission to break my own mother's heart, but I halted at the last second.

"Mom?" *Oh, fuck. Oh, fuck. Oh, fuck.*

Her glistening eyes softened for a moment as she sighed, looking up into my face. The anger floated away instantly. *Shit.* "Mom... I'm so—" Her hand was like a feather brushing my chest. "You, my sweet boy,"—tears continued to fill her big, chestnut-colored eyes—"are my greatest love."

"Heather." My father's voice was rushed, a gasp lodged in the back of his throat.

My mom's hand fell swiftly from my chest as she blinked away her tears. She turned around and walked back over to the stairs and descended them one by one. Her light-pink robe swayed as she continued down the stairway and all the way to the door, not looking back once.

A loud grumble tore from my father's throat as he rushed after her, calling out her name with every stride he took. I stood rigid in the same spot.

I knew I needed to move, especially before Madeline came out of her room with all the commotion. The last fucking thing I needed was to see her.

I dropped my gaze, wishing the anger would come back so I didn't feel the guilt of having kept the secret that my dad was a cheating bastard for so long, but it was there, and it was heavy. A held breath clamored from my mouth as I rubbed the gaping hole in my chest.

"Well, it's about time," a feminine voice floated around me as I reluctantly brought my chin up.

My eyes flicked over to her even though I begged myself not to look. *And fuck me.* Long, blonde hair fell down in waves over slender shoulders and a perky chest, leading down to too-short cotton shorts and bare feet with purple nail polish on the ends. I made myself stare at her legs instead of her face, because I couldn't fathom seeing her expression.

"What the fuck does that mean, Madeline?"

My chest heaved, and I was thankful because that meant my anger was coming back.

A light laugh tumbled out of her, and I couldn't help it. I zeroed right in on that pink, pouty mouth. "I mean, it took you long enough to catch on."

Did she...did she fucking know this whole time?

I crept along the hallway and made my way over to her,

finally locking onto those sky-blue eyes that held so much depth that she always tried to hide. For a moment, I saw the old Madeline. The one that once made me a get-well card when I'd caught the chicken pox in sixth grade. The one that dropped off freshly baked cookies when I'd first moved into the neighborhood. The one that made me a friendship bracelet one summer evening after we'd stayed up until midnight playing basketball in my driveway. I got a mere glimpse of the fresh-faced, sleepy-eyed, no make-up Madeline. The one I used to crave before everything changed. The fleeting, distant feeling of losing her flew through me, making me even angrier.

My head dropped into her personal space, and I softly pressed her back into the door jamb, angling her dainty chin up to meet my stare. *"You knew?"* I made no move to hide the utter disgust in my tone.

"Of course I knew. Your dad has been fucking my mom for years, Eric."

I didn't want to show my cards, but I couldn't help it. Every tight muscle along my face fell for a moment. *For years?*

Madeline's gaze bounced back and forth between mine, and for a second, she appeared remorseful.

If I wasn't so fucking pissed, I'd question the momentary dip in her bitchy, cold exterior. But I was pissed. *I was really fucking pissed.* My chest was touching hers, and I pushed away the burning in my core that told me I wasn't fooling the horny fuck inside of me before gritting out, "You fucking knew this whole time, and you didn't think to tell me? Or better yet..." I pressed even harder onto her, her back now smashed against the wood. Wisps of blonde hair flew out of her face, showing me those smooth, high cheekbones. Madeline was completely unreadable; she wore a mask at all times. It was hard to decipher what went through her head, but I could sense the discomfort I was inflicting on her. "Why didn't you tell your mom to close her fucking legs?" A sarcastic laugh erupted from her as I reached up and slowly moved a piece of her hair out of her face. Her breath hitched as her lips parted. "I guess the apple doesn't fall far from the tree, huh?"

Her lips slammed shut as she quickly turned her head to the side. I sighed angrily, the bare skin of my chest rubbing over her covered breasts. I hated that I could feel the tightening of her nipples through the thin cotton. I hated even more that I enjoyed it. "It's on now, Princess." I backed away slowly and saw her hands planted firmly on the wood behind her, white knuckles and all. "You think Christian was bad after he made a fool out of you at the party a couple of weeks ago?" I turned on my heel and shook my head, sparing her a wicked glance over my shoulder. "You just *fucking* wait."

She called after me as I descended the stairs, trying to catch my own breath. I wasn't sure if I was out of breath from feeling her body pressed along mine, or if it was from my anger, but either way, it felt like I'd just run three hundred suicides back to back on the football field.

"It's not my fault your dad is a fucking pig, Eric."

I paused, not turning back to look at those soul-sucking eyes of hers. "No, but you're a fucking bitch for not telling me. I'd always given you the benefit of the doubt, Madeline— old flames and all. But turns out, that nice girl I met years ago truly is gone."

She waited until I was almost to the door before shouting down the stairs, "I'm not afraid of your little games, Eric. Nor am I afraid of Christian's."

Before walking out the door, I huffed, "You should be."

CHAPTER ONE

MADELINE

THEY SAID high school was the best time of your life. That those memories of late-night football games underneath the lights, cheering along with your classmates, would be forever cherished. The pep rallies, pop-quizzes, prom dates, all of it. But I'm here to tell you that high school is *not* the best time of your life. It couldn't be, because if it was, then my future was looking very, *very* grim.

The sound from my alarm drove the knife in my back—that I, unfortunately, put there myself—in a little further, reminding me that I had to walk into that stupid, prestigious place in the next hour. Not only did I have to walk into English Prep with a target on my back, but I also had to do that on thirty seconds of sleep—*again.* The nerves in my stomach amplified as I scanned my phone for new messages, but I had zero. *Surprise, surprise.*

My finger swiped over the screen as I reread the unanswered texts I sent to Sky, my not so much friend but more so acquaintance that helped me in her own roundabout way.

Me: Sky, please text me back.

Me: I heard all about the races. I know shit hit the fan, but I'm desperate over here.

Me: I'll pay triple the price.

Me: I haven't slept in a week. At least direct me to someone else that can help me.

I clenched my phone in my hand, breathing deeply through my nose. If anyone were to read the messages on my phone, they'd think I was some crazed drug addict, but I wasn't. Sleeping pills weren't exactly a hot, new popular street drug, according to my knowledge. If I were to go to a doctor, I was sure they'd give me something, *legally*, to help aid sleep. But then they'd ask why I wasn't sleeping, and there was absolutely no way in hell I was going down that rabbit hole—I'd never be able to climb out.

I slowly sat up in bed, throwing my phone down to the bottom of my feet with frustration as I swung my legs over the side. Everything in my body hurt with an ache nestled inside each and every last muscle. I hadn't cheered in months, but it felt like I'd stunted for hours upon hours the night before. My head was ready to explode, and one look in the mirror had me cringing. The bags underneath my blue eyes were there, and they were *angry*. My skin even looked tired. *How was that possible?*

My plaid English Prep uniform laid on my desk in the far corner of my room, taunting me with another day of hell. Usually, I'd wear my devil horns with pride as I walked into school, taking in the dirty looks from my peers, but with three hours of sleep for the last week, I was feeling too weak to do much of anything. Even getting dressed was a hard task. I wanted to rip my blonde hair out instead of brushing it, but that seemed like more effort than even performing the task in the first place, so in the end, my light strands laid over the English Prep bulldog logo as I buttoned up my blazer.

Walking into school each day was a harsh dose of reality that I was forced to swallow with pride. On days like today, where I truly just did not have the energy to put up my malicious smile and flawless shield, I wanted to yell at the top of my lungs how sorry I was. How sorry I was that I treated people like they were *nothing*. How sorry I was that every friendship I ever had was forced and one-sided. How sorry I was that I pushed everyone away because I was too scared to let anyone in.

But I wouldn't say sorry. Not today, at least.

My teeth ground along one another as I stared at my computer chair pinned underneath my bedroom door. My heart thumped a little faster as I went over to my window, peering out the glass, trying to see if my mom's plaything was gone yet, but the only car I saw was the same silver Maserati parked along the side of the road as the night before.

I sighed, rolling my eyes.

Why was he still here? They were usually gone by now.

I bounced my attention back to the chair and then back to the green grass below my window. It'd been done before. I'd climbed out of my window in a poor attempt to avoid a slimy run-in with a man twice my age several times in the past. But that was with more energy. That was with more than five seconds of sleep.

I brought my thumb up to my mouth and nibbled as I decided my next course of action. I'd never seen this car before, so I wasn't sure what type of man my mom had decided to bring home. It was daylight, so it wasn't like I was going to find myself in the same situation as last time. This man probably wasn't going to pin me against our fridge and assault me with his mouth, or run his hands over my curves, making me panic. *But...*

A cold sweat started to trickle along my temples.

Nope. Not doing this again.

After moving the chair from underneath my door for when I got home after school, I dashed and grabbed my keys off my desk, along with my backpack, and threw my phone inside with the hopeful thought that Sky would finally text me back with a location to meet. I walked the few feet over to my window and opened it with barely any effort. I popped the screen out and pulled it inside before it fell to the ground below. I breathed in the fresh air for a moment to calm the erratic thoughts going through my head. *There. Just breathe.*

I pulled my hair to the side as I reminded myself that I'd flown through the air enough times in cheerleading that jumping a few yards below me from the gutter wasn't going to kill me. After all, I'd done it before, and I'd likely do it again.

As soon as my leg was hitched over the side, I pulled my slender body to the right and inched my other leg out. My arms were shaking, and my legs felt like actual lead hanging from the bottom part of my body, but nonetheless, I was able to grab onto the drainpipe beside me and hold on for dear life.

I breathed in and out through my nose a few times before I started to shimmy down, my plaid skirt hiking up so far that it was likely touching my bra. My heart halted as I heard a voice skim through my ears and land right inside the deepest part of my chest.

Eric.

The only boy I'd ever truly cared about. And unfortunately, I'd ruined us before I even knew what we were.

My mind scrambled to put up a good front. My heart rushed to put up that thick and heavy shield for protection. Every last nerve ending in my body screamed to act accordingly so he couldn't see how much I regretted becoming the person I was today. How much I regretted making him hate me.

Because let's be honest here, if there was one person on this earth that I didn't want hating me, it was him.

Eric's voice was just as dark and moody as he was. "Need some help, Maddie?"

I *hated* when he called me that. And he freaking knew it.

"Like you'd ever actually help me," I grunted out, preparing myself to jump down from the drainpipe before I landed in the rose bush below. I caught a brief glimpse of his dark hair as I glanced at the thorny bush underneath my dangling feet. The dark strands were pushed to the side in that lazy, I'm-sexy-as-fuck way that made girls sweat.

"You're right. I wouldn't help you even if it was the last thing left to do on this earth." His feet shuffled along the grass as he walked closer to the side of my house. The task to focus on the rust-colored brick in front of my face instead of meeting his eye was a lot harder than I'd ever admit out loud. He dragged his words out as he finally made his way over to me. "But I think I'll casually stand here and watch you fall. That sounds like a great way to start my day. So, please, carry on."

Before I pushed off the side and jumped to the right, missing the rose bush all together, I gathered the courage to meet his stare. Everything about me repelled him. His lip was lifted but not with that sexy, mischievous, bad-boy grin he gave to other girls. No, this was a snarl. A hateful gleam was evident in his steely glare as he waited for me to fall. His navy school blazer was pulled firmly over his shoulders, his arms lazily hanging by his sides with one foot kicked up behind him, resting on the bones of my house.

I wished, for a single moment, I could have gone back in time and made different decisions. Would we have ended up like this? Would I have ended up like this?

Probably not, no.

But now it was too late. There was too much *bad* associated with me. I wouldn't even know where to start if I ever decided to make amends.

My feet landed with a thud onto the soft ground, only a few feet away from him. No more than a second later, he pushed off the side of my house and started to walk away with his hands deep in his pockets. His locked jaw twitched at his temple as he shook his head.

"I guess you'll have to find another way to brighten your day, Eric." My voice came out strong, but on the inside, I was shaky and a little disappointed that he was walking away so soon.

He didn't even stop walking when he spoke, and I followed after him like a desperate fangirl. "I'm sure there will be another exciting English Prep episode at some point today, where you'll be the lead actress who has something terrible happen to her. I call it a feel-good show. It's my favorite one, actually." He finally paused and turned around to give me a smile that had my footsteps halting and my stomach dropping. It wasn't a genuine smile, of course not, but his perfectly plump lips split in two, and there was a tiny flicker of light inside of me. I straightened my shoulders, preparing for something hurtful to come out of his mouth. "What was it last week?" His head tilted, that dark hair falling into his eyes. "Fish in your locker?"

Ah, yes. How could I forget the fish in my locker? The smell was putrid, and I had to act like it didn't bother me at all. Otherwise, that'd put a crack in my I-don't-give-a-fuck-that-everyone-hates-me facade.

I pushed away the inklings of hurt that were trickling in and angled my chin up so I looked poised and unbothered. "Was it you?"

"Hmm?" he asked, raising his eyebrows.

A car drove down our quiet street, probably a neighbor on their way to work. Once I took my eyes off the black SUV, I met his cocky grin. "Was it you, Eric? Did you put the fish in my locker?" I crossed my arms, waiting patiently for his answer. "Is this all part of that lovely threat you gave me a few months ago?" I threw his words back at him. *It's on now, Princess.*

Almost every single day, something happened to me. Fish in locker? Check. Slashed tire in the parking lot? Check. Chair breaking in the cafeteria, sending me to my ass within a second? Check. The list went on and on. And again, I had no one to blame but myself. I had more enemies than Hitler.

Eric stood, twirling his keys in his hand over and over again as he stared at me. Shifting on my feet was absolutely not going to happen, but I wanted to squirm in every single way. When his dark eyes dipped down my body and back up again, my throat sealed shut.

I hated that he hated me.

I hated that I *cared* that he hated me.

Finally, he broke the silence. "I guess you'll never know. Maybe it was me. Maybe it wasn't." He shrugged nonchalantly, biting his lip in a way that made my heart light on fire.

Nothing like being mysterious.

Just then, I heard the latch of my front door opening, and I panicked out of instinct. My fingers clutched onto the straps of my backpack as my hair whipped around my face with the light breeze. I rushed past Eric, ignoring how good he smelled, and quickly climbed into my car without looking back. I was out of the driveway before he even made it to his Range Rover. I didn't give the man climbing down my porch stairs once single glance—too afraid he'd see me and get a nasty idea in his head that I was just like my mother.

I couldn't take another freaking nightmare roaming the halls at night and "accidentally" opening the *wrong* bedroom door. Being at English Prep was hell, but so was being at home.

CHAPTER TWO

ERIC

HEARING your own mother cry should be forbidden. It shouldn't exist. It was a conundrum. What was I supposed to do? Comfort her? Pretend I didn't hear her? She was in private, so the latter was probably the right choice, but something ignited inside me as I stood there listening. Every time I saw her sad eyes, I felt the burning. Like a fire that had just been put out, but the embers were still glowing. And every time I saw him—my father who I no longer addressed by name—I felt the flame catching. Like a fire roaring with anger.

"Mom?" I half whispered through her closed door. "I'm heading to school." Her sniffle was deafening as I rested my forehead along the wood.

"Okay, sweetie. I won't be home much this weekend. I picked up a few shifts at the hospital." The fake cheer in her voice did not go unnoticed, but I wasn't about to call her out on it. I understood her need to appear strong in front of me, but I wasn't nearly as dense as she thought. Apparently, the same went for my father. How he didn't think I'd eventually catch on to his behavior was beyond me.

"Alright, Mom. I'll see you Sunday, then. I love you."

She cleared her throat. "Love you, honey."

I sighed as I turned around and headed downstairs to my car, noticing all the housework that needed to be done. Dishes were piling up, and laundry was overflowing from the laundry room. The blanket on the couch was messy, likely because my mom had slept there the night before. She didn't think I'd noticed that she continued to sleep on the couch instead of her bed, but I did. I assumed it was because she didn't want to be anywhere that my father had been, even if he hadn't slept in their bed since she caught him fucking someone else, but it probably bothered her all the same. Just like it bothered me when I'd watch his name flash on my phone.

We'd talked a handful of times since I saw him railing Madeline's mom from behind, and each time, it ended the same: him threatening to cut me off and me hanging up on him.

Only, his last threat was no longer a threat. He had cut me off. He was still trying to make amends with my mom, but she cut him off in her own way. She went back to work, and she refused to take a single dime from him.

You could say our family dynamics were slightly complicated (read as: completely fucked up).

Before closing the front door, I made a promise to myself that I'd clean up the house before going out tonight.

Just as I was pulling my phone out to tell Jesse—last year's football captain who went to the closest college, aka the guy I now partied with since both of my best friends were knee deep in their girlfriends' vaginas—that I'd be at the party later than usual, a flash of platinum hair caught my eye.

Don't do it. Don't look over there.

I glanced over at the side of the whore house—I'm sorry, I mean *Madeline's* house, and saw her dangling from her window in her English Prep uniform. Her short, plaid skirt was pushed up way past her hips, and my tongue unknowingly darted out of my mouth to lick my lip. If it were anyone else, I'd indulge in the sight of smooth ass cheeks split down the middle with a lacy piece of pink fabric, but it was Madeline, and that was a no-fucking-way zone.

Regardless, I made my way over there to see what the hell she was doing hanging from her window.

Madeline. The girl who kept getting herself into sketchy situations that I seemed to always be present for. As of late, Madeline was my favorite pastime.

For months I'd sat and watched her, trying to decide how I wanted to proceed with my threat. I'd always had a soft side for Madeline, giving her a slight pass on her behavior and changed personality from the girl I used to know to what she became. I'd make excuses up in my head even when, deep down, I knew I should have hated her all along. We were close once—*really* close—but then she changed. She started ignoring me, distancing herself, pretending I didn't exist all together—and I did the same to her. Even when she dated Christian—my best friend—I pretended she wasn't a part of our group.

And somewhere along the way, my denial of living in a world where Madeline existed caught up to me, and it bit me right in the ass.

Every single memory of her flooded me the day I found my dad fucking her mom. Her words had sucker punched me. *"Your dad has been fucking my mom for years."*

Hate. I hated her in that moment. I hated her because I let my guard down, and it was the wrong move. Hurt flashed in between the bones of my rib cage when I'd realized she knew all along that my father was a cheating bastard, and she didn't tell me. A whole fuck-ton of hurt could have been avoided if Madeline had thought of someone other than herself for once.

So, for months, I'd been contemplating what to do. I'd been waiting, pacified by watching the Queen Bee of English Prep turn into the school leper. It definitely bought me some time. It was nearly every single day that someone bullied her in the same way she bullied them.

I wasn't going to lie; Madeline deserved everything she got, which is why it annoyed me that there was a small, and I mean *really fucking small,* part of me that felt bad. Maybe it was because I knew the old Madeline—the nice girl with two french braids and metal braces on her teeth. I didn't know. Regardless, I pushed away that pesky feeling and indulged in the feelings of raging anger and hate.

After all, it wasn't hard to hate a girl like Madeline. The pretty ones were always the meanest.

"Need some help, Maddie?" I loved using her old nick-name. I knew it bothered her beyond belief. I basked in watching her shrink into herself every time I used it.

She barely glanced down from holding onto the rain gutter. "Like you'd ever actually help me."

I grinned, staring at her ass once again. "You're right. I wouldn't help you even if it was the last thing left to do on this earth." I began walking closer to her, taking my traitorous eyes off her dangling body, and pushed myself up against the side of her house. "But I think I will casually stand here and watch you fall. That sounds like a great way to start off my day. So, please, carry on."

For a moment, Madeline's head dipped. Her light eyes met mine, her face shadowed with a passing cloud, but I still witnessed the disappointment. It was a short-lived moment, but I took pride in knowing my words got to her.

Madeline quickly jumped off to the side and landed on the

grass below, pulling her skirt down her long legs as she straightened her body. I wiggled my jaw back and forth, shaking my head. I placed my hands in the pockets of my khakis and began walking away, eager to put some distance between us.

Her voice sounded from behind, but I kept pushing one foot in front of the other. "I guess you'll have to find another way to brighten your day, Eric."

I called over my shoulder as I reached the driveway between our houses. "I'm sure there will be another exciting English Prep episode at some point today, where you'll be the lead actress who has something terrible happen to her. I call it a feel-good show. It's my favorite one, actually."

A dirty smile found itself on my face as I turned around to eye her. I wanted to see the hurt flash across her features. I wanted to have the upper hand in this situation, especially because my dick was still caught up on her bare ass. My head hitched to the side, my hair climbing into my eyes. "What was it last week? Fish in your locker?"

I had no idea who'd done it. The entire fucking hallway smelled like rotten vagina as Madeline opened her locker that morning. I did give her props, though. There wasn't even a slight muscle twitch on her face. She was a damn good actress. Always had been.

"Was it you?"

"Hmm?" I asked, acting as if I had no idea what she was talking about. Madeline's eyes flitted away, watching a car pass by behind me.

I gave her my best grin when she asked again, "Was it you, Eric? Did you put the fish in my locker?" Her arms moved across her chest, hiding her perky tits. "Is this all part of that lovely threat you gave me a few months ago?" Her voice lowered as she repeated my words. *"It's on now, Princess."*

My fingers clutched onto my keys in my pocket as memories from that day came swooping back in. It was months ago, but it somehow felt like seconds. Playing it off, I took my keys out of my pocket and began twirling them around and around, staring at her, waiting for the rising anger to simmer. I ran my gaze down her golden hair, past her heart-shaped lips, and all the way down to her knee-high stockings and back. I swallowed, fighting like hell to stay level-headed. Everything spiraled out of control after that day. Was it her fault? No. But could she have helped in some way? At least have given me a slight warning that my family was about to blow up? Yes. Yes, she fucking could have.

My words almost sounded like a bark. "I guess you'll never know. Maybe it was me. Maybe it wasn't." I shrugged, trying to appear unfazed.

Madeline's mouth opened slightly as she continued to stare at me, but the sound of her front door opening had her quickly rushing away. She moved around me gingerly, putting enough space between us to fit a freight train, and almost dove headfirst into her car. She was out of her driveway and down the street before I even opened my Rover's door.

I ping-ponged my attention to a man leaving Madeline's porch and to her fading headlights before I shook my head and turned my key in the ignition.

Nope. I didn't even want to fucking know.

Things were off with Madeline; that much was made very clear to me in the last several months, but that was her problem.

She didn't help me when I had problems, and I wasn't helping her.

It was as simple as that.

A commotion near the lunch line had me pausing with the banana in my mouth. My teeth sunk into the softness as my eyes skimmed over everyone, who was also rubbernecking it over to the loud bang. I bit off the end of the banana, chewing slowly as I watched Madeline sigh dramatically as she bent down to the floor to pick up the contents of her tray. A brown-haired girl, someone I was sure Madeline had bullied in the past, was laughing from behind her. The girl huddled in with her friends as they pointed and laughed even harder at Madeline as she scooped each and every last spaghetti noodle back onto her tray. I took my gaze off Madeline and turned to look at my friends.

"I feel bad for her," Hayley mumbled, stealing a fry off Christian's tray.

He pushed it over to her, urging her to take more, when he asked, "Who? Surely you're not talking about Madeline."

Ollie, Christian's brother, scoffed. "How can you feel bad for her? She was such a crazy bitch to you, Hayley." He paused. "She was a crazy bitch to everyone."

He wasn't wrong. Madeline *was* a bitch to Hayley and everyone else. She would tear others down to the ground, flip her blonde hair over her shoulder, and go about her day.

Hayley shrugged, wiping her hands on her school blouse. "She was definitely mean to me. A big bitch, to be frank. But..."

"There's a but? From you?" Christian asked, leaning forward onto the lunch table and looking at her like she was fucking delusional. His eyebrows rose to his hairline. "She dumped food onto your uniform your first day at English Prep."

Hayley raised her eyebrows right back at him, giving him a stern look. "Because *you* told her to."

Christian was Madeline's ex-boyfriend. The two of them were quite the power couple, although their relationship was nothing more than a show. I didn't know that for certain, not really wanting details about my best friend and the girl I once looked at with stars in my eyes, but Christian had never looked at Madeline the way he looked at Hayley. And Madeline had never looked at Christian the way she looked at me.

But that was then. This was now. Madeline didn't look at anyone anymore. Not really.

Piper, Hayley's best friend, snickered under her breath before burrowing her face in Ollie's neck.

"That's not fair," Christian groaned. "I had a reason to bully you. She did not."

Hayley sparred off with him. "So what? You're the only one allowed to be mean to me?"

He nodded with confidence. "That's right."

Hayley rolled her eyes, dismissing him quickly. "I'm just saying, I feel bad for her. There's a reason she's mean to everyone. I can see it."

"I don't know about that," Christian bemused. "I think she's just a cold bitch."

I swallowed my soda slowly, shifting my eyes to Madeline at her lone lunch table by the trash cans and then back to Hayley and Christian arguing about her.

"You can't judge a book by its cover, Christian. You should know that by now."

He chuckled. "I've been in between her pages. She has no excuse."

Piper gasped as Hayley turned to look at him once more. I waited with a slack jaw to see how Hayley would retaliate. Those two had a weird relationship. They fucking loved each other, but sometimes their little playful fights got dirty.

Christian was a dick, but Hayley didn't take his shit.

It was entertaining, to say the least.

"But"—she leaned in close to his face, her mouth almost

touching his—"did you happen to *read* those pages, Christian?"

I watched him gulp back a feral growl. Hayley knew how to press his buttons and how to make him swallow his words. Leaning back in my chair, I crossed my arms and grinned.

Hayley's hands clamped down onto Christian's thighs, really fucking close to his dick, as she waited for his answer.

Piper was smashing her lips together as she glanced up from the crook of Ollie's neck, who was barely keeping himself from laughing.

Christian licked his lips before smirking. "I didn't read her pages like I read yours…"

Hayley smiled before pecking him on the mouth. "Good answer."

A few seconds went by with everyone laughing at their show before Hayley turned her attention to me. "What are your views on it, Eric? You're awfully quiet over there."

My mouth slammed shut as I flicked my eyes up to Piper. She quickly glanced away, not meeting my eye.

Unfortunately, Piper knew there was something going on with me when it came to Madeline. She was observant. Too observant. She knew I watched Madeline like a hawk. She knew that Madeline dove underneath my skin and made me itch with unease. I was guessing that Piper had told Hayley.

Those two were trouble sometimes. But not the type of trouble that Madeline was.

I huffed out a breath, pushing my tray away with force before announcing—very *loudly,* might I add—what I thought about Madeline. "I think Madeline is a selfish bitch who only thinks of herself. She deserves every bit of what she's getting."

Something flew through my veins with my words—something similar to unease, guilt even. But I pushed it away as I found her stoic, yet soft face staring at me from her lunch table.

We kept a hold of each other's stares for no more than a passing second, but in that second, I saw a whole lot of emotion pass behind her blue eyes.

"Damn straight," Christian grunted, throwing up his fist to pound mine.

When I dropped my hand with a smirk, I glanced back at Madeline, but she was quickly leaving the lunch room, her plaid skirt swaying and her shoulders bunched up to her ears.

Before she walked through the doors, she paused and glanced down at her phone. Her shoulders dropped in a whoosh with what appeared to be relief.

I couldn't help my eyebrows crowding in together, wondering just what was on her phone that seemed to make her relax.

My jaw popped as I glanced away, ignoring all the weird signs that Madeline was giving off the last few months.

I don't care.

She didn't deserve the amount of thoughts I gave her. Madeline was like a passing season, changing every so often, only to leave you longing for more. But I was through longing for Madeline. That boat shipped out years ago.

CHAPTER THREE

MADELINE

SKY: FOR FUCKS' sake, Madeline. 2418 East Corbin St. Alpha Phi frat house tonight at 9pm. He goes by Atticus. He'll be waiting for you. I took off after Tank got arrested. I'm not selling anymore. Cops have been snooping around. Don't text me anymore.

Relief. Instant relief. That text couldn't have come at a better time, either. As soon as I got home from school, I rushed upstairs, thankful there were no new vehicles parked out front, and I stripped out of my uniform. I kicked my navy blazer and skirt halfway across my room and ran over to my closet, pulling on my black mini and fishnet tights. I pulled my oversized cream sweater down off the hanger, tucking it into the front of my skirt, and slipped on my black Doc Martens. Hair spray coated the top of my head and washed down to my shoulders as I fluffed my hair up. My red lipstick went on smooth, and my concealer hid the dark-gray color underneath my eyes.

There.

I looked hot. I looked the part of a college girl instead of some loser high schooler walking into a frat party to score some drugs that weren't even the good kind.

All I needed was some sleep, and I'd feel better. All I needed was one good night's worth of blissful shuteye, and my head wouldn't be so fuzzy. I wouldn't feel so anxious.

I pulled my phone up and reread the message again before typing the address in my phone. It was going to take at least an hour to get there, especially with the afternoon rush from work as I traveled through Pike Valley and the city. The college wasn't too far in terms of miles, but with traffic, I'd better leave soon.

I shoved my phone and keys into my cross-body purse and checked out my window once more to make sure no creepy guys were making their way to our front door.

One in particular.

Two, if you counted my own father who hadn't been home in months.

The tightly coiled nerves in my belly loosened as I saw that the coast was clear. I quickly glanced at Eric's Range Rover parked in his driveway. Why did I glance at Eric's car? I had no idea. I just couldn't help wondering what he was doing and if he was home.

It was a sickness, thinking about the guy who hated me the most, but whatever.

The second my Doc Martens stepped foot on the landing below the last step, my mom's voice called out, "Madeline? Is that you? Where are you headed? Christian's?"

I rolled my eyes. *When are you going to tell her you're not dating Christian anymore? In fact, when are you going to tell her you're the school loser instead of the school queen?*

I put on my best smile. "Yep. I'll be back later tonight. Bye, Mom."

"Hey. Wait a second."

My back went stiff as my mom came around from behind and ran her fingers through my hair. "We could probably get your hair done again. Your dad likes it when it's light like this."

I spun around slowly. "Does that mean he's coming home?"

I wasn't sure what was worse: my dad or my mother's random one-night-stand boyfriends. Both had fear prickling my neck for two very different reasons.

My mom brushed her hand through her own platinum locks. They fell down to her hips with their shiny sleekness as she pushed them over her shoulder. Despite her behavior, my mom was actually a very pretty woman, even without all the makeup she wore. But she was also a broken woman. A woman who was lost and believed every word every man had ever told her.

Beautiful.

Sexy.

Slut.

Trash.

She didn't know who she was or what she was. She let whatever she was feeling in the moment drive her to her actions.

You're supposed to look up to your mother, want to become half the woman she is. But I wanted to be the complete opposite of mine. I just wasn't sure if I ever would be. Because from where I was standing, we were two peas in a pod.

Fear and dread. We both felt it, and we were both trapped by it.

"I'm not sure when he'll be home next, but it's always best to be prepared." She winked at me with a warm smile, but it lacked any real emotion.

"And how prepared are you to explain to Dad why another man is in your bed every night?"

My mom's green eyes fell to the floor in an instant, and I hated that it was so easy for me to be cold and callous. My tone wasn't soft. The words were cut and dry, a meanness dragging with every syllable, and it wasn't fair. My dad scared me too. She was trapped and lonely.

I should have said sorry. I should have taken her hands in mine and told her I understood, but resentment had me stepping backwards, one foot after the other until I reached the front door. Before I turned and left, I called back to her, "I wasn't saying that to be mean. I just want you to be prepared for an unannounced drop-in from him, and if he finds you in bed with someone else..." I swallowed back the panic in my voice. "Well, we know how that'll end."

My mom slapped her mouth shut and gave me a single nod before I opened the door and let the fresh air wash over my sticky skin.

This time, I made my way to my car without once glancing at Eric's house. My mind was too wrapped up in other things to worry about what the boy next door was up to.

CHAPTER FOUR

ERIC

MY BACK RESTED along a dingy sofa in a large living room that had a mix of both old and new furniture. The room was dark and dull with a few standing lamps for light and one overhead light fixture that I was pretty sure had only one of three lightbulbs working, but the frat party was a nice change of pace to the cabin where most of the parties were.

Every Friday and Saturday night, I'd throw a party at my parents' cabin on the outskirts of town, but ever since Ollie and Piper started their thing and got into some trouble with street racing, things had been slower than usual.

And not to mention, the cabin parties were becoming tiresome. I'd been with half the girls that showed up every weekend, so none of them were keeping my interest any longer, and everyone and everything seemed to be irritating me lately.

I felt myself closing off. Ollie and Christian had both asked me what was wrong, but I'd told them I was fine, because I didn't want to talk about it.

Even the mere thought of diving into the shitstorm that my father created a few months ago made me want to chug the entire keg that was set up just a few feet away from me. Warm beer and all. I didn't care.

But for now, I'd sit right here on this couch that likely had enough cum on it to get every single girl in this room pregnant and enjoy the fact that I was out of Pike Valley for the night and away from everyone that knew me.

Except for Jesse, who was currently playing beer pong with two girls clung to his side. He caught my attention and angled his head for me to come over all while waving a red cup full of beer in my direction.

I glanced down at my phone, seeing the text from my mom, thanking me for cleaning the house, and the three from my dad that were left unopened.

Yeah. I need a drink. Right fucking now.

"Wanna be my partner, bro?" Jesse asked, shooing the two college girls wearing skin-tight dresses away. "I've seen what that arm can do during football."

I chuckled. "Yeah, yeah. You're the one playing with the big boys now."

He tapped my chest with the back of his hand before aligning the beer pong cups perfectly symmetrical on the table. I bounced the ping-pong ball in my hand, eager to get started so I could drink away my own fucked-up version of reality. "Bro, you're gonna be playing against me in less than a year. Did you get your acceptance letter from UCLA yet?"

And with that question, I locked my jaw and stopped bouncing the ball. Of course I got my acceptance letter. UCLA had all but sucked my dick to get me to apply. With my father being an alumnus and donating his money every year, they probably didn't even glance at the contents of my application. They saw my name and immediately put it in the "accept" pile.

The only problem now was that my father had cut me off. He hadn't given me a dime since I'd thrown him under the bus. Don't get me wrong, he tried to talk to me. "*If you'd just talk to me so we can work this out as a family...*"

But I refused. Every time I heard my mom crying or looked into her tired eyes as she worked another long shift at the hospital, unwilling to rely on my father for anything, I'd get angry all over again.

If she was gonna ice him out, so would I. I was on her side. Not his.

So anyway, according to my father, he wasn't going to pay for my college until I *grew up* and talked to him. Well, I'd stay a fucking toddler for the rest of my life if it meant he'd leave us alone.

Chances were, he wouldn't. But for now, he was staying true to his word. My bank account had slowly dwindled down to nothing.

"Dude, you good?" Jesse nudged me again, and I shook myself out of my thoughts. I leaned back and hitched one of the pong balls into a cup across the table. I grinned, my cheek rising to one side. "I'm good. Just getting in the zone."

He laughed. "Aww, shit. I've seen that look before." Then, he cupped his hands around his mouth and yelled, "Oh, ladiesssss? My man Eric is in the house tonight, and let me tell ya, he's on the fucking prowl."

Several girls cat-called throughout the room, a ripple of high-pitched voices straining against my ears. I wasn't going to lie; my dick twitched at the thought.

New pussy.

Fresh meat to take my mind off the only one at English Prep that continued to catch my attention. The one that I swore to hate so I wouldn't love. That pesky little unhealthy obsession of mine.

Just as I threw another ball into a cup, I caught the blur of golden hair moving through the crowd behind the opposing team.

My chest zinged with a little ping. I hated how the mere thought of her got me all twisted inside. My heart stuttered to a sudden stop when I continued watching the blonde weave through the crowd. It only took three seconds to realize it was her in the flesh, and only four to succumb to that feeling of pure exhilaration.

My, oh my... Look what the fucking cat dragged in.

So much for curbing that *unhealthy* obsession of mine.

A crooked smile fixed itself onto my lips as she finally glanced over her shoulder at me. Our eyes met instantaneously.

My grin did *not* mirror hers.

Madeline's shadowed face lit up like a damn firecracker. Her high cheekbones blazed with a red I could see clearly from halfway across the frat party of bustling college students. I wasn't sure if the red tint was from embarrassment or from anger. Either way, I'd take it.

I set down the cup I'd been holding and slowly brought my hand up to wave. My fingers wiggled toward her in a menacing way. I was certain the grin on my face was full of sarcasm with a sliver of malice on the side.

Madeline quickly darted away, pushing and maneuvering around groups of drunk girls clinging to equally drunk guys, to get clear away from me.

I laughed under my breath.

As if it'd be that easy to hide from me, Madeline.

CHAPTER FIVE

MADELINE

ATTICUS. Atticus. Atticus.

All I had to do was find a guy who looked like his name was Atticus. Funny, because there wasn't a single guy here who looked like he belonged to that name. What kind of name was that?! What was this? To Kill a fucking Mockingbird?!

I kept searching through the sea of people, annoyed that everyone around me was having the time of their life while I was just trying to find a faceless person so I could maybe, just maybe, get some fucking sleep.

Oh, and let's not forget that prickling feeling I had at the base of my neck that *someone* was watching my every move.

Of course Eric would be here.

Because why *would* the universe be on my side for once?

It was karma. It had to be.

I pushed my hair behind my ear as I slid along the wall that felt sticky against my sweater, making sure not to touch the couple that was dry humping along with the beat of the music, and continued surveying faces of guys that looked like they sold drugs—as if that narrowed it down any.

My eyes scanned the crowd, my nose upturned as warm beer splashed out of a full-to-the-brim cup and landed on my Doc Martens. I hurriedly pushed the drunk girl away, an irritated breath leaving me quickly as I zeroed in on a guy leaning back onto a drab-looking couch with his two arms hitched up behind him as they rested on a pair of girls' shoulders. He looked dirty. His hair was sticking to the sides of his head underneath a dark-gray beanie. He had those droopy, puppy-dog eyes that I'd recognized before. *He was high. Bingo.*

The second I stepped forward, I heard a voice. "Hey there, *Maddie.*"

I felt the widening of my eyes for a brief moment before I recovered, turning around to face Eric, who I'd hoped would just leave me alone. This was too important to get all wrapped up in his hot scowl.

"Leave me alone, Eric," I said, rolling my eyes so hard into the back of my head that I was impressed.

Eric ran a hand through his messy, dark hair, throwing his head back in the process and letting out a deep chuckle. I watched with a slightly parted mouth as his Adam's apple bobbed up and down. I clenched my jaw shut when he stopped laughing abruptly to stare at my lips.

His expression changed quickly. "Gonna tell me what you're doing here?"

"Why do you care?" My arms found their way across my chest as I bounced on my feet.

Eric leaned against the sticky wall, the one that I was pretty sure had fuzz stuck to it from my sweater, lifting a shoulder slyly. "I'm just wondering why you keep showing up at the same places I'm at." His eyebrow raised at the same time his jaw twitched. "Stalking me?"

A tight laugh escaped me. "As fucking if. I should be asking you the same."

Now it was my time to act cool and nonchalant. We *did* seem to keep showing up at the same places at the same time, but I was certain they were total coincidences. Fate's way of dangling something I wanted right in front of my face, knowing I would never, ever get it. I could be the last girl on this earth, and Eric wouldn't dare touch me. I could see it on his face. It was clear the day I had casually told him his father had been fucking my mom for years. He hated me then, and he hated me now.

He grunted, pushing off the wall to stand *way* too close to me. I kept my face completely relaxed. "I've got shit to do, Eric. So, if you'll excuse me." I went to move around him, but he quickly dodged right in front of me, causing me to hit my face off his hard chest. I got a whiff of his cologne, and I almost went in for a second sniff. Eric smelled exactly how he looked: dark and mysterious with a little bit of spice.

He took a step back, peering down at me with that cocky grin. "Things to do? Or *people* to do?" He shrugged again, putting one hand in the pocket of his jeans. "I mean..." His tongue slowly swiped a line over his plump bottom lip, and I was beginning to sweat. "A girl like you? I can only assume it's the latter."

His words flipped me completely inside out. He wasn't wrong. The Madeline he knew would fuck a random guy at a college party that she had no business being at, but that was *before*. That was before everything turned ugly.

"Get out of my way, Eric," I managed to croak out, hoping like hell my voice didn't break like I was breaking on the inside. He went willingly as I pushed against his chest. I swore I heard his laugh the entire time I walked over to who I assumed to be Atticus.

I gulped back my nerves and put on my mask of pure

confidence. "Are you Atticus?" I asked, looking down at the guy on the couch cushions that looked as if they were going to swallow him and his two girlfriends whole.

His cheek lifted as he ran his lazy gaze down my body. Chills coated my arms, and the hair on the back of my neck stood erect. "I am. And..." He began sitting up, using the two girls' knees as handles. "I'm going to bet you are Madeline."

I nodded once as he stood peering down at me from his tall stature. He had to be at least six feet, if not more.

"Follow me," he coaxed, grabbing onto my hand softly.

Alarm bells went off in every single crevice of my body, but I was too desperate to do anything about it.

I told myself not to let my guard down ever again, and here I was, following a strange guy up the stairs of some dirty frat house.

Pushing the fear away, I made sure to have one hand in my bag, holding onto my pepper spray I had put there months prior—just in case—and followed him anyway.

Once we climbed the flight of stairs, dodging a few couples making out, and rounded the line to the bathroom, Atticus stopped in front of a single door and slowly opened it.

He stood half in the hallway and half inside the room and barely flicked his head once for me to go inside.

A steady breath filled my lungs as I walked over the threshold, my hand slippery with sweat as I clutched onto the pepper spray even tighter.

Once the door latched behind me, my stomach dropped. *It's fine, Madeline. Breathe.*

"So," Atticus started, walking over to a small desk that was pushed up against the wall. "Ambien. That's probably the weirdest request I've ever gotten for a drug."

I ran my gaze around the room, staying quiet. It was a dark room with a deep-tan color all over with random posters of bands taped haphazardly around the space. There was a single bed in the middle of the room with messy covers and mix-matched books on the floor.

"I'm sure it was," I finally answered, taking my gaze off the *Pride and Prejudice* novel and landing back on him. Atticus took his beanie off his head, throwing it onto the desk behind him, and ran his fingers through his long hair.

"Can I ask why?"

"Why what?" I stood near the door, my hand still inside my purse. I shuffled on my feet, ignoring the need to pull my skirt down. *This is a normal guy, in a normal situation. Kind of...*

He eyed my hand in my purse for a second before answering. "Why the need for sleeping pills?"

Oh. Thoughts of my dark room and hands that didn't feel familiar started to creep in. It almost took my breath away. "No. You can't ask."

He chuckled, dropping his head. "Okay, fair enough." He turned around and grabbed a small plastic baggie and dangled it in front of me. I almost ran over to him and wept at the sight of it, but he pulled it back within a second. "How are we doing this?"

A tight band squeezed my ribs. "Doing what?"

He gave me a skeptical look. "You didn't think you were getting this for free, did you?"

I rolled my eyes. "Of course not."

"Okay..." he dragged the word out. "So, are you paying cash or in another way?"

"Another way?" I asked cautiously.

He chuckled, and it sounded a lot like he was laughing at me. "Some girls pay in cash, and some pay..."—he glanced down at my mouth—"in other ways."

Fuck. Don't panic.

I straightened my shoulders and raised my chin. I inhaled

through my nose before I let my words slice him. "The only way I will *ever* pay is in cash."

He grinned. "Shame."

My feet were urging me to back up. They wanted to drag me to the door and back outside to my car as Atticus crept forward. "It'll be four hundred."

I pulled back. "Four hundred?!" I stuttered over my words. "That's, like, triple the price of what I paid Sky!"

He shrugged, throwing his hand out. "It's not exactly easy to get my hands on something so unusual. Take it or leave it... or pay me in a different way." He winked, and I almost threw up.

This fucking guy.

I reached into my purse with force, pulling out all the cash I had—which wasn't four hundred dollars. Then, I all but snapped, "What's your app name? I'll wire the rest."

He held out his hand, and I thrusted my phone into it. He typed something quickly, and I paid him the rest of the money.

Atticus handed the bag to me, letting his finger swipe the inside of my palm before I snatched it back and stepped into the hall. I quickly shoved the bag into my purse.

"Hit me up when you want some more. I put my number in your phone." I didn't so much as even nod at him before I was rushing down the stairs and weaving through the party.

I got what I had come for, and now it was time to get the fuck out before I had a panic attack at the mere look from another guy.

CHAPTER SIX

ERIC

MADELINE WENT UPSTAIRS with some dude who looked like he snorted cocaine for fun, and even though I told myself not to care, I did anyway.

I fucking hated her. I hated her so much because I *couldn't* hate her. I hated that, years later, after watching her turn into an uppity, imperious girl who bullied her way to the top, I still got a twinge of jealousy knowing she was with someone else.

I'd tricked my mind in the past, ignoring the way her hand would wrap around my best friend's arm, looking the other way when he'd nip at her ear, but there was absolutely no way I was tricking my heart or my dick. Both had a mind of their own, and they weren't so easily swayed.

Regardless, I did what I did best, and I pushed back on every single feeling flying through my body, and I went numb. *I don't care. I don't care about anything.*

I swung my arm back and dropped another sinker into the cup across from me.

"My boy is on fucking fire!" Jesse slapped my back,

pointing at the duo in front of us. "Did you hear that? I said he's on fire!"

"Yeah, we fucking heard you. You're three feet away from us," one of his frat brothers slurred. Jesse and I were obviously very good at pong, and they weren't. They'd drank almost all of the cups on their end, and sadly, Jesse and I had both only had one cup each.

One cup of beer didn't even put a single dent in my mood. I needed much more alcohol if I wanted to feel even the slight tingle of a buzz.

After we'd won the game, I started to rearrange the cups again, waiting for the next team to demolish. I glanced up at the stairs for the fifteenth time in three minutes and gritted my teeth.

There she was.

Fucking finally.

I assessed her hair, seeing if it was messy in that I-just-got-fucked type of way. Her clothes were on straight, her sexy-as-sin fishnet tights still tight on her legs. I found her lips to be normal-looking and not all red and swollen from rough kissing.

She looked okay physically, but the way her shoulders were crowding her ears, and how she was pushing and shoving people all while holding onto her purse like it was her lifeline to flee to the door, had my suspicions rising.

Madeline, the ever-so-poised girl who was consistently on her A game, never backing down from a fight, was running. If I wasn't mistaken, she even looked a little scared.

I looked to the stairs and back to Madeline a few times before deciding I'd rather go after her than beat the fuck out of some guy who may not have deserved it.

For all I knew, Madeline was the one who did something wrong. Not him. She had a way of skewing things to benefit herself.

"I'll be back, bro," I said to Jesse. "Have this pretty little thing"—I grabbed onto a girl's hand, the one that kept staring at me and batting her sparkling green eyes in my direction, and pulled her in close—"take my spot." I smiled at her. "You'll do me proud, right?"

She giggled, her cheeks reddening in the process. "Sure. As long as you'll reward me in the end."

I winked. "You betcha."

Then, I rounded her cute self and caught up to Madeline just as she was descending the front steps of the frat house. There was a bite to the evening air as I stepped right in line with her. "Where ya off to, Maddie?"

She froze, her back going ramrod straight on the sidewalk littered with empty beer cans. "Quit calling me that, Eric."

Then, she took off again, her round ass in that stupid fucking skirt catching my attention as I stayed put. I tore my eyes away after a few seconds and followed after her, eager to know why she was running off so fast.

"What was that all about?" I asked, tilting my head to the party behind us. "Did you really come here just to fuck someone?" I laughed under my breath, hating the way being around her made me feel like I was constantly trying to win her attention. "I mean, I know you can't get any dick at English Prep or, fuck, even Wellington Prep... But to come here and pick the scummiest looking guy? You've really lowered your standards."

We were at her car now, my Rover parked just a few spaces up from hers. She swung around quickly, a raging fire in her eyes that set me off inside. "What do you want, Eric? Go back inside and get fucked up. Do whatever it is you like to do. Just leave me the fuck alone. I am so sick of you following me around like a lost puppy and getting into my shit! Why won't you just leave me be?"

My teeth ground back and forth as I watched her pretty

little mouth spout off to me before I leveled her with a glare. "I told you months ago. Don't you remember?"

She rolled her eyes before looking through her purse for her keys. "Oh, right," she gritted out, glancing up at me once with those light eyes. "*It's on now, Princess.*" She went back to ignoring me as her hand started to move faster inside her purse. She mumbled under her breath a few times before dropping her shoulders. She quickly spun around and peered inside her car window. "Fucking shit. Of course." She looked up at the sky and groaned before slapping the window.

"Lock your keys in your car?"

She shot me a steely glare, which only made me laugh. "Why do you care?"

"Oh," I mused, putting my hands in my jeans pockets casually. "I don't care, even in the slightest. Have fun getting home. Maybe you can ask that guy you went upstairs with to give you a ride."

I fought to keep the lazy smile on my face.

As soon as I mentioned the other guy, Madeline's face changed. She went from angry to blank in three seconds fast. I narrowed my eyes, wondering what had gone on upstairs.

Who cares, Eric? Go back inside.

I dropped my eyes to her purse, bouncing my attention to her eyes that were showing absolutely nothing, and noticed how her small hand clutched it closer to her body. She teetered back and forth on her feet, adjusting her skirt a few times, darting her eyes away before my lazy smile turned into a wicked grin.

The loose pebbles underneath my shoe creaked as I took a step closer to her. Madeline wouldn't meet my gaze. Instead, she looked to the left, pressing her purse even tighter to her stomach. I almost laughed, wondering if she was going to go as far as shoving it up underneath her cream sweater to hide it. "So, what exactly were you doing upstairs...Madeline?"

My shoe touched hers, and she pushed back onto the side of her car, her back resting flat against the window. I invaded her space, my breath falling down in between us. Her head tipped upward, her pretty eyes locked onto mine, and for once, they appeared soft. *She* appeared soft. Delicate. Breakable, even.

It was a shame that I was about to break her.

And girls like Madeline? They deserved to be broken.

One of my fingers swept a stray hair away from her cheek, tucking it behind her ear. A minty, faint breath gracefully fell from her lips as I tipped her chin up. "Did you fuck him, Madeline?"

Her mouth slammed shut, and I laughed, snatching her purse out of her arms so fast she didn't even have time to react.

"Hey!" she shouted, reaching out.

I quickly turned around and jolted to the front of her car, tipping her purse out onto the hood, letting the contents fall swiftly.

"Eric, no! Stop!" she yelled, attempting to push me away, which, of course, didn't work.

Madeline tried to scramble and put things back to where they belonged, but her gasp had my smile fading. "No, no, no," she mumbled, falling to pick something up.

I glanced down and saw small pink pills scattered all over the road, some even falling into the storm drain that was just a foot away from where I was standing. I moved back, accidentally stepping on a few in the process.

Drugs? That was what she went upstairs for? It all made sense now. The exhaustion I saw on her face every day at school. The hanging around at the street races last month with the homely looking chick. *Shit.*

Madeline was doing drugs.

"So that's why you went upstairs?" I asked, crossing my

arms over my t-shirt. "To buy drugs?"

Madeline ignored me completely. She was on the ground, picking up half-dissolved pills that had fallen onto the still-wet road from the quick rain shower that came through. She glanced up at me, a mixture of emotions on her face. "Do you fucking know how much I just spent on these?" Her head fell quickly when her eyes grew watery.

My breathing had picked up as I watched her on the ground in her stupid tights, getting all torn and dirty, holding back tears. She flipped around, sitting on the wet asphalt, and brought her knees up to her chin, resting her back along the front of her car. Her hands came up and covered her face as her shoulders shook.

Oh my fuck.

I stood there, completely fucking dumbfounded that Madeline was crying.

I was even more dumbfounded that I wasn't rejoicing with fucking glee. Instead, I found myself wanting to make it stop.

Something had to be truly fucking wrong for Madeline to cry—especially in front of me.

And to be honest, I was so sick and tired of hearing people cry. This was the second female I'd heard cry in less than twenty-four hours. That was plenty.

"Come on," I said, sighing. "I'll give you a ride home. You can come back tomorrow with your spare key or call a locksmith."

Madeline's hands fell from her tear-streaked face as she glared up at me. "I'd rather walk than get a ride with you."

A blurring line of anger cut through me. I wasn't even necessarily pissed at her. I was just pissed that I had offered her a lending hand—the first in a long, long time—and she threw it back in my face. "Fine," I snapped. "Better get to walkin' then."

"Fine!" she huffed, climbing to her feet. She threw everything else that I had dumped out of her purse back in, scooping every last thing up, except for the now mostly dissolved pills, and flung the strap over her head and laid it across her body. "Fuck you, Eric."

I huffed out a laugh, watching her stomp away. "Fuck you too. I hope you enjoy getting man-handled walking down those dark alleyways because you're too fucking stubborn to get in my car."

Madeline stopped dead in her tracks at my words. I'd apologize for being so crass, but the words were truthful. It wasn't smart for a girl as hot as her to be walking these streets littered with drunk college guys at night. She was stupid for doing it.

And I was stupid for being worried about her.

Madeline looked over her shoulder, just once, but I saw the minor dip in her stubborn facade. "Don't act like you care now, Eric. Don't you have a threat to follow through with?"

I only stared at her, knowing I should go back into the party and let her figure everything out on her own. It was Madeline, after all. She always had a way of coming out on top.

But when she continued down the sidewalk, hugging her arms to her chest, I pulled myself over to my Range Rover.

Every one of my muscles was coiled tight, ready to snap, as I opened my door and put my key in the ignition.

I could tell myself I hated Madeline all I wanted. I could fuck with her and laugh when someone put fish in her locker, but if something happened to her, something *bad,* I wasn't sure if I'd be able to look myself in the mirror.

There was a very thin line between hate and love, and for this very brief moment, I was going to straddle it.

For my own sake. Not for hers.

CHAPTER SEVEN

MADELINE

CRYING WAS A USELESS ACTION. Crying didn't make your problems disappear or create some amazing plan out of thin air to fix things. No fairy godmother was going to show up at the mere sound of my tears falling to the ground to help me.

But I was doing it anyway. Hot, angry, betraying tears streamed down my cheeks underneath the pitch-black sky as I walked down a cracked sidewalk, staring at my phone with directions pulled up that said I'd be walking for *hours* before I made it home.

I couldn't decide what would set me off more: walking down unfamiliar roads in the dark, wearing a short skirt and fishnet tights with things (read as: men) lurking in the shadows, *or* calling an Uber and having a panic attack in the backseat from being in a small, dark space alone with a man I didn't know.

Technically, it *could* be a woman driver, but with how fate had been treating me lately? It would be a man, and he'd be creepy as hell with some fucking porno 'stache.

At least out here, I had Eric following me in his Range Rover. I was still furious with him. So mad I couldn't even see straight. But I also couldn't deny feeling a little bit better with him trailing me.

He was likely only following me to see how far I'd make it before I *asked* for his help. There was no way he was following to make sure I stayed safe, because if it wasn't evident before that he hated me, it was most definitely evident now. His harsh words were still stinging my skin. *"I hope you enjoy getting man-handled walking down those dark alleyways."*

If he only fucking knew.

I furiously wiped another stray tear off my cheek, flinging the wetness into the dark abyss that surrounded me. The amount of disappointment in my stomach was almost enough to make me double over and puke. I was so close. So close to getting some sleep, to turning off the fear and anxiety and pushing away those pesky nightmares. And Eric ruined it.

Four hundred dollars down the freaking drain—literally.

Another four hundred sleepless nights laid in front of me, and the nightmares that I knew would come taunted me, laughing at me, making me feel even smaller than I already felt.

I sighed, my tears eventually coming to a stop, as I glanced at the time. I'd been walking for at least forty minutes, and Eric was still driving behind me, loose embers of asphalt crunching with each slow motion of his tire.

My left pinky toe had a blister on it from the walk, but I'd rather amputate my foot than get into his Range Rover.

Eric and I were at war now.

I let this little charade go on for far too long, the guilt finally catching up to me and making it hard to breathe, but now I was downright pissed off.

He had no idea what he'd done. He had no idea how badly I needed those tiny pink pills. He likely thought I was a druggie, but what did I care about his thoughts of me? They probably couldn't get much worse than what they already were.

My eyes darted to the left as his headlights got brighter. I kept walking, even when I heard his window roll down. His car continued to move forward slowly for another five or ten minutes before I heard his exasperated sigh.

It drove a hot stake into my back. "Why the fuck are you following me?" I gritted, stopping on the sidewalk to cross my arms over my sweater. "Want a front row seat in watching me get raped?"

My teeth clinked together as the words flew out. The beating of my heart went into triple speed, and I struggled to keep my breathing level. *Why did I just say that?*

"You're so fucking twisted, Madeline. Get the fuck in my car before I really do leave your snarky ass out here."

I couldn't believe I just said that, given my circumstances.

Sweat beads instantly formed on my forehead. I pushed my hair out of my face, feeling the strands stick like glue to my skin. I swallowed back a tight lump, a sour vomit taste burning my throat. Flashes of suppressed memories cut through my brain like slashes of a knife. I turned my back to Eric, gasping for the night air to calm my spiraling panic.

Just get in the car, Madeline. I knew I needed to. I knew I wouldn't last when I reached the city. Goosebumps coated every inch of my skin with just the mere thought of those alleyways that Eric had brought up.

"Clock's fucking ticking," Eric said with a tightness in his tone.

I spun around quickly, my mini-skirt rising with the motion. "The only reason I'm getting in your car is because you owe me now."

The tick of his jaw didn't go unnoticed as I climbed in the front seat. Neither did the snarl in my direction. "I fucking owe *you*?" My face burned as he threw his head back and howled with laughter. "You've got to be fucking kidding me, Madeline." He pulled back onto the main road, whipping by parked cars on the side. "First, you freeze me out when we're younger, morphing into some haughty, psycho little bitch." I winced internally at his words. "Then... *then*," he groaned, taking his hand off the steering wheel, flexing his fist before running it through his inky black hair, "you all but throw it in my face that my dad had been fucking your mom for *years*." I swallowed, taking my eyes off his veiny forearm as he gripped the leather wheel even harder. "You could have told me. But instead, you only cared about yourself. You're fucked up, Madeline. I'd always given you the benefit of the doubt, but not after that. It's true that you only care about yourself. And fuck, I'd love to know what goes on in your home behind closed doors. Your mom is a slut, not only taking my parents' marriage down, but likely hers down too. I wonder how many other marriages she's fucked up." He slowly looked over at me, and I saw the reflection of what I'd put there the second I ended our friendship: betrayal. He felt betrayed by me and rightly so. I was selfish, and I *did* only care about myself.

But if I didn't protect myself, who would?

So, of course I froze him out when we were kids. How could I be his friend—or *more*—while I knew his father was being a sleaze with my mom? How could I trust him not to ruin everything and somehow my father finding out?

"You have no fucking clue what you're talking about, Eric. You know absolutely nothing about what goes on in our home."

And trust me, you don't want to know.

I made Eric hate me for a reason.

I made everyone hate me for a reason.

We were nearing the outskirts of Pike Valley when he said five words that had my shoulders tensing.

"Maybe I'll just find out..."

I tried to keep my voice steady. "What does that mean?"

A deep, sarcastic chuckle came from his chest, and I swore it sucker punched me.

"Maybe I'll just find out what goes on in your home. Maybe I'll wait until your dad is back home and put a little bug in his ear that your mom is the neighborhood slut, and"—he clicked his tongue—"I guess I can let him know his daughter is a druggie as well."

My hand slapped on the side of the passenger door, and Eric's face split in two. He was smiling like the cocky fucking asshole that he was, and it only made my nerves amplify. My skin was itching. Hives were likely covering my chest.

I breathed in and out of my nose, steadying myself before I completely lost control of everything. But that was exactly how I felt. I felt out of control. Every single thing in my life was spiraling and twisting in unfathomable ways.

"Stop the fucking car."

For once, Eric actually listened and slammed on the brakes. My hand shot out to protect myself from plowing into the dash, and I quickly opened the door, allowing the cool air to coat my body like a blanket.

I wasn't even halfway out the door before I glared over at him, blood filling my mouth with how hard I bit the inside of my cheek. He was glaring at me too, his gray eyes looking like pools of complete darkness. "I'm not a fucking druggie. You have no idea what you're talking about or what you'd be doing if you said anything to my father."

My voice broke at the end, and Eric's eye twitched, telling me that he noticed the small dent in my armor.

If he tells my father...

I couldn't even let the thought consume me. I slammed the car door closed with all my might, which wasn't much, and Eric sped off in the opposite direction. I heard the squealing of his tires in my ears the rest of the walk home.

CHAPTER EIGHT

ERIC

MY FINGERS HOVERED over my phone as I continued arguing with myself about what I was about to do. I glanced around the cabin, noting that all my friends were busy partying with beer splashing out of their cups and flirting with one another incessantly like annoying-ass middle schoolers. I leaned back onto the couch, waving my attention over my best friends and their girlfriends who were all four in their own little fairy-tale world, and typed a sneaky little description into the search engine.

No.

I erased the words with so much force I thought my phone was going to crack. It'd been exactly a week since I gave Madeline a half-ride home from the frat party. I'd avoided her as much as I could during school this week. Someone tripped her in the hall, a mere foot away from me, and she fell to her knees onto the porcelain floor with a loud thud. A former football player and one of our closer friends,

Taylor, made a comment that had me dipping my attention to see how she'd react.

"Oh, look. Madeline's on her knees. No surprise there." Everyone around us laughed, except me. Instead, I leaned my shoulder on my locker, pulling my books to the side so I could watch her every move.

It didn't take long for her to stand up, rubbing her red knees in the process. Her face never wavered, though. Every single flawless feature was smooth and in place, as if she were bored with the entire thing. But I saw right through that. Madeline was exhausted. The makeup she'd caked on did nothing to hide the puffiness around her baby blues. Her movements were slow and lazy. She wasn't *not* reacting because she wanted to appear tough and unbothered. She just didn't have the energy.

And that, my friends, was exactly why you shouldn't do drugs. The after effect just wasn't worth it.

Curiosity was killing me, though. Not just with the drugs that she was very obviously using, but with other things too. Something just wasn't quite right with her.

I squeezed the life out of my phone, standing up abruptly in the middle of the party. All eyes were on me. "Let's go start a fire. I'm fucking bored."

Everyone cheered, following me through the cabin and down to the hill below the deck. All except Ollie and Christian. They both stared at me with their pressing eyes, but I brushed past them, grabbing a beer out of some girl's hand in the process. I downed it within seconds, not even tasting the malty flavor.

After getting the fire started, too stuck inside my head to converse with anyone, I ended up sitting back down on a folding chair, but just like that, the thoughts were back. It was like an itch on my back that I couldn't reach. A scratch in my throat that nothing soothed.

My heart ricocheted off every hard plane in my chest as I pulled my phone out once again.

I typed the words "*pink pill AMB*" and waited.

My eyes flew over the illuminated screen as I gulped in every last word that the search engine threw out to me.

After a few seconds of processing the information, I slowly clicked my phone off, sliding it back into my pocket. I stared at the fire; different hues of reds and oranges danced in front of my eyes. Ollie, Piper, Christian, and Hayley were all sitting to the left of me, some other people mingling around, shouting and laughing at nothing important, but I continued to stare.

I tried pushing away the nagging questions by joining in on conversations and even asking Piper how her brother was doing in rehab. But nothing, and I mean nothing, could curb the annoying fucking need to know more.

I wanted to hurt Madeline so I could make myself stop feeling things I didn't want to feel. I knew I was taking my anger out on her, and it wasn't wholly her fault. I was furious at my dad, pissed that he hurt my mom—*for years, apparently* —angry that he kept texting me and calling the house. I was just fucking mad.

All the time.

Hayley called me *brooding* earlier today at school when I basically threw my lunch tray at the mere presence of Madeline. Of course, no one knew I was throwing the little hissy fit because of her. But that was exactly why I acted the way that I did. Madeline. Seeing her, even a slight glimpse, made me feel things and think things that I didn't want to be thinking about.

She was that annoying little reminder that things were fucked up.

"Bro, are you good?" Ollie asked as Piper climbed off his lap and headed for the cabin.

I swallowed back the rage that was simmering below the surface. *Why the fuck am I so pissed?* "Fucking dandy. Just enjoying the show."

"What show?" Christian asked, chuckling. "You mean the fire?"

I nodded, leaning back even further into my chair, trying to escape their nagging questions. "The girls."

Ollie snickered. "You haven't given a single girl a glance, my dude. What's going on with you?"

Not this shit again.

The words rushed out. "My dad's pissed at me. Things are just fucked up. I don't want to talk about it. Family problems."

His expression fell for a moment, one side of his face shadowed by the darkness, the other lit up by the fire. "Uh. Yeah. Christian and I know all about family problems."

"Same," Hayley piped up from sitting beside Christian.

"Pipe, too," Ollie agreed, resting his elbows onto his knees, coming in a little closer to me. "You know we've got you, right?"

How the fuck could I explain years' worth of shit to them, mostly relating to Madeline—Christian's ex fucking girlfriend, main bully to his now *current* girlfriend—without fucking up everything else in my life?

Oh, hey. Yeah, so here's the deal: Madeline and I were once something, but then she stopped talking to me and started dating Christian, and I was basically in love with her the entire time but had to act like I wasn't, and then I found out my dad has been fucking her mom for years, and Madeline knew the whole goddamn time and didn't say a single word. I also can't stop thinking about her and fantasizing about what her mouth can do, but I also fucking hate her, too. How fucked is that? And my mom is depressed, and my dad won't back the fuck off. I also have no money because he's freezing me out. Good fucking times.

Even the thought exhausted me.

"I'm gonna head home. I'm not in the mood for a party." I stood up from my chair, my fists clenching by my sides. "You guys will make sure no one breaks shit?" I asked, looking down at my friends who were all clearly fucking confused.

"Yeah, man. We got you. But seriously, are you okay?"

"Are you even okay to drive?" Hayley asked, fully sincere. "I can take you home. I haven't had any alcohol."

"I've had one beer. I'm fine." And with that, I turned around and stomped my way to my car, pulling out of *my* party, not really giving a shit if people destroyed the cabin.

Once I got home, I ignored the texts lighting up my phone from a few people asking where I'd run off to and slowly made my way around the couch. Every light in the house was off, except for the small one above our stove in the kitchen. My mom was sleeping on the couch again, this time with her white shoes and blue scrubs still on. It was still weird seeing her working, given the fact that she hadn't had a job since before she and my father got married. My father made more than enough money to support us, so my mom had been a stay-at-home mom my entire life—up until she found my dad fucking the neighbor. It pushed her into this independent version of herself that I'd never seen before.

My mom's dark hair was splayed all over her face, and her arm was flung off the side of the cushion, dangling. I gently pulled the blanket up and tucked it around her body before glancing at her phone on the marble kitchen counter.

I made sure she was truly asleep before I stealthily walked over and pulled the screen open, typing in her password—my birthday, of course—and reading every last text from my father. I grunted with amusement at his name in her phone.

Asshole: I don't understand why we can't talk about this in person.

Mom: There is nothing to talk about.

Asshole: There is plenty to talk about. And what's going on with Eric? He won't return a single message of mine. I cut him off, thinking he'd come begging for money, and he hasn't.

Mom: He's hurt and confused. He found you having sex with his friend's mother. Did you think he was going to forgive you, just like that?

Asshole: I think we all three need to sit down and talk.

Mom: There is nothing to talk about. Eric will forgive you in his own time. As for me? I'm in contact with a lawyer.

Asshole: This is ridiculous.

Asshole: There is no need for a lawyer. We are not getting divorced.

Asshole: Please call me back.

I didn't even realize my chest was heaving until I felt the throbbing muscles inside working overtime. I loosened the grip I had on my mom's phone and placed it back down onto the counter as it was before. There was a manila folder pushed off to the side, and I knew that it was probably from the lawyer.

This was the first I was hearing about a divorce. I mean, it made sense. Why would she stay married to a man like my father? It shouldn't have surprised me, but it did.

Divorce.

I wasn't sure how I felt about that.

Was I relieved? Angry? Happy?

The entire time I showered, I kept trying to decipher my

feelings, but I came up empty-handed. I didn't know what I was supposed to be feeling.

I hated my father.

I hated him for putting us in this fucked-up situation.

Fuck.

After throwing on my gray sweatpants, I leaned back in my computer chair and peered out the window.

The glow from Madeline's window caught my attention—not that it was out of the ordinary; her light was always on. The chair moved up and down as my foot bounced on the floor below. Too many thoughts, too many questions, too many feelings.

There was way too much shit going on in my head to put up any of my usual walls when it came to Madeline tonight. Her face snuck in there, her pouty lips and high cheekbones. My earlier Internet search was like a neon sign flashing behind my eyes.

Why was she taking sleeping pills?

My leg stopped tapping up and down as I continued to stare at her window. There was no movement on the other side, no passing shadows behind the closed curtain, but her light was on, and it was like a beckoning call to me.

I sighed as I stood up and walked a little closer, peering down onto the ground below. Her mother's car was gone. Madeline was the only one parked in the driveway. Her father wasn't home either—no surprise there.

It was time I paid little miss Madeline a visit.

Was it a smart decision?

Probably not.

But it absolutely served as a decent distraction, and maybe it'd stop some of these nagging thoughts I couldn't seem to escape from.

CHAPTER NINE

MADELINE

A WEEK FROM HELL. That was what this week had been. A week from actual hell. Not necessarily at English Prep. I just meant in general. I'd gotten a few hours of sleep here and there—at least one hour in my World History class. Hayley Smith knocked a book off her desk seconds before the bell rang, and although she didn't look back in my direction, I was pretty sure it was to wake me up. I couldn't decide if she was trying to help me out or if she was being mean.

I deserved the latter, but knowing her, it was probably the former.

Headmaster Walton called me into his office a few hours after that, during lunch. Mrs. Boyd, the old, widowed secretary with her hair tied in a bun at the nape of her neck, gave me a strange look before I headed for his office. The plump man sat behind his expansive desk, and when the door latched behind me, I couldn't help but jump in my spot. His brow furrowed, his deep wrinkles looking more like hidden caves on his face. "Madeline, have a seat, dear."

"What is it this time?" I asked lazily, taking a seat in the leatherback chair while pretending I wasn't bothered that I was called down in the first place. The last time I was called into his office was because someone let it slip that I had stolen Hayley's uniform after gym one time. I had to buy her a new one. I liked to call that time in my life the I-hated-everyone phase.

I still hated everyone, but I hated me more. I supposed a rude awakening would do that to you. Trauma had a way of changing you from the inside out.

Headmaster Walton took his glasses off the bridge of his nose, resting them gently onto his desk. "I called you in here because a few of your teachers are concerned."

I fought hard to keep my shoulders level and chin raised. *Give him no reason to call your father, Madeline.* "Oh? About what? My grades are superb."

He beamed, flipping through a few papers on his messy desk. "Yes, they are. I'm sure your father is proud. I heard you got into Stanford."

I nodded, a burning pit burrowing deep in my belly. "Yes, I did." I had no idea if my father was proud or not. I hadn't talked or seen him in several months. He always disappeared after a fight with mom.

"So..." He raised his eyebrows expectantly. "Why exactly are you falling asleep in class?"

I fall asleep one fucking time...

"It was only one time, Headmaster Walton. I stayed up too late."

He eyed me suspiciously.

Right then, I knew I needed to get my shit together. If he called my father and raised suspicions with him, dear ol' Daddy would come crawling back home for a weekend to check in, and that was the very last thing I wanted. And it was the last thing my mom *needed*.

I had to get my shit together, and the first step to doing that was sleep.

Unfortunately, it didn't come that easy once I was home.

My back was flat against my already made bed, and I'd been like that for at least an hour or two. Something about sliding in between the mattress and blanket sent me into a panic. I didn't want to feel trapped. I just wanted to lie here, in the brightness of my room, and breathe.

Part of me wished sleep would come. The other part was terrified out of my mind.

I tried to think of everything good and fluffy, pushing the horrendous memories to the very last edge of my brain so I could relax. It wasn't even the actual memory that was bothering me so much; it was the nightmares. Because it was like reliving it over and over again.

If it was just one and done, maybe I'd be fine.

But no, I kept hearing the same voice every single time I closed my eyes.

It was exhausting.

The fluttering of my eyes startled me at first as I tried to hang on, but soon, I couldn't fight it any longer. The fear and anxiety were still there, but eventually, sleep won.

The darkness was bleak when I pulled myself awake. I blinked a few times, trying to allow my eyes to adjust, but it was no use. I couldn't see. I was pretty sure I heard the latch of my door, which was what had woken me up in the first place. I shoved the soft covers off my legs and turned my head to the red glowing numbers on my night-stand, but they were nowhere to be found. My hand reached out to find my clock, thinking it'd gotten turned somehow, but I'd hit something hard instead.

Instantly, I pulled my hand back.

"Sorry, I'm trying to be quiet," a deep voice said.

I must have still been a little disoriented and confused from sleep, because I didn't understand. My voice was raspy and broken. "What?"

"I'm trying to hurry. Scoot over, pretty."

"Scoot over for what?"

Finally, I realized what was happening.

"Whoa, jackass." Anger had me waking up pretty fast. "You're in the wrong room. My mom's room is two doors down."

I huffed, flying back onto my bed with a whoosh. The room wasn't as dark as before, my eyes now well-adjusted to the abyss. My mom had some fucking nerve. It was only a few days ago that Eric had found his father fucking her. She had been ashamed. She even apologized to me, saying sorry for having sex with my friend's dad. She didn't know we weren't friends anymore, but that was beside the point. Here she was, already beckoning a new guy into her life temporarily to keep my father's side of the bed warm until he deemed to show his face again. I never wanted to be like her. Ever. Which was why I had just mouthed off to a man I didn't know.

There was no way I would ever let a man treat me the way she lets them treat her.

It was why I was always in charge, making others fall to their knees at my wake.

"I know where your mother's room is, sweetheart."

My eyes flew back open, my back still turned to the man standing beside my bed. I felt a small trickle of anxiety prickling my neck, but I ignored it and slowly rolled back over.

"Then get the fuck out of my room." My tone was calm but sharp. I was looking at his silhouette as he loomed over me, trying to make out his features. An outside light from my window—probably Eric's headlights—shined through long enough that I could get a quick look at him. He was older—much older than me—with short, dark hair. His jaw was angled with a slight scruff on it. I couldn't make out the color of his eyes, but the way his features were drawn tight told me that he didn't care for my tone—at all.

"Don't you want to know how it feels to be with a man?"

My heart flew to an unhealthy speed.

Before I could say anything else, his hand clamped down onto my mouth fast and hard. My eyes grew wide. For a moment, I just lay there. Stunned. He took me by surprise.

I was never surprised. I was in control of every situation I was ever in, unless it came to my father, but that was a whole different ball game.

But so was this.

Finally, I regained my courage, and the anger came flying back. How dare he touch something that wasn't his? *My hands flung up, and I clawed at his skin, trying to pry away his fingers that were squeezing the life out of my face.*

This wasn't happening. This could not be happening.

When the man hooked a leg over mine and straddled my body, the fight inside of me left. Tears flung to my eyes. Wait. Why wasn't I still fighting?

It was karma. I'd made one too many bad choices. Said one too many evil things. I was getting what I deserved.

Why was I not fighting back? Why was this happening?

Knee him in the fucking dick, Maddie!

The last voice had me wavering. Eric? *Why was Eric here? That was not how this memory went. I knew what happened next, and it was enough to make my entire body go into shock.*

My eyes flew open as I gasped for air. I pushed away the covers that weren't even there and flipped over onto my stomach, falling to the ground with a thud. Pain radiated to my hip, despite the soft carpet below, and I jolted to my feet before running to my bedroom door. My hand hit the cold metal doorknob, and I twisted it no less than five times, making sure it was locked. Sweat trickled down the side of my face as I turned around to grab the computer chair to push up against the door for extra caution, but I screamed instead.

My hand flew up to cover my mouth as I stood there, all sweaty and panting, looking at Eric who was sitting in my chair in nothing but a pair of gray sweatpants with a book propped in his hand. His dark hair was damp, not moving an inch when he sliced his dark eyes my way.

"Have a nightmare, Maddie?"

My eyes closed tightly. *I'm still in a fucking nightmare, Eric.*

CHAPTER TEN

ERIC

MADELINE'S front door was locked, but being her neighbor for many years taught me where the spare key was. I moved the potted plant to the far left of the front door and found it within a second. I chuckled under my breath as I opened her door quickly, noting there was no alarm.

The entire house was dark. Madeline's mother was long gone. And her father? Well, who the fuck knew where he was.

As I climbed the steps one by one, remembering the last time I'd done just that, I stopped in front of her bedroom and listened for a moment.

Nothing. I didn't hear a single peep. A wicked part of me wondered if Madeline was in the shower, and I gave myself three seconds to imagine her wet and naked before I pushed those thoughts away and remembered that I hated her and her pretty face.

Should I knock?

No. I'd rather barge in and catch her off guard. As soon as

I turned the doorknob, the question about her pill usage on the very tip of my tongue, my shoulders slumped.

Locked?

The disappointment was there, and it was loud.

I was disappointed because I wasn't going to see her, and that didn't sit well with me. I needed to turn around and go back home. I could find a distraction elsewhere. It was really fucking low of me to come here anyway. Nothing good was going to come from it.

I hated her.

And even if I didn't, nothing beneficial was going to arise from digging into her life. Madeline had her own shit to deal with, and there was no fucking way I was going to help her with it.

She pushed me away a long, long time ago. I needed to accept that—regardless if she was no longer dating my best friend.

My head snapped to the sound of a door opening down-stairs. *Fuck.* A woman's laugh echoed through the house and carried itself to my ears.

Her tone was disgustingly flirty. "Shh. My daughter is probably asleep. We need to be quiet."

Fuck. Fuck. Fuck.

Don't get this twisted. I didn't *really* care if Madeline's mom saw me in their house or not. I just didn't want to see her. If you thought Madeline's face pissed me off, what do you think her mother's did?

So, instead of plunging myself into an even deeper pool of hate, I slipped into the room right beside Madeline's and shut the door quietly. It only took a few seconds to realize I was in Madeline's bathroom and another few after that for two voices to float on by. I rested on top of the vanity quietly, eyeing all the makeup splayed on the counter as I weighed my options and argued with myself about whether or not I should leave. I picked up one of her lipsticks and twirled it around in my hand, snickering at the name on the bottom: Pretty Liar. *How fitting.* I set the lipstick back down and continued glancing at the door opposite of the one I came through. *Did that lead to Madeline's room?*

A little wickedness seeped into my blood as I hopped to the floor and walked over to the other door. I ignored my pleas to go home as I opened it quickly, prepared to scare the hell out of her with the menacing grin on my face, but I wavered for a moment when I saw her lying on her bed.

The fancy, glittering chandelier above her was glowing brightly, as was a small light on the edge of her desk. In the far corner of her room, there was a standing lamp that was on too.

Strange.

I wasn't sure of my next move, but I found myself walking over to her pink computer chair and relaxing back in it, crossing my ankles in front of me. My gaze danced around the room as I took in her decor, stunned with confusion.

This was nothing like her.

Madeline was bold and bitchy. A little dark and sadistic at times. But her room was the complete opposite. My arms fell to my thighs as I looked up at the sparkling chandelier again, and then over to the sheer white curtains draped to the floor. Her walls were light pink, and her fluffy carpet was a shade away from white. A few teddy bears were propped up against a fur rug in the corner of her room, near the standing lamp, and there were stacks and stacks of books all over the place. A few of them were even flipped open. Everything, and I meant *everything*, in her bedroom was soft and feminine. Almost angelic. It was like seeing something forbidden. Like a villain stepping into a fairytale ending. It felt wrong to see her in a space that was probably more her than she ever wanted people to see.

I swiveled the computer chair around, grabbing a book off her desk that was stuck on page 127, and turned back to face her bed.

My eyes were just beginning to scan the pages, realizing it was some romance book, when I heard a whimpering noise. *Oh perfect. She was waking up.* I couldn't wait to see her face when she found me sitting here, all nonchalantly.

Another moan came from her, and I couldn't help the laugh that was bubbling up in my throat. *Was she having a wet dream?* I would never, ever let her live this down. It was more ammunition for torture. This was *fucking* gold.

I began to grin as I continued watching her, but my smile slowly crumbled as Madeline started to kick her legs, whimpering even louder. Her blonde hair was tangled around her face, little crinkles appearing around her clenched eyes.

The book fell to my lap as I sat up a little taller. My brow furrowed as her head snapped back and forth. Her voice sounded far away, pained even, when she mumbled, "No. *No.*"

Something about the way she said the word caused my fists to clench. My chest felt like it was caving in on itself, almost making it hard to breathe.

"*No.* Don't touch me!"

The chair creaked as I went to stand so I could wake her. This was wrong. This was no longer fun.

Was she crying?

Madeline's legs started to kick back and forth. She was clearly trying to get away from something. My mind was going a million miles a second. I could tell myself I hated her. I could remind myself of every last mean thing she'd ever done. But there was nothing that was going to make my heart stop beating like I was seconds from falling off a cliff. I'll admit, I enjoyed bullying her a little. I liked seeing her face fall when I reminded her how much I hated her.

But I wasn't a sick fuck.

I wasn't enjoying this.

It was real. Too real.

Just as I climbed to my feet, Madeline gasped, and I froze. She flung off her bed in record time, landing on the floor. She flew to her feet and darted over to her door, jiggling the handle so hard I thought it was going to snap.

I slowly sat back down onto the chair, washing away the worry from my face. I thought fast on my feet, telling myself not to act concerned in any way whatsoever, because she'd only push further if she knew I was worried. Madeline had a thick wall in place when it came to others, which was exactly why she was cruel to people. I wasn't dense. I'd watched her from afar. Her cruelness would climb to its highest peak when someone got too close. I'd always known there was a reason behind it.

When Madeline turned around, blue eyes wild with fear, she let out a yelp.

Not a single muscle on my face moved. I flicked my attention to her as she stood by her door in nothing but cotton shorts and a loose shirt. Wet tears glistened on her pale cheeks.

Madeline placed her hand over her heart and clenched her eyes shut as faint lines formed at the corners. Her blonde hair was sticking to the sides of her temples with sweat. I had no idea what she had dreamed about, but I intended to find out.

I stayed calm. My voice was almost eerie. "Have a nightmare, Maddie?"

The book I was casually skimming through a few seconds ago was back in my hand, making it look like I had been sitting here for hours, reading leisurely as I waited for her to wake up.

Madeline moved a few pieces of hair behind her ear with shaky fingers that she desperately tried to hide. Her tiny hands formed into fists by her sides after the small gesture.

"What the fuck are you doing in my bedroom? How..." She looked back to her bedroom door, her supple body glowing from the lamp behind her. "How did you get in here?"

I inclined my head to the bathroom door before putting my attention back on the book. I couldn't stand to look at her. I was worried. *I was fucking worried about her.*

The feeling *almost* had me throwing the book across the floor and storming out of her bedroom. I was disgusted. I shouldn't have been worried about her.

My head was all sorts of fucked up. I eyed the door behind her, ready to dart out of it.

"Shit," she muttered, rubbing her hand down the side of her face. Much to my surprise, her face turned even whiter. I expected her to be embarrassed that I was here watching her. Maybe a little flushed in the cheeks.

But no. She was pale. A sickly pale.

I continued to watch her every movement. The darting of her eyes to the bathroom door and to the chair I was sitting on. Her tiny rib cage heaving underneath her t-shirt. The shaking of her hands.

Madeline finally seemed to remember that I was in her room, because she settled a glare on me and bit out, "Why are you here, Eric?"

I clicked my tongue, taking my attention and putting it back onto the book in my hand. I lazily flipped a page. "Well," I started, "I came to ask you why you were taking Ambien, but I think I already know."

I brought my eyes back to hers purely to see her reaction.

This time, her cheeks did flush. A small spread of pink washed over her sculpted cheekbones. Her plump, curved lips fell into a straight line as she glanced away.

"What were you dreaming about?" I asked.

She gritted through her teeth. "None of your fucking business."

"Hmm." I clicked my tongue. "Try again."

"Get out of my room."

I chuckled, throwing the book onto the desk behind me. It landed with a small thud. "What were you dreaming about, Madeline? Why are you taking sleeping pills?" My eye twitched as I tried to appear relaxed. But I wasn't. I felt a little crazed. No matter what she did or said, I still had this small, miniscule part of me that cared about her. It was the most agonizing feeling in the world—caring about someone who didn't deserve it. It was like having some deviant form of Stockholm syndrome, and being alone with her was only making it worse.

Madeline padded over to me as I sat in her computer chair, feeling all sorts of pissed off about feeling shit I had no business feeling.

"Why do you even care?" she asked, stopping just a few feet away from me.

"I don't," I rushed out. "Just curious, that's all." My head tilted back as I met her stare, evening my tone. "It's not every day I see a girl like you crumble. I'd been wondering what was so important about those little pink pills since I witnessed you acting so damn pathetic over them the other night. So I went ahead and did an Internet search earlier and found out just what they were. So, Maddie...what's keeping you up at night?"

She laughed sarcastically under her breath. "It sounds a lot like caring to me, Eric." She crossed her arms over her perky tits. "Wouldn't want to confuse that with *hating* me, right?"

"Oh, I still hate you, Madeline. Don't think for a second that I don't."

She laughed sarcastically again, throwing her delicate chin back. "Oh, right. I forgot. You hate me because your dad fucked my mom. Sounds legit."

I stood up quickly from her chair, peering down at her. "That's not why I fucking hate you, Madeline."

She threw her hands up, feigning innocence as she mocked me. "Oh no. He used my full name instead of the cute little pet name. That must mean you're *mad,* huh?" Madeline stepped closer to me, her soft scent wrapping around my body like a fucking thorny vine, suffocating every last ounce of oxygen from the room.

"I am fucking mad." *I was.* I was so fucking mad all the time. It wasn't even really directed toward her most of the time, but it was there, lying underneath every single fake laugh and forced smile.

Madeline rolled her eyes. "For fucks' sake, Eric. Get over it." She slammed her hands onto her hips after throwing them up in the air. "So what, I knew your dad fucked my mom, but there are much worse things out there to be pissed about. Just leave me alone. Go hate-fuck some girls. Get it out of your system. I don't have time for this bullshit." She threw her hands up again, but this time it wasn't for show. She was getting riled up, her voice rising, her cheeks growing even redder. "Does your dad hit you? Or your mom? Does he choke her with anger?"

I laughed out loud. "Yeah, fucking right. I'd break his goddamn arms, and he knows it."

"Then quit being a little bitch, Eric! Get over it. Men cheat. It's not the end of the world. If I knew you were going to be this fucking ridiculous over it, I would have told you back in seventh grade. I could have avoided this entire thing."

Everything stilled. My arms dropped to my sides. My heart thumped painfully slow in some sort of calculated rhythm as I stared at her heaving chest. *Wait a fucking minute.* I paused before meeting her face. "That's... That's why you stopped talking to me?"

Madeline paused too. She looked away quickly, glancing at her window so all I could see was the dainty little curve of her nose. "Get out of my room, Eric."

"Not until you answer my question."

Silence fell between us, but it wasn't the quiet kind. No, it was loud and heavy and cold.

"That's why you stopped talking to me, isn't it? Because you found out my dad was fucking your mom."

She whipped her head over, her blue eyes piercing me. "Yes, now get the fuck out of my room." She stomped her way over to her bedroom door, unlocked it, and threw it open.

I didn't waste any time. I needed to be far, far away from her right now. One second I was fucking fuming, wanting to throw shit across her room, and the next I was itching to wrap my hands around her hips to fuck the heightened emotions right out of her. I was hot as hell on the outside but freezing cold on the inside.

I strode angrily all the way to her door but paused right in front of her. I stared at the dark and empty hall right over the threshold of her room before giving her a questionable look. "Why did you ask that?"

Her eyes dipped for a moment, but her voice was still as sharp as a butcher's knife. "Ask what?"

"Why did you ask if my dad hit me? Or my mom?"

Her mouth opened, the sound of her lips parting falling in between us. "I... What?"

My brow furrowed. There was an invisible hand wrapped around my throat, squeezing and squeezing until I couldn't breathe anymore. "Does..." *No. Don't go there. Don't ask.*

"Careful, Eric," she whispered. "You're starting to act like you give a fuck about me again."

A sinister laugh came out of my mouth before I moved in close, invading her space, breathing down onto her half-hidden face. "We wouldn't want that now, would we? Otherwise, I might just see through that thick wall you put up to keep everyone out."

Madeline didn't say a word.

Before I stepped into the hall and descended down the stairs, I whispered loud enough for her to hear, "I wonder just how fucking ugly it is behind that pretty face of yours."

I wasn't sure if Madeline said anything in response, because I booked it out of there before I gave her the chance.

Madeline was more fucked up than I thought, and apparently, I was too, because all I wanted to do was fuck her senseless and crumble each and every last wall she had put up.

CHAPTER ELEVEN

MADELINE

WHEN YOU DIDN'T GET an adequate amount of sleep, your decision-making skills lacked. When you didn't get an adequate amount of sleep, you started questioning things that you shouldn't even be questioning. When you didn't get an adequate amount of sleep, you started imagining things that weren't true. When you didn't get an adequate amount of sleep, you grew weak—and I didn't just mean that physically, but emotionally too.

It'd been four days since I found Eric in my bedroom.

My thoughts were scattered around like ashes in an ashtray. I kept going back to our conversation—or should I say *argument*. Eric and I couldn't have a normal conversation without spitting insults at each other, but I kept questioning his reactions that night. He watched me like a hawk, his eyes tracing over my body, running his attention all over my face, trying to decipher my every move. He wanted to know what was going on with me.

But it was truly none of his business. It wasn't anyone's business.

Sure, it was lonely dealing with things on my own, and it was exhausting pushing everyone away and creating this hateful aura around myself, but it was better that way.

Soon, I'd be off to college—Stanford (my father's wishes) —and I would start over. No one would know me as the mean girl of English Prep. No one would call me a slut, indicating that the apple (me) didn't fall far from the tree (my mother). I wouldn't have to lock my door at night or peer out my window each morning, wondering if I needed to escape down the drainpipe to avoid a trauma-inducing run-in with my mother's fuck buddy. I could leave this place behind and hopefully get some decent sleep without a nightmare.

Anxiety was a wicked bitch, creeping in at the last second before I fell into a deep slumber, awakening me with fear clawing at my throat.

I felt small and inferior.

My gaze wandered over to Hayley Smith.

She once said something to me, after I'd given her my best bullying tactics, that hadn't left my thoughts. She looked down at me, with her pretty face and soft expression, and said, "*Someone made you feel inferior once; that's why you are the way that you are.*" At the moment, I was angry. I felt her closing in. Hayley Smith was no fool; she saw right through me, and it made me panic.

But she was right.

I *did* feel inferior. Someone took the crown off my head and bent it before putting it back. Just like my father did to my mother. I promised myself I'd never allow anyone to treat me poorly or look down at me like I was *nothing*, but now look at me.

"Madeline?"

I blinked several times, breaking my stare. My moist,

burning eyes gazed around the locker room, and I realized almost everyone from PE was gone. I was still sitting on the wooden bench, my plaid uniform clasped tightly in my hand.

"Madeline? Are you okay?" I gave my attention to Hayley, who was still getting dressed. She slipped her blouse over her black bra and started buttoning it up, tucking it into her plaid skirt, all while staring at me hesitantly.

I couldn't pretend Hayley wasn't beautiful in this tough, I've-been-through-some-shit type of way. Her chestnut hair barely fell below her slender shoulders, and her face was clear of any makeup, but she was still pretty.

Envy hit me square in the face so hard I turned away. I was jealous of Hayley, but it wasn't because she was madly in love with my ex-boyfriend. It was because I knew she'd had a rough life, and I knew she'd been through really fucking shitty times, but she *still* came out on top. She was the nice girl. The one who people worshipped because they wanted to. Not like it was with me. I scared people. They followed me because I forced them to. Hayley was all things good, despite the bad. I was the complete opposite.

I finally answered her, still sitting in the same spot. My muscles were sore from playing volleyball in gym, but it was likely because I was just too tired and weak to recover like usual. "No, Hayley. I'm not okay."

I snuck a quick peek at her, feeling indifferent with my not-so-subtle answer. The concern etched on her soft features had me backtracking. *Why did I say that?* I stood up quickly, still gripping my clothes. "But it's really none of your business."

She nodded, agreeing with me. "You're right. It's not."

Good. Now leave me alone.

I turned around and began stripping out of my gym clothes, pulling my stockings on so fast I thought they might rip. The shuffling of feet had me biting my lip. For some strange reason, tears formed behind my thick eyelashes. I was blaming it on lack of sleep, but I knew it was because I was breaking. I was breaking in half. I was tired, physically and emotionally.

Going home later wasn't even a relief. It was Friday. I should have been thrilled to have the weekend away from everyone at English Prep, but the weekends were almost worse. Hell was hell, no matter where I was.

"Madeline?"

A lump rested at the very edge of my throat. I didn't answer Hayley, too afraid I'd either say something callous as a form of self-preservation or completely succumb to the weight on my chest and crack in half right in front of the one person who should probably hate me the most.

I almost wanted her to hate me. I basically craved the punishment that I deserved.

What was wrong with me?

"Madeline," she repeated as I kept my back to her. I stopped fiddling with my skirt and dropped my eyes to the floor. The air conditioner kicked on with a buzz, a cold draft coating my cool skin. "Do you need help?"

My voice came out weak, and my face flamed with embarrassment as a result. "Help with what?"

"Are..." She paused, her voice closer. "Are you in some sort of danger? It's just... I know what fear looks like. I know what it feels like. You're afraid of something. I can see it in your eyes. I can see it in your posture. I see the way you push people away."

I tried to come up with some insult, something nasty to say to her. Something that would make her face tighten and cause her to flee the locker room, but nothing came out.

I began turning around. To do what? I had no idea. I wasn't sure what to say or do, but for some reason, I had the urge to look her in the face. Maybe I'd ask her how she did it.

How she came out on top after going through trauma. But a familiar voice had my spine straightening and my resolve falling.

"Babe? Are you still in here?"

"Yeah, give me a sec," Hayley yelled back, but it was too late. Christian was definitely in the locker room. I could feel his presence. I quickly threw on the rest of my uniform.

"Oh," he snarled. *"Madeline."* He paused before spitting the words, "Get out."

"Christian," Hayley warned.

I was still facing the lockers, unable to turn around to face the power couple of English Prep. I began threading the buttons on my blouse as his words rang out.

"What?" he asked innocently. "I could have said '*get the fuck out,*' but I refrained from being mean—not that she deserves it."

"Christian," Hayley chastised him. "Stop."

My uniform was on fully now. My shoes were untied, but that didn't really matter. I gathered my blonde hair to one side of my neck and slowly turned around to face Christian and Hayley. She was angled toward him, half in between us, with her arms crossed over her blouse. Her big round eyes were raised high, a warning look flashing. Christian was glaring at me with his smoldering look, hating me just as everyone else did.

"He's right," I said, almost whispering.

I must have caught Christian off guard, and honestly, in the few years that he and I had dated back and forth, I'd never ever evoked a single emotion from him. We were superficial, using each other as a distraction. Curving our boredom.

He was hot, I'd give him that, but I knew nothing about him. And he knew nothing about me.

"What do you mean, *I'm right?*" Christian strode over to

Hayley and stood with his hands on his hips, pulling back his navy English Prep blazer some.

I eyed Hayley, and she was watching me with patient, doe-like eyes. Usually, she and I glared at each other or ignored one another completely, but it felt like she was looking right through my wall. She knew what struggle looked like, even if disguised. She knew I was fucked up.

"You're right," I repeated with more confidence. "I do deserve it." I grabbed my backpack and flung it over my shoulder. I whisked past the two of them quickly, making it out the door before I hyperventilated. I rushed to the end of the hall and pressed my back along the metal lockers to get my breathing intact. These moments of weakness were no longer few and far between. They were coming more frequently and lasting much longer than they should have.

I pulled my phone out and shot a quick text to Atticus, asking him to meet up again for more Ambien. I needed to sleep. I needed to heal. I needed to hold myself together until college.

Then I could breathe.

Then I wouldn't have to lock my door.

And I wouldn't have to fear my father's car in the driveway.

Just as I shoved my phone back in my pocket, I heard familiar voices coming down the hallway. I rushed to the bathrooms just past the locker room and pressed my back into the corner so I'd be temporarily hidden.

Ollie's laugh boomed and echoed along the lockers, and even though it was faint, I could tell Eric was chuckling beside him.

I took a teeny, tiny peek around the corner, catching a fleeting glimpse of him. A warmness coated my belly, and a faint, content smile ghosted over my lips. Eric was grinning at Ollie and Piper, happiness evident in his dark eyes. It was rare to see him happy. Whenever he was around me or glanced in my direction, his cheery attitude would fall, and he'd turn that cheeky grin into a malicious scowl.

I quickly pulled myself back, tucking away that rare visual of a happy Eric into my back pocket for later, and continued to listen.

God. How the tables had turned for me. Here I was, on the other end of the English Prep popularity stick, hiding away and lurking in corners to hear what the cool kids had to say.

So pathetic. Yet, I couldn't seem to stop.

I nibbled on my lip, straining my ears.

"That was fucking weird."

"What was?" Piper asked, talking to Christian.

He and Hayley must have come out of the locker room when I was in my Eric trance.

"Madeline...in the locker room."

Hayley huffed. "I told you to stop being a jerk. Something is totally off with her. She hasn't said a snide remark to me in weeks. Not even a dirty look. Has she to you, Pipe?"

Piper spoke. "Actually...no. I noticed something off with her at the dress shop a few weeks ago. Do you remember how she looked like she wanted to tell us something, Hay? Then she clammed up at the end?"

"Yeah. I know something is wrong with her. Something bad. I can see it."

"Who cares?" Christian said. Their voices were getting farther and farther away, and I had to force myself to stay hidden against the wall instead of following them around. I wanted to hear what Eric had to say, even though it would likely hurt me.

Apparently, I liked the feeling of a knife twisting my insides.

"What happened in the locker room?" My heart sparked at the sound of his voice. My stomach dipped.

"She pretty much said she deserved the bullying when I threw an asshole remark at her." He paused. "Surprised the shit out of me. I never thought I'd see a day where Madeline actually looked remorseful. Sad, even."

Silence filled the hall, and I wasn't sure if they'd left or if the conversation ended.

Just as I was about to step out into the hall, Hayley spoke. "Something made her the way that she is. It's just catching up to her now. I think we should help her."

My body stilled.

I started to feel a little unsteady on my feet. My skin was clammy to the touch.

I heard the sound of lips smacking. "And that, babe, is why you're *you*." Christian must have given Hayley a kiss for being nice. The thought used to make me snarl, but now I was hopeful. Hopeful that someday I'd feel like I deserved that type of love.

Once I felt the coast was clear, I hurriedly darted down the opposite hallway and out the side doors of English Prep. The parking lot was basically desolate, everyone on their way to their happy fucking weekend parties and whatnot, living their best high school lives.

I looked over to where the guys usually parked, where *I* used to park, and I stopped my feet just along the patch of grass separating the parking lot from the sidewalk.

Eric was leaning back along his Range Rover with his arms crossed over his button-up shirt. His tie was loosely hanging around his neck, the first two buttons undone, showing off his tanned skin. My mouth went dry as his gray eyes surrounded by long, dark eyelashes squinted. Too many empty parking spots laid between us for anything more than a long glance, but I saw the way he questioned me with the tilt of his head.

Eric was beginning to see a lot more than I wanted him to see. He was paying attention to my subtle mood changes and behavior. I wasn't sure why, because he had a serious vendetta against me. Maybe he wanted to watch me crumble. Maybe he wanted to make my life even harder by gaining some recon.

I didn't know, and I really didn't want to find out.

I pulled my attention away as I unlocked my car and climbed inside.

As I was pulling out of the parking lot, pretending I didn't notice Eric still leaning against his car, all hot and mysterious, I got a text from Atticus.

Atticus: I'll get them. Meet me at 9. Same house. Same room. Same price.

I rolled my eyes at the last part, but I'd still show up. And this time, Eric wouldn't be there to interfere.

CHAPTER TWELVE

ERIC

THE MUSIC in Christian's Charger rattled the change in the cup holder beside me as we headed to Jesse's frat house again. Usually, he and Ollie would both be with Piper and Hayley on a Friday night, but they were having some girls' night or something with Ann, Hayley's ex social worker.

I wasn't even sure what a girls' night was. I'd never been in a lengthy relationship before, and I was an only child—meaning I didn't have a sister. I had nights *spent* with girls—multiple, even—but I didn't think that was anything close to what Hayley and Piper were doing with Ann. I surely hoped not.

My mom was working a late shift again at the hospital, and I couldn't bring myself to ask about the impending divorce. The papers were moved from the counter to her bedroom, so I assumed that meant she wasn't ready to talk to me about it. Which was fine. I'd be here when she needed me.

As for my father... Well, he'd given up on the threatening texts and now called me once a day. I ignored every last ring.

Just like I had ignored the light being on in Madeline's bedroom every night for the past week. I was pretty good at denial.

Madeline's car was gone when Christian picked me up, and I couldn't ignore the thrilling thought that she might show up at Jesse's again. I mean, it was likely, considering every single pill she bought from the party last weekend was gone. But if she knew what was good for her, she wouldn't be here tonight.

Madeline was playing a very dangerous game with taking those sleeping pills. I'd learned enough about drugs lately that I knew nothing good came from them if being taken illegally. She didn't know what she was fucking doing.

"Why are you shaking my entire fucking car?"

I whipped my head over to Christian who was eyeing me. "What are you so mad about, bro? Look at your fists." He nodded his head to my thighs, where my hands rested in achingly tight fists on top of my jeans.

"Nothing," I snapped. "Let's go."

I pulled the handle on the door as Christian just barely got his car into park. The rumble of the engine cut off quickly as I began rounding the steps of the frat house.

The sun was finished for the day, the moon well above my head. But even in the bleakness of night, I could tell the classic, Victorian-looking frat house was a hunter-green color. The peak had scalloped siding, and it reminded me a little of a gingerbread house. I bypassed a few groups of college students loitering on the lawn with red cups in their grasps when a hand clamped onto my shoulder. The grip was firm, and it felt like claws shot out from my fingers.

"What, Christian?" I asked, spinning around. Ollie was smirking from beside him, waiting for us to have words.

"Are you going to act this uptight the entire night? Because I'm about sick of the whole angry, pensive vibe you've got going lately."

Ollie rubbed his lips together, chuckling under his breath.

I ran my tongue over my teeth angrily. "You've got to be fucking kidding. You were a fucking ass for the last few years of high school. Just because you've got Hayley now, and you're all fucking happy, doesn't mean the rest of us are."

Christian's hands flexed. "Then why don't you do something about it? Go fuck someone. Go fuck lots of someones. Get whatever the fuck is up your ass out, because we have a few months left of school, and then we're off on our own. Do you really want to spend it being like this?"

As if it were that easy to just snap out of it.

My long strides brought me over to him quickly. We were like two angry bulls, ready to fight, both of our brows bundled together with anger. "You have no idea what you're talking about. Did you hear me or Ollie asking you to quit being a depressed dick when you were hating the world?" I got closer, my voice rumbling out of my mouth. "No. We fucking backed you up—*always*. Now, I'm asking you to back me up. Let me be mad. Let me hate everyone. Let me work through my shit. Jesus. You're as bad as my fucking father." I wanted to hit him. I wanted to punch his stupid straight nose and make it crooked.

Fighting wasn't foreign to me. Or to Christian. But it'd been years since he and I had fought. We had once gotten into a fight, freshman year, which was what had decided our fate at English Prep. He thought I was fighting him to prove a point in front of everyone, but I wasn't. I was fighting him because he took Madeline from me, and I was so fed up with pretending like it didn't darken my soul a little each time they kissed.

I remembered pounding his face until I caught a glance at

Madeline's heart-shaped mouth pursed into a frown through the formed crowd. I let Christian win that day. I let him win because I knew I'd always be on the losing side if I kept chasing her. That I'd continue resenting him for being with her even when he had no idea.

A couple of college girls roamed past us as I came back to reality. Christian was about to spit something else in my face, but his phone rang. He sighed angrily and took a step back. Once he pulled his phone out, he turned around and answered.

"Hey, baby."

His tone was no longer pissy and domineering. He was obviously talking to Hayley.

"Yeah, we just got here. Don't worry. I'm the DD. Ollie and I just came to hang with Eric." He looked over his shoulder at me and glared, as if he were telling me we weren't done with the conversation.

Fuck him.

Ollie sauntered up beside me and nudged my tense shoulder. "It's honestly astounding how quickly he can go from fucking pissed to a whipped boyfriend in three seconds flat. Isn't it?"

I didn't answer, but apparently, Ollie didn't catch on to my don't-fucking-start-with-me mood. There was some serious pent-up aggression trying to claw its way out of my chest.

Between my family shit and the unyielding thoughts of Madeline and her stupid fucking light glaring into my window each night, I was drowning in shit I wanted no part of.

It wasn't even that I was denying the fucked-up shit going on in my life currently. I just wanted to stop caring for the night.

Ollie was still talking. "It's almost sickening. Listen to him talking all sweetly to Hayley, and I bet when he gets off the phone, he'll turn back into his true alpha form and start on you again."

I grunted in response. Christian was an alpha, but I was too. People didn't fuck with me. People didn't talk back to me. I wasn't an easy-going guy, by any means.

The only reason Christian dominated the halls of English Prep was because I had let him back when we were freshman. There was no fucking way I was fighting for that role, because if I did, that'd mean I'd have to put up an even bigger fight of denying my feelings for Madeline. Because up until recently, she was the queen of English Prep. I wanted absolutely no part in her world.

Yet, somehow, I kept finding myself circling the pits of hell with Madeline right in the center.

"Eric, you do you. We're here for you, even if you do have a pole up your ass."

I finally let my gaze wander to Ollie. He was smiling in his typical happy-go-lucky way, but I saw the pointed look in his eye. It twitched at the last second. He knew something was going on with me, and I wasn't sure what Piper had told him. She was the most invasive of all of us, yet in her own secret way.

"Thanks," I managed to force out, side-stepping him and leaving Christian, who continued talking to his girlfriend on the phone.

I scanned the cars lining the street and didn't see Madeline's car anywhere. It seemed she went somewhere else tonight, which was good. I was going to grasp tightly to that little break in my spiraling thoughts for the next few hours.

Madeline wasn't winning this one. I wasn't going to feel bad for her or wonder why she slept with her light on every night.

Maybe Christian was right. Maybe I *did* need to fuck someone else.

CHAPTER THIRTEEN

MADELINE

I PULLED up to the frat party right before the clock hit eight and felt relief settle into my bones. Eric's car was parked in his driveway when I'd gotten home from my hair appointment—the one my mom had set up for me to keep my hair the platinum blonde that it was to please my father who only popped up into our lives occasionally—so I knew Eric wasn't going to be here tonight.

I needed to get in, get out, drive back home, and sleep for the rest of the weekend without the anxiety of another nightmare waking me up.

Kicking an empty beer bottle out of the way, I made my way through the opened door of the house. The party was much busier tonight than last weekend. Too many people were crammed into the open floor plan. Weed and stale beer lingered in the air, along with cheap cologne and perfume from those who were trying too hard to get laid. I hardly managed to swallow back the putrid smell.

I skirted my gaze over the room quickly, trying to spot

Atticus. There was a young couple arguing in the corner, a few girls gathered together on the disgusting couch, talking with their heads down low, and a lonesome dude with long blonde hair in the other chair, typing on his phone. I glanced to the other corner of the room, past a few girls dancing drunkenly, and my eyes widened. The heel of my Doc Martens squeaked on the hardwood as I spun around quickly.

Shit! What the hell are Wellington Prep boys doing here?

I bristled at the very vivid recollection of when I inevitably fucked my entire existence at both English Prep and Wellington Prep—the opposing prep school in the area—with an awful rumor I'd started revolving around one of their own.

I don't even remember why I did it. The old Madeline was malicious in an attempt to protect herself and her tough-girl image. The new one realized that no matter how malicious or forthcoming you were, you still weren't invincible.

And not long after I'd started the rumor and everything fell apart, karma made her stop at my house and completely ruined me. Everything before that moment became one giant blur. It was cruel how the worst memory of your life was the one that stood out the most. Fear was a strong and blinding emotion.

I shuffled my feet to the stairs, keeping my back to Cole, the one guy who should hate my fucking guts the most, and began climbing them hastily.

The damaged girl that now lived within my bones begged for me to apologize, but I was too ashamed to even look in his direction. I was a little afraid too.

I did him dirty.

Really dirty.

Each door in the upstairs hallway was shut, even Atticus', but I wasn't wasting any time. I raised my shaky fist to knock, and that was when Cole's smooth voice sounded from behind.

"Did you think you could sneak past me?"

Since your back was to me, yes. I actually did, Cole.

My hand dropped to my side slowly, and I had to make the decision between fight or flight. My limbs ached to take me into the room in front of me and to slam the door in his face. But I was stronger than that. I was. *At least I used to be.*

I ran my tongue over my lips before spinning around and locking onto his green eyes. Cole was an attractive guy. He was a bad boy through and through. Dark, shiny hair. Thick eyelashes and a strong jaw. His bottom lip had a tiny, faint scar in it that led down to his chin—the perfect touch to his bad-boy appeal.

"Cole," I managed to croak out. It infuriated me that I could hear the fear in my tone.

"I knew it'd only be a matter of time until I ran into you."

I nodded my head as my eyes dropped.

I heard him shuffling closer to me. There was no one else in the hallway. Everyone was locked behind closed doors, doing God knew what in random bedrooms. For a moment, I took my eyes off my shoes and glanced over at the landing of the steps. Cole's entire crew was staring up at us in the midst of the party around them, all with swag-like grins covering their faces.

Oh, God. What does he have planned?

I began panicking. The floor felt like Jell-O under my feet. "Listen, Cole," I started, backing up just a hair. "I'm..." I darted my gaze away from his haughty one.

He took a step closer, taking advantage of my paranoia. "What's that? Cat got your tongue there, Madeline? It's funny, because it didn't seem to have your tongue when you told that nasty fucking rumor to Christian fucking Powell." His wide shoulders came closer to mine, caging me in against the door. I wished that Atticus was on the other side and he'd open it so I'd fall backwards and out of Cole's trap. Atticus likely wasn't the hero of any situation, but for now, he could be mine if he'd just open the fucking door. My breaths were coming in short spasms. My skin grew clammy.

I used to be strong. I didn't put up with people's shit. People were scared of me, not the other way around.

But now I was weak and scared. I wanted to turn around and bang my fists on the door, begging someone to save me.

Cole's knee went between my legs as his hard chest pressed against mine. He smelled like the ocean, and it would've been refreshing if I wasn't frozen with fear. *I deserve this.* Just like I deserved the karma I got served after.

A whimper came from deep inside my chest, and Cole's glare vanished for a split second. "You told him I was a rapist."

My eyes shut as the word assaulted me.

Darkness clouded my vision as I tried to push away the thoughts scratching at the walls of my brain. My hands reached up on their own, and I put them on Cole's chest. "I'm sorry," I whispered, about to shove him away.

"Why'd you do it, Madeline? Huh? Were you that desperate to fuck me?"

I shook my head hastily, my eyes still sealed shut. "I—I..." I couldn't think straight. "I'm sorry, Cole. I wasn't..." I swallowed, trying to catch my breath. "I wasn't in my right mind. I was trying to prove..." The words were lost on my tongue.

When I'd started that rumor, months ago, I was at my lowest. I was trying to prove to everyone that Christian was my knight in shining armor, that I still had a hold on him, because I felt him slipping from my grasp. I felt my entire existence at English Prep slipping. I wanted to prove to everyone that Christian loved me, but my plan backfired.

"Trying to prove what? Huh?" I jumped at the coldness in Cole's tone.

Just as a mortifying tear was beginning to fall over my cheek, Cole's threatening shadow was ripped from my vision.

A thundering, rough voice boomed throughout the hall. "Tell me one good reason why I shouldn't throw you over this fucking banister and break your body in half."

My mouth fell open at the sight of Eric holding Cole by the collar of his shirt over the hall banister. Cole's face turned beet red, angry lines running all over his features.

Eric's back was to me, but I could see the tenseness in his broad shoulders. The veins in his forearms bulged with rushing blood. He was going to fucking kill him.

Oh my God.

"Eric!" I shouted, rushing toward them. "Stop! What are you doing?" Never mind the mind-blowing fact that Eric was coming to *my* rescue. But he was dangling Cole over a sea of people who were beginning to give us their attention. People had their phones out, recording the incident. *This was bad.*

"Eric, let him go!" I said between clenched teeth. My skin was hot and itchy, the bothersome feeling creeping up my neck.

Eric's fists were as white as a ghost as he clung onto Cole's shirt. He shot me a look that felt like a knife cutting my throat. "Was it him?" he demanded.

I stared into his stormy eyes that were clouded with anger. "Was what him?! Eric, let him go right now. You're going to kill him."

He chuckled sarcastically. It was sinister-like. "That's the fucking point, Madeline." He turned back to Cole who was actively trying to stay still. "Did you fucking rape her?"

Cole looked at me like he wanted to wring my neck. "What the fuck, Madeline?! Again?"

"No, no, no!" I slapped my hand on Eric's forearm. "That was a rumor made up months ago, Eric. Let him go! I was apologizing to him."

Eric shook his head angrily. "That wasn't a fucking rumor, Madeline."

Oh my God. "What? Yes, it was! Cole did not rape me. Or Cara!"

Cole scoffed, trying to push Eric's vise-like grip off his shirt. "Fucking finally. Can I get that on camera?"

"Shut the fuck up," Eric seethed in his direction.

Movement below caught my eye as I saw the Wellington Prep boys starting to edge closer to the stairs. Each and every last one of them looked lethal as they kept their eyes locked and loaded on Eric.

Cole grunted. "I didn't fucking rape her, man." He glared at me for a moment before continuing. "Although she probably fucking deserved it for making up that rumor."

My heart bled inside my chest. *He was right.* A dark cloud started to crowd my vision again as my breath began to hiccup. *Nope.* I shoved the memory away as hard as I could and squeezed my eyes shut. When I opened them again after regaining my composure, I locked onto Eric who was observing me intently.

He gave me one more quick glance and then pulled Cole away from the banister before hitting him so hard I heard something crack. Cole bent over at his knees and shouted. Blood began to rush from his face onto the floor. Eric snarled as he took a step back. His dark hair was sweaty on his head, sticking to his forehead. The muscles in his jaw ticked back and forth as he rubbed his knuckles. Over his shoulder, halfway down the stairs, I saw Christian and Ollie running with all of Cole's friends behind them.

It was going to be a brawl, and I was the one standing in between the two opposing sides.

"What the fuck is going on? Why the fuck is Eric fighting on your behalf?" Ollie demanded, rushing in front of me as Christian strode to stand beside Eric. I heard Christian make a snarky remark to Cole as Ollie snapped his fingers in my face. "Madeline? What the fuck did you do?"

I began shaking my head. "Nothing! Eric misunderstood. I told him to stop!" I stumbled over my words. "He thinks..." Loud commotion had Ollie and me ceasing our conversation.

Cole was yelling at Eric, telling him to come at him again. And Christian was holding Eric back, telling him to stop. "Eric, calm the fuck down. There's three of us and ten of them. We'll have to pick a fight another time."

Eric yelled over Christian's shoulder. "You're fucking sick, saying shit like that! You deserve more than a fucking broken nose."

Christian snapped his head to Ollie and me as he struggled to hold Eric back by his shoulders. "A little fucking help? Madeline, get him out of here! Fix whatever you did to cause this." I didn't waste any time running over and grabbing Eric's forearm to pull him away.

Christian yelled at Ollie, "You're tight with Piper's cousin. Go fix this shit so we don't get fucking ambushed." He grabbed onto Eric's face—hard. "Go. Right now. Calm the fuck down."

Eric ripped his jaw from Christian's grasp and locked onto me. I turned around quickly, unable to stand being scrutinized, and pulled his arm along with me. I whisked him into the door at the end of the hall and locked it behind us, ignoring the sign taped to the front that said *Out of order - go pee outside.*

The light was on within seconds, and his arm was ripped out of my grasp even quicker.

He stormed the tiny room, walking over the dirty vinyl floor. Back and forth. Back and forth. His shaky hand reached up, and he shoved his now curling black hair off his forehead and continued to breath heavily through his nose.

The hollow parts of his cheeks were tinted with an angry red. His eyes were darting. He looked everywhere but at me. Which was fine. I could hardly form words without his eyes on me, let alone if they were.

Almost as if he heard my thought, he stopped pacing and stood right in front of me. I kept my eyes on the tan bathroom rug that laid in between us, feeling like my lungs were going to explode.

"Who fucking touched you?"

My stomach dropped, and I somehow found the strength to raise my gaze, but I was too ashamed to look him in the eye. Instead, I looked in the mirror just over his shoulder and held back a shudder.

Strands of blonde hair framed my face, but it did nothing but accentuate my pale cheeks. My blue eyes glittered with unshed tears, and my lips were trembling. *Fuck.*

I pulled myself out of the trance and tried keeping my eyes unreadable as I placed them on Eric who was waiting for my answer. His strong, straight nose was flaring as he breathed deeply.

"What are you talking about?" I tried to deflect. "I told you it was a rumor I made up months ago. You remember. You were at the party when I told Christian."

There was a slight twitch to Eric's eye. "Who fucking raped you, Madeline? Was it him? Because I will snap his body in half."

My voice was shaky. *Fuck. Fuck. Fuck.* "I told you... It—"

Eric rushed at me, and I pressed my back along the locked door, my breath catching in my throat. "Stop lying."

I swore, in that moment, Eric was peeling back my layers one by one, and he was seeing all the little truths that laid behind. I swallowed, trying to even my breathing. "Eric—"

His hand wrapped around my chin. It wasn't a tight, angry grasp. It was gentle, but his eyes were anything but. The dark pools were filled with anger and all things alpha. He was angry. And that set an entirely new batch of anxiety into my already-in-overdrive body.

"It wasn't him," I finally choked out, almost doubling over with queasiness.

Eric's eyes shut, his temples wiggling back and forth. His dark eyelashes danced as he kept his lids closed. The calloused hand on my face tightened just enough to bring me back to reality. *What did I just do?*

At the last second, his eyes fluttered opened. They were no longer filled with rage but with something else entirely. "But someone did? Someone raped you?"

There was that word again. The word that dragged me underneath the high tide and kept drowning me all together. *Raped. Someone raped you.*

My eyes were stinging, and my throat was closing. I'd never in my life wanted someone as much as I wanted him in that moment. I wanted to cave into him. I wanted to bury my head in the crook of his neck and have him make me forget everything.

So I did the only thing I could think of to get out of the predicament. I glanced down to his mouth and pressed my lips to his. His hand quickly dropped from my chin as my tongue met his. His mouth was warm and tasted like cheap beer. My back arched as he gripped my hips—hard, his fingers biting at the skin underneath my shirt.

I waited for him to push me off and tell me he hated me. I wanted to make him mad. I wanted him to hate me again. The kiss was supposed to be a move in a chess game. I wanted to remind him that I wasn't worth saving. I needed him to stop looking at me with pity.

But the kiss was the opposite. It was like opening a floodgate of trapped emotions inside my heart. I expected it to trigger something dark and unforgiving, but the kiss was anything but.

Briefly, *very* briefly, I wondered what it would feel like to be loved by a guy like him. How it would feel to be worshiped by a guy like him. How it would feel to be protected by a guy like him.

The room spun around me as he picked me up and slammed my butt down on the bathroom vanity, spilling random products to the floor. I scooted forward and pressed my middle to the bulge in his jeans as his hands cupped my face. His fingers were tangled in my hair, his teeth scraping over mine.

My body was on fire.

The only thing I could see was him.

The only thing I could taste was him.

A loud bang hit the bathroom door, and instantly, I knew the moment was gone.

Eric's mouth left mine, and his hands were ripped out of my hair. He put much needed distance between us. "God-damnit, Madeline," he growled. "I should have seen that coming! You play fucking dirty." He looked appalled. "That was the last thing I intended to do tonight. *Especially* now."

I hopped off the vanity on trembling legs, annoyed that I was enjoying myself. The kiss was supposed to put a wedge between us. He was supposed to push me away and remember that he hated me. I needed him to stop prying. But he wasn't.

"What's that supposed to mean?" I asked with a bite in my tone, but the truth was, I felt more embarrassed than ever. I knew what he was thinking. He thought I was damaged now. He thought I was weak.

Eric wiped the back of his hand over his mouth like he

was ridding himself of my kiss. "Did you think that kissing me was going to make me forget?"

My stomach flipped with unease. "Forget that I betrayed you? Forget that I ruined our friendship all those years ago? Forget that you hate me?" I began shaking my head. "No..." *That was the point.*

"No," he answered angrily. "I'm referring to the fact that you got fucking raped by someone. That's why you don't sleep, right? Because you keep having nightmares about it?"

My lungs began to burn. My heart thumped loudly behind my ear drums. *I am weak.* I stole one tiny glance at Eric and felt myself crumble. *I need to get out of here.*

I didn't usually run from confrontation, but if I didn't run right now, I'd likely pass out, and I wasn't doing that. A weird rush of feelings I'd never felt before were pelting my skin, and I needed it to stop.

Before Eric could say anything else, I flew past him and threw the door open. I ran down the hall, bypassing Ollie and Christian, along with the Wellington Prep gang, and I didn't stop hyperventilating until I made it to my car and down the street.

I parked off to the side, just underneath a flickering streetlight as my eyes began to blur. A loud sob erupted from deep inside my chest.

I hated myself.

And I hated Eric for bringing up the one thing I wanted to forget.

I was angry, sad, ashamed, and all sorts of other things.

Exhausted being one of them.

I got even angrier, realizing I didn't even meet up with Atticus. My hand stung from smacking my steering wheel.

Shit!

CHAPTER FOURTEEN

ERIC

"YOU MEAN TO TELL ME..." Ollie pushed his head in between the driver and passenger seats where Christian and I sat, parked in my driveway. "That your dad fucked Madeline's mom?"

"For years," I answered bleakly, staring at her stupid window that was—you guessed it—*glowing*.

I finally had to come clean and fill them in on what had been eating away at me for the last few months. Although Ollie and Christian were the two people I trusted most on this godforsaken earth, I couldn't bring myself to tell them about Madeline. They knew I hated her; they knew that she knew all about my father fucking her mom, but that was it.

I wasn't about to tell them what I'd found out. I wasn't about to tell them that I had this indescribable pull inside my body that had me considering barging into her bedroom right now to finish our earlier conversation.

She fucking kissed me. *She* kissed *me!*

For the past few years, on my worst days, I'd let myself

imagine what kissing those hot lips would feel like. How it would feel to wrap my hands in her golden hair and make her crumble in my arms. I'd wondered what she'd taste like and what she'd feel like against my palms. And it was nothing like I'd ever imagined.

I hated it but loved it at the same time. Story of my fucking life when it came to her.

And now that she was away from me and I was able to calm down and get my thoughts straight, I was so pissed. I wasn't mad that she kissed me, but I shouldn't have kissed her back. Not because I was back to my right mind and hating her again; it just felt so fucking wrong. *She was raped.* My head was spinning as Christian's voice rang out again.

"Her mom always did seem slutty. Much like Madeline." My chest tightened; my neck stiffened. I pressed my back into the seat to keep myself steady.

I knew Christian despised Madeline. To be honest, he despised anyone who wasn't Hayley, but he was still a good guy. If he knew what I knew, he wouldn't have said that.

"Yeah," I finally answered. "Things are just fucked up right now. I'm certain my parents are getting divorced, and good fucking riddance, but my mom is throwing herself into shifts at the hospital, and it's probably because she can't stand to look over at Madeline's house without being reminded of it."

Ollie grunted. "I'd say. What a fucked-up thing to do. Fucking the neighbor, only a few yards away from your wife."

A piercing pain shot into my chest.

"Yeah, my father is a fucking ass." I sighed, unclenching my tight fist. "So anyway, that's what's been going on. That's why I snapped when I saw Madeline."

Not exactly true.

I glanced in the rearview mirror, barely able to see Ollie's expression due to the darkness inside Christian's Charger, but I felt the suspicion lingering.

"Why were you about to kill Cole then? It looked like you were mad that he was hitting on her or something." Christian was apparently also a little leery.

I shrugged, giving him a side glance. "Maybe I'm taking a little page out of the almighty Christian's handbook. Madeline is my enemy. I'm the only one who can fuck with her." I cocked an eyebrow. "It wasn't too long ago that you threatened everyone that even dared look in Hayley's direction. 'She was *yours* to bully,' I think is what you said in the locker room."

Christian scoffed. "That was different."

"Nah, brother. It's not," Ollie joked. "It's *literally* the same fucking thing."

I chuckled when Christian scoffed again.

"Fine. She's yours. I'll give you that." He gave me a long look, as if he were trying to unravel my thoughts. "But don't fall for her, bro. I don't want to see you get wrapped up in the Madeline web. She has issues."

Yeah, just like Hayley did.

"What kind of issues?" I asked patiently. *Does he know more than he's letting on?*

He shrugged, turning back to face the road in front of us. "I don't know. Maybe Hayley was right. Maybe something happened to her to make her the way that she is, but that girl has fucking thorns. If you get too close, she'll cut you."

Swallowing back the words I wanted to say, I nodded. "Don't have to worry about that. I want nothing to do with her. I just like making her suffer. She deserves it, right?"

The words tasted bitter on my tongue. I'd basically just repeated what Cole had said. *I didn't fucking rape her, man. Although she probably deserved it.* My lungs burned at the thought. My pulse skyrocketed. The remnants of anger were still coursing through my veins like a dam being broken. Blood rushed fast and hard.

My hand shot out to the door handle. "I'm tired. Those vodka shots I took with that annoying chick are catching up to me."

"She was annoying," Ollie agreed. "Why was she squealing like a seal every time you took a shot?"

I had no fucking idea.

"I'll see you guys Monday," I said, stepping out of the car. I bent down at the last second. "Thanks for having my back with Wellington Prep."

Christian shook his head before glancing out the window. "Not the first time we've had to have each other's backs when it came to those fucking pussies."

I chuckled, slamming the door and walking up to my dark house. My mom was working again—the fifth night in a row. She'd texted me earlier and asked to spend some time together the following weekend, though, and I assumed she'd be telling me about the divorce then.

I fiddled with the front door latch until Christian and Ollie drove away. Then, at the last second, I turned and looked at Madeline's window, only to find her staring at me. Her blue eyes widened when she saw that she was caught. The curtain closed quickly, and her shadowed silhouette disappeared.

I stood there, staring at her window for at least another five minutes before I found my feet dragging me over the driveway and into her house.

The front door was locked again, so I grabbed the key from under the pot and unlocked it. I climbed the steps slowly, trying to come up with a reason as to why I was in her house, but nothing came to mind.

I shouldn't have been there.

But I was.

The glow from her light shone underneath her bedroom door into the dark hallway. My hand reached out to barge in, but I reconsidered.

Typically, I would. I wouldn't give a fuck if I scared her. In fact, it would have been better if I did. But now, I felt at odds with it.

I pulled out my phone and brought up her name, **Shedevil,** and typed, "I'm coming in. Unlock the door."

Her phone faintly pinged from close by, and I smiled. Then, I quickly wiped the smile off my face.

I shouldn't be fucking smiling.

Shedevil: No

I rolled my eyes and said through the door, "I know how to pick a lock, Madeline. Unlock the fucking door."

My phone pinged again.

Shedevil: Good luck. There's a chair pushed up against my door for extra caution.

My brows furrowed. There was a nuisance-like tug in my chest. I eyed the door to the bathroom that led to her room and grinned.

"Fine," I finally said before walking over to it and whipping it open. Madeline was smart, always one step ahead of everyone else, so the chances of her rushing across her room to lock the adjoining bathroom door was likely, but unless she pressed her bed against it from the other side, I'd be able to pick the lock, and then she couldn't hide *or* run like at the party.

Just as I stepped onto the tile, Madeline yelled, "Eric!"

My eyes grew wide, and I felt the actual dilation of my pupils when I found her. Water cascaded out of the tub and onto the floor with a splash as her naked legs came up to hide her body.

My jaw went slack. I should have turned around and

banged my head off a wall to get the visual out of my brain, but I was nothing but weak when it came to her.

I moved my gaze from her slippery, shiny knees to her plump lips and was taken back to a couple of hours ago when they were on my mouth. The kiss tormented me because I was starving for more, but I knew I shouldn't have been. Madeline was poison. She only kissed me because she knew I was circling in on her. She used our attraction against me.

And I didn't like that very much.

I didn't like it because now I could feel her all over. Slithering into my veins. Wrapping around my dick.

"What are you doing here?" Madeline asked as she wrapped her arms around her knees.

Thank fuck there were bubbles all around her in the bath; otherwise, I'd continue grazing her naked body with my hungry gaze.

What was I doing here?

I shut the door behind me, watching her flinch as the door latched.

"You didn't answer my question, so why would I answer yours?" I tipped my chin at her, raising an eyebrow in her direction.

Madeline's blonde hair was falling into the tub around her, floating out on top of the bubbles gracefully. Her arms wrapped even tighter around her legs, and she pressed her flushed face to her knees, moving away from my pressing stare.

"What's your question?" she sighed, glancing to me for a moment.

I licked my lip, crossing my arms against my black tee. "Did you, or did you not, get..." I paused, unable to say the word. My throat tightened at the last second, and I fought to keep my arms crossed instead of clawing at the unwelcome feeling.

"You can say the word, Eric."

"Fine," I said harshly. "Who raped you?"

Madeline turned her head abruptly, resting it along her knees again. She might have thought I didn't see the way she flinched at the word, but I did.

"Who told you I was raped?"

I held back a snarl as I pushed off from the door. "Well, considering you can't even stomach hearing the word, I'd say *you* told me." I stopped just a foot away from the tub, glaring down at her hidden face. "And not to mention, the nightmare."

Water splashed as she peered up at me, all doe-like and innocent. Two things I never, ever expected to see from her. White cloud-like suds laid along her chest except for the tiny sliver of cleavage peeking up at me. "What do you mean?"

"You talked in your sleep the other night. I heard you."

The pink on her cheeks disappeared.

"Yeah," I reiterated, taking a step back before I did something I'd regret, like pull her out of the tub and kiss her again. "So, who did it?"

Her innocent act faded. Her anger came back, slashing at the vulnerable girl in front of me. "Stop looking at me like that!" Her words snapped like a rubber band, so I snapped right back.

"Like what?"

A tiny yet angry noise came from her. If I didn't have that voice in the back of my head, reminding me of all the reasons I hated her, I might have thought it was kind of cute. "Like you want to be my hero. And what exactly did you tell Ollie and Christian when they saw you were about to kill someone for me?"

I glared at her. "Stop evading the question."

"Why do you even care?!" she yelled, her arms falling from

her knees for a brief moment. I tore my eyes away, glancing at the ceiling. "You hate me so much I figured you'd be glad."

My blood pulsed. "You never knew me at all if you truly thought I'd want something like that to happen to anyone—even *you*." My voice picked up in volume. I turned around before I got even angrier. *This is what she wants. She wants you to get mad and leave her alone.* Madeline's greatest defense mechanism was pushing people away, but I wasn't letting that happen again.

"Do I know who it was?" I asked, keeping my back to her. *I will kill him.*

It took her entirely too long to answer. "No."

My shoulders sagged. I don't know why I'd hoped she would deny it again. Something about her admitting that she was raped made me feel fucking sick. It confused me, worried me, and pissed me off all at once.

"Finish your bath and get dressed," I demanded, knowing I was five seconds from punching something in this girly ass bathroom. It smelled like her. All flowery and intoxicating.

"What are you doing?" she asked hesitantly. I was pretty sure she was crying, but I was too afraid to look, so instead, I opened her bedroom door, stepped inside, and slammed the door behind me.

CHAPTER FIFTEEN

MADELINE

MY BATH WATER WAS COLD. Goosebumps broke out all over my arms and legs. I knew it was time to climb out, but I was still too angry. Each tear that trembled down my face betrayed me.

I hated crying.

But I was so worked up I couldn't stop.

My chest heaved as I dried my body off, and the skin on my cheeks screamed in agony as I took the towel and roughly wiped away my weakness. I wasn't going to cry in front of Eric. I had to quickly put on my armor, my cool facade, and deal with him inside my bedroom.

I wasn't even sure what he was doing in there. Waiting for me? But why?

My fingers shook as I tied my drawstring shorts that rested along my hips and as I pulled my shirt over my head. My hair was still damp, little trinkets of water falling off the ends and onto the floor.

I couldn't even glance at myself in the mirror. I was afraid I'd start crying again—or get too angry and break it. I knew that the girl staring back at me was a shell of who she used to be. She was fragmented. And she was angry and hurt. I felt betrayed by myself, and that was a truly disturbing and lonely feeling.

My cheeks puffed as I blew air out of my mouth and reached for the doorknob. I gave myself a five-second pep talk to keep my composure as I rallied against Eric and his confusing actions. He was awfully quick to remind me that he hated me every day, but his behavior completely contradicted that.

As soon as I was inside my room, closing the bathroom door behind me and double-checking to make sure I locked it, my shield started to shake. Eric was perched on the end of my desk, his long, jean-clad legs still touching the floor. A small dip in my stomach told me all I needed to know about my feelings for him. It had been a really long time since I'd felt those magical butterflies in my stomach at the sight of a boy, and here I was, swatting them away furiously as I fought to remind myself that Eric and I would never be more than what we were now—a cross between enemies and forgotten friends.

"What do you want, Eric?" I sighed. I was proud of how annoyed I sounded. But the truth was, I wasn't annoyed at all. In fact, him being in my room somehow clamped down on all my usual anxiety.

"I'll give you one night, Madeline. That's it."

I slowly padded over to my bed, pulling my long shirt down to cover my legs more before sitting on my fluffy blanket. "What are you talking about?"

Eric picked at his nails, avoiding me. His hair looked like he'd tugged the ends of it forcefully before I came out of the bathroom. His strong jaw was clenched. His cheekbones were sharper than usual, like they would cut me if I dared touch them.

A breath escaped me when I found my way back to his eyes. He was staring at me intently before he glanced out the window, crossing his arms over his t-shirt. "I'll give you one night to sleep, and that's it." I bit my lip when he sighed exasperatedly. "I'll wake you up at the first sign of a nightmare. You obviously fucking need sleep if you're trying to get more sleeping pills—which, by the way, is so fucking stupid."

I ignored the emotions clouding my vision. "Why?"

His strong brows lifted as his stormy gaze met mine. "Why is it stupid?" He rolled his eyes dramatically. "Well, for starters—"

"No," I interrupted him. "Why would you do that for me? Why would you sit in here all night while I slept, just to make sure I didn't have a nightmare?"

I still couldn't believe I had talked in my sleep the other night. Apparently, my subconscious dream-like psyche was betraying me too.

Eric's nostrils flared as he pinned me to my spot. He instantly went from annoyed to angry. A small wrinkle formed in between his eyebrows, and his perfect lips that had savaged mine earlier were pulled taut. "Because I'm feeling fucking generous. Take it or leave it."

My resolve fell, my armor shattering to the ground. I bit my tongue to keep from thanking him in a blubbering mess. I wasn't going to thank him. I didn't ask for his help, so I surely wasn't going to pretend like he was doing me a favor.

But he was.

He had no idea how badly I wanted to weep.

The thought of sleeping, knowing someone—that, believe it or not, I actually trusted—was going to wake me before I reached that point in my dreams that had me rushing to the bathroom to vomit, was enough to make me break myself in half.

"How bad was it?" I whispered, lowering myself to lie down. I lay flat on my back with my arms resting over my belly. "My nightmare, I mean. What did I say?"

Eric waited a little while before he answered, which only made me more jittery. His tone was clipped and to the point. "It was bad. Now go to sleep."

"Did I cry?" I asked, shutting my eyes, not because I was trying to sleep but because I was too nervous to watch his expression.

"Yes," he answered matter-of-factly. "And that's not all. Now go to sleep." He paused. "And stop taking sleeping pills that aren't prescribed by a fucking doctor."

A bite was at the very tip of my tongue. A snapping remark was locked and loaded, ready to fire out of my mouth, but something held me back. Eric was giving me an olive branch, and I was holding on for dear life. I knew it'd break eventually, and he'd go back to being mean to me and glaring at me from across the cafeteria, but for now, I'd let myself hang on to it.

After a few minutes of tossing and turning, my body finally started to relax. I peeked at Eric a few times, lifting only one eyelid, until he'd snap his stoic attention in my direction. At first, I thought I'd feel uneasy with him in here, given everything, but deep down, I knew that Eric would never hurt me. He may have hated me, but I knew he wasn't a bad guy. The twelve-year-old girl inside of me trusted Eric with her whole heart, and I was trusting her. But then again, could I trust anyone these days?

That was the last thought I had before I felt myself fall asleep.

The low chatter of my mom and dad startled me from a deep

sleep. My eyes felt groggy, and my mouth was parched. I opened my lips, desperately needing water, but that was when I realized my mouth wouldn't open. There was something over it.

Tape?

My hand went to reach up to move it, but my limbs wouldn't work. My parents' voices grew louder, my dad's familiar yells plowing through my bedroom walls. When did he get home? And why was he already angry? It usually took at least a few days for him to snap.

I tried wiggling my arms, my eyes adjusting to my dark room, but it was like I was in quicksand. My limbs were heavy.

Why couldn't I move? Panic started to seep into every outlet of my body. Skin smacked against skin, and a loud whimper from my mom had me kicking my legs out from my blankets, but it was no use. They weren't working either.

What is going on? Was this sleep paralysis or something?

Just then, my heart began to race as if it knew something was coming that I didn't. A scream was lodged in my throat as I began to feel the looming presence of something dark and heavy on top of me. My eyes wouldn't adjust. I might as well have been blind.

Why wasn't my light on? I always kept my light on.

"Hold still, baby."

The voice had me completely shook. I knew that voice. It haunted me. Replayed in my head whenever I'd let my guard down. I started to breathe heavier, tears gathering in my eyes.

I tried to scream and claw as the presence grew heavier. My father's loud voice boomed in the background, and my mom screamed out. I needed to get to her, to help her, but the man on top of me was overpowering everything.

No. No. No.

A large hand cupped my thigh, ready to spread my legs, and I sobbed on the inside.

Not again.

My stomach convulsed as my entire body shook and trembled.

"Goddamnit, Maddie. Wake the fuck up!"

My eyes popped open at the sound of Eric's voice. I shot up out of my bed quickly, my eyes barely adjusting to the dim light.

"The lights. Turn the lights on!" I screamed, hurriedly crawling off my bed. As soon as my feet hit the floor, I rushed past Eric and latched onto the bathroom doorknob. My fingers moved quickly, unlocking it swiftly, and as soon as my knees hit the bathroom tile, I heaved into the toilet, acid burning the back of my throat.

My eyes grew even more watery as I laid my sweaty head down on my forearm. My entire body was racking with trembles, and sweat beads slowly ran down my spine.

I hate this.

As soon as I knew I was done puking, I flushed the toilet and tried standing, but my legs gave out, and I fell to the floor on my butt. I clenched my chattering teeth and sucked in my lips to keep myself from crying again as I backed myself up against the tub, closing my eyes.

I was stronger than this. Why couldn't I get my shit together? Why did the nightmares keep coming back? And why were there two unnecessary evils in this one?

I breathed in and out of my nose, calming my body down for long, agonizing minutes before regaining the strength to stand again. As soon as I unclenched my eyes and stood up on two feet, ready to walk back into my room to face Eric, I stopped. He was standing there, just inside the bathroom, staring at me like he'd seen a ghost.

My lip trembled when we locked eyes, and I wanted to hide. He was seeing a part of me that even I didn't want to see. And I hated that he was staring at me so stoically. I had no idea what was going through his head. There wasn't that evil glint in his eye he often gave me, and there wasn't that cocky, smart-ass grin on his face either.

He just stared, his blue-gray moody eyes on me.

I suddenly felt even smaller than usual.

Embarrassment had me darting past him. He moved just enough that I wouldn't touch him and then slowly turned around and continued staring at me.

When I sat on my bed and pulled my knees up to my chin, not daring to sneak another glance at the boy who just saw me completely raw, he whispered, "I assume it happened in the dark."

I still wouldn't look at him. Instead, I stared at the teddy bear my grandma gave me when I was seven perched on the floor in the corner of my room. "Yes." It absolutely killed me that my voice came out raspy and broken. I didn't need Eric to see me like this. I didn't need anyone to see me like this.

"Did it happen here? Is that why you lock your doors? Did someone come in here and hurt you, Maddie?"

Mortification swirled in my belly. I dropped my head to my knees and slowly nodded as a tear escaped.

I paused at the sound of Eric's knuckles cracking. I stole a peek at him, and by the looks of his tense shoulders and wiggling tight jaw, I could tell he was angry. That was the conflicting behavior I was talking about earlier. Eric was mad.

And for a fleeting moment, I let myself relish in his sudden protectiveness, but only for a second, because I knew, without a doubt, that he'd go back to disliking me eventually. This was a minor time lapse in our story. Maybe if we were in a different reality, in a different time, this could have played out differently.

"I'm fine, Eric. You can go home now. I won't be able to sleep for the rest of the night." The clock on my table read just after three in the morning, which meant I'd actually gotten a decent amount of sleep for once.

Eric's broad chest rose swiftly underneath his tight t-shirt. His arms were still crossed, and his expression was unreadable. When he flicked his eyes to me, I jumped. "Who else knows about this?"

I gulped, clutching my knees even tighter. *God, I have to look so...vulnerable.* "No one."

His eyes widened for a split second. "No one? No one at all?"

I shook my head slowly. Of course no one knew. Who would I tell? All my friends? My boyfriend? That's right, I had neither. "No." Panic hit me fast. I snapped my spine into place. "Please don't tell anyone."

Eric didn't move his attention from me. Not even a slight dip of his eye. Nothing. He just blinked a few times before letting his arms fall.

"Here's the deal," he started, advancing toward the bed with a wide, confident stride. "Tomorrow, you can go back to being your strong, I-don't-give-a-fuck, thorny self...poking anyone who comes near...and I'll go back to remembering all the reasons I absolutely fucking hate you." My eyebrows hunched together as I angled my chin up to meet his stance from above my bed. He swallowed, his prominent Adam's apple bobbing up and down. "But for now...what do you usually do after a nightmare like that? You said you don't sleep, so what do you do?"

I licked my dry lips, confused as hell. My heart flew through my chest at the prospect of Eric not hating me for just a few more hours. "I...I read...or binge-watch a show. Something interesting...to keep me awake."

He nodded, looking all around my room before he landed on the remote laying on my dresser. He walked over briskly, snatched it with one swift hand, and then came over and flicked his chin at me.

I scrambled to move over, all way to the very side edge of

my bed, and sat up tall. The mattress dipped as Eric sat down and flipped his legs onto it. He smelled clean and fresh.

What was he doing?

"Stop looking at me like that," he said before snapping his attention to me. Our eyes met, and I felt myself jerk back. Eric may not have been the star quarterback or the alpha in his trio friendship with the Powell brothers, and he may not have been labeled the king of English Prep, but he was every bit as intimidating. His steely eyes, dark features, and the knife-like cut of his jaw angled in my direction paired with the low raspy bite to his tone and subdue attitude... Eric was every bit as terrifying as he was hot. And that meant a lot coming from a girl like me. I didn't usually allow men to intimidate me, but Eric did just that. Maybe it was because I knew he hated me, or maybe it was because every male was now skewed in the worst way possible inside my brain, or maybe it was because I was so attracted to him. Either way, I was thrown off course.

"Look at you like what?" I finally croaked, looking away.

"Like I'm some hero. Wasn't it just a few hours ago that you told me to stop looking at *you* like I wanted to be such a thing?" A light chuckle came from him, and the butterflies came back. They stunned me so much I actually looked at my stomach, but at that moment, a noise echoed throughout the house, followed by faint laughter. I felt Eric's entire demeanor change. His back straightened up, and he hissed through his teeth.

My mom was home.

And she wasn't alone.

The hair on my arms stood erect as my heart galloped in my chest. The thumps were hard and painful. I peeked at Eric from the corner of my eye, and he was wound tightly, ready to snap something with his clenched fists. A man's slurred voice floated underneath my locked door, and relief kicked in. I didn't even realize I was holding my breath until I gasped for air. Eric's fists loosened, and it seemed we were both swimming in relief.

I was relieved it wasn't the dark voice from my nightmare. And he was likely relieved it wasn't his father. What a predicament he and I were in.

Minutes passed, the clock ticking by slowly. The remote was still laying between us, neither one of us touching it.

Before I could backtrack and put my walls back together, I blurted out an apology. "I'm sorry."

The entire room froze like we were in an ice castle. Not a single sound was heard. Not a single movement was made.

"You're sorry?"

A breath floated out of my mouth, and I honestly expected to see it in the ice-cold room. "I'm sorry my mom slept with your dad."

Eric laughed sarcastically, shaking his head. His tone was sharper than before. "That's not what you need to be sorry for."

I picked at the little threads on my blanket. "I know."

Painfully long seconds passed, the room somehow even colder than before.

"Why didn't you just fucking tell me?"

Because I couldn't risk my father finding out. There was too much to explain. Too many questions Eric would ask if I told him the whole truth. So I didn't.

"Because I'm selfish, Eric." As soon as the words were out, I caught his eye. I dug my fingernails into the palms of my hands, almost recoiling at the validity in my response. I truly was selfish. It wasn't a lie; it just wasn't the whole truth.

Eric's stern expression never wavered. We were locked and loaded. He was angry, and I was angry. The only difference was his anger was directed at someone other than himself. But me? I was mad at myself. I was mad for letting myself feel this way. For letting myself feel guilty with my self-ishness.

Who would protect my mom and me if it weren't for me?

I shouldn't feel guilty about that. But I did. I did because looking at how hurt and angry Eric was made me feel things I hadn't felt in a long time.

I was growing weaker each second I was alone with him. I was allowing hidden truths to dictate how thick my steel wall was.

Eric's harsh gaze was ripped from mine. I gazed at the tick in his jaw as he grabbed the remote and turned the TV on.

We stayed eerily stiff on my bed, not touching or looking at each other as some Netflix show played in the background. As soon as the sun started to peek in, we both glanced at my window.

Eric finally moved, swinging his legs over the side of my bed, and stood up. He didn't look at me once as he moved the chair from underneath my door and unlocked it, stepping over the threshold. He left without a single word.

It was as if the entire night never even existed, and it was probably better that way.

CHAPTER SIXTEEN

ERIC

"THE SEVERITY of the war was unmatched. Tens of thousands of young soldiers died, never going back to their families or loved ones."

Mr. Kahn's voice was monotonous. His teachings were similar to watching paint dry for hours upon hours. I liked to consider myself a good student. I got excellent grades—you kind of had to in order to attend English Prep—but when Mr. Kahn went on a rant over a war that could have been summed up in ten minutes or less, there was no end in sight. He droned on and on and on until the bell sounded and he was summoned back to reality.

Pair his annoying voice and twitch of his nose every three seconds above his graying mustache along with Madeline's head bobbing up and down from falling asleep every so often, and I was agitated.

Every time I'd glance at her, with his voice in the background, I'd get even more irritated. I was on pins and needles when it came to her. When I'd left her house Saturday morning, I jumped into the shower and banged my fist against the tiled wall. Blood seeped from my knuckles and washed away down the drain along with every rational thought in my head. Her scream was on repeat, and the need to pick up her broken pieces was a substantial weight on my conscious. I barked at her for the rest of the night, acting as if I was doing her a favor by staying in her room, but really, I was doing *me* a favor. I knew if I left her room, I'd do nothing but lose my shit over the fact that someone had touched her like that.

The vulnerable, sobbing girl with hair as bright as the sun standing on shaky knees shook me to my core. I was angry. So incredibly angry over the fact that someone took her and broke her.

I was also shaken to my core over the fact that I was losing my cool. I was supposed to be hating her. Fuck, what would my mom even say if she knew I was at their house in the first place? If she knew I was lending a helping hand to the daughter of the woman that had a hand in ruining her marriage, how would that make her feel? Probably just as betrayed as she felt when my father cheated.

I was torn. Pissed off even more than usual. Madeline was fucking everything up. I wished I could have let it go. I should have ignored all the clues that something big was going on with her because now look at me. I was stuck in a tangled net over her.

Madeline's head fell forward again, and the pencil in my hand snapped in half. Hayley glanced at me from behind and gave me a questionable look. I ignored her, and thank God the bell chimed throughout the room, and everyone started gathering their books. Madeline jumped up, her light hair swaying back as her head snapped to attention.

A few snarks and giggles sounded from around us. I couldn't bring myself to look down at her tired eyes, knowing it was only a matter of time before that, too, would haunt me.

As soon as I was in the hallway, meeting up with everyone before lunch, my shackles rose.

"Did you see the way her head was bobbing? I think my dick is still hard."

I swallowed harshly, focusing on Hardin and his childish laughter at his own joke. He was a lowerclassman but often hung around us and the rest of the football team because he was actually pretty good on the field. He'd likely be the quarterback next year since we will be off to college. He was a sharpshooter with the girls in the classes below. They oohed and awed at him every chance they got, hanging off his arm during the on season at a chance to become popular. But his pussy-eating grin made me recoil because of the words coming out of his mouth. "No, no. For real. Do you think I could tap that?" He grew serious, taking a step back and glancing down at Madeline digging in her locker. Her long legs, both toned and smooth below her plaid skirt, caught my eye too. I'd give him that. But he didn't get to say those types of things. Not now. Not after I knew what I knew. He laughed, and Christian and Ollie rolled their eyes jokingly. "No one else wants her anymore. Not after our king tossed her out." A few girls snickered around us as we began walking down the hall to the lunchroom. I kept my attention straight ahead, trying to tune out his tiresome voice and her legs.

Don't do it. Don't do it. Keep fucking walking, Eric. I wasn't going to be her hero.

My heart strummed violently behind my rib cage, climbing, climbing, climbing...

"Okay, wait. With her bobbing like that in class, I bet she gives really good head. Someone hurry, push her down to her knees and hold her hands behind her back. I bet she'd be all over me fucking her vile little mouth."

Snap.

I was over to him within half a second, his body flying back into the metal lockers. "Take it..." I pushed my forearm up to his windpipe, hearing him gasp for breaths. "Back."

His eyes grew dark, his brows furrowing with confusion. I could feel the depth of my anger, and it rolled off me in crashing, thunderous waves. "How would you like it if I pushed you to your fucking knees and held your arms behind your back... I'm sure someone in this school would fuck that annoying little mouth of yours, Hardin."

"Bro...what the fuck are you doing?" Ollie's face came into my vision, his eyes widening. "For fucks' sake, let him go before a teacher comes out. There's only so much Christian can do with the headmaster to evade punishments for the three of us. Don't fucking start a brawl. *Again.*"

I forced my anger to dissipate, trying to push the unleashed emotion down. My pulsing arms slipped from around Hardin's neck, and he wheezed. "If I ever fucking hear you talk about her like that again, I'll snap that glorious throwing arm in two. Do you fucking hear me?"

My peers murmured around me, trying to confirm whether or not I was referring to Madeline.

Fuck.

I growled, shoving my finger into his chest. "If you talk about *any* girl like that, I'll snap it in half. You got that? Be a fucking man. Not a cocky little boy who thinks girls are toys. Grow the fuck up."

Ollie was still giving me a look, his stern jaw clicking back and forth. I finally dropped my hand, and the entire hallway grew quiet. Christian stood back, just far enough away not to interfere but close enough that I knew he heard everything. He looked skeptical and disapproving at the same time. His eyes moved from mine, and as I turned around to see what he was looking at, I felt like I'd just given up my reins.

Madeline was standing there, her books clutched tightly to her uniformed chest. She was fuming. Her pretty features, that just a couple days ago appeared so utterly broken and sad, were skewed together in roaring, dismayed betrayal. She turned around quickly, pulling her attention from everyone that was now staring at her, and rushed down the hall. The door that led to the stairs slammed so hard people in the crowd jumped.

"Now what's your excuse?" Ollie half-whispered to me.

"What are you talking about?" I ripped my tie from around my throat and loosened it.

"That's twice now that you've stuck up for Madeline. Still going with that whole "I hate her" lie or...?" He looked amused, and I wanted to push him up against a locker too.

"Fuck off," I ground out before plowing through the dispersing crowd to find the one person that should have been thanking me instead of throwing a dirty look my way.

Madeline had a lot of nerve acting like *I* was the bad guy in this situation.

I pushed through the door she had run through and instantly scowled. She was pacing with her books splayed all over on the shiny floor as if she had thrown them the second she was alone. Her tiny feet stomped back and forth, lingering echoes reaching up the stairwell and down again.

"I told you I don't need a hero, Eric!" she shouted when she pierced me with those blue eyes. I ripped my backpack from my shoulders and dropped it to the ground with a loud thud. It was like we were getting ready to step into the ring. Fists up and all.

My hands went to my hips as I dropped my head in a low chuckle. Dark strands of my hair fell into my eyes. My words were cool coming out of my mouth. "Well, you surely fucking act like you need one."

"I don't need anyone!" she shouted again. I could hear the

rising panic in her voice that she was desperately trying to cover up with anger.

Her legs carried her over to where I stood, and my heart thumped hard. I could hear it pounding viciously in my eardrums. "Now everyone is going to be suspicious! I hate you for bringing that unwanted attention to me!"

My head snapped up fast, and her eyes widened. I put my hands on her waist and flipped her around, backing her up to the door behind us. Her back hit it with a soft bump, and I bent down into her face. "You don't want me to be your hero, Maddie?"

Her strong facade started to slip just slightly, like a veil being dropped just far enough that I could see the girl behind the blind rage. "No. I don't need you or anyone else."

I chuckled, still caging her in with my body. My hands flexed on her hips, and her lush, baby-doll lips fell apart just enough that I felt myself burn on the inside. "Good," I seethed. "'Cause it's the last thing I want to be."

Her eyes dropped to my mouth, and something inside of me was bending in unimaginable ways. If there weren't that tiny voice in the back of my head, reminding me of what she'd been through, I'd rip off every last article of her uniform and fuck her.

Shit. Panic clawed at me, and I was seconds from dropping my hands and leaving her pressed against the door, all out of breath, but her words stopped me from doing anything. "Then stop acting like it."

I can't fucking help it.

My hands slowly left her slender hips, and I watched her breathe a sigh of relief.

"Fine," I blurted out before reaching down and snatching up my backpack, unable to look her in the eye. She had her wall up again. And it was thick. Madeline's features were coiled together, small divots on her pretty skin. But I couldn't get those sad eyes out of my head. I couldn't stop hearing her racking sobs that I somehow felt in my own chest.

"Fine!" she snapped back.

I gave her one last chance. One longing look. She knew what I was saying without saying the words. I'd protect her if she needed me to. I'd be a hero for the day, or night, if it meant she'd stop being so fucking wrecked. It was a contradicting lapse of judgment. A minor dip in my own personal beliefs when it came to her, but either way, I couldn't make myself move without giving her one more chance.

My heart stood at attention when her eyes fell to the ground. I caught her lip trembling as she hid herself from me. *There you are, Maddie.* The air cracked with a high-strung energy when her blue eyes caught back up to mine. Her attention shifted from my mouth to my eyes several times before she gingerly walked past me and began picking up her books.

I kept my back to her as the words came out strong. "Last chance, Maddie."

What the fuck was I doing?

She softly answered, "I have no clue what you're referring to. You said you'd go back to hating me...and you're doing a poor job of it. If I didn't know any better, I'd say you still had a thing for me."

I spun around fast, catching her off guard. Her blonde strands shot past her high cheekbones as she leveled her shoulders. I scoured my gaze across her flawless features. "You're not fooling me, Madeline. You can't hide from me. I know why you act this way. The second someone gets close to you, and they start seeing past all your barriers, you start pushing them away. You treat people like shit so they *can't* get close to you. But I see you. You do need a hero. You're just too fucking stubborn to admit it."

Her little body quaked with anger. Or maybe embarrassment. I wasn't sure. I only knew that I'd struck a chord when a breath left her mouth, cutting through the tense air. If I stayed near her any longer, I was certain the entire school would blow up. I was angry, and she was angry. And the fact that I wanted to devour her mouth with mine was a pressing issue too.

"I don't need a hero!" she spat between her perfect, white teeth.

A snarky grin etched on my lips. "Well, have fun with your nightmares tonight." I cocked an eyebrow before lazily spinning on my heel and walking back out into the hall.

A heavy sigh clamored out of my tight chest as I closed my eyes. I had no idea what had come over me.

One second, I was hating Madeline, and the next, I was begging her to let me in. I was blaming it on the girl I saw two nights ago. The weak part of her. The version that made me want to pick her up and press my lips to hers, coaxing her into believing that she'd be safe with me.

I was hot and cold—and obviously completely fucked up in the head. But that was Madeline. She was always fucking with me, even if she didn't mean to.

Once I opened my eyes and regained my composure, I was met with two familiar faces.

Ollie and Piper.

They both had shit-eating grins plastered on their faces.

Fucking eavesdroppers.

I walked past them briskly. "Not a fucking word."

Neither of them answered me, which only irritated me more.

CHAPTER SEVENTEEN

MADELINE

EIGHT O'CLOCK on a Saturday night and I was so pathetically lame that my nightly entertainment was staring out my window at the side of Eric's house, hoping I'd get a glimpse of him.

No matter how malicious and intimidating Eric tried to appear, I knew, deep down, he was all things good. He was the boy who used to let me win when we'd play basketball in his driveway. He was the boy who caught me fireflies one night and put them in a jar so I could see them up close and personal. He was the boy who'd wait each night to wave goodnight to me from his bedroom window before we both turned out the light and went to sleep. And he was the boy who continued waiting at his window even when I'd iced him out.

I'd always wondered how he never caught on to his father sleeping with my mom. Maybe he hadn't glanced over at my house as much as I'd glanced over to his, because if he would have just *looked,* he would have seen what was happening.

But that was the problem with most people. They looked, but they never truly saw. If that were the case, maybe people would have noticed that I was a broken girl hidden behind nice makeup and a blistering attitude.

That was what I wanted, though. I wanted to fool people. I didn't want them to see me. So their faults were to my benefit, I supposed.

Except for Eric. He was seeing right through me. He thought I needed a hero, but I didn't. Not anymore. The damage was already done. Eric couldn't save me even if I wanted him to.

I still couldn't help but wonder what he was doing tonight. I'd already creeped on social media, pitifully searching to see if there was a famous English Prep cabin party that *used* to be my go-to, but as far as I could tell, there wasn't a party tonight.

Then, where was he? Probably with some college girl. Maybe he went back to the frat party since last week was cut short because of me.

Speaking of... My fingers rapidly typed another text to Atticus who was likely ignoring me.

I knew how risky and dangerous it was to be taking pills, even if they were as harmless as a sleeping aid. The problem was, I just didn't give a shit.

Sometimes, in the morning, even in my groggy-no-sleep-state, I'd give myself a pep talk in the mirror. I'd roam my eyes over my faint freckles on the high arches of my cheeks and peer into my light-blue eyes. I'd tell myself that everything was okay and that I was safe now. That when I locked my door at night, no one could come in. That I wouldn't make the same mistake twice.

But of course, now that it was dark outside and sleep was rapidly approaching, a chill ran down my spine. I shivered, clutching my phone even tighter in my hands, before I flopped onto the bed.

I sighed anxiously. "You are stronger than this." I gulped some water nearby and lay back down on my bed, my phone still laying on my chest. I crossed my ankles and gazed at the ceiling, trying to convince myself to relax.

What used to relax me? I wasn't sure. The old Madeline was such a blur in my head that I didn't even remember what I used to be like. Though, the harsh looks and everyone hating me at English Prep reminded me that I'd never really been a nice person.

That I'd always been one step ahead of everyone else, putting myself up on a pedestal so no one could touch me.

Until they did.

I lifted my head with the thought and made sure my chair was still pushed up against my doorknob. I shifted my gaze over to my bathroom door and saw that it was locked too. *I desperately needed to get another chair in here for that door.* I sighed again and went back to staring at the ceiling above me, my sheer canopy laying gracefully over the sides of my bed.

I ran my finger down the soft fabric until my phone vibrated on my chest.

Atticus: No can do. Your boyfriend came to my room last night and ransacked it until he found the Ambien. He flushed them down the toilet before I found him. He also fucking punched me, which was followed by a threat, so this is where our platonic relationship ends, sweetheart. Gonna have to find some elsewhere.

My mouth was unhinged from my face. My chest burned, and my eyes watered. Not from sadness but from pure fucking loathing.

How dare he?!

I flung up from my bed and rushed over to my window to

see if he'd somehow come home in the last ten minutes. My hand ached to slap him across the face. I *told* him I didn't need him to be my hero. As soon as he left me in the stairwell yesterday, I knew our little fucked-up version of a friendship was over.

Last chance, Maddie. His words echoed in my head all night, but I knew I'd done the right thing.

Eric couldn't save me now. The damage was done.

Plus, I didn't deserve him, even in the slightest. Why couldn't he see that?

And why the hell would he go to Atticus and threaten him? Was this some sick form of retaliation? Was it part of his grand plan to ruin me?

Newsflash, Eric: I'm already fucking ruined.

I could see the reflection of my steely expression in the window. It didn't look as if anyone was home at Eric's. Not yet anyway. But that was just fine. I'd stand here all night long and wait for him to come home, and then I'd confront him. It wasn't like I had anything else to do.

I groaned, running my hand through my long hair.

I hate him.

But then why was there this small part of me that almost relished in the fact that he had threatened some guy over me? I knew it was highly unlikely that he was doing it to protect me. But for a moment, I let myself believe it. I let myself bask in it.

Butterflies were overtaking the anger that was slowly carving my stomach out, but before I could focus on that, my entire body grew cold.

I shook in my very spot. My legs grew unsteady. My upper body swayed.

No.

Fear like no other slapped me across the face, and my internal voice screamed, "*Run. Now.*"

I backed away from my window that displayed my worst nightmare—*literally*. He was walking around the front of a bright-red Porsche to open my mother's door, and my throat closed. One slice of his eyes to my bedroom window had bile burning the back of my tongue, but I had absolutely no time to perform such an act. Vomiting would have to wait for now.

I ripped open my closet door and threw on a pair of leggings and my blue jacket. My hair was gathered into a high pony within seconds, and I was shoving my phone and random things into my backpack at the speed of lightning. My mom's slurred laugh lingered up the stairs and underneath my door as a stray tear fell down my face. *How did she have this bad of taste in men?* Didn't she get that sick feeling in her stomach with him? Didn't she get that sick feeling in her stomach with my father?

I knew she did with my father. But unfortunately, my mother lived in a land called denial, and it pushed her into making the worst decisions ever.

The smooth, deep voice that I'd heard over and over again the last few months was loud as it passed by my bedroom door. He wanted me to know he was here.

It sent me into action. My window was open, and my leg was over the edge. I moved over to the gutter quickly and hung on for dear life. Something sliced my stomach as I began sliding down. I yelped when whatever it was cut my hand too. It burned, along with my lungs that were gasping for air as I landed on the grass below. My ankle twisted, and I knew I was moving too fast, wild with fear and chaos. I glanced at my window and saw nothing but my sheer curtains innocently dancing with the breeze, but the fear of seeing his face had my legs pushing through my ankle pain and all but running over our driveway and to the next house.

The fucker had parked behind my car so I couldn't leave,

unless on foot. It was as if he knew I'd make a run for it once I saw him.

Did he think three months was enough time for me to just forget? Or was he just hungry for more? Fear flew down my spine, and my legs moved even faster.

I stared at Eric's yellow front door like it was beckoning me with its sunshiny color to open it. And I did just that. I opened it as all rationality left my brain and the cloudiness of poor decisions filtered in.

Nothing really mattered anymore, other than getting away from my house.

I just had to hope I could hide out until morning without anyone figuring out I was here.

Eric was likely back to hating me. And his mom? Well, she probably hated me too. But who could blame her?

CHAPTER EIGHTEEN

ERIC

THE TAKEOUT BOXES slid around on the leather of my front seat as I rounded the street to my neighborhood. I came to a halt at the stop sign and answered my phone, the Chinese damn near spilling onto the floor.

"Mom?" I answered. "I'm almost home."

She breathed a sigh of relief into the other end of the line as I began driving down one of the side streets. "Oh, good. We can just talk when you get here. I made brownies, and I have ice cream in the freezer."

I grinned. "Sounds good, but what do we need to talk about?"

I hated when someone said that. *We need to talk...but not now, later.* What a pointless thing to say. Just say whatever it is you want to say in the moment it's meant to be said in. No use in skirting around a subject. Just spit it out.

My mom must've thought I needed some cushioning for whatever it was she was going to tell me if she was pulling out the big cards like taking off the entire weekend from the hospital and buying ice cream. This was a cautiously similar situation to when I was ten and Sammy got run over. *We need to talk, sweetie. It's about Sammy. But oh, I got ice cream for you.* As if ice cream would help me cope with my dog getting run over.

I was about to pull onto our road, but I still questioned her anyway. Half of me wondered if my dad was going to be waiting at the house, both of them ready to tell me they were getting a divorce.

My chest burned with the sudden thought of her doing the opposite.

Holy shit. What if she took him back and that was what she wanted to talk to me about?

My foot slammed on the brakes, the containers of food flying forward, but I blocked them with my arm.

"Oh no, we can just talk when you're here. I think it's better if you just see for yourself."

"Mom," I forced her name between my teeth, trying to sound casual. "Dad's not there, is he?"

She gasped. "No. Of course not. I wouldn't trick you like that. Although, I do feel that you should talk to him eventually."

No can do.

Relief had me pressing on the gas again. "I'm almost home. I'll see you in a sec."

Once I pulled up into my driveway and cut my engine, I glanced to Madeline's window. I knew she'd be home tonight. Her light was on, as usual, but her window was open. I squinted before looking down at my busted knuckle and then shook my head.

Not my problem. Last night was another lapse in my sanity, but I was back. I was no longer concerned about Madeline. I did my public duty, and now she could deal with her shit all by herself like she wanted.

I didn't allow myself to look at her window again as I rounded the front steps to the porch. The smell of brownies wafted around as I pulled open our front door, carrying the takeout. I strode into the kitchen and walked over to my mom, placing a swift kiss on her cheek. "Hey, Mom. Smells like I'm back in the sixth grade when you made brownies to soften the blow of telling me we were moving." *Another time she tried using brownies to help me cope.*

Her cheeks rose as she pushed her hair out of her face. "It worked, didn't it?"

A guttural laugh came from my throat. "A little." *That and the fact that our new neighbor was hot as hell.* Too bad she turned out the way that she did. Madeline was still hot, though—one of the many reasons I had a hard time being in the same room as her.

"I know why you're making brownies tonight—at least, I hope I know."

My mom's hazel eyes were glossy as she looked away. "We *should* talk about your father and the future." She sighed, placing the knife for the brownies on the counter. "But we need to discuss something else first."

I stood up a little taller, concerned. "What's wrong, Mom? Did Dad threaten you or something?"

Her tiny smile calmed me. "You're such a good boy, Eric. So protective over me."

My brows crowded. "I'm not a boy, but of course I'm protective over you. You're my mom."

She shook her head softly, edging toward the stairs. "No, my sweet son, you just have this fierce protectiveness inside of you that begs to be released. I've seen it over the years. With me, your friends, for those that you love."

I snickered, following her up the stairs. "There's not much I love, Mom. You and a few friends. That's all."

She laughed softly and shook her head again. We were

standing outside my bedroom door now, and I was one hundred percent confused. "What's going on?" I glanced at my bedroom door and then back to her.

"You tell me."

My mom opened the door quietly and pushed it forward. My bedside lamp was bathing my room in a soft glow, and when I looked at my bed, my expression fell. *What the hell? Madeline?*

There she was, curled up on her side on top of my covers, spreading her flowery scent all over my shit. My pillow was likely engulfed with the smell of her shampoo. Madeline looked so small and fragile lying there. Her arms were wrapped around her middle, her knees tucked up to her chin. She was in the fetal position with her hair pulled up in a high ponytail. Her soft, heart-shaped face that often resembled a stoic statue was soft and relaxed. If I looked hard enough, I could probably see the line of dainty freckles on her nose.

"What is she doing here?" I asked, looking back at my mom.

Her eyes were wide as she shrugged. "I found her asleep in your bed when I brought in some clean clothes."

I didn't detect any resentment from my mom. Only curiosity. But that didn't stop me from feeling guilty. I was sure that Madeline, the daughter of the woman my dad fucked, was the last person my mom wanted to find in my bedroom. *God. I felt like shit.*

"Give me a second, and she'll go home. I have no clue why she's here."

I hesitated for a moment, almost feeling bad that I was about to wake her. I knew she rarely slept, and she looked so incredibly peaceful. *No. Fucking no.* Madeline didn't get to make me feel this way. She was always fucking with my head.

I took one step in my room, but my arm was tugged, pulling me backwards. My mom shut the door quietly.

"What are you—"

She shushed me and pulled me back down the stairs and into the kitchen. The smell of brownies hit me once again.

"Mom, what are you doing?" I asked.

She dropped her hand from my arm and gazed up at me. I was much taller than my mom at 6'1", but she'd always been on the shorter side. "That's Madeline, right? From next door?"

I swallowed, clenching my jaw as I looked away. My answer came out harsher than I meant. "Yes."

"Is she okay? Why is she here?"

Was she okay? No. No, she wasn't.

I kept my expression imperturbable. "I'm not sure. We aren't friends. I don't know why or how she'd be in my room."

Her brows knitted together as she looked away, staring at the untouched takeout on the counter. "But you used to be, right?" Her eyes moved all over the kitchen as if she were lost in her thoughts. "What happened between you two? I remember you were close. I found your cute little window notes that you two used to hold up at night when you were supposed to be sleeping."

I pulled back, my face feeling hot. "I didn't know you found those."

She smiled, and her eyes lit up like the jumbotron that laid at the end of our football field. "I found them all stuffed under your pillow once. Of course, I put them all back in their rightful spot so you wouldn't know I touched them. How did you think I wouldn't find those? I made your bed every day." She laughed, putting her hand on my chest. "I was certain you two were going to become a couple." Her hand dropped. "But then things changed."

I shifted my jaw back and forth, moving back to rest against the counter to stare at her. "What do you mean?"

She began grabbing silverware and plates, her back to me.

"I saw the change in you both. You became a little closed off. Grumpy, even. And then..."

"And then what?" Suspense had me clenching my fists. What wasn't she telling me?

She turned around, and her expression grew worrisome. "Madeline stopped waving at me and smiling. She wouldn't even look at our house anymore. I remember waving at her once when she got home from school, and the poor girl froze. She just stared at me before dropping her head and running inside to slam the door." She shook her head, clearing the memory. "It was so strange. I thought something may have happened between you two." My mom gave me a pointed look. "Did you break her heart, Eric?"

I laughed. I actually laughed. It came out loud and angry, sarcasm hanging off each echoing guffaw. "Can't break a heart that doesn't exist, Mom."

She eyed me. "What does that mean?"

Might as well get this over with. "Madeline knew Dad was cheating on you with her mom. For a long, long time. That's why she stopped waving at you, and that's why she stopped talking to me. She didn't want to tell their dirty little secret."

I hated the way my mom looked away at my words. I didn't mean for them to hurt her, but I also didn't like that she was insinuating that *I* broke Madeline's heart. If I was being honest, it was the other way around.

Her tiny sigh had me swinging my attention back to her. She walked over the few feet, and her warm hands grabbed onto my forearms. "Sweetie, you can't be mad at her for that."

I scoffed, my arms flexing under her grasp. "The hell I can't."

She peered up at me, her eyes so warm and comforting. My mom was the nicest person on this earth. I was sure of it. I hated what my father did to her. "Madeline was a child. A child that, under no circumstances, should have known such a thing about the adults in her life. She was probably confused and upset."

I shook my head. "She could have told me. She had years to tell me. Madeline isn't a child anymore."

My mom gave me a pitiful smile. "It wasn't her responsibility, and it wasn't yours." She moved away briskly and started putting food on our plates. "You know," she said over her shoulder. "I'm more angry with your father for putting you in such a terrible position than I am over him cheating on me." My mom turned around, and I bit my tongue. Her eyes were watery, and I swore if she started crying in front of me, I was going to hunt my father down and rip his fucking head off. "I'm so sorry for what you had to go through, knowing what he was doing and having to pick between keeping his secret or hurting me. That wasn't fair, and when he realizes that, it will wreck him, Eric."

My voice cracked under the weight of anger. "He won't realize it because he only cares about himself, Mom."

She looked away again. "He cares about you, sweetie. And one day, he will own up to his mistakes. He will apologize to you. I promise."

"Doesn't mean I have to forgive him."

My mom smacked my chest lightly and gave me a pointed look. "Eric."

But both of our heads snapped to the noise fleeing down the stairs. My eyes widened as my stomach tensed. *Oh, shit.*

My mom and I both paused for a few seconds before we heard it again. *Fuck. Madeline.*

Madeline's screams grew raspier, and my mom panicked, running to the steps, but thankfully, I was faster. "Mom, don't. She's having a nightmare," I said over my shoulder as I bypassed her. "I can fix it."

I very blindly let the statement fall out of my mouth with confidence. *I can fix it?*

Madeline's shrill scream had my chest splitting open. I scrambled up the last step, flung my door open, and all but dove onto the bed, ready to shake her awake.

Her screams felt like nails being drug across a chalkboard. They were loud and real. Very, very real.

"Madeline!" I shouted, grabbing her and shaking her shoulders. Her blonde hair was all over the place, falling out of her ponytail. She was no longer tranquil looking. Her face was wet with tears that were spilling out from underneath her clusters of long, dark lashes. "Wake up."

I knew she was in a different place, at a different time. Her head shook back and forth as her chest heaved. Her long legs kicked on the bed.

"Maddie!" I yelled, shaking her again. Her name on my lips sounded tortured. "Fuck this," I muttered as I pushed my arms underneath her body and ran to the bathroom. Her head was moving back and forth, and I had no fucking idea how she hadn't woken up yet.

Who has you, Maddie?

Whoever the fuck it was, was going to let go in 3, 2, 1.

The cold water hit us both, washing down on our heads like a downpour in the middle of spring.

Her blue eyes sprang open as she gasped for air. She almost flipped out of my slippery arms before I coaxed, "Madeline, it's me. You're okay."

She snapped her head to me, the showerhead still raining down on us. Tiny beads of water ran down her face and blended in with her tears. A whimper of relief sounded from her pressed lips. I turned the water off at the same time she threw her arms around my neck even tighter. Her body shook and trembled as if she, herself, were an earthquake wrecking the world. *Wrecking me.*

"You're okay," I shushed, stepping out of the tub. We were sopping wet, dripping water all over the tiled floor.

What was I doing?

Madeline slowly pulled back to look at me, her arms still clutched tightly around my neck with mine underneath her legs.

I wanted to save her.

We locked eyes for what felt like years, but she didn't let go. Her pink lips didn't move an inch. Her eyes never strayed from mine.

And for once, I was actually okay with that.

I was okay with wanting to save Madeline, and for a split second, I think she was too.

CHAPTER NINETEEN

MADELINE

ERIC'S ROOM was so unlike the version of him that I was accustomed to. It was warm and inviting. I'd never seen the inside of his room, not up close and personal. I used to see small slivers of it when he would hold up those notes for me back in middle school, but since I cut him out of my life, he'd kept his blinds closed at all times.

His walls were a dark-navy color, but somehow, they made me feel warm. His furniture was the darkest and richest of wood. Even the lamp had a soft glow to it, like a cozy fire glowing on a cold night.

"Here." Eric walked back into his bedroom as I stood there, peering down at the covers on his bed that I'd messed up in my psycho night terror. His stormy eyes wouldn't meet mine as he thrusted clothes in my direction. "You can wear these."

I couldn't believe that I'd fallen asleep—on his bed, none-theless. The blinds were open across the room, and I had been staring at them for at least a few hours. I knew his mom was home, so I didn't turn his ceiling light on, only the little lamp on his bedside table. My plan was to just stay in his room with the faint glow of his lamp until my perpetrator left. I'd climb out the window, just like I did mine, and go back home.

But his pillow smelled so good. Just like him. All woodsy and clean. The last thing I remembered doing was trying to figure out exactly how to describe the scent when I'd closed my eyes and fell asleep. *This was so embarrassing.*

Before taking the clothes from his hands, I moved my gaze cautiously to the window. The car was still there. That stupid fucking red car.

Maybe I should have told my mom. But there were too many unknowns tied to that. I was afraid she wouldn't believe me, and I was even more afraid she would believe me and tell my dad, causing a whole clusterfuck of bad.

I felt dirty. And guilty. And a little deserving. I was embarrassed to tell anyone. I hated that Eric knew.

"It's...it's okay." I shook my head, my arms still wrapped around my middle. "I'll just go home."

I couldn't go home. But I couldn't stay here either. I'd just have to figure something else out.

I began walking to gather my bag that held nothing but my phone, keys, and a random book, and winced when I remembered my ankle hurt.

"Why are you here?" Eric threw the clothes that I was assuming were his mother's onto his bed when I didn't take them. *I cannot wear her clothes.*

I pulled my bottom lip between my teeth, basically hiding my limp as I reached down to grab my bag. I went to fling it over my shoulder, but Eric snatched it out of my hand at the last second, causing me to tumble forward.

"Ow." I grabbed at my stomach. I'd forgotten I scraped it too. I was such a mess. So different to how I was just months ago when everyone in the school thought I was put together with the pretty little navy bow that graced my ponytail on game days.

Nothing about me was pretty. Not then, and not now.

When I finally allowed myself to see Eric, he was staring at my hand clutching my stomach. I dropped it and pretended to act fine. "Give me my bag, Eric."

He didn't say a word. The room was heavy. His lingering gaze never moved from where I was clutching my stomach. "Lift your shirt."

I was suddenly standing on hot embers; every single part of my body was bathed in heat. "Excuse me?"

"I said..." Eric started toward me, and my heart seized to beat. "Lift your shirt."

"No." Oh my God. Could this night get any worse?

Yes. It could. You could be over at your house, hyperventilating in the fetal position.

Eric was so close to me that I felt his warm breath wash over my features when he sighed exasperatedly. "Madeline. Fucking show me what you're hiding underneath your shirt. I'd rip it off myself, but I think you've been violated enough, don't you?"

I raised my chin as I choked back the overpowering need to cry. I wanted to be angry at his words, but he was right. And it meant something to me that he wasn't going to overstep boundaries. It meant something that he was actually respecting me for once. He may have despised me, but he was further proving that he wasn't the monster he pretended to be.

My fingers trembled as I fiddled with the hem of my shirt. Slowly, I pulled the cotton fabric up and glanced down to the thin, reddening scrape on my belly. I saw it earlier when I'd first come into Eric's room, but I'd pushed the concern away, too hyped up on the adrenaline from climbing out my window and being inside his house.

Eric took a step closer, invading every bit of my air. That woodsy smell hit me head-on, and I tried to even my breathing. He appeared so concerned yet contradictorily angry at the same time. His black hair flopped forward with a bounce, covering up the two worry lines in between his naturally sculpted brows. His already cut jaw was even firmer than before. He was flawless up close and personal. The skin on his face was clear of any imperfections at all. Eric was cold with his dark features, but he was also breathtaking. Like an icicle —so incredibly beautiful, but he could cut you too.

When his hand reached out, he peeked at me for a quick second, gauging my reaction. When I didn't so much as blink, his warm fingers landed softly on my skin around the scratch. I almost swayed. They were warm and tender as they all but caressed me. He trailed his pointer finger along the redness, and goosebumps scattered over my arms. A familiar pull tugged on my insides, and I was too far gone in his touch to even care.

His voice was low when he flicked his dark eyes to me. His other hand wrapped around my lower back when he peered down, stealing every single breath out of my lungs. "Why are you here, and why are you hurt? Did someone do this?"

Not technically.

My attention shifted from Eric to the window when the flash of lights moved through the room. I stepped away, breaking the intense moment between us, and ran over to the glass.

He was leaving.

The fucker was leaving.

My eyes clenched shut, my breathing coming back and resuming to normal.

Thank God.

I spun around quickly and rushed to my bag that Eric threw onto his bed, ignoring the slight twinge in my ankle. I was eager to get out of his bedroom with all of his things surrounding me that made me feel things I had absolutely no right to feel. "I...I have to go." As soon as I stepped toward his bedroom door, I paused.

Wait.

I couldn't face Eric's mom. It was the very last thing I wanted to do.

But my options were limited. I could either climb out the window and injure my already sore ankle, or I could come face to face with my guilty conscience looking Eric's sweet angel-like mother in the eye. She probably hated me just as much as she hated my mom.

"You are not leaving until you tell me what's going on, Madeline." Eric slid right in front of me and backed himself against the bedroom door. I peeked up at him and took a step backwards. Why was I letting him get to me? Was it because I'd gotten a glimpse at the tender side in him? Was I getting my hopes up and allowing that little crack in my wall to split even more by letting him in?

"I shouldn't have come here," I answered, being completely truthful.

Eric was acting in such conflicting ways that I was finding it hard to think straight around him. One second he hated me, and the next he was caring for me. One second he was glaring at me, and the next he was scorching me with a heated look.

What did he want from me?

"What's that all about?" He tilted his head to the side, bouncing his eyes back and forth from me to the window.

"What?" I asked, crossing my arms over my chest. I could feel myself closing off, the wall going back up, pushing him away. It was aggravating that I was doing it, but it was the only way I knew how to be.

Even with him.

Eric's mouth twitched. "Didn't you say, just a day ago, that you didn't want me to be your hero?" My mouth opened and then closed. He took the opportunity to continue on, pushing off the door and slowly backing me up across the room. "Yet, here you are. In *my* bedroom. So tell me, why are you here?"

"Do you really want to know, Eric?" I was flying blindly. I had no idea what to say or do. I was trying to dig out the old Madeline. The unbreakable girl who pushed everyone to their knees in her wake, but it was different with him. With his soul-sucking eyes and sharp tongue. Eric didn't put up with my shit. And he'd seen me break more than once now.

My shoulders squared, my head tipping to meet his. I could feel the strands of my high ponytail swaying against my spine. "Wasn't it just yesterday you told *me* that being my hero was the last thing you ever wanted to do? So get out of my way, Eric. I'm going back home."

"Stop it." His words were sharp and actually caused me to flinch. They were a slap across my face, stinging my tender skin. He was suddenly in my space again and had somehow backed me all the way up to the wall across the room. His large hand wrapped around the small of my back. An emotion I hadn't felt in a long time clouded my vision, breaking down my walls one by one. "You've already pushed me away once, Madeline. You closed yourself off to me and the rest of the world. I know why you did it. It was some type of twisted form of self-preservation. But there's no fucking way I'm letting you do that again. I'm the one in charge here, and you're going to tell me why you're in my bedroom."

I swore that the floor under my feet shook. My entire body vibrated with anger, and fear, and everything in between. I felt myself combusting from the inside. "Fine!" I shouted in his face, tipping my dainty chin up to meet his steely one. My lips were almost touching his. "I'm here because the man who raped me came home with my mom. So, I jumped out my window, hurting myself in the process, to get away before I came face to face with him again. I had nowhere else to go. I just knew I had to get away and go somewhere, and somehow, I ended up here. In your room." My lungs burned. My throat was tight. Even my tongue was tingling.

Eric was unreadable. Completely blank. The only thing I noticed was that his grip on my back grew heavier as my shouts grew louder. After a moment of my labored breathing, with us at an impasse, his eyes shifted slowly from mine and over to the window.

"He's gone now," I managed to whisper, breaking the tightness in the air. I could feel the risen tension from both of us slowly fall to the ground in the form of relief.

"You know who did this, then?" Eric didn't look back at me. He didn't move at all. He just stared very sternly at the window with his tight grip on my body. His hand was starting to sear the skin underneath my shirt. It was driving me mad. Not because I didn't like it, but because I liked it too much.

My voice was still a whisper. "Not necessarily. I just know what he drives, and I caught a glimpse of his face. It...it was dark the night—"

He interrupted me with an ice-cold tone. "And what does he drive?"

I traced the side of his face, wishing he'd move away so I could go back to building my walls. But he was too close, and too warm, and too protective. "Why does that matter now?"

"What does he drive?" he demanded.

"If you're wondering if it was your dad, you can relax, Eric. Your dad may have cheated on your mom, but he isn't a creep."

"What the fuck does he drive?" he growled, pinning me with a murderous glare. He shook his head, closing those deep dark eyes for a moment before opening them back up and calmly asking, "Just tell me what he drives. Please." My heart twisted inside my chest as I watched the anger leave only to be replaced with pleading.

"He drives a red Porsche." My answer was weak. I glanced down to his mouth and noticed his lips formed a grim line. Then, he nodded once before backing up and giving me room to breathe. My shoulders fell, and I tried to catch my breath that I wasn't even aware I was holding.

Eric began pacing back and forth in his room with his hands on top of his head. He was wearing dark jeans and a gray Henley shirt that clung to his body, and I couldn't stop staring at him in awe. He seemed so protective of me all of a sudden, and even though I denied it until I was blue in the face, his protectiveness was the one thing I desired the most.

Fear was knocking on my back door, ready to tackle me down with its heavy presence at the thought. I'd been pretending I was the bravest person of all for years, telling myself that fear was a useless emotion, but I *was* scared.

I was leery of men.

I was afraid of the ones my mother brought home.

I was afraid of my own father.

And I was afraid of Eric.

I wasn't afraid because I thought he'd hurt me, but because I knew there would be a time in the future where I'd have to let my guard down and trust someone enough to be *this* vulnerable with, and deep down, I wanted it to be him.

Eric growled as he spun around, and my crossed arms fell as I pulled myself out of my panic-inducing thoughts. My heart skipped a beat when he picked the clothes up off the bed and threw them in my direction again. "You're not going home. Put these on and come downstairs. There's Chinese...and brownies."

No. No. No.

"Eric—"

He gave me a stern look, his jaw ticking back and forth. "You're not going home."

"Why?" Why was he being like this? Why did he care so much?

"Because what if he comes back tonight?"

My shoulders dropped. *Oh. I didn't think of that.*

"I'll just watch out the window, and if he happens to come back again, which I don't think he will, I'll just jump out my window and shimmy down the drainpipe again."

"No," he snapped. "If he comes back, I will rip his fucking arms off his body to teach him that he shouldn't touch things that don't belong to him."

Whoa. My face flamed as desire wrapped herself around my body. Eric didn't waste any time barking at me to get dressed before he left the room, and for once, I listened.

The second I stepped out of Eric's room and into the hallway, my muscles grew tight. I felt like a small child getting ready to tell her parents that she'd done something bad. Like I was awaiting some form of punishment.

I remembered Eric's mom being the nicest adult I'd ever met. My mom wasn't "mean" by any means, but she was selfish—just like me. Eric's mom wasn't. Heather was the type of woman who made homemade cookies for the bake sales at English Prep Middle, and who yelled for Eric in the stands of a football game, wearing war paint on her face to match his. She was genuinely nice. Which was why it made me feel even worse when I'd found out that her own husband was cheating on her. I couldn't even look her in the eye after I'd found Eric's father leaving my mom's bedroom the first time. Even at age twelve, I wasn't naive enough to believe he came over to fix a leaky sink or something. It was right after my father had disappeared for a few months, which was right around the time things became very real in my life.

I stood on the second stair up after taking my sweet time descending the steps, wearing Heather's clothes: a black pair of comfy joggers and an English Prep shirt that had "Eric's Mom" on the back. Did she hate me? She probably hated me. I looked just like my mother, too. Both with golden, salon-like hair. Bright-blue eyes. Slender bodies. Would she even be able to look me in the eye? All signs pointed to yes, because of how nice she'd always been, but I was still worried.

No. I tightened my ponytail harshly in the form of discipline. Being worried that she hated me was beyond selfish. She was allowed to hate me. After all, I could have told Eric and put a stop to the entire thing years ago.

But of course, my selfishness got in the way.

Pick a side, Madeline. Mean or nice? What'll it be?

Sometimes I wished I could just go back to being a selfish bitch who cared about nothing other than herself. But now I was a little jaded. Split in two right down the middle. I was knocked off my high horse, and I was having a hard time climbing back up. Everyone at English Prep thought Christian's very public break-up with me was the reason I was a recluse now, but they were wrong.

Someone else ruined me.

And it wasn't him.

"I told you," Heather sang. "You *are* protective."

Eric's voice was gruff. "What are you talking about?"

"Did you know, when you were little, you used to check

under my bed for monsters?" I heard some shuffling around as I took another step down to hear better.

"What?"

Heather's soft laugh moved up the stairs to where I was eavesdropping. "Yep. Instead of being worried monsters were under your bed to get you in the middle of the night, you would check under my bed. You used to say, 'Mom, I'm just making sure you'll be protected from monsters at night.'" She laughed again. "It was so cute. And further proves my point that you are fiercely protective."

"Whatever," Eric said nonchalantly, as if he weren't even paying attention.

"I'm just saying. You're protective by nature, sweetie. And you just proved my point by what just happened upstairs."

She was right. Eric *was* protective, even if he pretended not to be. I felt my heart awaken with his words, "*If he comes back, I will rip his fucking arms off his body to teach him that he shouldn't touch things that don't belong to him.*" I knew I had absolutely no right liking it, but I did.

"Should we go check on her? You gave her the clothes, right?"

I glanced down at the white English Prep shirt. Maybe his mom didn't hate me? She didn't sound hateful at all, but again, that wasn't surprising. Heather was simply nice. She was the type of woman who was still able to smile even after her husband fucked the next-door neighbor.

"She's fine," Eric sighed.

I gulped up the last of the oxygen on the stairs and leveled my shoulders, preparing to be swimming in my guilty conscience as I took the final step down.

"Hi," I whispered as I walked into the living room.

Eric and his mom both glanced up at me, and I froze. My stomach fell to the floor with a clunk. I was jittery and filled to the brim with nerves.

"Hi, sweetie." Heather's face split in two with the warmest smile I'd ever been graced with. "Are you feeling better?"

Heat coated my cheeks, and I fluttered my eyes away. "Yes. I'm fine. I'm sorr—"

"Nope!" Her voice was cheerful. "I won't hear of it. No apology necessary. We all have bad dreams sometimes."

Not like this.

"Eric used to have them too. I can't tell you how many times I found him standing in my room, asking if he could sleep in there."

Eric's dark brows crowded. "Mom. Stop."

My lips twitched when she smiled innocently and rolled her eyes. "Well, come on in here. Would you like some warm tea? Or we have brownies and Chinese."

Why was she so nice? And welcoming?

It only made me feel worse.

I took a step further into the living room, my bare feet sinking into the comfy rug. "Oh, no," I answered softly. "I don't want to be a bother." My arms went directly to my torso as I pulled into myself. Eric gave me a weird look, like he couldn't believe that I was acting this way. I couldn't believe it either. *Snap out of it, Madeline!* Every word I said so far nearly trembled coming out of my mouth. My guilty conscience was whispering uncertainties in my ear to the point that I almost just walked out the front door.

I have to apologize. My mom was selfish and was too busy chasing after her own happiness to care about anyone else's— even mine. I didn't fault her for it. I understood. But just because I understood something didn't mean that I thought it was the right choice. She made bad choices all the time.

"You are not a bother! I'll go get you some tea."

I went to protest again, but Eric spoke up. "I'll make it. You two can pick something to watch." His voice was relaxed and smooth, but when he glanced my way, his eyes told a different story. There was a lot going on in his head. He was probably getting whiplash with my behavior just like I was with his.

I wasn't acting like the Madeline of English Prep. Eric was seeing more and more of the girl who was ruined instead of the girl who did the ruining.

"Will you make me some too?" his mom asked, smiling over at him.

"Of course, Mom." My heart stuttered to a complete stop when I watched Eric's rock-hard jaw soften into a relaxed smile. His lips showcased a glimpse of his white teeth, and his dark eyes somehow turned light.

"Thanks, sweetie."

When he cut his gaze back to me, his smile disappeared just as fast. He turned around and walked into the kitchen, leaving me and my stuttering heart alone with his mom.

"Here." Heather handed me a gray knit blanket as she pulled me over to sit on the love seat. Their living room was large but still cozy. A flatscreen TV hung above a fireplace mantle with a ridiculous number of pictures of Eric on top, showing just how much he had grown over the years.

"Thank you."

Once I sat on the couch and curled my legs up underneath my butt, I draped the warm blanket over my body and bit my lip. Being alone with Heather had me panicking. It was almost as bad as being in my house at night, fighting off sleep because another man was in bed with my mom. My entire body was tensed up to the point that my muscles ached.

"What would you like to watch, Madeline? What do you like?"

I slowly turned my head and looked at Heather. Her chestnut hair was tied in a low pony, and her warm eyes were pouring into mine so intently that I couldn't stop the words from cutting through the air. "I'm so sorry."

Her perfectly sculpted brows knitted together as she witnessed me breaking. I bit my lip even harder to keep it from shaking. I knew Eric's dad and my mom were the ones at fault. The first time he'd come over to our house was when he'd made his mistake. But I could have told Eric. I had the power to stop it before it went on for too long, but I didn't.

"No," Heather said softly. Her features fell, her lips forming a frown. "You have nothing to be sorry for."

Yes, I do.

I gulped back the tight lump squeezing my neck. I knew why I hadn't told anyone, and I knew why I had stopped talking to Eric—why I'd cut him out of my life. But again, just because I understood why I did it, that didn't necessarily mean it was the right choice.

It was just hard to know what the right choice was when you weren't sure of which consequences were worse.

Was it worth my guilt? Was it worth losing Eric? Because from where I was currently sitting, it wasn't.

Even more so when Eric came walking into the living room, balancing two cups of tea in his large hand and a container full of homemade brownies in the other.

He appeared so nonchalant at school, so lazily cool and unperturbed by much. The only expression change I'd ever seen from his relaxed features was a glare in my direction or he wouldn't look at me at all. But here, in his house, he was relaxed in a harmonious way, shining his heart-stopping smile toward his mom, giving her a blanket, and laughing freely at something she said as he handed her the brownies. It all seemed so *normal*.

"Why are you looking at me like that?" he whispered as he sat down in the seat beside me. There was a large fold-down cup holder in between us, blocking us from touching. Thank God.

I shrugged shyly, taking the cup of warm tea from him. "It's just weird. Seeing you so... nice."

He sat further back into the couch cushions but not before speaking low enough that his mom wouldn't hear. "Nice people deserve nice treatment. Why do you think I've been mean to you for the last few years?"

I took a sip of my tea before I put it down and turned toward the TV. I was hoping Eric's mom didn't hear me when I said, "It's okay to hate me, Eric. I hate me too."

Especially now. Heather didn't deserve what Eric's father did to her. And Eric didn't deserve what I did to him.

I had shut him out, and I was regretting it.

CHAPTER TWENTY

ERIC

DENIAL WAS A BEAUTIFUL, beautiful thing. I loved how easily I could deny everything my brain was telling me.

Madeline needs you. No, she doesn't.

You need her. Absolutely not.

You should help her. She could help herself.

As soon as my mom fell asleep on the couch, I turned the TV off and glanced at Madeline, trying to remember that she and I were nothing more than passing enemies.

I still felt the slight simmer of rage inside, knowing the man who made her into this weak, breakable girl was just a house over from me hours ago. If I would have known from the start why she was in my bedroom, I would have walked right over to her house and into her mother's room—*again*—and punched the fucker—mid-thrust or not—over and over again until he admitted what he'd done. Then, I'd drive him right to the hospital so they could reconstruct his face, only for me to fuck it up again.

If I truly hated Madeline as much as I told her I did, I

would have made her leave when we were sparring off in my bedroom. He was gone, no longer upstairs, fucking her mom, so it wasn't necessarily unsafe for her to go back home. But the truth was, I felt better knowing she was with me, over here in the safety of my house.

Which only proved I was in way over my head with her.

I hated her. But I didn't hate her.

Maybe I hated her because I *couldn't* hate her.

I groaned, rubbing my hand over my face. What a fucked-up thing to say. It didn't even make sense. None of this did.

Madeline shifted beside me, the blanket falling into her lap. Her slender arms were wrapped tightly around her stomach, and the shirt my mom lent her was pulled up just enough so I could see the soft skin gracing her hip bone. Her lips were shaped like a pretty little bow, her eyelashes fluttering like the wings of an angel.

She was the furthest thing from an angel.

"What?" she asked, groggily sitting up. "Why are you looking at me like that?" She suddenly went stiff. "Was I dreaming again? Did I say something in my sleep?" Her shiny blonde hair wisped in between us as she searched the room for my mom. Her shoulders fell in relief when she saw that she was asleep.

"No, you weren't dreaming."

"Oh, good. Then why were you looking at me like that?" Her look was quizzical, if I had to describe it, but also a little hopeful.

If I allowed the truth to come out, I would have said, *"I'm looking at you like that because I want to kiss you."* Because I did. I really fucking did. I was crazy attracted to her, my blood spiking when she was near. I had a hard time keeping my hands to myself, which was why every single time we were alone in a room together, I found myself crowding her space, wrapping my hands around her lithe waist. But I was exceptional at evading one truth with another. "I'm wondering why you haven't told your mom."

That was not precisely why I was looking at her, *but* the question was in the back of my head.

Madeline glanced away quickly, her bright-blue eyes shying away. There was a slight pull in my chest, and I honestly wanted to split my own rib cage open to make my heart stop skipping beats with her near. It usually thumped with hidden rage when she was close, but now it was skipping beats and fluttering like I had some type of heart murmur.

"Can we talk upstairs? I don't want your mom to hear."

Madeline began folding the blanket and draped it over the couch.

"Lead the way." I ushered, nodding my head to the stairs.

I pulled the blanket up to my mom's chin and flipped the lights off before going after Madeline. I wanted to give her some time to get upstairs so I didn't have to pretend like I wasn't going to stare at her ass the entire time she climbed the steps.

As soon as I shut the door of my room, the latch echoing, I watched Madeline jump. Her eyes went directly to the doorknob before she turned around to stare out the window that sat across from hers.

"Tell me," I intoned, striding over to sit in my computer chair. Madeline turned around slowly with her pink bottom lip tucked in between her white teeth.

"No."

I dropped my head, the weight of it stretching the knots in my neck. A deep, sarcastic chuckle rumbled out of my chest before I sat back and hiked an ankle over my knee.

"How's your hand?" she asked.

I shifted my gaze to her and tilted my head. My mouth twitched as I held back a smirk. "What are you talking about?"

Her dark lashes fluttered against her skin as she shook her head. "So, was it before or after you said being my hero was the last thing you ever wanted to do that you broke Atticus' jaw?"

I brought my hand up to my chin. "Mmmm. Ya know, I just can't remember."

Madeline's arms dropped to her sides. She stomped her foot, and I had to fight the urge to laugh. "Is this some game you're playing? What? Is it a form of retaliation? Fucking with my head?"

"Oh, you mean how you fucked with mine?"

She scoffed. "How have I fucked with yours?"

I suddenly sat forward, resting my elbows on the top of my black jeans, glaring at her. The hardening of my jaw made my teeth hurt. "One day you were my best friend, and the next you weren't. One day you were flirting with me, and the next you were dating my best friend. One day you rubbed it in my face that my dad was fucking your mom, and the next you were apologizing." I scoffed right back at her, crossing my arms over my expanding chest. "Excuse the fuck out of me if I don't feel like explaining myself."

Madeline's pouty mouth opened and then closed, only to do the same thing again. She huffed and turned around quickly, putting her back to me.

I didn't have to answer to Madeline, and she had no right asking me to explain myself. I wasn't sure why I was going against everything I stood for when it came to her, but that was what I was doing.

Of course I didn't threaten Atticus as a form of retaliation. Of course I wasn't playing a fucking game. That was the last thing she needed. Madeline had been put through enough. Did she deserve the hiatus she was getting from everyone at English Prep? Probably. But I knew there was much more to her behavior over the last several years than she was letting on. Which reminded me...

"When did it happen?" I questioned, relaxing my arms back down to my knees. I hoped she knew what I was refer-ring to.

Madeline glanced over her shoulder for a second before answering, "Right after Christian and I broke up."

That proved my point that something else made her into the callous girl that she was. She pushed people away. She was in control of every relationship she'd ever had. Madeline craved that control. But why? She had shallow relationships with everyone, and I just couldn't understand why.

"You should tell your mom," I finally said, pulling myself out of an internal war of unanswered questions about Made-line. They were dropping like atomic bombs all around me.

"I can't," she answered quickly.

"You can. You just won't."

Madeline turned around slowly, and I swore I saw the conflict presenting itself right behind her eyes, like she was trying to justify not telling her mom, but we both knew she should. She should have told her right after it happened. She should have told someone.

My windpipe felt like it was being crushed as I thought about how alone and scared she must have felt afterwards. If it was shortly after Christian broke up with her, she had *no one* in her corner. But did she ever truly have anyone in her corner? I could guarantee no one knew the real Madeline; they only knew the one on the surface.

"You can take the bed," I said, flicking my chin over to it. It was an abrupt shift of whatever the hell she and I were doing at the moment, but I needed it to pass before I said or did something I regretted in the morning.

She looked at my bed for a second before glancing back at

me. "Why are you being so nice to me, Eric? Is it because you feel bad for me?"

Yes. No.

I shrugged. "Sure, if that's what you want to hear. But really, you're in no position to be asking such things, so why don't you just accept it and get some sleep while you can." I was being harsh. I knew I was. But it was the only way I could be without being submissive when it came to her.

She looked over to the bed again, hesitating. "Where will you sleep?" Her voice was unsure as she stayed rooted in the middle of my floor, swallowed up by my mom's clothes.

"Don't worry. I'm not going to crawl into the bed after you fall asleep." Probably not the best idea, considering her situation—or mine, either, if I was being honest. Getting too close to her was a bad, bad idea. I was already toeing the line between hate and love, even if unintentionally.

Her tiny shoulder lifted. "You can, you know. I'm not afraid of what I can see. Only what I can't. Hence the lights needing to be on at night."

I understood that. "If I get tired enough, sure. But for now, I'd like to sit right here and watch if a certain red Porsche decides to come back."

I wish we had security cameras so I could catch a plate to do some digging, but my mother and father both thought a top-notch security system was aimless because we lived in a gated community.

I heard Madeline sigh.

I wasn't kidding when I said I'd rip his arms off his body.

That fucker better never come back in this neighborhood again.

CHAPTER TWENTY-ONE

MADELINE

I NEEDED FLOATIES. Or maybe an anchor. I needed something to keep myself from drowning, but to also keep me from floating away.

A trickle of anticipation danced over my skin as I sat on top of my bed, still in my school uniform. My plaid skirt fell over my thighs as I sat cross-legged, finishing up a chapter in my calculus book. It was nearing dark, the sun setting behind the trees, no longer shining down on Eric's Range Rover parked in between our houses. I'd noticed he'd been home a lot more often lately. Ever since he found me in his room last weekend, he'd been home each and every night with his blinds open. I wanted to believe it was because he was checking in on me, but that couldn't be true. Not only did he go back to ignoring me at school, but he also made a point to laugh when Missy, in all her spray-tan-gone-wrong glory, accidentally "tripped" and dumped her entire tray of food on my lap during lunch this week. I couldn't help but see the irony in *that,* considering I'd done the same thing to Hayley Smith months ago.

My first reaction was to shriek while grabbing a handful of her poorly done platinum-blonde hair and banging her face off the table. But then I reminded myself that this was karma, and the only thing I could do was bask in it until it finally fucking stopped.

The cherry on top, though, was when Hayley and Piper had both come over to help me clean up the mess. People snickered as they walked by, pointing and whispering, but eventually Christian and Ollie grabbed their girlfriends by wrapping their hands around each of their waists and pulled them into the hallway when the bell rang. I shot them both a half smile, barely noticeable to the naked eye, but I was hoping they could sense my gratitude. They owed me nothing. In fact, they should have been the ones dumping their tray on me instead of Missy. I had been a lot meaner to them than I was to her.

My mom had been going out more and more lately, bringing men home almost every night. She did this whenever my father would call and tell her he was coming home soon. It was as if she used other men to curb her anxiety until he got home. She'd go out and flirt, show her panties to some handsome sleaze, and then bring him home to fuck the stress out of her system.

My mom and bad choices went hand in hand. It was nothing new.

As soon as I closed my calculus book, I snuck another peek at Eric's window. I froze when I saw that his light was on. His blinds were pulled up so I could see directly into his room. The gray computer chair he sat in all night last weekend, while I slept on his bed, was still facing my window. I hadn't seen him sit in it since, but I found it strange that it was still facing over here, just like I found it strange that his blinds were still open.

Eric was nothing but perplexing lately. He had ignored me at school for the entire week, but each night, when my mother would arrive home with a new fuck buddy, he'd immediately text me to let me know it wasn't a certain red Porsche that I'd come to dread. I'd reread the three messages he sent in the last five days over and over again, pretending that he actually cared about my well-being.

And maybe he did a little. But he also liked to remind me that he hated me and that he owed me nothing. And he was absolutely right. He didn't owe me a single thing. I just wished I knew why he kept getting all warm and fuzzy on me one second and then ice cold the next. I really had no business worrying about Eric's feelings, but it was hard not to when my twelve-year-old heart still belonged to him.

I tucked a few strands of hair behind my ears, looking out the window again. *Oh shit.* A faint squeal flew from me when I saw him standing there from behind without a shirt on. His back was perfectly sculpted with rippling muscles as he moved his arms up to pull a different one on. I could tell he'd just showered when he'd spun around as his damp hair fell into his eyes. My face grew warm when I started imagining him in a hot and steamy shower, washing his body as water droplets fell over sculpted cheeks. My face was on fire when I felt the tingling in my lower stomach.

A weird feeling started to slip its way in, taking my desire and attraction and twisting it all up, making me feel uneasy.

Shortly after the incident, I'd had sex. I quickly wanted to wash away the filth I felt, so I replaced it with a teenage boy who had no issues letting me be in control. It was quick and seamless with absolutely zero feelings involved.

It didn't take the nightmares away, though, and it didn't make me feel any better about wanting something like that with Eric. I knew it was because I wasn't just feeling an attraction with him. It was more. So much more. And as much as it killed me to admit it, that scared me.

A faint tapping noise sounded from the window, and I quickly shook my head, allowing my thoughts to scatter. I began to smile when I found Eric staring back at me. He was standing there, fully clothed now—thankfully—holding up a piece of torn notebook paper below his chest with a smirk on his face. It read, *Enjoying the view?*

I hurriedly ripped a piece of paper of my own, feeling giddy inside, and hopped off my bed. I grabbed my purple pen and wrote, *I don't know. Are you?*

The rise of my cheeks felt alien as I held up the torn paper. Eric rolled his gray eyes, and I was pretty sure I could hear his scoff through the window. He shook those dark strands out of his face and walked over to his desk, resting one arm on it as he tore the cap from his marker with his teeth. After he scribbled something else, he popped the cap back on and walked over to the window.

It read, *Where's your mom? Fucking another rando I take it?*

Eric's feelings toward my mom hadn't changed a bit. He hated her, and maybe I should have stuck up for her, but she'd made a lot of bad choices. There was no taking back what she'd done. There were no valid excuses.

Grabbing another piece of paper, I wrote, *Vulgar much?* and held it up.

There was a brief moment where I almost scribbled, *Where's your dad? Fucking another blonde?* But I just couldn't bring myself to do it. The old Madeline was rolling around in her grave, kicking and screaming to be let out, but something held me back. *Maybe I truly have changed.* Maybe I just wasn't that girl anymore. Maybe that version of me was gone forever.

I wasn't sure if that was a good thing or a bad thing. Was

it okay that I was becoming submissive and holding back the mean, crass comebacks that used to lift me up? Was I suddenly turning nice?

That wasn't a very comforting thought, because nice girls got stomped on, and I'd be damned if I got stomped on again.

Once I glanced at Eric's window again, after holding up the *Vulgar much?* note, he was gone.

The disappointment was like an oncoming train heading right through the window and into my room. I could basically see the steam from the engine as I began to turn around, infuriated with myself that I was actually allowing myself to feel let down over the boy next door who still very well hated me, but then something caught my eye.

What are you doing, Eric?

Eric was in his driveway, wearing black joggers and a long-sleeve English Prep shirt pulled up to his forearms, bouncing a basketball with his hands. I couldn't remember the last time I'd seen him outside playing basketball. It had been years.

Memories of us that I'd had locked away started to surface, and my heart grew warm. Those were the memories I'd always shied away from because they reminded me of what I'd left behind in my selfishness.

When the ball stopped bouncing and Eric snapped a smirk in my direction, I bit down on my lip. He raised an eyebrow, flicking his hair off his forehead.

Does he...?

He mouthed the words, *What are you waiting for?*

I was waiting for the other shoe to drop. That was what I was waiting for. Did he really want me to go down there and play basketball with him? Like we were back in middle school again?

Do not go down there.

What if I went down there and he turned around and

went inside, only to make me feel like an idiot for believing that he wanted me to play basketball with him? I would not let myself look like a desperate girl with high hopes for a guy who wanted nothing to do with her.

Eric and I were nothing more than long-lost friends turned into rivals.

I was his foe.

And embarrassingly enough, he was my ally.

We were on opposite sides with very different feelings.

I gave him another quick glance, ready to shake my head, when he threw me for a complete loop.

He smiled.

Eric just smiled at me.

And it was beautiful. It was a quick glimpse of that twelve-year-old boy who I was happiest with. My phone buzzed as I pulled my dazed gaze away.

Eric- Stop trying to fool yourself into thinking you have big plans for tonight...get down here, loser.

I texted back quickly, swatting at the butterflies.

Me- Or what?

Why was I flirting with him? Why was I flirting with the guy who told me he was going to ruin my life?

My resolve fell just as fast as it climbed. *He's also the guy who has been chasing away your nightmares.*

Eric- Or I'll come and get you.

The thought excited me. A rush sparked my blood. When was the last time I'd felt this? When was the last time I'd felt so exhilarated by the prospect of a guy? It felt good to be wading in unknown waters. To feel something real. Did Eric hate me? Maybe. But even if he did, I couldn't deny that he had just ignited a faint amount of happiness in me that I hadn't felt in a really, really long time.

I knew it wouldn't last long, but at least I wasn't so ruined that I couldn't feel it again.

CHAPTER TWENTY-TWO

ERIC

MY GUARD DROPPED when the sun went down. Every single night, I found myself sitting in my computer chair, inevitably facing Madeline's house. Even if I'd turn my chair around and pull it up to my desk, I'd somehow swivel back and be left staring at her bright room with the flowing curtains again.

I kept catching small glimpses of her. Her blonde hair would snag my attention like a spotlight, and I'd sit up a little taller in hopes she'd be having some crazy fit of a nightmare and I'd have an excuse to run over there.

Usually, when that thought would filter in, I'd have a sobering realization that what I was doing was purely selfish and totally out of character. I didn't care about many people, especially not her, so to be wrapped up in her shit was a big step off the what-the-fuck-are-you-doing cliff.

But it seemed no matter how many times I'd told myself she didn't matter to me, and that she was a callous bitch who cared about no one other than herself, I still found myself revisiting the past, wondering why she had turned against everyone.

I deserved an Emmy for the acting I'd performed all week at school, pretending that I was back to hating her. Even Hayley and Piper got onto my case when I'd laughed as one of my old hookups "dropped" food all over her lap. But when it was just Madeline and me, at our houses, all alone with only a simple patch of grass in between us, my guard completely vanished.

I craved to be in her vicinity.

I forgot why I hated her. I forgot that she left me behind years ago. And I realized that, despite her tears and night-mare-inducing screams, she was probably one of the strongest people I knew.

Madeline thrived on being independent. She pushed everyone away and still stood tall.

Then, here I was, waiting for her to grace me with her very presence so we could take a fucking stroll down memory lane together with an old game of one-on-one. *Stupid.*

I snapped to attention as I heard the opening and closing of her front door and then again as she walked underneath the moonlight. I ran my gaze down her body, lingering on the tight black leggings she was wearing that no doubt made her ass even rounder. Her long blonde hair fell down in waves over her shoulders, and her lips were glossy, as if she'd put on some lip gloss before coming down.

"Trying to impress me?" I asked with a smirk, feeling right at home with my teasing.

"No. Why?" she asked, putting her hands into her hoodie pocket. Her eyes darted away, and I knew right then that I was right.

I lifted a shoulder, holding the basketball under my arm casually. "You just look like you spent some time getting ready before coming down here."

Madeline's blue eyes sparked, and I felt the jolt. Her little hands graced her hips. "Is that your roundabout way of telling me I look good, Eric?"

I wasn't sure I liked the way my name sounded on her lips. Actually, I wasn't sure I liked the way my dick *liked* the way my name sounded on her lips.

"Trust me, Maddie." I inched an eyebrow up. I ran my gaze down her body again before locking eyes. "You'd know if I thought you looked good."

Her mouth opened with an audible gasp.

I spun around fast, putting my back to her to shoot the basketball like I wasn't at all affected by her sexy little frame. It was her eyes that did it. I watched them come to life as a shotty remark tumbled out of her mouth, and I liked it. I liked it too much.

Maybe there were some parts of the bitchy Madeline that I liked. Maybe I'd take a mixture of the two.

"You can be a real jerk, Eric. You know that?"

"Only to you." I threw the ball her way without allowing my lips to creep into a smirk. I had to give myself props. I was damn good at dissing her when need be.

Though, on the inside, it was a goddamn war zone of unshed feelings, hidden memories, and lustful thoughts all ambushing me from every fucking angle.

"Why am I even down here?" She rolled her pretty eyes that glittered right along with the stars above our heads. "Why aren't you out with your friends? Or at some frat party with college girls? Huh? Is tormenting me really that fun?"

She was right. I should have been with my friends or at some frat party, but I was no longer welcome at Jesse's frat house—something about breaking his frat brother's nose. Whatever.

Regardless, I knew exactly why I was home on a Friday

night, playing one-on-one with Madeline. I just couldn't admit it aloud.

"Yes. Tormenting you is *that* fun. It's what I live for, actually."

She made an annoyed sound, throwing the ball back to me with a little too much force. I caught it fast.

"I have an idea," I said, feeling the excitement in my bones. "If you win a game of one-on-one, I promise I'll stop hating you. I'll even go as far as friending you at school so everyone else leaves you alone."

Not a chance in hell she was winning.

"And if you win?" Her voice was hesitant, like a tiny mouse trying to beg for its life in front of a lion.

I looked her dead in the eye. "Then you tell your mom about what happened."

Her head dipped, her blonde hair covering her soft features. I barely heard her when she said, "No."

"Fine. Then tell your dad," I countered.

My hands tightened on the ball when her head snapped up. Her soft features were drawn into sharp lines, showing just how mortified she was at the thought. *Interesting.* I'd like to know more about this father of hers who only showed up on occasion. I knew all about fucked-up marriages, but it seemed there was a bit of fear lying there.

"No. Pick something different. I'd rather stand up in the middle of English Prep and apologize to everyone I've ever been a bitch to rather than do that."

"Hmm," I hummed, feeling mischievous. "How about this? If I win, you have to tell me why you're so afraid of your own father."

I swore, every single noise outside stopped. There were no crickets chirping. No rustling of the wind. The world very well could have stopped spinning. Madeline was frozen in her spot. Her eyes were like saucers, and her glossy lips fell apart as she sucked in oxygen. She redeemed herself quickly, snapping that mouth closed and crowding her perfectly arched eyebrows together. But I saw it. I saw how shaken she was.

"Who said I was afraid of my father?"

I tipped my chin, erasing the space between us. "You really think you can hide from me, Madeline? If I didn't know any better, I'd say I'm the only person on this planet who truly knows what lies beneath all the fake beauty." I glanced at her glossed lips and back up to her horrified expression.

"You don't know me like you think, Eric." Her words were laced with venom. It was cute that she thought she had an upper hand with me.

I chuckled, gripping the basketball so hard I thought it might combust. "That's where you're wrong, Maddie. Don't act like you've forgotten each and every time we caught each other staring over the last few years. Don't act like you didn't notice when I was glaring at you as you sucked on my best friend's neck, leaving those stupid fucking hickies as a reminder that you were his." Madeline's chest rose and stayed that way as if she couldn't even take a breath. "Do you know that every single time you laughed, it sounded like nails dragging against a chalkboard to my ears? Because guess what?" I took a step closer to her, the basketball the only thing separating our bodies. "I'll never forget the way your real laugh sounds. When was the last time you truly laughed?"

This got way too deep, way too fast. Why was it always like this between us? Things could never be left unsaid; shit couldn't be left untouched. I wanted to know more about her. I wanted to help her get back to that girl I once looked forward to seeing every single morning.

Madeline finally spoke, staring directly into my eyes without an ounce of her earlier anger. "I don't want to tell my mom, and I *can't* tell my father. Under no circumstances can he find out."

I lifted my head in question, but instead of asking any more—because it was completely redundant at this point—I took a step back and held the ball out to her. "Then I guess you better win, huh?"

It took her a moment, but she snatched the ball away quickly and went to our original starting spot. She shot me a glare as she started dribbling the ball, her small hand slapping the leather.

I had to turn around so she wouldn't see me smiling like a fucking fool.

Things were definitely about to get interesting.

CHAPTER TWENTY-THREE

MADELINE

THERE HE WAS with his glorious, yet annoying smirk slanted in my direction. Eric stood with his hands on his hips, his sturdy chest expanding quickly even with his top-notch endurance, the moon and stars both gleaming behind his body, outlining him in the way my heart wanted to see in real life, instead of in this weird, fantasy-like bubble we were currently in.

He was glowing, happiness evident on his flushed cheeks. A bead of sweat was dripping down over the edge of his straight jaw, falling to the concrete below.

I was buzzing with memories that I'd pretended never existed. The sound of a basketball slapping on the concrete driveway, the smell of the cool night sky, so fresh and invigorating, the familiar look in Eric's eye when he'd snatch the ball away from me and make a one-pointer. It was almost too much for me to handle.

If there was one thing I was good at, it was turning off my feelings. I was good at making people hate me.

But I didn't want him to hate me anymore.

It took years of acting like Eric meant absolutely nothing to me to really believe it. It was easy when I thought he hated me. But standing in his driveway, dashing out of his grip and watching the basketball cascade through the air and into a hoop...it was hard to get my heart to play along. It was hard to remember why I had pushed him and everyone else away in the first place.

A gush of warm air fluttered around me as Eric was back, trying to slap the bouncing ball out of my hands. "We're tied, Maddie. One more point and I win."

His large hand quickly jolted forward, and I spun around with an excited squeal. "You're right," I said breathlessly, "but that also means one more point and I win, too."

My back was to Eric as I continued dribbling the ball in front of me. It was funny how being alone with him, doing something so harmless, could make me forget about all the bad that had happened. My heart was beating with freedom, a flutter dancing throughout my lower belly, my lips tingling as my cheeks burned from a smile.

"Knock it off, Madeline," he whispered into my ear, jolting his hand out again. I may have been smaller than him, but I was also a lot faster.

"Knock what off?" I asked with fake innocence, feeling brazen with him behind me.

I yelped when both of his hands fell on my hips, holding me in place. A breath was stuck in my throat, and a skitter of juicy anticipation flushed my skin. His warm breath tickled my ear. "I know you're using this tight little ass as a weapon, just like you used that pouty mouth a few weeks ago at the frat party."

A faint smile graced my lips. I hadn't even realized what I was doing, but he was right. I *was* rubbing on him as he stood behind me, and I was pretty certain it was because I wasn't stuck inside my head for once.

"I'm immune to your tactics. It's not going to work." His hands gripped me harder, but he didn't move.

I was still feeling bold. Maybe a little high with ecstasy from being so close to him and feeling so free.

I smiled even wider and pushed myself back even harder. He groaned, his fingers digging into my skin. I tilted my head back, still holding the basketball. I met his steel-colored eyes. His pupils were dilated, and his jaw was taut. "Are you sure about that, Eric?"

One tilt of his head and he was gone within a second. I turned around quickly, only to freeze. Eric was standing there, looking at me like I was fucking prey. His mouth curved into a menacing smile, his inky hair framing his forehead, making him look like the villain. "Two can play that game, baby."

Desire washed through my body. I shifted on my feet, squirming from the feeling. I felt alive with his eyes on me, and that was something I wasn't sure I'd ever feel again.

Eric reached underneath the hem of his shirt and tore it over his head within the blink of an eye.

I had to keep my face steady so I didn't show just how much his bare chest enticed me. He was toned with round pecs sitting nicely above his washboard abs that slanted into that delicious V that led to the waistband of his pants.

He was dangerously attractive. So hot he made my mouth tingle.

Pushing my blonde hair over my shoulder, I clicked my tongue and played it cool. "I've seen better."

Eric's mouth fell before he threw his head back and laughed loudly. My cheeks rose even when I told them not to. Once he stopped laughing so hard, he shook his head and smiled at me. "You can't lie to me, Madeline. I see right through you."

My cheeks were still lifted as I stood back, staring at him with his half-crescent smile and gleaming eyes, and just like that, I was taken back to the past. I wasn't staring at the boy who I'd hurt deeply and who hated me, but instead, I was staring at the boy who made my entire body sing, even as young as we were.

And the longer I stood and stared at Eric, the more it hurt. My smile fell swiftly, and I was suddenly met with a heart-stopping loss that was like a punch to my chest. My arms dropped, and the basketball slowly rolled to where he was standing. My throat burned as I forced the words out. I was treading lightly. My voice shook. "I...I am so sorry."

I could barely see him as he walked toward me, too stuck in my spot with earlier memories assaulting me.

His feet stopped shuffling, and the surrounding air suddenly felt suffocating. The small brush of his hand tipped my head back, and I was at a complete loss for words. His eyes bounced between mine for far too long before he whispered, "I know."

I swallowed back my emotions, my mouth suddenly very dry. "I hate myself for turning into this detached person. For pushing you away. For making you hate me."

"You pushed everyone away...not just me." His thumb caressed my cheek, and it took everything I had to keep my feet rooted to the ground instead of reaching up and kissing him. My lips felt like they were going to shrivel up and die if they didn't touch his, and where that should have shut me down in every single way, it didn't. Instead, it awakened me. It opened my eyes. What a stupid, stupid mistake I made.

"It was easier that way."

"Why?" he asked softly, gazing down into my eyes just as deeply as I was gazing up at his.

The truth felt vile as it tumbled out, the vulnerability making me shudder. "Because if you don't allow anyone to get close to you, then they can't hurt you."

His thumb grazed my bottom lip. "That's not true. You and I have been strangers since the day you shut me out, but every day after, one look from you and the cut just went deeper. We were so far apart you could have stuck a continent in between us, and I'd still feel that pain and resentment. The *hate*."

Suddenly, everything was closing in. My throat was tight. "I don't want you to hate me anymore." The words were no more than a whisper, and I was pretty sure I'd surprised us both by letting it out.

Eric's voice was low, too. "What happened to you that was so bad you didn't even want me on your side? Huh? It wasn't the rape. Something else happened." He shook his head, both of his hands now cupping my face. His need to fulfill this gaping hole of lingering confusion went deep. I could see it behind his eyes. He wanted me to let him in. "Tell me what made you like this. Tell me why you made me hate you. Why you made everyone hate you."

The moment was right there.

The words on the very tip on my tongue.

My lips parted as my stomach rolled.

My breathing quickened as Eric's finger laid over the pulse point in my neck. He had to have sensed my rising anxiety.

It all came down to one single moment that had me pushing him away, along with everyone else. I could tell him. I could tell him the truth. I could tell him about my dad. I could trust him.

Headlights caught my eye from the side, and as soon as Eric and I saw his mom pulling into the drive, we both immediately stepped apart. The distance between us broke the moment, the night air whooshing in and slicing it in half. I wrapped my arms around my torso and took a deep breath.

"Hey, you two!" Eric's mom stepped out of her SUV in her blue scrubs and with a tired face, giving us both a warm smile. "Eric. Why is your shirt off? It's not that warm out."

I snuck a glance at him as he bent down to snatch his shirt from the ground. He pulled it over his head in one quick movement before giving me an unreadable look.

"Madeline, would you like to join us for dinner? I can order pizza. I didn't know you'd be home tonight, hun." She directed her last sentence at Eric. "You're usually out on the weekends."

"You know, that's okay," I said as I started stepping backwards. I didn't stop until I got all the way to my front steps. "I'm feeling tired. Thank you for inviting me, though." I quickly smiled before rushing up to my porch and shutting the door behind me. I slid down to my butt the second I was alone and banged my hand against my head.

What are you doing, Madeline?!

Being around Eric was a dangerous thing.

How stupid would I have been to put my trust in a boy who swore he hated me?

The next day went painfully slow, and the number of times I'd checked my phone to see if Eric had texted me was downright embarrassing. When did I become this needy girl who was all caught up in a guy? I almost gagged at the thought. But it was Eric. He snuck in my head and made me question every ounce of strength I had left.

I'd already given myself a talk as I lay in my bed all night long, getting minimal amounts of sleep—although, a little more now that I felt like Eric was watching out for me—about how to avoid the lingering question that he kept throwing my way.

He wanted to know why. He was starting to dig. The hate that laid between us seemed to be slowly dissipating at times.

I knew it was in my best interest to avoid him, but tell that to the desperate girl inside of me who forced me into putting on my best leggings and light-blue sweater that I knew looked great with my eyes, just in case I saw him tonight. I even graced my lips with cherry lip gloss and did my hair.

Absolutely pathetic and completely desperate.

"Madeline?"

My head turned toward my bedroom door as my mom called out. She walked in and glanced around the room for a moment before finding me at my desk.

"I'm going out, not sure when I'll be home." Same story. Different night. "What are you up to tonight?"

I sat back in my computer chair, closing my book. *What was I up to? Staring at Eric's house like the desperate loser that I now was. Will probably stalk social media and feel that tiny bit of resentment over the fact that everyone is having fun except for me.* "Not sure," I answered instead. "I'll probably go out with friends."

She smiled, pushing her glossy hair—same exact shade as mine—behind her shoulder. "Okay, then. Be careful."

She went to turn around, but I stopped her. "I thought you said Dad was coming home soon."

My mom paused with her back turned toward me. Her short red dress barely hit mid-thigh. "You know how it is. He comes home when he feels like it."

And we mustn't question it. The words were up in the air, like an unspoken sin we both hated so much but couldn't seem to avoid. Except, something was stirring inside of me. It wasn't anger. Not even resentment.

"Why?"

Her cheeks flinched as she turned around. "Why what?"

I swallowed, pulling my knees up to my chin before gaining courage. "Why are you still with him, Mom? You are so much more than just a pretty housewife. You could get a job; we could move away. Just you and me."

Her expression softened, her thick mass of fake eyelashes fluttering against her cheeks. "It's not that simple. And don't forget, Madeline, he's your father and he loves you."

Love. What a corrupted word.

"You're not supposed to be afraid of the people who love you, Mom."

And that was how I knew every single relationship I'd ever had, friendship or not, wasn't of real substance. Most of my "friends" feared me—they used to, anyway, until I lost my status at English Prep.

Her eyes dropped, her plump mouth curving into a frown. When she looked back up, I saw the fear lying there. The fear and the animosity.

I didn't understand. I didn't understand how she could be so afraid of my father but still love him the way that she did. She bent over backwards to please him when he was home, only for him to hurt her in the end.

"One day, you'll understand, Madeline. I promise."

I had a hard time believing that, but I nodded anyway.

"I'll see you later, okay?"

"Okay. Be careful."

My mom looked wary of my warning, and I wanted to smack myself for saying it. But she turned around and left anyway. I got up from my chair and glanced at Eric's. His light was turned off, his car no longer in the driveway.

I flopped on my bed and told myself it was better this way. Eric and I were dangerous territory. I was going to end up getting hurt, and if that was the case, then I'd just wasted my entire high-school existence protecting myself for no fucking reason.

CHAPTER TWENTY-FOUR

ERIC

I SAT AT THE CABIN, drumming my fingers against my leg to the music pounding through the speakers. It wasn't my idea to have a party tonight, but I figured it was a good thing, considering last night I'd almost kissed Madeline into a frenzy until she spilled every dark truth that laid behind her pink lips.

Ollie and Christian were casually sitting on the couch beside me, watching their girlfriends beat a pair of beefy underclassmen at beer pong. I laughed when they'd send glares to the poor bastards playing against their girls, and I smiled when Piper and Hayley would jump up, yelling that they'd made a shot. But even through the motions, my head was someplace else.

Pulling out my phone, I typed a text to Madeline but then quickly erased it, shoving it back into my pocket. I ran a hand through my hair and leaned back onto the couch cushions again. I was going crazy wondering if her mom was bringing home another lay and if he was going to keep his hands to himself. I was infuriated that I kept circling back to that feeling of missing out on something—that something being Madeline.

When did the shift happen? When did I find myself wanting to see her instead of thriving in the midst of a notorious cabin party full of willing girls and alcohol? I'd somehow replaced those two vices with another, more potent one.

Fuck.

My mom was working tonight, so I wouldn't be able to get updates on who was pulling into Madeline's driveway. I'd given her just enough information on the nightmare that Madeline had last weekend for her not to question when I'd asked the favor. She smiled at me and said, "*See. Protective. But yes, dear. I'll make sure nothing suspicious goes on over there, although her mom has made quite a name for herself.*"

Then, like clockwork, I felt like shit because I'd let it slip my mind for a split second that my dad fucked Madeline's mom and my parents were likely about to get divorced over it. She still hadn't brought that up, and I still hadn't talked to my father. Because fuck him.

That was all the more reason to keep my distance from Madeline. She and her mom were both in the middle of *my* family drama.

I cut one glance to Christian and Ollie who were seconds from tearing off Piper and Hayley's opponents' heads before slowly standing up and lazily moving around tipsy, slutted-up girls who kept purring at me and the rest of my drunk peers. I got into my Range Rover and waited until I was halfway home before texting Ollie and Christian in a group text.

Me: I left. Make sure nothing gets broken. I'll be back to clean tomorrow.

I tossed my phone in the cup holder, turning up the music to block out any incoming texts. I purposely waited to text them instead of telling them in person where I was headed, because I wasn't ready for their incredulous looks.

Ollie and Christian both knew me like the backs of their hands, and they both knew when something was wrong. I'd suspected they knew I was headed to Madeline's, and I didn't particularly enjoy lying to them, so avoidance was key.

Pretty much what I should have been doing with Madeline.

I chuckled at the lack of grip I had on the situation with her. She'd somehow crept into my head with her sobering blue eyes and beckoned me to invade her life. To take her privacy and throw it out the goddamn window. I wanted to know everything. She gave me small glimpses, like a peek at the sun behind dark, troubling clouds.

It hadn't always been easy to ignore her when she was fucking my best friend, but it was awfully easy to hate her when I blamed her for my mother's pain. She took it, too. Madeline wanted me to hate her. She did things to make everyone hate her.

But now, things were changing.

She had it easy the first time she pushed me away. I let it happen. But I wasn't going to make it that easy this time.

We had a conversation to finish.

And a game of one-on-one to complete.

When I pulled into my driveway, I immediately peered up to her bedroom window. Her light was on, as usual, but I didn't see her gazing down like she was a real-life Rapunzel or anything. If one thing was for certain, Madeline was not a princess. She was more like a wicked witch disguised as a princess with her pretty looks and golden hair.

And if I knew her at all, she was likely planning on avoiding me because of how close I was to unraveling her last night. She knew I was caving in on her, and if she was feeling anything like I was—and let's face it, she was—she wouldn't be able to put up much of a fight.

I closed my car door with a loud slam, waiting to see if she would peek down between our driveways. But she didn't. There wasn't even a lingering silhouette behind her curtains.

I chuckled as I jogged up to her front door, using the spare key that was always in the same spot. When I latched the door behind me, I massaged a spot over my chest, rubbing away at the cotton that laid between my hand and my heart. It was thumping harder than usual. Fast and loud, climbing with each step I took to her bedroom.

My fist raised to knock, but instead, I dropped my head against the wood, placing both hands on the hard oak. "I know you're in there, Madeline. Open up."

I glanced down to the light pouring out from the bottom of her door, grinning at the small shadow from her standing just on the other side. "Let me in."

I meant that both physically and metaphorically.

"Why?" she asked through the wood.

I chuckled. "Because we have a conversation to finish."

Her sigh was barely audible. "You should go home."

Did she truly think it was going to be that easy to get rid of me once she let me in?

"I'll break down the door if I have to."

I heard her soft laugh. "You will not."

"Try me." I grew serious, and I guess she knew me better than I thought, because she opened the door after only a few seconds.

The first thing I noticed was her glossy lips again. They were redder than usual, and I licked my lips as I continued to stare. Her blonde hair was silky and falling down over her perfect boobs. A thin, blue, long-sleeve shirt was the only thing keeping me from seeing her in that lacy bra that was taunting me from the top.

I didn't give her a chance to say anything as I strolled inside her room. I immediately went over and sat in her chair, grinning at the book on her desk. It was the same book I'd picked up a few weeks ago when I'd snuck in.

"Doing a little naughty reading tonight, are we?"

Madeline shut the door behind her and rested along it. She was trying to put as much space between us as possible. Her pink cheeks caught my eye when she glanced at the book in my hand.

"What? No." She shook her head quickly.

I leaned back and started flipping through the pages. I could see her squirming, moving back and forth on those cute bare feet. "You know," I started, slowly flipping the pages. "I didn't know you were an avid reader, Madeline."

"There's a lot you don't know about me, Eric." Her arms crossed over her chest in her typical aloof behavior.

We had made so much progress last night, much to my dismay, but she had me hooked. She truly did.

I placed the book down slowly, not once taking my gaze off her. "Precisely why I'm here." My heart was thumping faster, things inside my body going haywire with her standing across the room. I wanted her near. "You never answered my question."

I expected Madeline to play coy. To pretend she'd somehow gotten amnesia in the last twenty-four hours, acting as if she had no idea what I was referring to, but to my surprise, she didn't. "I want you to go back to ignoring me. I don't like this, Eric. Stop fucking prying."

"Mmm," I hummed. "There she is." Madeline rolled her eyes, crossing her arms even tighter across her chest. "There's that prickly girl I've watched over the years, pushing everyone away when they get a little too close for comfort."

Her expression never changed. She just continued glaring at me, her bow-shaped lips pursing.

I shot up from the chair, and her eyes widened just a fraction. If she had any room to move, I was certain she would have taken another step back when I'd gotten closer. "You said you didn't want me to hate you anymore, right?"

Her eyes lingered a little too long on my mouth before she darted her gaze away, and that was the wrong thing to do, because something was exploding inside of me. *Want.* I wanted her. I wanted her snarky little mouth on mine. I wanted to devour her and show her just how much I *didn't* hate her.

"This is you not hating me?" Her warm breath hit my face, and a rough swallow went down my throat. "Because from where I'm standing, it looks like you're trying to intimidate me into telling you shit that is none of your business. That seems a lot like a hateful power play, doesn't it?"

I said nothing. Instead, I shot her a grin as I felt her nipples harden on my chest. *Tread lightly, Eric.*

"I think you like where I'm standing. I think you like it a lot."

Now it was her turn to swallow. Her cheeks went back to that rosy color that told me all I needed to know.

"Why are you afraid of your father, Maddie?"

"You can't intimidate me, Eric."

I smiled at her, inching my knee in between hers. Madeline tilted her head up, and our mouths were so close to touching I instantly got hard. There was no denying it now. Hate or not, I wanted her. I wanted her bad.

"I can, Madeline. Or..." My grin faded as I felt the desire surging through my veins. "I can just work it out of you."

Her blue eyes became hooded, her chest rubbing against mine with heavy breaths. Was I really going there with her? Right now?

"And if I tell you to stop?"

I paused, my hands holding onto her waist gently. Just enough to let her know that I wasn't going to overstep like her mother's boyfriends that had no fucking manners. "Then I'll stop. But just know...your body tells me a different story." I pushed up against her, and a breathless moan escaped her. *Fuck.* I needed to back off. If I didn't, I'd kiss her. I'd kiss her so fucking hard and fast, just like at the frat party, and if she told me to stop, I might have to throw myself out the window to do so.

"Quick," I whispered along her ear, dragging my mouth away from hers. "Better make me hate you before I do something we'll both regret in the morning."

"Shh," she snapped, placing a hand on my beating chest.

I paused, pulling back from her just slightly. She was glaring at her window. I felt the change in the mood almost instantaneously. Her eyes widened, her hand pushing at my chest harder. She was over to her glass before I even had a chance to get my dick soft again.

"Oh no." The fear in her voice was back. It was the fear I'd heard the other night when that fucker was at her house. I strode over to her, ready to feel that red-hot surge of anger whoosh through my body, but it wasn't who I thought it was.

"Who is that?" I asked, glancing at Madeline's pale face. She looked sick. The rosy blush on her cheeks was completely washed out. *Please tell me it wasn't another fucking pervert.*

The man was tall with long, lean legs and a muscular upper body. You could tell he spent hours in the gym, perfecting his physique. He had light-brown hair with a chiseled jaw and a large hand clamped down on Madeline's mother's arm like he was ready to snap it off. *Wait. I recognized him.*

"Madeline?" I repeated. She gave me one glance, and it rocked me to my fucking core. "That's your father, isn't it?"

Her tone cut right through me. "*Yes.*"

CHAPTER TWENTY-FIVE

MADELINE

MY HAND WAS FASTENED down on Eric's so hard I thought I might bruise him. He asked what was going on as I pulled him over to my bedroom light, flicking it off, and again as I threw us both into my dark closet.

I hated the dark.

But I hated my dad more.

Fear was lying in my stomach like a bundle of sticks that were ready to be lit on fire, my father's voice being the gasoline and my mother's scream being the match. I knew how this was going to go. From the second I saw his hand on her arm, dragging her to the front door, I knew.

"Madeline," Eric repeated for the third time—or maybe it was the thirtieth, I wasn't sure. I might've spaced out by the pleading in his voice. "Tell me what's going on right now, and why the fuck we're crammed in your closet with you on my lap."

I glanced down, which was stupid because it was so dark I couldn't see anything. Was I sitting on him?

I moved to climb off, but Eric's hands pulled me back. A shiver went through me, making me tremble.

I whispered, "I don't want my dad to know I'm home."

I shifted on top of him, trying to calm my breathing. God. It was really dark in here. Heat started to prickle my scalp.

I'm fine. It's just Eric.

Rationally, I knew it was Eric. But the thing with trauma and fear? It had a nasty way of warping reality.

"Stop moving like that," he rushed out, his tone low and gravelly.

"Like what?" I paused at the sound of my voice. It was all breathy sounding.

He gritted into my ear. "Like that." His hands crushed my hips to get me to stop moving. *Oh.*

"I'm sorry, it's just..." I tried to even my breathing. "It's dark in here."

"Yes, I'm aware."

"I don't like the dark, and I don't like—" The sound of something crashing echoed through the house, and I jumped, feeling like a child again. "I don't like what's coming."

Eric's hand unclamped from my hip, and I felt it wrap around my arm gently. His forehead rested on the back of my shoulder as he ran small circles over my skin. "Tell me what's coming, Madeline. Why are we in here?" I wasn't sure if he was trying to soothe me or not, but it was working a little. It worked enough for me to catch my breath.

"Remember when you asked me if the reason I shut you out so long ago was because I found our parents sleeping together?"

His thumb stopped moving for a second as he nodded against my back.

"That's true, but—" Another loud bang from downstairs and a brief shout from my father had me jumping again, so I rushed the words out. "There's more to the story." I took a deep, shuddering breath before spilling. "I wanted to tell you so bad. I wanted to tell you because I knew how wrong it was that they were cheating, but I couldn't risk you telling your mom and then her telling my dad."

"Why?"

"Because my dad is a psycho, Eric. He hits my mom. Then he leaves for months and comes home to apologize after his time away. Only to do it again. If he found out my mom was sleeping with your dad—or any of the men she brings home— I don't know what he'd do. He hits her over stupid shit. He just loses it."

Just as the words came out, the shouts grew louder. They were upstairs now. I could hear the spook in my mom's voice much clearer.

"You need to calm down. Have a drink. Let's just talk." She was pleading, and that was never good.

My chest was tight. My stomach filled with heavy, impending dread.

My father's voice roared, and I clenched my eyes shut, pushing my back even further into Eric's chest. "Does Madeline know what you've been up to? How you've been slutting it up since I've been gone? What a great fucking example you've set for my princess."

Princess. I was the furthest fucking thing from a princess.

"What a great example *I've* set?" My head snapped up as my mom's fear-laced voice turned into something more powerful. *This is the time she stands up for herself?* "What about you?!" she screamed, her voice growing raspy. "You rarely come home, and when you do, you come home to fuck me like old lovers and then throw me around like a rag doll! I am so tired of this! So fucking tired. Of course I'm fucking other men! At least they have the decency to say thank you at the end."

Slap.

A soft whimper escaped me, and Eric was hastily moving me off his lap. I panicked, grabbing onto his arm so hard he very well could have been bleeding.

"No!" I whisper-yelled. "You'll make it worse!"

Eric stopped as I pulled him back farther. His body heat was surrounding me, his spicy cologne invading the entire closet. "Madeline, I know I'm not your mother's biggest fan, but I cannot just fucking sit here and listen to a man hitting a woman who's not even half his size."

"Eric, please!" I pleaded, pulling him back to where we once were. "I promise you will make it worse. He'll get angrier, and he's scary when he's mad. His rage is endless."

"Has he hit you?" His voice was a bite to my very flesh.

I hesitated before answering. "Once." I pushed away the memory, my hand absentmindedly going to my cheek as if the mark was still there. "I got in the way."

"Madeline." I was facing him now, on my knees, so our faces were level. My eyes had adjusted some in the pitch black, but all I could see was his outline. His hands found my face, and although they were rough to the touch, he held my cheeks like they were made of glass.

"My mom made me promise to hide if this happened again. And to never *ever* come out of my room." I shook my head. "He'll stop. He will. He'll say sorry. They'll fuck." I choked on my words and pushed like hell to get my tears to evaporate. "And he'll leave us alone again, and things will go back to normal."

"You mean normal as in locking your bedroom door so men don't come in here to get a taste of you?" Eric slowly dropped his hands from my face, and for a moment, I was left feeling completely vulnerable. But then he pulled me into his body and placed me on his lap again. My closet was big, but the space we were tucked in, behind the rack of shoes, was barely big enough for us both. His legs hit the wall in front of us, and mine hit the wall beside us. We were tangled up in each other, but instead of it making me antsy, it made me feel safe.

"So, this is why," he whispered into my hair, his head falling onto my shoulder again. "This is why you shut me out? Because you were afraid I'd tell my mom and she'd tell your dad?"

My mother and father were still yelling. He was accusing her of all sorts of things, and she was urging him to calm down. It was a lot like being on a merry-go-round—a fucked-up one with rusty carnival animals that didn't stop spinning until someone got hurt.

"Yes," I whispered. "I couldn't risk it. And I couldn't fathom still being your friend and not telling you. It felt wrong."

Eric muttered something as we continued listening to my parents. My father hadn't hit her again, not yet, but their voices were growing louder. Like, right-outside-my-room loud.

"Where the fuck is Madeline? I'll just ask her. She won't lie to me."

Wrong. I would very well lie to him. My father didn't know me at all. We were complete strangers, although I could play the innocent-daughter part very well when he was around.

My heart started to beat a little faster. My throat began to close. I couldn't breathe. I tilted my head up, looking for an escape, but there was nowhere to go. There was no other oxygen source. It was just Eric with me inside my closet as I hyperventilated.

I choked for air, and Eric shushed me. "Turn around and put your hand on my heart."

My chest heaved as I choked out, "What?"

Eric quickly swiveled my body so I was facing him. My legs went on both sides of his hips, so I was straddling him, but I was too concerned with not being able to breathe to care much about it. His palm wrapped around my wrist as he took my hand and crept it underneath his shirt. His chest was warm to the touch, and the skin underneath my fingers had a special feel to it—like nothing I'd ever felt before. Soft, but coarse. A little comforting, but dangerous all the same. His words wrapped around my body like a familiar cocoon. "Do you feel my heart beating?"

I nodded, although he couldn't see me.

"Count the beats in your head, okay? Try to get yours to beat with mine. You've gotta calm down, Maddie."

My chest was lifting fast, but I concentrated on the beat of his heart. *Thump, thump, thump, thump.*

I held my breath when I heard my mom pleading with my father. "Madeline isn't home. I've already told you that."

Eric's hands cupped my waist, keeping me steady as my hand still rested on his chest. "That's it. Just focus on the beats."

I nodded again, slowly relaxing my shoulders and breathing. I felt myself falling into him, collapsing into his shoulder. My forehead landed on the hard plane, my middle pressing down on him as my body grew heavy.

Thump, thump, thump.

"That's it," he coaxed as one of his hands came and rested behind my head. "You're safe with me."

I'm safe with him. Am I?

My father's voice boomed as I heard a door crashing into something. I shot straight up, my head swiveling to the light pouring underneath my closet door.

A barely noticeable whimper crawled out of my throat.

"Madeline!" My father's voice felt like needles being pricked into my skin, over and over again. I was always afraid of shots when I was little, my mom having to hold me down at the doctor's office. But now I'd take a million of them over hearing the rage in his voice. "Where is she? Do you even know where she is? Her car is parked outside."

Oh my god. He's going to come looking for me.

Eric cupped my face and brought my forehead down to his. His whisper eclipsed my fear for a moment. "I won't let him hurt you."

"Madeline is out with friends. They picked her up as I was leaving. It's just you and me here." *She's covering for me. Does she know I'm in here?* "Please just calm down. Let's just go downstairs and talk this through like adults. I don't understand why you're so angry. It's not like you aren't having affairs when you're gone."

I was coiled tightly; every last muscle in my body was locked. It felt like there was an anvil tied to my ankles, dragging me under.

"You've known that for years! You knew that when you married me. But I never said it was okay for you to fuck other men. Maybe I should just fuck them out of your system. Is that what you need?"

"What I need is for you to calm down, *please*." My mom's request was more of a beseech. The pleading was at an all-time high. That meant she noticed the look in his eye. That scary, causes-chills-down-your-spine look.

"I'll calm down when you say it."

I gulped, pushing myself even further onto Eric, as if he was going to make everything disappear.

"Say what? Can we please go downstairs and talk? Or at least get out of our daughter's bedroom."

"Maybe I'll just fuck you in here."

Eric's hands clamped down on my thighs, as if he couldn't believe what my father had just said.

"Tom. Stop—" *Slap.*

I smashed my lips together, suddenly feeling very, very pissed. What was wrong with him?

"Say it. Say it now."

"What do you want me to say?"

"That you're mine. You're mine even when Madeline turns eighteen. That you know I'll still ruin you, even if I can't take custody. I'll turn her against you so fucking fast you won't know what to do."

Wait. What?

Shock replaced the anger and fear I'd been feeling. It had me slowly rising from Eric's shoulder. My hands somehow found their way to his as they sat splayed on my thighs. I sat back on my heels, still straddling his lap. I had absolutely no idea what my father was talking about, and I was too shocked to make any sense of it.

"I'm yours, Tom. You know I'll never leave you. I'm sorry I was out with another man. I just miss you."

I knew what my mother's submission meant. It meant that their fight was almost over. It meant that she was backing down and letting him get his way, as usual, but had she been staying with him this entire time because of me?

A choking sob was knocking at the back of my throat.

"Good girl," my father purred, and just like that, my bedroom light was shut off, turning the closet into an abyss of endless black again.

And here I thought my mom was one of the most selfish people on this earth.

But I was wrong. So very wrong.

CHAPTER TWENTY-SIX

ERIC

THE CLOSET that Madeline had stuffed me inside was dark and stuffy, filled with a soft scent that shouldn't belong to a girl like her. Everything suddenly made sense. The way that she was willfully closed off and fearful if anyone got too close to her. My chest was cracking as she trembled on my lap. It surprised me how badly I wanted to wrap my arms around her and take her out of this stupid fucking closet and put her in the crook of my arm for the rest of eternity.

There was too much that was wrong with this entire situation.

The anger directed toward her father was lying nice and still underneath the pain I felt for her. She was cut open, yet I was the one bleeding.

The yells from earlier were gone now. We'd been cooped up in this small space for so long everything felt stagnant. Madeline hadn't moved even an inch since her parents left her room. Not even a small twitch of her leg.

"So, this is why?" My hands were resting on her thighs, my

back hard against the wall behind me. "This is why you've never let anyone get close to you? Why there has never been a single friend at your house. Why there has never been a guy here. Not even Christian."

The admittance I was giving to her, the one that confessed how closely I'd watched her over the years, meant that I was calling a truce. I was done with my little charade of hating her. There were much bigger things at play than me blaming her for my parents' rocky marriage. *Fuck.* Madeline said she was selfish, but she was the furthest thing from selfish.

"You noticed that?" Her voice cracked in spots that had me recoiling.

"Yes." I paused. My hands were unmoving on her legs. I wished I could see her face, her expression. Was she still on the verge of breaking? Was she still afraid? "I know you much better than you think."

The parting of her mouth sounded out around us in the small space. You could hear every last breath the two of us took. "I painted you out to be the villain, Madeline." I chuckled softly, my fingers clamping down on her thighs to garner her full attention. "You're not a villain at all."

She was quick to rebut. "Yes, I am. I have done a lot of bad shit over the years. I'm vindictive and selfish."

"You're the least selfish person I know. You gave up real friendships to protect your mom. How is that selfish?"

She sighed, her warm breath mingling with mine. "Doesn't explain why I was a bitch to everyone." She paused for a second before whispering to herself, like she was coming to the realization for the first time. "Maybe Hayley was right. Maybe I was a bitch because someone made me feel inferior. I acted that way, tormented people, made them fear me instead of love me, because I wanted to feel superior. I wanted that power to hurt them first." Her light laugh was sarcastic. "I'm no better than my father."

"No." Now my fingers were digging into her skin. "That's not true."

How could I make her see herself the way that I did? She wasn't selfish; she was afraid. She didn't want anyone to come close to her because she was protecting herself and her mother without even realizing it.

Madeline pressed herself into me hard, and my dick basically convulsed underneath her warmth, but I was quick to ignore it. Her hands clenched onto my wrists as she lifted them off her legs. "Do I need to remind you of all the mean things I did? Do I need to remind you that I knew our parents were fucking for years? Do I need to remind you that everyone at school fucking hates me?"

I flung her hands off my wrists harshly and pressed her closer to me with a force that awakened something buried inside my chest. "Stop trying to make me hate you." The words gritted through my teeth like sandpaper across my tongue. "Not now."

"You need to hate me," she gritted back, her hair surrounding us both, tickling the skin on my arms. Her breath was warm as it lingered in front of me like a juicy steak in front of a starving dog. My heart thumped; my blood pulsed all around me. My hands gripped her body like she was the only thing holding me to the ground.

"You want me to hate you? You want me to leave you in here all alone after everything you just told me?" I gripped her hips, and her breath caught. "That's too fucking bad. I will not let you push me away again."

Hot, heavy seconds passed between us. The closet was eerily silent except for our breathing as we both let the sentiment linger in the air. I finally heard her take an inhale of breath before she slowly started to move over me in a way that had me closing my eyes and holding back a groan. Madeline was a hot little grenade in my hands that was ready to combust. I could feel it. The electricity. The spark. The pull between us. The emotional downfall.

"You're playing a dangerous game right now with all these mixed rules." My hands went to her face, my fingers getting lost in the silky stands of her hair. "One second you're pushing me away, and the next you're pulling me in. What do you want, Madeline? Do you want me to hate you? Or is it the opposite?"

"Right now? I just want you." She was breathless, barely getting the words out. Her chest pressed against mine, her tight nipples rubbing along my t-shirt. "This feels good, and I know it's fucked up after everything we just heard between my parents, and after everything you know about me, but it's been a long time since I've felt like this. You can go back to hating me in the morning."

I stifled a groan. *Fuck me.*

My dick was instantly hard as she ran her hands up my chest and around my head. I gripped her harder, pressing her pussy onto my dick. "Madeline..." I warned. *We shouldn't be doing this.* Her firm little body shook in my hands. and I was quickly losing a hold on all the rationality in my head. "Are you sure about this?"

"*Yes.*"

CHAPTER TWENTY-SEVEN

MADELINE

THIS WAS SO wrong on so many levels. Completely fucked up. I was grinding on Eric, moving my body in ways that I hadn't done in a very, very long time. and I couldn't seem to find even a flicker of redemption inside my head.

My emotions were running rampant. Fear, anger, embarrassment, anger again, and now desperation. Being shut away with Eric in my very dark closet was like an illicit potion being forced down my throat. I was turned on, my body taking hold of every ounce of reality and making it vanish completely. I just wanted to feel good, and I was turning to sin to make that happen.

My mother just got man-handled by my father, and in the midst of that, I'd learned she'd been staying with him for me. Guilt was creeping around the corner, lurking like a predator in the shadows on a dark and gloomy night. But I was pushing it all away so I could just have one single second of bliss before everything came crumbling down.

Maybe this was my body's way of protecting me from the pain I was about to feel.

Whatever.

I didn't care.

All I could focus on was Eric's rough fingers gripping my body like he was going to devour me.

"Have you been with anyone since...?" Eric's mouth grazed over mine in a hesitant way, and I felt like I was dying a slow, painful death. My entire body was strung tight. I ached.

"Yes."

He groaned, and his teeth sunk into my lip. My core flamed. "Who?" he asked as he let go. His hands were roaming my body, one finger skimming down my spine, making me shudder.

"None of your business." I was panting as Eric's nose rubbed along my cheek. He growled as his teeth scraped me. *Oh my God.* "I was desperate. I wanted to replace the bad with the good. So I used someone in haste. I'd hoped it would stop the nightmares."

He pulled back, and not only did I hate the dark for other reasons, but I also hated it because I couldn't see him. I pictured his gray eyes, all hooded with ecstasy and lust. "And it didn't work," he stated.

I moaned when his hips pushed upward, momentarily pausing the ache in between my legs. "No."

His hands stopped moving over my body, and I heard him take a rough swallow. "Maybe we shouldn't..."

My palms found his shoulders, and I pushed down onto him again and whispered, "Please don't make me feel any more damaged than I already am."

He rubbed his hardness over my middle, as if he was unable to stop. "Madeline, I'm trying to be a good guy right now. I'll make you feel good, if that's what you want. But not if you're going to regret it later."

"I'm sure we will both regret it later, but don't make me beg, Eric." My stomach dipped when I felt his warm breath linger over my mouth.

"Tell me if you want me to stop."

I didn't have a chance to tell him okay, because seconds later his mouth covered mine so roughly I lost my breath. His hands were on my hips, moving me back and forth over his hardness as his tongue assaulted my mouth. I moaned, the friction from below making me act downright desperate. He bit my lip hard, bringing me back down from my high before whispering, "If you're not quiet, I can't do what you need."

I nodded, unable to speak.

"The last thing we need is your father to come looking."

I clenched my thighs around him. *Jesus.* What was wrong with me? That thought should have scared me to death. I should have climbed off Eric's lap at the mere thought of my father being near, but it did the opposite. For some reason, the thought of getting caught made me burn even hotter—which was so fucked up.

He was right. I was playing a dangerous game. Eric made me feel invincible. And he was causing my body to react in ways that I'd never ever be able to replicate. I was begging for him to touch me, for him to make the ache disappear, and that was a welcome thought because I wasn't sure I'd ever feel like that again.

Eric's hand left my waist, and the disappointment was like getting hit by a truck, but when his fingers skimmed the skin above my hip, the disappointment evaporated. I lost focus. I felt dizzy. His lips were back on mine, and they were so soft and plump that I had a hard time not sinking my teeth into them. He was driving me wild.

When his hand crept underneath my bra and the pad of his thumb brushed over my nipple, my eyes shot open. "Eric." My whisper turned into a breathy moan.

"Shh," he hushed. "Just enjoy the ride. I know what you need. Let me give it to you."

I ground my hips over him, needing to feel that rough sensation. I threw my head back and gasped as he pinched my nipple. Warmth washed over me, and my toes began to tingle.

"Please," I begged, not caring how desperate I sounded. I'd get on my hands and knees if I had to. "Mmhm." His teeth grazed my ear, and goosebumps covered my body. His other hand, the one moving me back and forth over his jeans, went into the front of my leggings and underneath my lacy underwear.

Yes. Yes. Yes.

I lifted my body up, needing his fingers to do their magic. His thumb flicked over my clit, and I pushed my hips forward. "This...this is good."

"I know, baby. Fuck my hand, Madeline. Make yourself feel good. You said you were selfish. Show me how much."

Death by Eric's dirty mouth sounded like a great way to go. I sunk down when his finger entered me and pressed my forehead to his. "Oh my God," I croaked, moving my hips back and forth. "*Eric.*"

"Shh. That's it, baby. Find that spot."

He needed to stop. He had to stop talking like that. I was on the urge of professing my love to him. I was high. Eric was a drug. His fingers, his mouth, his voice. His heart. All of it.

"It feels too..." My hips were moving; his fingers were pumping in and out, his thumb brushing over my sensitive clit.

"Good. It's too fucking good."

Eric's mouth was on mine, and it only made things that much hotter. I felt the tightening down below and the spark of warmth start on my scalp.

"Come for me, Maddie."

My hips moved faster, chasing a high that I was absolutely and irrevocably in love with. My entire body went into shock as I came. Eric's lips sealed my mouth shut, drowning out any possible noise that wanted to come out.

A heavy breath left me as I collapsed on him, my entire mind and body sated.

I wasn't sure how long it took, but eventually, my chest stopped heaving, and my eyes grew heavy. Eric pulled his finger out of me slowly, and I whimpered as the sensation rippled through me. Suddenly, I wanted more. I wanted more before it was morning and we went back to our fucked-up version of *us*. I started to move, but he stopped me. "No more tonight; you need to sleep."

I could barely form words. "Nuh-uh."

His lips brushed my forehead in a sweet way, and a tiny piece of my damaged heart mended. "You've been through hell emotionally, Maddie. Go to sleep. I'll stay with you until daylight, and then I'll sneak out. Just sleep, okay? I'll chase away the nightmares."

Somehow, Eric had maneuvered my body without me even knowing it, and I was curled up on top of him with our legs intertwined. It was a small space, but I didn't care because that meant I was closer to him. His arms were wrapped around me, and it felt so good.

I knew in the morning things would be ugly, but right now, they were beautiful. *I* felt beautiful and worshiped. *Whole.*

So I did exactly what he said. I went to sleep and pretended like everything was fine.

CHAPTER TWENTY-EIGHT

ERIC

KISSING MADELINE WAS like having one hand in hell and the other in heaven. Her lips were as sweet as an angel's, but her tongue was as seductive as Eden's. At some point through the night, I'd carried her over to her bed and laid her down. Her hair was a wild mess, the strands tangled from my hands. Her clothes were disheveled, her bra halfway off underneath her shirt, but fuck, she was still somehow tattooing her name in thick black ink on my heart.

I fucked up. I went against everything I'd told myself over the years. I let her in, and now there was no turning back.

I wanted to make her mine.

I wanted to protect her.

I wanted to wrap my hands around every last person's throat who dared make her feel inferior.

My heart was strumming behind my chest, my ribs cracking as I thought about how scared she was when she heard her father and mother arguing. The strong-willed ex-queen of English Prep was replaced with a fragile, fearful girl who took my heart in her shaky hands and squeezed the life out of it.

My mom was right.

Madeline wasn't the one to blame.

I glanced out the window just as the sun was beginning to rise. Oranges, reds, and yellows started to streak the darkened sky, letting me know it was time to untangle myself from her soft limbs and leave the room. I glanced down at her delicate cheek, wanting to kiss her one last time before leaving, but I refrained.

She'd been sleeping since around one in the morning, and I didn't want to wake her up. Mostly because I didn't know what to say or do, but also because she needed sleep.

Her lean body was snuggled up to me, making it hard to disappear. One of her legs was hooked over mine, her head resting just below the beating of my heart. When I'd inched over to the side, her leg clamped down, trying to trap me. Her arm moved just below the button on my jeans, and my dick got hard within one second.

Great.

I locked my jaw, slipping out from her quickly before I flipped her on her back and woke her up like I truly wanted to—with my head in between her legs.

She and I crossed over a line last night, throwing caution to the wind and letting our hormones do the talking for us. I'd tried telling myself that Madeline was fragile, whether she wanted to admit that or not, and that I needed to hold back on my impulses, but the way her body sung when I touched her caused my brain to misfire. It was much too dark in the closet to truly see her, but she was so fucking hot. I was pretty sure I could still taste her tongue on mine.

After glancing out her window and realizing I'd likely break the drainpipe she used to shimmy down when sneaking out of her room, I peeked my head out her bedroom door and listened.

It took a few seconds before I heard shuffling down the hall. Part of me wanted her dad to find me in here. Maybe he'd take a swing at me and then I'd have an even better excuse to rip his head off. Sure, her father may have been a little bit bigger than me, but I'd been picking fights for as long as I could remember. Even Christian and I had gone a few rounds.

Rage had a way of making you stronger than you really were. And I'd be raging a lot more than him if we ever came face to face.

Madeline wasn't his little *princess* as he called her last night. She was mine.

My foot teetered back and forth over the threshold of her soft carpet and the hallway, waiting for him to come strolling out of the bedroom I'd been in just months prior, watching his wife get nailed by my father, but the shuffling from a few seconds ago turned into low moans.

The repeated thumping noise was all too familiar to me.

Madeline's mother was moaning even louder now. *Too* loud. I'd say she was faking an orgasm.

I almost laughed as I walked toward the stairs, but the thought of leaving Madeline made me antsy, even if there was no other choice. I couldn't kidnap her from her house just because her father was a misogynist abusive ass to her mother, but I wanted to.

The worry was already eating away at me. I didn't like the idea of leaving her in a house with a man like that, which was exactly why I was already trying to figure out a way to see her tonight.

As soon as I made it down Madeline's front steps, I grabbed my phone out of my car and shot her a quick text, asking her to let me know when she woke up, and then scanned the group text from the night before.

Christian- Where did you go?

Ollie- I bet I know where.

Christian- Quit ignoring us. Are you with Madeline? Dude, don't do it. Don't get mixed up with her.

Ollie- For real. You'll likely get cat scratch fever.

Christian- This is Hayley. Don't listen to them. Do what you want.

Ollie- Or who you want. *devil emoji*

Christian- If you're fucking her, fine. But don't get wrapped up in her. Madeline is as unattainable as they come. She will burn you and laugh as your skin singes. And make sure you use a condom. I heard a rumor she fucked Benny Cline from Oakland High. He gets around.

I stopped walking. Was that who she fucked after everything?

Ollie- How do you know he gets around, Christian?

Christian- Stop while you're ahead Ol. I see where this is going.

An hour later, Christian texted again.

Christian- Eric, why are you ignoring us? Afraid I'll talk you out of fucking the girl you swore you hated?

Ollie- You swore you hated Hayley, and look at you now, big bro. Ready to propose.

Christian- Damn right I am. And you have no room to talk. You and Piper are the same.

Ollie- Da, da, da-dum. Da, da, da-dum.

Christian- Why are you so annoying? Even in text?

Ollie- Da, da, da-dum. OH! CAN I BE THE FLOWER GIRL???

Christian- You do not exist anymore.

I chuckled and continued reading the next texts, which came a couple hours later.

Ollie- ERIC! Someone stole your mom's vase. The one that sat on the mantel.

Ollie- OH MY GOD. NOW THEY'RE PLAYING HOT POTATO WITH IT.

Ollie- And... it's broken. Sorry, man. We tried.

Ollie- Okay, he must not have his phone. He would have flipped if he knew someone was messing with his mom's shit.

Christian- Or he knows that we would break their arms if someone touched shit they weren't supposed to.

Ollie- Truth. Alright, Eric. We're done texting you. Have fun fucking Madeline even though you'll deny it in the morning.

I shoved my phone in my pocket, ignoring my two best friends and their incessant texts, and started the trek back over to my house, which was a grand total of four yards away. Ollie and his wise cracks were nothing unusual, and I knew he probably didn't give two fucks if I was involved with Madeline. But Christian was a different story. He wasn't making light of the situation. He didn't trust Madeline, and he was letting me know every chance he could. He knew I'd do what I wanted in the end, because that was who I was, but he also wanted to put the warning out there. I respected that. Christian was the king of English Prep, but I was the furthest thing from noble. I didn't take orders from him. I did my best to turn off my feelings when he and Madeline were together, because he was my best friend and my ignorance for her turned into hate, but now things were different. They weren't together anymore, and I didn't hate her.

Madeline was fair game.

"Funny seeing you this early."

I snapped my attention to my porch, finding my mom smiling into a steaming mug. I glanced back to the driveway and saw her SUV parked behind my Range Rover. *When did she get home?*

"I thought you were working an overnight shift?" I slowly started to walk up to the porch, my shoes shuffling over the steps with ease.

"Slow night in the ER. I have overtime, so I was the first to go."

"Ah, gotcha," I said, nodding as I sat beside her on the swing. It creaked as it dipped down, and my mom let out a laugh, eyeing the springs.

"So," she began, taking a small sip of her coffee. Once she was finished, I shot her a half-grin, and she rolled her eyes, handing me the mug. The warm Colombian brew coated my tongue, and for a moment, I was a little resentful that it replaced the taste of Madeline. "Where were you?"

I slid the mug back over to her, and she took it gracefully.

"Why ask a question you know the answer to?" I lifted an eyebrow, and she grinned into her mug again.

"Is everything okay with Madeline?"

I thought back to a few days ago when I'd given her *very* minimal details about Madeline's screaming-in-my-bedroom ordeal. She didn't ask many questions, but I knew she was concerned.

Glancing back to Madeline's house, I answered with integrity. "Not really."

"Anything I can do?"

My chest burned, and it had nothing to do with the hot coffee I'd just drank. I felt myself splitting in two, like a torn piece of notebook paper. I was getting a slight glimpse of how Madeline felt when she'd found out my dad had cheated with her mom. It would have been difficult to ask me to not say anything in fear that her father would find out. Just like it was difficult that I was about to ask my mom that same favor. "Yeah." I ran my hands down the front of my jeans. "Can you not say anything to Madeline's dad? You know..." I gulped, unable to meet her eye. *Was it right for me to ask this of her?* "That her mom and...Dad..."

My mom's hand landed on my clenched fist, unbundling my fingers from digging into my palm. "Eric." I couldn't meet her eye. I felt like shit. It wasn't fair that I was asking this, but it also wasn't fair that Madeline was in the situation she was in. "Do you really think I'd do something like that? Their marriage is none of my business."

"No," I rushed out, locking eyes with her. My mom was a saint. There was nothing vindictive about her. "I don't. But I just had to say it, just in case."

She nodded slowly, her face morphing into worry. "What's going on, baby? You're worried. I can tell."

I wavered for a moment, looking over at Madeline's house again, eyeing her father's Jaguar in the driveway. I wasn't sure what telling my mom would do, but it seemed unhealthy that no one knew what Madeline was going through. I wanted to come to her defense for some reason. I wanted to prove that Madeline wasn't this awful person everyone thought she was. I wanted to prove her worth to my mom.

But I kept my mouth shut as my phone vibrated in my pocket.

Maddie- I know you're back to hating me, but please don't tell anyone about last night. No one can know, Eric.

I wasn't sure if she was referring to her dad or the part where she came all over my hand.

Me- Tell your mom you're staying with a friend tonight.

She texted back instantly.

Maddie- Is that supposed to be some joke about me not having any friends?

I chuckled under my breath, eyeing my mom from the side who was staring directly at me.

"Movie night tonight? And do you care if I bring a friend?"

She smiled. "Tell Madeline it's a pj party. No pjs, no admittance."

I laughed, shaking my head. She and I used to have pj parties all the time when I was younger, especially when my father was on a work trip. It'd obviously been a long, long time since we had done something like this, but it sounded just about perfect for Madeline. She needed a little normalcy in her life, and she needed to get out of the house and away from her parents' fucked-up marriage.

Me- My house, 7pm. My mom said you have to wear pjs.

Maddie- ...what?

Me- See you at 7, and don't even try to make up an excuse. I know where you live, and I will come get you if I have to. Father home or not.

I slipped my phone back in my pocket, knowing she likely wouldn't text back. My mom nudged me with her shoulder, handing the cup of coffee back to me.

"I'm here for you when you want to talk about it, okay?"

I didn't answer her. Instead, we both sat on the porch in silence as I tried to sort through my thoughts which all revolved around the girl next door that I swore I'd never ever let back in.

CHAPTER TWENTY-NINE

MADELINE

It BAFFLED me how my father could morph from monster to hero in a matter of a few hours. How he could sip on his coffee with a radiant smile, ruffling my hair and wrapping his arms around my mother's waist like she was his own personal home.

She was stiff, unbeknownst to him, but her posture was nothing near relaxed. She stood at the sink and stared through the window as my father sat with me at the table and had breakfast like he hadn't smacked my mom around the night before.

When I'd woken up this morning, the first thing on my mind was Eric. I could smell him on my covers and feel his kiss on my lips. My body felt sated and relaxed. Full of light. Until I remembered what led me to that feeling.

I shot out of bed, almost toppling over onto the carpet, and ran to my window. Dread weighed heavy on me when I saw that my father's Jaguar was still there, which meant last night wasn't the start of a nightmare that turned into a blissful dream. It meant that my father was home, and I had completely lost it in front of Eric.

It was probably wrong what we did. I knew, deep down, that I'd be the one hurt in the end. For all I knew, Eric was only fucking with me. Playing me. It could be part of his game. After all, he did say he'd ruin me.

But I didn't care. The pain was worth the high. Eric made me feel so good and safe. I was full to the brim with emotions. He was all I could think about as I ate breakfast—until my father smacked his hand on the table.

I jumped as the silverware clanked together and looked at him. His bright-blue eyes were beady, but they softened at the last second, little crinkles forming around the edges. "Princess, I asked you a question."

"Oh, sorry," I muttered, looking around the sparkling kitchen for my mom. *Where'd she go?* "What did you ask?"

He shifted uncomfortably in his chair, his shirt unbuttoned at the top. "Have you noticed any new friends of your mom's? Anyone coming over recently?"

I didn't miss a beat. "No. Why?" I took a big bite of my pancakes, giving me time to spare before answering another question. I sat back in my chair, appearing bored.

"Are you sure?"

I swallowed, placing my fork down. "She's been home except for a few meetings at the club here and there and the normal things she does, like grocery shopping." It didn't faze me even a second how effortlessly the lie came out. I'd been practicing these lines for years.

He didn't seem satisfied with that answer, but he let it go. "Okay, well, I'm taking her out tonight, but I have to leave early tomorrow. Would you like to go too?"

Absolutely not. Please just go.

"Why don't you two just go and have a date? It's been a while since you've been home, Daddy. She misses you." *Sell it,*

Madeline. Make him think he's her world. Just like she told you to do.
If they can just get through tonight, things would go back
to...normal.

He smiled as his eyes glossed over. "It's been a while since
you've called me that, princess. And you're right. It has been
a while. Don't worry, I'm changing that soon. I've almost
turned the entire company around. I'll be home more when
things settle."

My cheeks continued to lift, but on the inside, I was
completely frazzled. All I wanted to do was go back into my
cocoon of thinking about Eric so I could pretend that
reality—this *awful* reality full of fear and hate—was
nonexistent.

How was I ever going to go to college when I knew my
mom would be locked away with him?

I forced the rest of my pancakes down without ever
breaking conversation with my father. Playing make-believe
was second nature when he was home, but I was getting really
tired of being the princess he thought I was.

———

When I'd found my mom later on in the afternoon, she was
in their bathroom, putting on her red lipstick that my dad
had always loved. Her mouth was puckered, the red stain
effortlessly gliding over her lips.

"Getting all dressed up for a date?" I hated how disapproving my voice sounded. She didn't deserve that.

My mom found my eyes in the mirror and nodded. "Yes,
he's taking me to his favorite restaurant."

No surprise there.

I nodded, pushing my hair behind my ear nervously. I
glanced behind my shoulder and quietly shut the bathroom

door. "Dad is on the phone with a security place. He's installing cameras."

Her head dropped, but I said nothing more. We both knew why he was doing that. He'd threatened it in the past but had never followed through, probably too afraid there would be proof that he hit my mom.

"He found me on a date last night," she whispered.

I walked farther into their expansive bathroom, propping myself on the edge of the tub. "I know. I was home."

She nodded. "I thought so."

Silence rushed in, both of us unable to say what we wanted to say, too afraid he was outside listening. That was how he was: sneaky and unrelenting in his ability to gain control. So, instead of saying anything, I stood up and walked over to her. I wrapped my arms around her from behind and rested my head along her back. Her Chanel perfume hit me head-on. "Leave him, Mom. I know how well I can play the good-daughter-who-adores-her-father role, but I would never *ever* choose him over you. He may be my own flesh and blood, but he is incapable of love."

Her shaky hand sat on top of mine as she breathed heavily through her nose. "There's a lot that goes into it, Madeline. I'd have nothing if I left."

I hugged her tighter. *That's not true.* "You'd have me." I wasn't sure that was enough for her, but I said it anyway.

Her chest shuddered, but I quickly left her before the conversation turned into anything else. I didn't want him to suspect anything weird. I didn't want to set him off. Before I left their bathroom, I whispered, "Just...stay safe tonight. We both know how he can get." In other words, *love him like your life depends on it.*

One slight nod was all I got before I left and went to my room. I sat on my bed and stared at Eric's house, not even needing to reread our texts from this morning.

I wasn't sure if he was playing games with me, but I didn't care. I'd likely do anything to get out of my house for the night. When my father was home, it felt like my house was a battlefield with live mines all over. One wrong look, one wrong move, and the beautiful illusion that everything was rightful would be destroyed in a second.

CHAPTER THIRTY

ERIC

"THOSE AREN'T PJS." My mom pouted as she came into the kitchen.

I glanced down at my gray sweatpants and t-shirt. "This is what I sleep in."

"You do not." She pushed me out of the way, taking over the popcorn. "You sleep in boxers."

I raised my eyebrows as I pulled out my phone to check to see if Madeline had texted. She hadn't. Though there were a few missed texts from my father that I hastily deleted.

"Well, it'd be a little weird if Madeline showed up and I was watching a movie with *my mommy* in my underwear, wouldn't it?"

My mom swung her gaze to me and laughed. "Yes, you're right." She turned away. "I need to tell you something."

My heart slowed, and my hand dropped to the counter as I placed my phone down. "Let me guess, you're divorcing Dad?"

I knew this talk was coming. I'd been waiting. And *God, I*

fucking hoped that was what she was about to say. It'd been a couple weeks since I'd heard her crying in her room, and it was so relieving, except for the fact that I'd replaced my worry for my mom with worry for Madeline. But at least one female I cared about was smiling again.

I paused. *When had I started caring about Madeline—or at least admitting it?*

"Did your dad say that?"

"Huh?" I shook myself internally. "Oh. No. I don't talk to him, remember?"

Her eyes softened around the edges before pouring popcorn into three bowls. The smell of butter had my hand reaching out to snag some. "You can't hate him forever."

"But you can?" I questioned before throwing the popped kernels into my mouth.

"I don't hate your father, Eric. I'm angry. A little mortified. But I don't hate him. I can't hate the man I created a life with. That's not fair to you."

I scoffed, grabbing my phone. "What's not fair to me is hearing you cry in your bedroom when you think I'm asleep." Her almond eyes widened. "I hate him for hurting you, and I think you deserve better. If you're hesitating with the divorce for any reason at all other than your true happiness, then that's what won't be fair to me."

"Sweetie—" There was a soft knock on the door, and I silently thanked God that Madeline didn't make things difficult and act as if I really wouldn't come get her. Because I would have.

"Dad is a selfish asshole, but if staying with him makes you happy, then whatever. Fine. But I don't know that I can ever look him in the eye and not get the urge to spit right in his face. Not after what I saw."

Her eyes welled up, but she nodded, understanding my

anger. Before I got all the way to the door, she said, "I'm sorry you saw it. And I'm sorry you heard me crying."

"You're not the one who should be apologizing, Mom."

Her cheeks barely lifted before turning back around to the counter.

My chest grew tight, and my shoulders tensed, but somehow, it all disappeared when I opened the door and saw Madeline standing there in the cutest fucking get-up I'd ever seen.

I couldn't help my lips splitting. She peered up at me from those beautiful blue eyes, her cheeks pink and full of life.

"What?" She crossed her arms over her chest and glanced away. "You better not make fun of me. I had to pull these out of the back of my bottom drawer because I'd never ever worn them in my life."

I held back a laugh and scoured my gaze over her. Her hair, the color of the sun, was in waves falling over her slender shoulders. Her skin was free of makeup but still so incredibly gorgeous. The light-pink thermal pjs were snug on her frame, outlining the two mounds on her chest and sliding over the curve of her hips. My mouth watered. How could someone be so cute but so fucking hot at the same time?

"Eric!" She stomped her foot. "Is this part of your game? Did you only invite me over here, in my dumb pjs, to make fun of me? Are you going to snap pictures and post them all over social media or something? Because let me save you the trouble; people will make fun of me regardless. You can't embarrass me further."

I rolled my eyes before grasping her wrist and pulling her into my house. The door slammed shut behind her as I caged her in. "Oh, we're playing a game, alright. But it's not what you think."

I grinned, and a switch of desire flicked on as I watched her pupils dilate. Her hooded eyes became glassy. "I invited you over because I was going absolutely fucking insane knowing you were just a few yards away, stuck in a house that is the furthest thing from a home. It's not safe there. It is here. Thus, why I invited you."

Madeline barely flinched, but I could see the wheels turning. "I didn't realize you cared so much about my safety."

I halted, slowly dropping my arm as I heard my mom coming through the foyer. I took a step away from her and all her natural beauty she liked to hide at school with makeup. "I didn't either."

"I know! He's my favorite too. I want to know more. I hope next season they give us some more background on him."

My mom nodded. "I bet they will! That was a good cliffhanger. I'm going to look up how many seasons there are. We might need to make this a weekly thing!"

Madeline sat up and crisscrossed her legs with excitement. Her pink thermal pants rubbed along my thigh, and every single nerve ending in my body fired to attention. "Good idea!"

Rubbing a hand down my face, I glanced away from the two of them. They were lost in their conversation about whatever show we were watching on Netflix. I had no fucking idea what the show was called or what it was about because, the entire time, I was too concerned with the way Madeline's leg kept touching mine, and how she'd gasp at a twist in the storyline, or how her features would soften when the main character would kiss the girl. She was mesmerizing. It was one of the first times I'd let myself loose, allowing myself to truly take her in, but now, I couldn't seem to stop.

"Hello?" I turned my attention to my mom as she answered her phone. "Oh hey, Cammie. What's up?" Her face dropped as she glanced to Madeline and me. She waited a few beats before saying, "Sure. That's not a problem. I'll be in."

My mom hung up the phone and gave us a sad smile. "Sorry, guys. I have to cut this short. They need someone at the hospital. Apparently, a few nurses caught food poisoning from the night before when they ordered takeout." She made a worrisome face as she stood up and began folding the blanket. "But do not let me put a damper on the night. Keep watching." She turned to Madeline with a bright face. "You can fill me in next weekend, and we'll pick up where you left off. Deal?"

I stopped existing all together when Madeline showed off her perfect, white teeth. Her smile was breathtaking. I was suddenly taken back to middle school when she'd shown up on my doorstep with homemade cookies, welcoming us to the neighborhood.

"Deal!"

My mom smiled one more time before walking off to throw her scrubs on. Her leaving changed the charge in the air almost instantaneously. Madeline shifted uncomfortably, tucking her legs underneath her. It was like she was trying her hardest not to touch me.

Her lips rolled together as she let out a shaky laugh. She appeared...nervous?

Well, shit. *Was she afraid to be alone with me?*

A hidden chuckle left my throat, just barely, but it was enough for her to whip her head in my direction.

"What?" she snapped, angry lines crowding her eyes. "Why are you laughing?"

I started up again, this time throwing my head back as it rumbled out of my chest. "I just..." I tried to regain my seriousness before meeting her eye. The smallest smile was gracing her mouth as she watched me. "I've just never seen you nervous. Ever. Not like this."

I'd seen her scared...and worried. But nervous? Over being alone with me? No way. She was as tough as nails. The leader of the pack. Pulling guys by a leash instead of the other way around.

"I'm not nervous." She shifted again, pushing herself even farther away from me. If she went any farther, she'd likely flip off the side of the couch.

I grew serious, wiping the smile off my face. "Are you...are you nervous to be alone with me after last night?" *Fuck. I hoped not.*

She rolled her eyes, glancing at the TV. "Why would I be nervous? I'm not nervous."

I tsked my tongue, sitting further back onto the couch. "Are you embarrassed, then?"

She shot me a glare. "Embarrassed that you heard my father beating up on my mom? Um, yeah. It is embarrassing."

I shook my head. "That's not what I'm talking about, and you know it."

Her face turned fifty different shades of red, her gaze dipping to my mouth and then back up to my eyes. "No." Her dark lashes fluttered. "I don't know what you're even talking about."

My eyes grew wide, and I laughed again. Was she really going to pretend? Was she out of her mind? I leaned in close, our legs brushing again. My dick started to move, her scent filling my senses and fucking them all up. "I'm talking about when you fucked my hand and came so hard you collapsed afterwards."

Madeline sucked in air, stealing oxygen right out of my mouth. Her chest pushed out as she bit down on her lip. "Oh. That."

"Yeah," I answered. "*That.*"

"Okay, you two!" My mom bounced down into the living room, her chestnut hair tied in a bun on the top of her head.

She was wearing her navy scrubs with her ID tag dangling off the front. "Have fun. Lock the door behind me. I'll be home in the morning sometime."

I slowly backed away from Madeline as she grabbed the remote to press play on the TV. "Alright, Mom. Love you. Bye."

Madeline cleared her throat. "Bye, Heather."

As soon as the front door latched, my dick hardened.

Madeline and me all alone in my big, empty house.

Whatever will we do?

CHAPTER THIRTY-ONE

MADELINE

GET YOUR SHIT TOGETHER! Letting out small puffs of air, I continued reprimanding myself in my head, desperately trying to calm myself. Eric was so close to me I could smell his clean, spicy scent. His body heat wafted over me, making me sweat in places that didn't even exist.

Every single time our legs brushed accidentally—or maybe on purpose—my thigh would tingle.

He was all cool, calm, and collected over there, leaning back on the couch with his legs propped up on the coffee table, unknowingly being super fucking hot. His dark hair was ruffled on top, effortlessly disheveled in a sexy way that he likely didn't even mean to do. His sharp cheekbones begged for me to touch them. His lips were unmoving, so plump and inviting.

I was pretty sure he was toying with me, saying things to make me feel uncomfortable on purpose. He was killing me slowly and painfully with sex appeal, making me so turned on I'd have to beg him to touch me so he could put me out of my misery. He said we were playing a game, and maybe we were, but I had no idea what the rules were. Was he making me fall for him so he could break my heart in the end? Was he pretending to care about me so I'd feel safe, and then he'd leave me to the wolves when he knew I was hooked? Or was he truly trying to kill me with sexual tension?

I froze, my thoughts scattering like lost marbles, when Eric's hand clamped down on my ankle. He swung my legs up and over, landing on his thighs as my head softly hit the couch arm behind me. "What are you doing?" I asked, sitting up, all out of breath. *Now he was touching me?!*

"You won't stop squirming, clenching your legs together. You're restless. Just lay your legs here and watch your show."

I didn't want to watch the show anymore. I couldn't focus on the show. His mom had left for work, and we were just sitting here, alone, in the dimly lit living room with colors from the TV dancing all around us.

Maybe I should have gone back home.

I glanced to the window, wondering if my mom and dad were back yet. A part of me was worried that she'd make a wrong move or glance at a waiter for too long, causing my dad to get angry. But I had to remind myself that my mom was a grown woman, and she knew how to play her cards right—most of the time, at least.

"So, what did you tell your parents about tonight?" Eric asked, his hand still resting on my ankle.

I cleared my throat so my voice wouldn't sound as desperate and frazzled as I truly felt. "I told them I was going out with friends and that they should have a date night." I kept my eyes on the TV, but I wasn't really watching it. "I wanted to sell it to my dad that my mom missed him so maybe he'd forget that she was on a date with another man the night before."

I felt the couch move as he nodded. His thumb started to

skim the bare skin of my ankle, back and forth, back and forth. Something began swirling deep inside my stomach, but I was enjoying it too much to make myself get up and move.

I continued watching the show, gazing at the colorful screen, but I couldn't register a single second of what was happening. As every minute passed and Eric's hand crept higher up my leg, running his fingers back and forth, I was wound so tightly I couldn't help my outburst. I flung myself up, the couch swallowing my body. "What are you doing?!"

Even my voice was tight, the words almost choking me as they came out.

Eric slowly turned his stormy gaze and latched onto me so hard I almost grabbed his hand and shoved it between my legs.

"I'm enjoying the show."

I was huffing, my chest rising and collapsing at an increasingly fast pace. "Well, I'm glad one of us can pay attention to it! You're driving me crazy!"

His grin was dark and sexy, the edge of his jaw becoming sharper. "No. I mean *this* show." He pointed his chin to me, his eyebrows raising to show off his dark eyelashes.

I gulped. "Wha—what?" His finger was still toying over my ankle, rising up to my knee and back. Even through my pjs, the friction was causing goosebumps.

I wanted more.

"I'm enjoying the show you're putting on, Madeline."

"What show?" I was panting, and it was so embarrassing, but I couldn't make myself get up and leave. I didn't want to. His touch made the room sway and rock in the most delicious of ways.

More.

I felt myself scooting down farther, my legs enveloping his. My face was hot. It was like slipping into a hot tub, feeling the warmth of the water flush my skin.

"You enjoying my touch." He licked his bottom lip, his tongue darting out quickly before disappearing. I pouted when he pulled it back into his mouth. "You squirming... unable to stay still because the chemistry between us is at an all-time high." He turned away, his finger creeping higher. "Thanks to last night."

"Why are you doing this? Is it part of the plan to ruin me? Destroy me like I destroyed you?"

He smirked. "You didn't destroy me. You only made me mad. You made me hate you." His hand stopped moving, and my hopes came crashing down.

No. Please don't stop.

I shivered.

"But..." My eyes widened as his eyes tore through me like an unstoppable tornado. "I don't think I hate you anymore."

I felt brave with his eyes on me. I felt the girl buried inside sparking to life with his hopeful words. I knew, outside of this house and back in our normal reality of our fucked-up, high-school-deemed hierarchy, we were nothing. I was the school leper. His friends *loathed* me, and even the teachers wanted to watch me crash and burn. I was damaged beyond reach, shoving away the trauma only for it to haunt me in my sleep. But here? Tucked away inside thick walls, all alone with nothing but worthless words separating us? I didn't care if I was worse off afterwards. I didn't care if I had the bitter taste of love left behind when we went our separate ways.

I wanted the boy next door, even if he did hate me in the end.

The leg his hand was burning opened farther, dropping to the side like a sacrificed invitation. "Hate or not..." I reached for his hand, crept it up past my knee, and placed it at the waistband of my pants. "I'd still beg you to touch me."

Eric's eyes were hooded, his nostrils flared. My middle

was throbbing, my nipples hardening with the single thought of our bodies colliding.

All I could think about as Eric peered down at me with his soul-sucking eyes and kissable mouth was, *mine, mine, mine.*

He was the furthest thing from mine, but right now, I could pretend.

His hands grasped my hips, and he pulled me down even further onto the couch. My head hit the cushion softly as he ripped my thin shirt up and over my head. I arched my back when his warm breath hit my chest, right in between the lace of my bra. He inhaled like he couldn't get enough. "Same thing applies," he whispered. "Tell me if you need me to stop." Then, he whipped himself forward and sealed a kiss on my mouth. His tongue swept in, swirling around with an urgency that we both felt. I spread my legs wide, pushing up on his hardness, wanting to rock away the ache that had only intensified.

"So fucking hot," he mumbled against my lips, biting and pulling, making me whimper with need.

I was so incredibly desperate; it was downright mortifying how obsessed I was with his touch. It was wild. *This* was wild. Eric and I were completely unstoppable.

When he took his mouth off mine, inhaling a lungful of oxygen, he ripped his own shirt off and threw it across the room. The lights on the TV danced along his rippling muscles, his chest bare of any flaws, only mounds and valleys of toned bulges, begging to be licked. He pulled himself back down, trailing his nose over the curve of my heavy breasts, both spilling out of my bra. When I felt the slickness of his tongue lick a line from my chest down past my belly button, I almost passed out.

"Eric, don't make me beg for it."

I felt him smile along my skin. "Begging sounds nice. Tell me how bad you want it, baby."

No, he did not just ask me to beg.

My hips jerked upward, and his hands grabbed them, pushing me down from rubbing myself on him. I traveled my fingers over my bra, needing some type of stimulation to keep me from crying out, but then his fingers found mine, and he intertwined them.

His gaze was dark and heavy, lust covering every single feature that I'd grown to love. "Let me hear you say it."

"Say what," I panted, still arching my body for his touch, like I'd die without it. "What do you want me to say?"

His eye twitched. "Say you never stopped caring about me. Say you always felt the pull that I felt. Tell me you want me as bad as I want you."

If only he knew.

My gaze never left his. "I want you." My words shook the room. "I always have." I glanced away, keeping myself from saying something that would completely ruin the moment.

Eric stopped breathing. His eyes ping-ponged back and forth between mine, a little worry line forming between his eyes as if he were trying to decide if I was being truthful or not. My hand wobbled as I reached up and smoothed the wrinkle out. "It's the truth," I said with conviction. "Now fuck me like you love me—or hate me. Either one. Just fuck me, Eric. Put me out of my misery."

His eyes flared, and I felt the hot burning stake go through my chest. My pants and underwear were both down and halfway across the room when his warm, wet mouth slipped down in between my legs and coated me from the inside out. Darkness crowded my vision, my fingers pulling at the thick strands of his hair.

This was such an intimate thing to me because I'd never done it. Most of the time, guys wanted me to suck them off, and then they'd finger me before we'd have sex. It was a fast exchange in getting five seconds of pleasure, but this? This made me feel worshiped. Like Eric cared that I felt good.

My eyes flung open as a mind-numbing roll of ecstasy started to seep all around me.

He was going to fucking destroy me, and I meant that both physically and emotionally.

CHAPTER THIRTY-TWO

ERIC

SHE WAS SO FUCKING WARM, and tight, and tasted like heaven on my mouth. Everything inside of me was corrupted. The only thing I wanted was to make this girl mine. I wanted her mouth, her pussy, her mind, her heart. I wanted it all.

Madeline's body moved like a stripper as she fucked my face. Her hips rolled and bucked, and I licked up every last drop that her pussy gave me.

That's right, baby.

I knew she was close to getting off because her hips moved faster and her moans were unrecognizable. My dick had never been so fucking hard in my life. It was painful, and uncomfortable, and the only thing I wanted to do was fuck her with it. But I was a patient guy. The girl always got first dibs; that was just how it was.

"Eric," she hissed between clenched teeth, so close to overflowing. I smirked against her clit and brushed my teeth over it, sending her into overdrive. My finger wasn't even halfway inside her wet walls when she clamped down and rode herself into bliss.

My eyes clung to her as her pink lips parted, making that adorable little *O* with her mouth. Her cheeks were blazing; sweat glistened on her hair line. Her body trembled in my hands, but we were far from over.

I could stay here all fucking night and fuck her on this very couch. I gave absolutely zero fucks that we were in my living room.

Her breathing was still rushed, her body quaking with sweet little shudders from the high. Her baby blues were hooded and lust-filled as she sat up on her elbows and gazed at me in all her glory.

In the past, I'd never let myself picture her like this. I'd always thought she was hot as hell, fuckable, one of the most attractive girls at English Prep—her blonde hair was like catching sight of the rising sun, her pink lips always appearing so soft and kissable. And although I'd always felt overly attracted to her, unable to keep my hands from touching her when we were alone, I didn't let myself conjure up this image, because I knew it would completely consume me. And it did. Her eyes held so much desire and need that even if it were a life-or-death situation not to touch her, I still would.

I always knew there'd be a day when I'd have Madeline at my mercy, and I knew when that day came, I'd destroy her in three seconds flat with vengeance.

But when it came to Madeline, hate was a fleeting emotion, because instead of destroying her, I wanted to do the opposite.

Madeline and I locked eyes as I wiped my mouth, the feel of my swollen lips rubbing over the back of my hand. She watched without trying to hide the rising desire, her eyes widening with each one of my slow movements. I crept down over her, pushing her body back down into a lying position.

Her bra strap was hanging loosely over her shoulder, her silky hair covering the lacy fabric.

The contact that our skin held was like a thousand fireflies lighting up the dark room. Everything felt warm and fuzzy. We were in a haze. Lust-locked.

My fingers tingled as I pulled the other strap down to meet the crook of her elbow, her chest almost fully exposed. She arched her back, never once leaving my gaze, and I unsnapped the scrap of fabric with one skillful click, and soon, she was completely bare.

The bulge in my sweatpants was pulsing, aching, almost so hard I thought it might fall off. The smallest brush of her knee against me had me sucking in air.

Madeline's head tilted just slightly before a mischievous twinkle appeared in eye.

Her shaky hand left my forearm as I rested above her, taking in her beautiful, toned curves. She was small but had an athletic build—years and years of cheerleading, I was sure. I lowered down to her, my covered dick resting on her warmth, as she trailed a line with her finger from the very top of her chest to the bottom of her belly.

What was she doing?

Madeline's eyes closed for a moment as her leg came up, and she hooked a toe in the top of my pants. They moved just enough for me to rise up and take them off all the way. I hovered above her, her thick eyelashes fluttering back and forth as her hand continued to trail up and down on her body.

Was she teasing me?

She was. She fucking was. Her hand stopped right above her clit as she peeked at me. Her lip was captured by her teeth suddenly, and when she started circling herself like I'd done just a moment prior, I almost came.

"Is this your way of begging, Madeline?" I asked as I

reached for my phone, snagging a hidden condom from in between it and the case. "Because I need you to know what you're asking for. Are you sure this is what you want?"

Part of me was a little on edge as the question left my mouth.

"I know exactly what I'm asking for, Eric. But I'll say it again in case you're stuck in that head of yours."

The condom was on, and my hands slapped her legs hard as I brought her down even further and positioned myself.

"Fuck me...*please*." Desperation looked good on a girl like her. I wanted every single part of her.

She was desperate for me to fuck her, and I was desperate for her to let me.

"Only because you said please." I smirked.

Her lustful gaze turned dark for a moment before she spread her legs far and reached behind me and thrusted me in hard and fast.

"Whoa," I grunted, euphoria making me lose all train of thought. *I was going to lose my fucking mind with her*.

There was no time to think. Once I was buried inside her, I couldn't stop. I thrusted, and she met me halfway. Her head was thrown back, shoving her perfect tits right in my face. Desire clawed at me. I was wrecked with the need to make her feel good again because, believe it or not, that made *me* feel good.

My arm cupped around her back, my other grasping her breast. Her small bud tightened under my palm, and I thrusted even faster. My lips were on her nipple, and once I grazed my teeth over her, her entire body shook as her pussy sucked every single ounce of life my dick had to offer.

"Maddie," I moaned, burying myself into her so deep I thought I'd be permanently embedded into her walls.

We were both out of breath, our limbs tangled around one another. I wasn't sure where she started or I ended. Our bodies were glued to one another, our sweat mixing, our separate scents becoming one.

I knew, right then, I'd never be able to go back from that.

"Wow," her sleepy voice finally whispered.

I eventually pulled out of her, but instead of rushing away, I continued holding her sated body in my arms.

"Mmm," I answered, unable to form a single coherent sentence.

"Tired. I'm...tired."

I nodded, pulling her in even closer. "Sleep," I hushed, brushing her hair out of her face. "I've got you." When I glanced down, her dainty ear was pressed against my heart, and she was already sound asleep.

CHAPTER THIRTY-THREE

MADELINE

PANIC DROVE into my body as my eyes flung open. I lay perfectly still on a soft spot, covered up by a thick blanket as my head rested on a cloud-like pillow. *Where—?*

I suddenly sat up, my eyes adjusting to the dim room. As soon as I realized where I was, my body started to relax a little. Eric wasn't anywhere to be found, but being wrapped in his covers made me feel safe, especially as I was on the verge of another dark nightmare. I glanced at his clock, which read just after midnight, as I dragged the covers with me to peek through his bedroom window. My father's Jaguar was missing in the driveway, and I wasn't sure if that meant he'd already left for his flight, or if he and my mother hadn't come back from their date yet.

I went to go text my mom to check in, but I couldn't find my phone. Or my clothes.

They were likely still downstairs.

"Dude, what the fuck?"

I found the door to Eric's room partly open, allowing faint voices to filter through.

"What?" Eric asked, his voice more distant than the first.

"Is this why you've been ignoring us? You really are fucking her?" That was Ollie, Christian's brother and Eric's best friend. *What was he doing here?*

"Who said I'm fucking her?" Eric's tone was nonchalant, and it set worry into every single hope-ridden thought I'd had since waking up.

"Her clothes...all over the floor." *Oh, goody. Both Powell brothers were here.*

"So what if I am?" Eric asked, sounding angrier than before.

"Dude. She is as unattainable as they come. What's your endgame here? Fuck the crazy out of her?"

Unattainable. Christian had some nerve calling *me* unattainable. And I would be lying if I said my feelings weren't hurt as he called me crazy.

"Shut the fuck up, Christian. You don't know a single thing about her. Why are you even here?"

"We're worried about you, man. You've been ignoring us— even more after you told us about your dad and Madeline's mom." Ollie's tone was softer than his brother's, as if he really did care.

He told them about my mom. Great.

"Is that your plan?" Christian boomed. "Are you fucking her to get back at your dad? And her mom?"

My heart came to a sudden halt. Heat coated every inch of my skin, yet my body was cold to the touch. I pulled the blankets up to my chin, listening even harder.

"Christian. Back off," Eric seethed, his voice near murderous. *He didn't deny it. Was that his plan?*

"No." My eyes widened with the bite in Christian's tone. Christian was as broody as they came. He fought with his fists and didn't think twice about it. He was demanding and even a little scary at times. There was a reason he was the ringleader at English Prep.

"I am not going to let you get sucked into her games. You're hurting, we get it, but Madeline isn't good for you or anyone else. She's mean and cold."

Ouch. But he wasn't wrong. I wasn't good for Eric. Not at all.

"Have you ever fucking asked yourself why?"

I ignored the burning itch on the back of my neck that usually indicated I was breaking out in hives.

"Why what?"

"Why is she like that?"

Ollie spoke this time. "Is this the part where you try to convince us that she's a good person? We're just trying to help you, Eric. We don't give a shit who you're fucking, as long as you have your head on straight."

I hated this. Here I was, sitting in Eric's room, eavesdropping on a conversation with his best friends over why he should stay away from me.

My feelings weren't exactly hurt because of their insults, but more so because they were speaking nothing but the truth.

"Christian?" Eric said his name in question. A long stretch of silence came after—so long I thought I might have been caught listening.

"No," Christian finally answered. "I've never asked myself why she was like that."

Someone clapped. "Exactly. You didn't ask because you never cared about her."

"Okay. So?"

I was sensing some serious rising tension even though I was upstairs in a completely different room. My skin was prickly.

Eric's voice was cool and calm. "Do you remember that time we fought freshman year out there on the lawn at English Prep?"

I did. I remembered vividly. It was mortifying for me to watch. They were going at it. Their navy ties were pulled away from their necks; blood and grass stained their white shirts and khakis. My stomach was in knots.

Christian was my boyfriend at the time, but I wasn't worried about him at all. I was worried about Eric. He was hurting, and there was nothing I could do to make it stop. And that was the start of me shutting off my feelings.

"Yeah, I remember. You gave up in the end."

Christian remembered the fight correctly. Eric *did* give up after we locked eyes. Something passed between us. Hurt? Sadness? I never did decipher what it was, because by that time, I'd pushed him so far out of my life it was like looking at a stranger.

"You and everyone else thought that was our fight to the top. Who wanted to be the almighty king of English Prep. Eric or Christian?"

I heard a faint snicker, which likely came from Ollie.

"I wasn't fighting to become the stupid fucking king, Christian."

Christian's voice wavered. "Then why were you?"

Eric's laugh was cynical. "I threw the first punch because I was so fucking sick of seeing you and Madeline together. I was so sick of hearing how you fucked her like she was nothing to you." There was a pause, and I was at the edge of the bed, eager to hear more. "I fucking had her first, and then she shut me out and somehow fell right in your arms, and you didn't care about her at all. You didn't even ask the important shit! Like why she never invited you to her house! Why you never met her father! Why she was so fucking standoffish to every single person she'd ever come into contact with."

Oh my God. This was bad. This was so bad. I felt so incredibly small hearing him talk like that. I hurt him when I shut him out. I hurt him even more when I dated his best friend.

I fucked Eric up. *Me.* I did that.

Christian was absolutely right. I was no good for Eric.

The first time I shut him out was because I was selfish—only worried about myself. This time? I'd be the selfless one. I was all wrong for Eric. And eventually, he'd see that.

CHAPTER THIRTY-FOUR

ERIC

MY FISTS OPENED and closed a thousand times as I stood staring at my two best friends with their slacked jaws and wide eyes. Ollie was bouncing his eyes back and forth between Christian and me, likely wondering which of us was going to throw the first punch.

I couldn't help myself from shouting. "So you're going to stand there and tell me she's no good for me? Well, then what the fuck were you to her for all those years? Huh?"

Red began to paint the corners of my eyes. The room was closing in. I was fucking pissed, and it was mostly irrational because Christian and Madeline both were nothing more than fuck buddies with a loose title, but still, the thought of her being so fragile and breakable was in the forefront of my mind.

Madeline hid some serious fucking shit. But no one even dared to dig a little, not even her boyfriend at the time.

"I never said I was good for her. We all know I was fucked up before Hayley." He looked concerned, his dark brows crowding together as he walked around the living room, step-ping over Madeline's bra with his hands on his hips. "So, what? What's so wrong with her life then?"

I paused, glancing at the steps that led upstairs to where she was sleeping. If there was one thing I knew about her, it was that she wanted to keep things private. It was the whole reason she'd been so detached.

"Just know you aren't the only one with skeletons in your closet, okay? And back the fuck off. You had your chance with her. You don't get to ask those questions anymore."

Christian's jaw ticked as he glared at me. Ollie stood up, half coming in between us. But after a few passing seconds, Christian's face relaxed like something came over him. "You know very well I'm not acting this way because I care about Madeline, Eric. Don't get jealous. I care about you, Eric. You are my—" He glanced at Ollie before shaking his head. "*Our* best friend. We just want you to be smart. You've been distant, and for a while there, you drank yourself into a fucking coma at every party."

I sighed, glancing away. *Yeah, well. Shit happens.*

"I don't approve of you and Madeline because I think she's sketchy. I think she'll fuck you over eventually. It's what she does. I've seen her do it to many, many people."

His words were digging himself into a bigger hole, but I still couldn't fathom telling him what I knew. What she was going through.

"People change," Ollie's voice barely registered. "You did." He was looking at Christian with his brows raised to his hair-line. "And not to pick sides or anything, but it's been proven to us, time and time again, that we don't always know what goes on behind closed doors." He shrugged. "Take my girl-friend, for example."

We all stopped and stared at each other, a trio of brothers at a loss for words. Christian eventually dropped his gaze and backed away. He gave me one more glance before turning around and stalking off to the front door. "You better watch her, Eric. She has sharp claws." Before he left my house, he stopped with one foot out the door. "And if I knew she was yours first, I would have never fucking touched her. You know that, right?" He glanced back at me, and for the first time in all of our lives, I saw a sliver of remorse in his eye.

I nodded. "It's true what they say, you know."

"What?" He half turned toward me, his hand on the doorknob with Ollie nearby.

"Hayley did thaw your heart."

Ollie snickered as Christian rolled his eyes aggressively. "Fuck off."

Ollie cackled as he followed him out after giving me a fist bump.

I craned my neck back to the stairs, ready to get back to Madeline.

I heard every last thing Christian and Ollie had said, but none of it really mattered. They didn't know her like I did.

No one did.

After scooping up Madeline's clothes and rearranging the pillows on the couch, I went back upstairs to check on her. My bedroom door creaked as I pushed it open. I leaned against the wooden door jamb and locked onto her curled body, tangled in my sheets.

Her hair was cascading in waves all over my pillow, the soft glow of the bedside lamp casting a delicate shadow over her high cheek bone. She'd make an amazing muse for a painter or sculptor with her soft, angelic features. I was almost jealous I couldn't capture her like this and bottle it up forever.

Was Christian right? Would Madeline end up fucking me over in the end? I gripped her clothes tighter, wondering if I had gotten myself into something too deep. She wasn't what they said she was. She wasn't some crazy, fucked-up chick with sharp claws. She was scared, and fragile, albeit distant when it came to others, but I was still swept up in her, wanting to protect her and be there for her.

After laying her folded clothes at the end of the bed, I sat on top of the covers and continued staring down at her face. Her eyes fluttered a few times before relaxing again, her chest rising and falling in a steady rhythm.

The shine of headlights caught my eye from the window, and I left her on the bed alone, wanting to get a better look.

Madeline's father's Jaguar whipped into their driveway, parking just behind Madeline's black BMW. His door swung open, and a tall leg popped out. He wore dark slacks and a crisp white button-down with the first few buttons undone. His light hair was gelled back, his jaw clean shaven. When he went around to the passenger side and opened the door, Madeline's mom stepped out, and she was slammed against the hood so fast I hardly had time to blink.

My heart ricocheted with rising stress. I didn't particularly care for Madeline's mom, and I'd never ever be able to get the visual out of my head of her ass up in the air and my father's dick buried inside her, *but* the thought of Madeline's father using his hands as weapons and his steely gaze as a warning had my entire body shaking.

I kept going back to the night before when Madeline was trembling in my hands. He scared her, and I didn't take kindly to that at all.

My jaw ground back and forth as he hovered over her mom, assuming the moon and stars were his only witnesses.

I rested my arm along the window, gazing down sternly as he pulled her dress up and wrapped her leg around his backside. Her head was turned as if she were trying to pretend he wasn't on top of her, fucking her with what seemed to be his hand. My stomach turned when he bent his face down to hers and kissed her. Her back arched up, and he smiled down like the fucking devil.

She was swiftly flipped around with her ass in the air, her dress bundled up to her hips, and he pounded her from behind. I had to turn and stop watching for a moment, because I was sickened by it. What a fucking douche. Could he not see that she wasn't enjoying herself? Or did he just not care? She wasn't pushing him away, not physically, but even from where I was standing, I could see that she was just waiting until the moment passed. There was no flick of desire on her features, no opened-mouth orgasm driven from pleasure. Nothing. The only thing I caught a glimpse of was a blank expression and downcast eyes.

After making sure Madeline was still asleep, I looked back through the glass only to see him zipping his pants and smiling like the snake that he was. He turned Madeline's mom back around and pulled her dress down before slamming his mouth onto hers. Her back was ramrod straight, her limbs stiff like she'd been paralyzed.

He'd mouthed something to her that barely had her mouth lifting to a smile before getting back into his Jaguar and backing down the driveway. She stood and waited, dress half on, until his taillights faded.

Then, she quickly darted for the bushes and bent over at the waist. Her body wracked and heaved. When she stood up, she wiped at her mouth and peered up at Madeline's window.

I dodged out of the way before she found me lurking like a fucking creep. It was no wonder she slept with my dad or any other men she brought home.

If I had to be with that man, I'd want an escape too.

Still didn't excuse her sleeping with a married man, but at least now I had a little bit of insight.

My father on the other hand?

He had no excuse.

None at all.

CHAPTER THIRTY-FIVE

MADELINE

I COULD COUNT on one hand the number of times I'd slept cuddled up to a guy. Once, I'd fallen asleep with Christian, but we weren't cuddling like long-lost lovers or even like the couple that we both pretended to be. To be honest, Eric had been the only guy I'd ever fallen asleep next to, with our limbs tangled like a knot, our skin brushing against one another like a live wire, ready to burn us alive.

I swallowed back my selfishness and slid out from his heavy arm. His features tightened for a moment, the mass of dark lashes outlining his closed eyes as they clenched, but soon, everything relaxed again, and I got to take in the softness of his sharp jaw and straight nose. Eric's dark, thick hair was laying over his forehead, grazing down onto his eyebrows. His cheek was turned away from me, the smoothness of it begging me to run my finger along the chiseled curve. Eric was dangerously attractive; he made everything awaken when he pinned me with a stare. There was always a slight dip in my stomach when he'd catch my eye, some automatic pull between us, like we were tied at the waist by the same rope. He was bare chested as he slept, his expanding chest moving effortlessly with each flowing breath.

Depression started to set in as I pulled my bra and panties back on. The fabric of my shirt and pants felt heavy against my body—uncomfortable—like it knew that, just hours prior, I had Eric's hands running along my skin.

There was too much bad shit that had gone on between Eric and me. It wasn't like we were best friends and had drifted apart due to age, or like I'd moved away and we had lost touch. Instead, it was years and years of me parading his best friend in front of his face after I'd inevitably hurt him and threw him out of my life so fast he couldn't even reach a hand out for help. Hearing him defend me to his friends made me feel warm all over, like the sun had dipped down and brushed over my shoulders, but it was wrong.

We had no future. I hurt him. My mom had a hand in ruining his parents' marriage. His friends hated me. Eric deserved so much better. Even when he spat hateful things my way and snickered when someone wrote *slut* on my locker in permanent marker for the fifteenth time since Christmas break, he still deserved better.

I gave him one last look before tiptoeing to his door, grabbing my phone on the way. My mom had texted at some point, after I'd gotten back in bed and fallen asleep after hearing Eric with his friends, that my dad had left for the airport hours ago. *Thank God.*

I told myself it was better this way. My mom and I could go back to our fake lives, revolving around hushed truths, and Eric could go back to hating me, and everything would be normal again.

There would be no more guilty thoughts, no more butterflies full of hope in my stomach, *nothing*. I could go back to feeling absolutely nothing, except that tiny bit of fear I'd continue to push away until it'd eventually fade.

One foot was in the hallway when I froze, my back snapping to attention.

"And where do you think you're going?"

Shit.

Slowly spinning around, pushing my hair over my shoulder, I bit down on my lip. I averted my eyes away from him, unable to say even a single word. *Say something, Madeline.*

My first reaction was to lash out, to be the meanest I could be so he would just let me go. But something inside of me began to mend the very second he protected me. It mended even further when he defended me to his friends.

"What's this?" he asked, his voice all sleepy.

I watched in dread as he reached for the note I had left, ironically on the back of the stupid piece of notebook paper he'd held up through the window the other day.

A gulp worked itself down my throat as I gripped my phone, glancing away.

He chuckled, and I winced at the crumpling of the notebook paper and then flinched all together when it landed on the floor.

Silence passed between us, each of us waiting for the other to break the ice. I knew I had to be the one to do it, so I did what I did best; I shut him out. "What did you expect, Eric?" I asked, placing my shaky hands on my hips for stability. His gaze lingered there for a moment as he sat up in his bed, the blanket falling to his lap. "Did you expect us to walk into English Prep Monday, holding hands, acting like a power couple?" A breath-filled laugh left me. "I heard everything Christian and Ollie said a little while ago, and they were absolutely right. I'm not good for you. For anyone." It hurt to say it, but it was the truth.

"So you heard the entire conversation between us then?"

Eric's jaw ticked back and forth with unshed anger. "Then you heard me defend you, right?"

My stomach began falling, dread pulling it all the way to the floor. "Yeah. That's part of the issue."

Eric pushed the blankets off his legs and stood up quickly, adjusting the waistband of his sweats around his slender hips. I hated how good he looked. It made me waver for a moment. "How is that part of the issue?"

I threw my hands up, looking past him at the window. "I'm not coming between you and your friends. You shouldn't be arguing with them about the girl you just fucked. They hate me. Everyone at school hates me. Your mom *should* hate me. And let's not forget that my mom ruined your parents' marriage! I could barely look your mom in the eye, let alone your dad! He knew I knew that they were fucking occasionally. He even waved to me afterward, like it was no big deal. Are we just gonna pretend like everything is all good with us? Because if there's anything I know, you can't just keep shoving the truth under the fucking rug. It'll all come out eventually."

Eric stared at me intently as I ranted. He stood in the same spot, right next to his bed, with the warm glow of the lamp outlining his body like he was a god. Seconds passed, maybe even hours, before he finally slanted his head and glared. "You don't get to do that again."

I fidgeted on my feet, backing up into the hallway so we weren't even in the same room. "Do what?"

"You don't get to shut me out again. I'm not letting you."

Anger came rushing to the surface. Anger and fear. I felt scrambled inside, unable to pinpoint exactly what I was angry about and what I should have been fearing. "You can't tell me what I can and can't do, Eric. I've never given anyone the power to boss me around, and I won't start now."

A dark chuckle came from him, and goosebumps rushed to my skin. He was in my face fast with his hand wrapped around my back like a snake striking its opponent. His stormy gaze fell upon me like a dark cloud over the ocean. "You don't want me to touch you? Fine." I gulped, my breasts pushing upward, rubbing along his chest. I ignored the way my body sparked. "You don't want me to kiss you? Also fine. I won't kiss you unless you beg for it. You don't want us to hold hands and act like some fucking power couple? *Super.*" His face crowded mine, his lips a breath away, making it hard for me to remember where I was. The floor thundered under my feet with the protectiveness of his tone. "But so help me God, if I see a red Porsche in your driveway, I'll be over to your house so fast you won't even have time to panic. And if I see that sleek, expensive Jaguar parked just behind your car, I'll be in your closet with you, holding your hand as your father demands that your mother bows at his fucking feet. And if either of them—or anyone, for that matter—lays a hand on you without your consent"—Eric reached up and grabbed onto my face so hard I couldn't look away even if I wanted—"I will rip their fucking arms from their body."

My lip began to tremble. A firework worth of feelings clawed at my chest, begging to be let out as I willed for them to stay put. *How? How could he still be so protective over me even when I was pushing him away again?* I swallowed back the sadness in my throat and bit my lip so it would stop wobbling like the weak girl I'd become. Eric's eyes drove into mine, his fingers digging into my skin. "You pushed me away once, Maddie, and I swore I'd never *ever* give you the power to do that again." His hand suddenly vanished from my face, and his fingers let go of my shirt he'd had bundled from behind. He bent at the waist and picked up the crumpled piece of notebook paper and held it up. "So no, I won't stop worrying about you. Thanks for the recommendation, though."

Leave, Madeline. Fucking leave right now.

I stepped one foot backwards, and then another, neither

one of us breaking the hold we had on each other. I was unable to grasp the fact that my plan didn't work. That he still wasn't giving up even after I'd reminded him of everything bad that came associated with me. *What do I do now?*

Right before I turned to dart down the stairs, Eric left me with, "Let me know when the nightmares come back, Maddie. I'll be over when you need me, even though I know you'll tell yourself that you don't."

Eric was wrong.

I did need him. He just didn't need me.

The next few days were some of the worst I'd ever had at English Prep, and that was saying something, because nothing out of the ordinary happened. No one messed with me. No one tried to trip me in the cafeteria or called me a cumdumpster as I walked by. *Slut* was somehow magically erased from the front of my locker too.

It was all very strange, but I wouldn't let myself ask Eric if he had something to do with it. Eric was a no-look, no-talk, and no-think zone. Of course, two out of three of those were nearly impossible to abide by. I thought of him 24/7. I even dreamt of him last night when I'd managed to let myself sleep, too afraid he was right, that the nightmares would start coming back. And they did, except it was an entirely new nightmare.

This one was all about Eric. Instead of some creep sneaking into my room to feel me up, it was Eric. I enjoyed it, even waking up with a wetness between my legs, but somehow my dream flipped, and he'd left my room and started fucking my mom down the hall.

To say I was fucked up would be an understatement.

It was even more messed up that I told Eric to stay away from me and to stop worrying about me, yet I couldn't stop searching for him every single time I walked into the lunchroom. Our eyes would meet briefly, and he'd hold my stare all while nonverbally asking, *Change your mind?* I'd quickly look away and pretend to go about my business.

For the entire time in history class, my neck prickled like little spiders were crawling all over. Whenever I'd brush my hair back behind my shoulder, I'd catch his lingering stare on me, causing my face to flush and my back to sweat.

I was exhausted when I came home from school, only to become even more exhausted as I tried to force myself to stop looking at his bedroom window, too afraid he'd be standing there like some bodyguard, but on the other hand, I was even more afraid he'd be gone, partying at the cabin.

What I needed was for him to leave me alone so I could bask in self-pity and fear. But what I wanted was for him to keep watching me and making me feel the sort of jitters you get when you're about to have your first kiss.

I was pathetic. I dug my heels in, wondering where that fierce, I-don't-need-anyone girl I used to be was.

I groaned, kicking my uniform skirt halfway across the floor of my bedroom. I put my back to my window, ignoring the fact that I could hardly keep myself from glancing at his every three seconds. My mom was gone, go figure, probably trying to gain back her self-worth after my father had crumbled it a few days ago.

After flinging off my shirt, I stalked to my closet to put on something comfy. I had the urge to text some of my old friends, those who didn't necessarily bully me after Christian shunned me from the entire school but also didn't reach out. I wouldn't mind wasting my time with them, even if they weren't really friends to begin with. That was, if they even wanted to be seen with me.

Rolling my eyes, I opened my closet and flipped on the light, only to scream bloody murder. My hand flew to my chest. "What the hell, Eric!" I scrambled backwards, tripping over my shirt that I'd haphazardly thrown to the floor and landing on my ass with a whoosh.

His palms were on me within an instant, pulling me to my feet. His large hand swiped my messy hair out of my face. "You good?"

If I had any will power left in my body when it came to him, I would have ripped my arm out from his grasp. But instead of doing that, I stood there, in nothing but my underwear, bra, and knee-high tights, completely out of breath. "I...I.."

Eric raised his eyebrows as his lips tilted upward. I took a step back, and he dropped my arm.

"What are you doing in my closet, Eric?"

Eric darted his gaze away momentarily, which was unusual for him. He was typically searing me from the inside out, his dark and moody eyes always trained to mine like they were sucking my soul. "Not worrying about you, that's what."

I squinted and crossed my arms over my chest. Eric wet his lips and swallowed, his throat bobbing up and down. My skin flushed.

I quickly moved around his body like he had the bubonic plague and reached up to snatch the first shirt I could find, which was an old English Prep Cheerleader shirt. *Good times.* I threw it on quickly and snatched up a pair of jeans that were laying on the floor.

Eric watched my every move with a careful eye. He reached up and rubbed the back of his shoulder and sighed loudly. I darted my gaze down to his neck, which was becoming redder and redder as the seconds ticked by.

"I see your mom isn't home again," he stated, still standing half in my closet.

I squinted again, ignoring him. "What were you doing in my closet?"

"You told me not to worry about you." His cheek twitched. "So this is me not worrying about you."

What was he getting at? "Wha—"

Eric's warm palm wrapped around my wrist as he pulled me into the closet quickly. He flipped around, putting my back to him and shut the door. The light switch was flipped off, and panic began to crowd me.

"Eric," I said. "You know I don't like the dark. Stop it."

"Shh," he hushed, rubbing his hands along my goose-bump-covered arms. He whispered down into my ear, his breath tickling something sensitive, "Look up."

My head tilted slowly, my hair falling down my back. I gasped. My eyes were blurry, and my heart cascaded to the floor in one single breath.

"Just in case I'm not here." His hands were still on my arms, rubbing back and forth in the most comforting way as we both stared at the ceiling that was lined in what seemed to be a hundred glow-in-the-dark stars.

A soft smile graced my lips as I continued to gaze up. "This..."

I didn't have any words. I hated how much I enjoyed him caring about me and protecting me. It went against everything I stood for, because deep down, I knew I trusted Eric with everything I had, and I couldn't remember the last time I truly trusted someone.

There was no corrupted plan for him to make me fall in love with him only to crush me in the end. He wasn't doing this to get back at his father and my mother. He was doing it because it was *him*. The boy who was fiercely protective above all else.

I was still at a loss for words as I gazed upward, resting my back along his sturdy front. "I don't know what to say."

"You do know what to say..." He paused before bending down to my ear again. "You just won't."

He was right. I was too afraid to say anything that I might regret later. Couldn't he see that this was me trying to be selfless? Couldn't he see this was me trying to change? Why was he making it so difficult for me?

Eric's finger brushed over my skin like a feather, causing my heart to skip a beat. His hand rested on my shoulder for a moment before he came up and caressed my neck. "I can feel your pulse sky-rocketing, Maddie." I stopped breathing, hoping it would help disguise the way that he was affecting me. I hoped he couldn't see the way he was making me trip on my words. "Do you know how many times I caught you staring at me today? With that sad, puppy-dog look in your eye?"

My head barely shook. His hand was still resting along my neck, and I found myself pressing into him even further. I couldn't stop. I couldn't fucking stop.

No one had ever affected me this way before. He was consuming me. I felt crazed. My blood was buzzing.

"Thirty-one."

No way.

"Thirty-fucking-one times I caught you looking at me. Want to explain that?"

Thirty-one?!

I shook my head again. I didn't trust myself to talk. Eric's hands suddenly dropped from my body, and the disappointment was ground-breaking.

He spun me around to face him, his hand grasping my chin. He tipped it upward, both of us now looking at the glow-in-the-dark stars above our heads, surrounded by hanging clothes rubbing along our arms. "Well, until you can admit that you want me in the same way that I want you—sans whatever the fuck anyone else says—at least you'll have these to remind you that you're safe in the dark."

I wasn't safe without him.

"Stars aren't going to protect me," I said breathlessly, looking him in the eye. Everything around us was shadowed, but with the neon stars above, our faces were glowing.

His head tilted. "No, but I can."

More heavy-lidded silence fell between us before he worked his jaw back and forth and took a step away from me. His hands fell as the light came back on and the door was swinging open. He put necessary distance between us, and I hated it.

"I don't hate you anymore, Maddie." Eric gave me a half-hearted grin, almost looking sad. "But you knew that already, right?"

I wanted to reach out to him so badly it hurt. Taking one step forward, I said, "Please stop."

"Stop what?"

"Stop making me regret being a good person. I'm really trying here, and you're ruining it." I took another step toward him. "I'm trying to be selfless, Eric. For once in my fucking life, I'm trying to do the right thing."

He scowled, meeting me halfway. "You think you're being selfless because you're pushing me away? Again? You think you're bad for me?" He laughed sarcastically, rubbing a hand feebly down his face. His angry eyes drove into me, and I licked my lips eagerly. "Since when do you care if you're bad for someone, Madeline?"

An exhausted sigh left me. "I'm trying to do better, Eric. I want to be selfless. You are better off without me. Have you seen me? I am a wreck." My chest began heaving, and my arms were shaking. My tone started off calm but suddenly turned chaotic. The words were rushing out of my mouth so fast I couldn't even catch my breath.

Eric threw his arms up. "Fuck that, Madeline! How can I make you see yourself the way that I see you?" He quickly spun around, putting his back to me for a second before whipping back and shouting, "You cut me out of your life because you were protecting your mom! She brings home fucking creeps who try to fuck you in your bed at night! You made yourself out to be this terrible mean girl all so you could protect the perfect image you and your mom had conjured up in your heads." The veins in Eric's forearms were bulging as he clenched his fists together. "Okay, you know what? Fine." He threw his hands up again. "Yes, you were a bitch. You were cold and calculating in your mean-girl efforts." I stepped back from the harshness in his voice. "Is that what you want to hear? Huh?" He got in my face. My eyes watered as I scanned the pain and fury coming off him in waves. "Well, guess what?" he spat. "I still fucking loved you, even then."

Tears rushed to the surface, falling down my cheeks so fast I couldn't wipe them away fast enough. "Well, that's too bad, Eric! You can't love someone like me."

"Says who?" He wiped my tears away with force, his dark brows crowding his face in a twisted bunch.

"Me!" I shouted. A sob was trying to wrack out of my body, but I broke it into pieces before it had a chance. "I'm messed up! My dad is abusive. I'm scared of the dark. I hardly sleep. I'm a fucking rape victim. Everyone hates me! *You* should hate me! Why are you so intent on fixing me? Protecting me? I'm not whole! I'm broken into itty bitty pieces. There's nothing left of me to love."

"That's not true. You are not broken." Eric's hands wrapped around the back of my hair, and he pressed our foreheads together.

My chest split open, and tears ran down my face like rain droplets dancing on a windshield. They were scattered all around, dripping fast. I cried even harder, and Eric tried his best to wipe every last tear away.

"How can I make this stop?" he finally asked, his thumbs coming in and wiping my face clean.

I swallowed, gaining my control back for a second. "You can't. The past is the past. Trust me, Eric, if I could change it, I would. I would do everything differently."

The slam of a car door had us both pausing. His thumbs stopped moving. I stopped sniffling. Eric craned his neck back, still keeping a hold of me, and then his entire body stiffened. He was like a brick wall, every muscle locked up tight.

"Eric?" You could hear the urgency in my voice. "Is it my dad?"

"No."

Oh no. "Is...is...is it...?"

Eric's features softened for a second. "Relax, Maddie. It's my dad."

"Your dad?" I croaked.

The vein in Eric's temple was out, and it was proud. "You stay here," he said before dropping his hands. "This conversation isn't finished. But I need to take care of something."

"Eric..." I warned. He was hurting. He was hurting, and he was using that hurt and turning it into rage. I watched the slow dip of his brow when he looked through the window. I felt the moment of betrayal go through his body. Then I watched as he hardened. "Don't do anything you'll regret."

He chuckled as he walked out of my room. His voice had a poisonous bite to it. "The only thing I'll regret is not doing this sooner."

Oh, Eric.

CHAPTER THIRTY-SIX

ERIC

THEY ALWAYS SAY you see red when you're angry. Red was the devil's color, an angry color, the color of blood. But all I saw was black. A deep, dark tunneling abyss of pure blackness.

The moment I saw his stupid sports car parked in the driveway, my blood ran cold. He wasn't allowed to just show up. It wasn't okay that he was going to try and swoop in and talk to my mother face to face because she wasn't answering his calls. I wasn't stupid. I knew what desperation looked like. To be honest, it looked a lot like me trying to get through to Madeline.

Like father, like son, I guess. But he had some fucking nerve showing up at the house. And that was exactly what I said to him as I crossed over the green patch of grass and landed on the concrete drive.

"You have some fucking nerve showing up out of nowhere."

My father spun around, glancing at me for a brief second and then at Madeline's house. Something flickered behind his gray eyes, and it was a slap to the face. "You have some fucking nerve looking over there, too."

"Eric," he warned. "I'm about half tired of this high-and-mighty attitude you have with me."

I laughed sardonically. "Just like I'm about half tired of you fucking around on Mom and trying to get me on your side."

Grabbing my phone out of my pocket, I read his last text aloud. *"Eric, I know you're still angry that I put you in an unfair situation and that you saw me in a compromising position..."* I snickered and continued reading. *"But please understand I love you and your mother. I want to fix things. I made a mistake."*

My phone clicked off, and I slid it back in my pocket. When I met his face again, he was clenching his smooth jaw, the muscle jumping in his temple. "Don't you mean...*mistakes*, Dad?"

Nothing on his tanned face moved. No dip of his eye, no twitch of the nose. Nothing. In fact, he appeared bored.

"What are you referring to, Eric?"

I smiled, and I hoped he could tell it was as conniving as he was. "I know you've been fucking Madeline's mom—amongst others—for years, Dad. *Fucking years.*"

His face blanched as he took a step back. "That's not true. Stop filling your mother's head with lies. It's no wonder she won't answer my calls and is threatening divorce."

Good for her.

"You really have the audacity to stand there and lie to my face?" I asked with an even tone. The rage was bubbling up, my mother's cries echoing in the back of my head, Madeline's sad face when she told me why she threw me out of her life so long ago. It was the calm before the storm. I was ready to punch my own father right in the fucking face. He was a selfish asshole.

"Eric." His voice grew deeper, like he was reprimanding me.

"Admit it. You've been fucking her since we moved into the neighborhood."

I heard a door open, and I wasn't sure if it was mine or Madeline's. I would prefer that neither she nor my mom heard this conversation, but that was inevitable. I continued stalking toward my father, watching him scramble for words.

"That is not true..."

"Yes, it is." A ding went off in my chest at the sound of Madeline's voice.

"Madeline." My father looked past me, and I almost snapped.

"Don't you dare say her name like that." I could feel the grittiness in my mouth as my words carved through. His face faltered for a moment before he put two and two together.

Yes. That's right. I'm fucking your mistress's daughter. How do you like that?

Another door opened, and my mother appeared on the porch steps. "What's going on out here? Brett? What are you doing here?"

"He was just leaving, Mom."

He snapped at me. "No, I wasn't." Then he turned to her, lowering his voice. "We need to talk, and since you"—he glanced at me—"both have been ignoring me. I thought I'd just come by."

"Brett." My mom was tired. She had worked a shift last night and didn't get home until after I had gone to school. I eyed her sleepy eyes and messy hair.

"Heather. We need to talk. You said so yourself."

Make him leave, Mom.

"Fine," she sighed. "Let's go."

"Mom." I pushed past my father, shouldering him hard.

His hand reached out, and he gripped my arm hard. "Get your hand off me," I snarled, hearing a gasp from ahead.

"Eric." My mom was warning me, but there was no need. I knew exactly what I was doing.

"I'm still your father, and you will respect me. You will *not* talk to me like that."

"Oh really?" I asked, ripping my arm from his grasp. "What are you going to do? Cut me off?" I laughed. "Oh, wait. You've already done that." I looked to the sky, the sun just beginning to set. "You won't pay for college? I couldn't care less." We met face to face, both of us the same height. "You always taught me to respect my elders, but you've ruined my respect for you, which means I will punch you right in the face if I learn you've mistreated her again. So, you go in there, and you hear what she has to say, and then you accept it."

"Eric, baby, calm down." My mom's voice was distant even though she was only a few yards away. Everything was distant except for the feeling of hot blood running through my veins. I couldn't stop the words from coming out. "And how *dare* you keep fucking Madeline's mom when you knew her daughter was keeping your secret. Do you even realize how much hurt you've caused? Not just with Mom, but with me and Madeline, too?"

My father looked flabbergasted. He was stunned, as if I truly had punched him. He opened his mouth, but nothing came out. I was ready to throw something else in his face, but then I felt two tiny hands land on my tight forearms. "Eric, come on."

I glanced down and saw Madeline staring up at me with her baby blues. She was worried. "Let's just get out of here. Come on."

"No," I said as she pulled me away. "I, at least, want him to admit it."

She shook her head lightly, rubbing her soft palm down

my arm. "He knows the truth. He doesn't need to admit it. Let's just go, okay?"

I glanced back at my father, who now had a pale face. He looked sick, but maybe I was the sick one because it made me happy to see him like that. To see him hurt. My mom shouted to Madeline. "Madeline, you drive. Okay?"

Madeline nodded quickly, continuing to drag me away.

"Call me when he leaves," I managed to say to my mom. She gave me a gentle nod and blew me a kiss. I could tell she was worried, too. I could see it all over her face. But she didn't need to worry about me. I may have been pissed, but I still meant every single word I'd said to my father.

"Where do you want to go?" Madeline asked as we exited through our gated community. Her little fingers drummed on the steering wheel in a jittery manner, and she kept glancing at me.

"Cabin." I stretched my fingers out on my jean-clad leg, curling and uncurling. The adrenaline was still running me high, and my skin was burning, likely hot to the touch.

I glanced at Madeline's now frozen fingers wrapped around the steering wheel tightly. "The cabin. Okay, yeah. I'll take you there."

Why was she so wound up?

"You okay?" I finally managed to ask, still staring at her tightened fingers.

Her blonde hair caught a shine with the interior lights as she briefly caught my eye. "Me? I'm fine. The question is...are you okay?"

I scoffed, relaxing back into the seat of her car. "I'm great. Never been better."

"Eric," she sighed. "You almost punched your dad in the face. You're not great."

The blinker switched on as Madeline climbed onto the highway. "He had it coming."

"Can't argue there. Your mom is literally the nicest person I have ever met. Your father is a complete idiot to let her go."

I chuckled. "Why do you think he's trying so hard to get her back?"

A sad laugh left her, filling the small space. "Do you think she'll take him back?"

I clenched my jaw and cracked my neck, staring at the blurring lines out the window. "I fucking hope not. She deserves better."

"I agree."

Neither one of us said anything else as she continued to drive us to the cabin. Soft music played through the speakers, and it did nothing to calm either one of us. My hand was still aching to punch something, and Madeline was still wound tight. She kept sighing, her fingers flexing every few seconds on the steering wheel. "What's wrong with you?" I finally asked.

"Huh?" She spun toward me for a moment before going back to the road. "Me? Nothing."

"You're nervous. Why are you nervous?"

"I am not nervous."

A choppy laugh came from my throat. "Yes, you are. Why are you nervous? Are you afraid to be alone with me again? Afraid you won't be able to keep up this little charade of yours?"

She gave me a dirty look, her round lips pursed. "No!"

I flicked an eyebrow, and her shoulders dropped as she turned onto the gravel road. "It's just...what are people going to say when I show up with you all hot and bothered at the cabin?"

Holding back a laugh, I angled myself toward her. "You think I'm hot and bothered right now?"

I watched the widening of her eyes, her thick eyelashes that barely had any mascara left on them from her earlier tears blinking. "That's not what I meant."

I chuckled, righting myself in the seat and glancing out the window. "Yeah, okay." I paused before saying, "You can stop worrying. No one is at the cabin."

Once we pulled up, Madeline shifted her car into park and twisted the key. "It's not me I'm worried about, Eric. It's you. Do you really want people to see us together?"

"You know very well I don't give a fuck what people think about me, Maddie."

She sighed, opening her door and pulling her keys from the ignition. Something caught my eye at the last second, and it put a pause on all the fuckery going on in my head. My rage had simmered.

I swiped her keys quickly, and she flew back into her seat. "What are you doi—"

Her expression changed from confused to ashamed—or maybe even embarrassed. The dome light shined on her pink cheeks, and I grinned. "What's this? Hanging on to our old friendship bracelets, are we?"

"Uh..." She looked away. "I don't know what you're talking about."

I smiled even wider. "It's absolutely adorable that you are pretending to not know what this is. Ask me where I keep mine."

Madeline gave me one last look before she realized there was no point in lying. She rolled her eyes playfully, and I saw the slight slip of her lips. "Oh, whatever." She snatched the keys out of my hand quickly and shot out of the car, slamming the door in my face.

I laughed, shaking my head as I climbed out of her car

and followed after her. The clouding thoughts of my parents were slowly coming back into view, and the pent-up aggression from holding back my fist from flying into my father's nose was beginning to flame again. I needed an outlet before I pulled Madeline's body into mine and buried myself in her as if she were my own personal safe haven.

I was being honest with her when I'd said I wouldn't kiss her again. Not unless she begged me.

She could pretend all she wanted, but she and I were inevitable. I was going to break her. I was going to break her into telling me how she really felt, listen to her beg, then I'd piece her back together with a single fucking kiss.

CHAPTER THIRTY-SEVEN

MADELINE

IT HAD BEEN a while since I'd been in the cabin. The last time I was here was when Christian had shunned me in front of everyone, and I'd acted like a desperate queen with a broken crown. My stomach turned at the thought.

I thought Christian breaking up with me was the worst thing that would happen to me during my senior year of high school.

How wrong was I?

I jumped at the sound of the door latching behind me. Eric came around, his annoyingly delicious scent wafting all around me as he turned the light on and walked into the den area. For as many parties as the English Prep boys threw here, the place was still in nice shape. Large, comfy couches surrounded a fireplace with a TV high on the mantel. The swirls of tans and browns on the marble countertop were glistening underneath the lights as if they'd been recently waxed. The floors were clean, not a speck of dirt to be seen. No littering beer cans or used condoms.

Nothing like it would appear the morning after a cabin extravaganza.

"Do you hire a cleaning company after the parties here?" I asked, my gaze lingering. It was surreal seeing it like this. It was way bigger than I thought without everyone crammed inside.

"Nah." Eric walked over to the fridge and pulled out a beer. "Christian, Ollie, and I usually clean up the next day. Or we make an underclassman do it."

I nodded, pushing my hair behind my ears awkwardly.

Why was this so awkward? Was it because he saw me at my worst earlier? Or was it because I saw him at his?

"Want one?" he asked, leaning back onto the counter. Eric was so tall he could have sat on the counter and his legs would have still hit the floor.

"What's the occasion?" I asked, eyeing him with a watchful eye as his lips wrapped around the beer bottle.

After taking a swig, he shrugged. "Not beating my father's ass in front of my mom, I guess."

I honestly thought he would have taken a swing at his father if I hadn't run down my porch steps and grabbed onto his arm. His skin was like fire, burning my palm when we'd touched. He was shaking, blinding anger laying right underneath the surface. Heather had taken one glance at me when he'd stepped into his father's face, and that was all it took for me to rush down as his barrier.

"Are you going to make me drink alone?"

I glanced up and saw Eric watching me with hope in his eyes. Drinking with Eric was likely one of the worst things I could agree to do, but I put one foot in front of the other, and soon, a beer bottle was thrust into my hand and the malty flavor was on my tongue.

His cheek lifted, his dark eyelashes fanning. "Thatta girl."

Eric walked past me, taking another swig of his beer. By

the time I wiped the smile off my face, I turned around, and he was sitting on the couch in the den area. The cushions molded perfectly to his body. He pushed his dark hair back with a skillful hand, showcasing all the defined lines of his face. "You can sit, you know."

I shifted my gaze to the spot beside him, and my stomach pulled tight.

"I wasn't lying the other day when I said I wouldn't touch you."

Shoving away the disappointment that I had brought upon myself, I took a step down into the den, still holding my beer bottle in one hand. I felt my disappointment slowly turn into jealousy. Jealous of what? I wasn't sure. The beer bottle that his lips were touching? The thought of him touching someone else because I had pushed him away?

You touched me earlier," I said, taking another step closer.

His stare darkened. "Not like I wanted to."

Mmmhm. Just light me on fucking fire.

"Eric," I warned.

"Sit down, Madeline. Let's just take a breather." He made a tired noise as he rubbed his hand down his face. "You and I have been going at it for weeks. I don't know if I have the energy right now. Not after almost beating the fuck out of my dad."

Right. I forgot all about that little incident for a moment. "Are you okay? Like, really okay?" I asked as I moved closer to him. Eric glanced up at me, and his lips straightened. "I don't know. I mean..." He glanced away, looking out the glass door that led to the deck. "I'm still so fucking mad." He gripped his beer bottle so tight I thought it might break. "I still feel hyped." He pointed the bottle at me. "Hence the alcohol."

Guilt tapped me on the shoulder. "I should have told you about him sooner."

He peered up at me, the gray in his eye a little less stormy. "You had your reasons."

I closed my eyes, finally sitting down on the couch and falling backwards until my back hit the soft cushion. I swung my legs over but kept them bent so they weren't touching him. "Everything is so messed up."

"Yeah, it is."

My eyes flew open when Eric touched my leg with the palm of his hand. Even through my skinny jeans, I felt the searing burn he left behind. I knew it was all in my head, but I still glanced down to make sure my leg wasn't on fire.

"Let's play a game," he mused, a smile in his voice.

"A game?" I asked nervously.

He nodded, his lips forming that dangerous grin that made me uneasy. I sat up, pulling myself to a sitting position with my beer tucked away in my thighs. "Like what?"

Eric thought for a moment, and when he shot me a mischievous look, my nerves intensified. A look like that from him was *never* good.

"You look awfully naughty over there, Eric," I whispered, taking another drink of my beer to hopefully calm the jitters.

"Truth or Dare?"

I looked away, unable to focus on really anything at all other than the fact that I was losing my battle of *Resist Eric* quickly.

"Do you really think that's a good idea?"

"All I have are good ideas, Maddie."

I snickered into my hand. His palm was back on my leg, and that was all it took for me to agree. "Fine. I guess if it'll help you calm down over there with all that angry testosterone."

He laughed as he stood up and went into the kitchen. I heard him mumble under his breath. "That's unlikely."

When he came back, he turned the lights down low and placed four beers on the coffee table in front of us.

"Really?" I asked, eyeing them. "Trying to get me drunk?"

He shook his head. "Nope. Trying to get me drunk. Now who's going first?"

"I am." I sat up, bringing my legs together to sit cross-legged. I pulled my hair into a high pony and took another baby sip of my beer before turning toward Eric who was looking at me with skepticism. "What?"

"You good over there, Bob Barker? Planning on winning a square game or...?"

A laugh bubbled up and flew out of my mouth before I slapped my hand over it. "Did you really just call me Bob Barker?"

"You've been prepping for this single game of Truth or Dare like you're about to host the world's greatest game show. Seemed fitting."

I laughed again before sighing and getting in the zone. It was going to have to be all hands on deck for this one because I had played Truth or Dare many times in the past, specifically at parties, and they *always* turned dirty.

"Okay, are you ready?" I asked, sneaking a glance.

Eric appeared completely unfazed and relaxed as he sat back on the couch with his one hand wrapped around the bottle and the other laying on his thigh.

"I've been ready. Go on."

"Okay." I took a big breath. "Truth or dare?"

He answered quickly. "Truth."

The choices were limited here. I didn't want to cross over that line I had drawn, making this sexual from the very beginning, because that wouldn't help me in any way whatsoever. I also didn't want to bring up anything dealing with our parents or the situation we had found ourselves in, so I asked the first safe thing I could think of.

"Is it true that you've never told a girl you loved her before?"

Eric pulled back, glancing down at me with furrowed brows. "What?"

I shrugged, bringing my beer to my lips. "I'm curious if the rumors are true. You're the talk of the girls' locker room." Especially now that the Powell brothers were taken.

"Explain."

I shrugged. "It's just...every girl that's ever been with you has compared notes. Kind of like a compare and contrast thing."

"They compare and contrast what exactly?"

I could already feel the shift in the conversation. "You know..." I beat around the bush. "Just stuff."

Eric's face was still confused, and I rolled my eyes.

"What do you expect when you've been with almost every single girl in the senior class, Eric? They're bound to talk."

He licked his lips, appearing curious. "Well, what do they say?"

I thought back to a few months ago when Sara, Cassie, and Missy, whom I used to be friends with, all cheerleaders of course, talked about how Eric had always been very accommodating in the bedroom but completely unattached otherwise. No matter the number of dates or hookups they'd had with him, he'd never once told a girl he loved her. In fact, Missy's exact words were, "I'm not even sure he *liked* me."

"They said that you aren't very...vocal."

"Vocal?" he questioned, grabbing a new beer.

I rolled my eyes, suddenly becoming very annoyed with the conversation. "They said you fuck so good that it feels like love-making, but you've never actually said it."

Eric threw his head back and laughed so hard the couch shook. My mouth opened as I watched him slap his knee hard.

"Why is that so funny?" I asked.

"They think I love them?" His eyes were wide, his cheeks flushed with laughter. "Are they serious?"

"No!" I half-laughed, attempting to remedy the conversation. "Not really. Well, I don't know. I think it was more that they were fishing to see if you loved anyone else."

His laughs were beginning to fade. "And did anyone fess up?"

My lips fell at the same time my hope did. "So you have told a girl you loved them?"

I only asked the question because I assumed it was true—that he hadn't told a girl he loved them.

"Yes."

Stake to the heart.

"Okay." I was quickly moving away from this topic before he saw how much that bothered me. "Well. It's your turn now."

His laugh was low, like he was trying to hold it in. I wouldn't dare look at him, though, in fear that he'd see how angry I was. I had no right to be angry, but I was. I was angry and jealous, and suddenly, I needed another beer. *Was this how he felt when I was with Christian?* Oh my God. I was a terrible fucking person. All the more reason he needed to stay away from me.

"Truth or dare?" he finally asked after I still wouldn't look at him.

"Truth." There was no way I was taking a dare from him.

"Does it bother you knowing I've told a girl I loved her before?"

I grasped onto the beer in my hand, concentrating on the cool glass beneath my palm. *Stay focused. Act cool.* Eric shifted beside me, and the hair on my arms stood up. "Nope," I answered.

Eric leaned in closer, and damnit, he smelled so, *so* good. "Need I remind you of the rules of this game?"

I looked at him out of the corner of my eye. He smirked. "Tell the truth. Does it bother you that I told a girl I loved her?"

Ugly jealousy surged through my veins. *Of course it bothered me!* I wanted to rip her hair out, and I didn't even know who it was. The old Madeline was creeping back in, and I needed to shut her out, but Eric's taunting voice was stuck on repeat. *Does it bother you?*

"I think it probably bothers me as much as it bothered you that I fucked your best friend."

Our eyes met, and the room was suddenly charged. If there were candles lit, they'd all be brighter, their flames burning everything in sight. Eric's gaze darkened, and mine did the same. He leaned into my space further, and I told myself to pull back, but my body was too stubborn.

"It's my turn again because you lied." His warm breath smelled of beer and something enticing. I said nothing as he asked, "Truth or dare?"

My eyes dropped to his mouth as the words piled out. His tongue slipped out to wet his lip, and my heart sped up.

"Truth." *Still not taking a dare from him.*

"Is it true you used to look for me in a crowded room after kissing my best friend?"

My face grew hot, like I was standing too close to a fire. *Shit.* "No."

His head slanted just slightly. "My turn again."

I said nothing because he was right. I was lying through my teeth.

"Truth or dare?"

I probably should have picked a dare, considering he was playing dirty, but then again, *he was playing dirty*, so a dare wasn't going to be in my best interest either.

"Truth."

Eric placed his bottle on the table in front of us, and his hand landed just below my crossed legs. The couch dipped down, bringing our faces even closer together. "Is it true you used to picture me when you two fucked?"

My heart slammed against my chest. Eric was playing *so* fucking dirty. He was doing it on purpose, wanting to get under my skin. He was proving a point. We both knew I wanted him. He just wanted me to admit it.

"Yes," I answered truthfully, taking a hold of the game in my hands.

His chin tipped slightly, his eyes becoming hooded. He liked to hear that I had pictured him, and I hated to admit it, but I liked it too.

"Your turn, *Maddie*."

Eric was playing dirty, but I could play dirty, too.

"Truth or dare, *Eric*?"

His eyes flared. "Dare."

Dare?

I smirked, moving closer to him. Our lips were grazing, and I felt electrified all over. "I dare you to kiss me."

His nose brushed over mine, and I braced myself for the impact. I wanted to see the stars behind my eyes. I wanted his tongue tangled with mine despite my earlier pleas for him to realize I was selfless and everything good.

"I told you I wouldn't kiss you until you begged for it."

"But it's truth or dare, and you picked dare." Our lips were brushing along one another just enough to make me throb. "Need I remind you of the rules, Eric?"

He growled, keeping his eyes on mine. His mouth opened at the same time his pupils dilated, and I stopped breathing when his lips crashed on mine. His tongue swept in, bringing me back to life, before he pulled away so fast I almost whimpered.

His voice was raspy as a swallow worked itself down his throat. "Truth or dare, Maddie?"

I was panting. "Dare."

He smirked. "I'll give you two options."

My eyes narrowed.

"I dare you to, one"—he held up a finger—"beg for me to touch you, since I won't do it otherwise, *or* two"—he held up another finger—"touch yourself."

The room grew hot with his enticing words. My mouth parted as I stared at him and his lust-filled eyes and plump lips. "This is a dangerous, dangerous game..." I whispered, pushing my beer bottle to the side.

He lifted a brow. "Which one? Truth or Dare? Or the game we've been playing for weeks?"

I licked my lips. "Both."

He nodded. "So, what will it be? Do you want me to touch you, Maddie?"

God, yes.

Something wicked stirred inside me as I watched his breathing become heavier. He was turned on, and I was feeding off of it like the devil feeding off a sin. "I do." I smiled coyly as I took my shirt off and dropped it to the ground. "But I want to touch me, too."

Eric's eyebrow hitched as his pupils dilated. I began tracing my finger around the lacy cup of my bra as he watched my every move. "Truth or dare, Eric?"

He kept watching me. "Truth."

"Is it true you want to watch?"

He blinked slowly, his mouth opening just slightly. "Yes."

My nipples hardened instantly, my finger moving danger-ously close to the edge of my jeans.

"Truth or dare?" Eric whispered, leaning back onto the couch cushion, giving me more space to explore.

"Dare."

He clenched his jaw, his hand fisting on his jeans. "I dare you to unbutton your jeans."

Done.

My finger shook slightly as I pushed the metal button through the slit and again as I unzipped them. The only sounds were the zipper and the shifting of Eric and me on the couch every few seconds. We were both basically foaming at the mouth, ready to strip each other bare, but if I knew anything about Eric, it was that he was stubborn. He truly wouldn't touch me until I asked for it. Maybe he was trying to be respectful, especially since he knew what had happened to me, or maybe he just wanted to win the game.

"Truth or dare, Eric?"

Eric kept watching my fingers as they fiddled with the top of my panties, dipping down for a moment and then back up.

"Dare." The single word felt like a brick falling to the floor.

"I dare you to touch yourself, too."

He groaned, throwing his head back, the cords of muscles popping back and forth. He unbuttoned his jeans, all while staring at me intently, and bundled his dick in his hand. It was hard for me to see, because he was working inside his boxers, but the look of relief on his face when he touched himself made me even wetter.

"So, who's going to break first?" I asked when his eyes flew to mine. "Is this going to end with me begging for you or you begging for me?"

"Oh, I'll absolutely be touching you, Madeline," he said through his teeth as he lifted his lap up and shimmied his boxers down past his thighs. He threw his head back again when he gripped himself hard.

Oh.

"But I promise you I'm more stubborn than you are." His

white teeth gripped his bottom lip as he watched my hand disappear into my panties. "You'll be the one begging."

I didn't recognize my voice when I said, "We'll see, Eric."

But I knew, deep down, I'd be the one to succumb. It seemed I had absolutely no self-control when it came to Eric.

CHAPTER THIRTY-EIGHT

ERIC

OH, fuck me. Madeline. Madeline. Madeline.

But for real. *Fuck me.*

I couldn't stop staring or pumping myself. I wanted to go slow so I could outlast her, but Jesus fucking Christ. *I dare you to touch yourself, too.* I swore I would never let this girl have the upper hand when it came to us, even if she was invading my brain every second of every day, but I was ready to bow down at her feet and beg for her to let me worship every part of her body.

There was a tiny freckle on her toned stomach, just above her right hip bone. I kept trying to focus on it instead of her hungry moans and lithe hand inside her panties, but it was no use. I could have been a blind man, and I'd still fucking come all over the place at the sound of her, let alone the sight.

Madeline's hips bucked upward as she pulled her jeans down to her ankles. I stopped beating myself off long enough to rip the denim the rest of the way before my hand was back on my dick.

I squeezed and pumped, watching her finger disappear inside her panties again, and I was flying with jealousy. *I want to touch you.*

Feeling myself tighten in all the right spots, I clenched my eyes. "Does it feel good, Maddie?" I asked, trying my hardest to get her to lose this stupid fucking game we had going.

"Mmhm," she muttered, barely making the sounds audible.

"It'd be better if I were in you," I whispered, forcing myself to slow my pumps. My hips wanted to inch forward. I wanted to fuck her so bad I couldn't see straight.

"Does it feel good for you, too?" she asked as her hand stopped for a second.

"Too good," I grumbled, pumping faster.

I glanced at her face, and she was watching me work myself with droopy eyes and wet, glistening lips that begged for me to fuck them. *She* was begging me to fuck them without saying a single word.

"Are you going to let me make you feel good, Maddie?" I asked, trying my hardest to tease her without actually touching her. "Don't you want my hands on your body? Roaming. Touching. Caressing."

My hand started to move faster as she continued to gulp up all my dirty words. She liked it. She liked it so much she couldn't even focus on herself. "Why did you stop?" I asked, going slower now. Precum glistened on the tip of my dick, and when I looked back at her, she was licking her lips.

Her eyes flung to mine so quickly I froze. My hand froze too.

"Fuck me."

Did she—?

"Fuck me right now, Eric, or I swear to God, I'll get off on my own in three seconds." Her hand dipped back down into her panties, but before she could get too far, I gripped her hips and crushed my mouth onto hers. She cried out, straddling my lap with her warm, wet panties. My throbbing dick pushed up onto her sex with a single thread of cotton separating us. Madeline threw her head back, thrusting her covered tits in my face.

I unclasped her bra and threw it behind me before burying my face in her chest, licking and sucking on the soft skin. She lifted her ass up, and I skimmed the pink panties down her thighs and past her ankles, dropping them to the floor. "Are you sure you want this, Maddie?" I asked, hoping she didn't deny me.

My hands gripped her bare ass, and if my dick didn't push into her warm folds soon, I'd fucking die. Madeline consumed every single part of me.

"I do," she whispered, pulling back slightly to peer down at me.

Unspoken words passed between us, something that only she and I were a part of. Broken pieces from the past were mending; hushed truths were coming to light.

"Good," I whispered, grabbing a condom and sliding it on quickly. "Remember this conversation when you go back to pushing me away in the morning. Remember this moment." I began pushing into her tight pussy, my chest constricting. "Right. Here." Cupping the back of her head, I pulled her face to mine and kissed her breathlessly. Our mouths were molded, warm and slow kisses shared between us. Her skin began getting slick to the touch, our bodies moving gracefully at first and then rougher toward the end. For once in my life, I wasn't driven by lust, but instead by something different.

Madeline tore her mouth from mine, throwing her head back as she rocked back and forth. I kissed her neck and her chest, thrusting upward to meet her steady rhythm.

"Eric," she moaned, her pussy climbing with a tightness that told me I'd be doomed for the rest of my life.

"I've got you," I whispered along her skin. "I've got you for as long as you need." I snuck my hand around to where our bodies met and brushed my finger over her clit, breaking her into tiny little pieces all around me.

Her hands gripped my head as she rode out her orgasm, and I gripped her even tighter as I rode mine.

We both crumbled back onto the couch, evening our breathing as I pulled out of her. Madeline never let go of me, her legs wrapped up in mine, and her head buried into the crook of my neck.

My mom texted at some point a little while later, telling me my father had left and I could come home.

But there was no way I was going home.

Not right now.

Staying in this recluse spot with Madeline was the only place I wanted to be.

Even if I knew she'd be pushing me away come morning.

CHAPTER THIRTY-NINE

MADELINE

NOT A SINGLE WORD was shared between Eric and me this morning. Nothing was said except for, last night, at one point when he'd carried me upstairs in the cabin, and laid me on the bed, and asked if I was still having nightmares at night.

I was sleepy, groggily answering him with nothing but the truth. "*I only have nightmares when I'm not with you.*" He pulled me into his body and wrapped my leg around his. His head nodded against mine, brushing along my hair. He kissed my forehead, and then we woke up this morning when his alarm sounded, and we both got dressed with nothing but our breathing shared.

My stomach was in knots the entire drive to our houses. Eric's hand rested on my thigh, and it only made things worse. The sun was beginning to rise when I pulled into the driveway, and I kind of hated that because then he could see me clearly now. He could probably see all the uncertainties going on in my head.

Eric kept a hold of my leg for a minute as we stared at each other. I think he was waiting for me to say something, to break the ice that had thawed the night before only to freeze back up by morning, but I didn't know what to say.

I wanted him. I wanted it all with him. The status. Calling him my boyfriend. Going on dates. Cuddling. Holding hands at school. I wanted the real deal, but how could that even be possible?

Just yesterday, Eric was ready to lay his father flat on his ass for something he did with *my* mother. There were too many questions and uncertainties when it came to us. I was hesitating on letting myself fall too hard for him because of the past.

So, for the entire day at school, I kept my head down. During class, I ignored the prickling along my neck that told me Eric was watching me. During lunch, I stared at my plaid skirt while I picked at my salad in fear that I'd catch his eye and see the disappointment he had there.

I had messed with his heart when we were barely teenagers, and here I was, doing it again—even if for the right reason.

My phone vibrated as I kept my back to my bedroom window, knowing Eric was likely standing there.

Eric- Avoidance. Always a great tactic.

Eric- I have to say, I'm enjoying the view.

My heart raced as I clutched my phone in my hand, unable to type anything back. The only thing I kept repeating in my head were his words from last night: *Remember this feeling when you go back to pushing me away in the morning.*

As if I could forget.

Eric- I'm going to the cabin for a party. It's Piper's birthday.

Something cold washed over me.

Eric- Plus my mom is working, and I need to let off some steam before we talk in the morning about what she and my dad discussed last night.

That was when I decided to text back.

Me- Let me know if you need anything after you two talk. I'm sure everything will be okay.

Eric- Why won't you turn around?

My stomach felt funny, like I was on a rollercoaster I didn't want to be on.

Eric- Is it because you know you'll feel something when you look at me? ... We wouldn't want that, would we? You might beg me to fuck you again.

I sensed some anger in his text, but I wasn't sure. Maybe that was better? Maybe making him mad at me was a good reason for him to stay away.

Eric- You're not fooling anyone, Maddie. Not even yourself. I'll see you tomorrow.

My brow crinkled.

Me- What's tomorrow?

He texted back quickly.

Eric- You said you have nightmares when I'm not sleeping beside you. So, I'll see you tomorrow night. Sorry I can't stay tonight...you could always come to the cabin with me.

I wanted to. I wanted to go with him so badly my eyes began to water. But I shook my head and threw my phone on my bed, hoping he didn't notice how annoyed and frustrated I was.

It wasn't his fault.

It was mine.

He texted one more time before I heard his car start up in the driveway.

Eric- Don't forget to lock your door, Maddie.

Part of me wanted to keep it unlocked in case he decided to come home early. But I knew it was unlikely, so I trudged over to it and locked it before I decided to follow him to the cabin to make a fool out of myself in front of everyone who hated me.

CHAPTER FORTY

ERIC

I'D RATHER BE ANYWHERE ELSE than where I was at the moment. The cabin was swarming with my friends, all intoxicated off cheap beer and even some weed lingering in the air. I was sitting in the same spot that I had fucked Madeline in last night, and the only thing I could do was watch Christian lean back onto the spot beside me, knowing she had lay there and fingered herself less than twenty-four hours ago.

My face felt hot, and the beer coating my tongue did absolutely nothing for me. I wanted to be with Madeline, tucked away somewhere with the lights down low, with her mouth on mine. Or fuck, maybe even cuddling. I didn't care. I just wanted to be with her, and I wanted to make sure she was okay.

"Christian, knock it off," Hayley bemused beside me as Christian nuzzled her neck. Ollie was in the kitchen, cutting the cake—that was, quite possibly, the ugliest cake I'd ever seen—that he'd made Piper, handing out pieces to whomever wanted one—which was really just anyone with the munchies.

"No," Christian murmured.

Resentment started to fill my head. Did he know how lucky he was to be sitting with Hayley, touching her in public? When would Madeline let me do that? *Would* she ever let me do that?

I thought I'd broken her last night. I thought I'd gotten it into her head that I didn't give a fuck what people thought, even more so what my father thought. Yeah, okay, our families were involved in some fucked-up drama that belonged on a soap opera, but it didn't really affect us any longer.

My father fucked up.

So did her mother.

No one had to tell her monster of a father what went on. I knew I wasn't going to tell him. In fact, I hoped I never had to come face to face with him *ever*.

Taking another drink of beer, letting it burn the back of my throat, I glanced at my phone, only to see no missed texts.

I wonder what she's doing.

I scanned the room, ignoring the girls who were batting their eyelashes at me, asking for a quick fuck without actually asking.

Then, it hit me.

My fingers flew over my phone quickly, a smirk dancing on my lips.

Me- How's it going? Mom bring anyone home? Specifically, someone in a red Porsche?

Her mom hadn't been home much since Madeline's father had left, but she hadn't brought anyone home, either.

Madeline texted back quickly.

Madeline- I'm fine. No. She hasn't come home yet.

**Me- Nice. I was just checking in. I gotta go,
though. Missy keeps trying to steal my attention.**

I chuckled, clicking my phone off. I was playing a hand
out of Christian's handbook. The number of times he used
another girl to make Hayley jealous, sometimes even using
Madeline, was almost cruel, but it worked in the end.

"Hey, Hayley?" I nudged her with my elbow. She turned
around from Christian's lap and peered down at me.

"Yeah?"

"On a scale of one to ten, how fucking livid were you
when Christian would dangle other girls in front of your face
to make you jealous? You know, before you two came to your
senses?"

Hayley pouted as she thought back to the past. "A solid
ten. In fact"—she let out a little growl and hit Christian on
the arm—"I think I'm still mad."

He scowled before grinning. "That's not fair. I was just
trying to get you to see that you had the hots for me even
when you said you didn't." His lips curved. "Now look at us."

Hayley rolled her eyes. "Of course I denied having the
hots for you. You told me you hated me." Then, a small smile
appeared on her face as she glanced back at me. "Why are
you asking?"

I leaned back and held my phone, waiting for the text to
come through. "No reason."

Missy caught my eye from across the room, and I gave her
a tip of my chin. She gave me a look, throwing her wavy locks
back. "Me?" she mouthed.

I nodded, pulling open my phone.

Madeline- Missy Rhodes?
Me- Yeah.

"Hey, Eric." Missy's voice was squeaky like a mouse, and I
thought my eardrums had exploded at the sound.

"Hey." I glanced up at her. "Want to do me a favor?"

She bit her lip in an attempt at being sexy. *Sorry, Missy. Been there, done that. Twice.* "Like what?"

"Sit on my lap for a few, snap a pic, post it."

Her dainty shoulders dropped, her crop top hiding the sliver of bare of skin below her belly button. "That's it?"

"Mmhm," I answered, shoving my phone back in my pocket.

"What's in it for me?" she asked, crossing her arms defiantly.

I lazily swung my gaze around the room. "Free beer, good weed, popularity points by sitting on my lap for a few."

"I'm already popular."

My gaze darkened. "For now."

Christian snickered, and Hayley buried her face in her hands. Missy shot them a wary look before changing her attitude. "Okay, sure."

I winked. "Thanks."

Then, she sat on my lap, snapped a picture, posted it, and stood up. "Sure that's all you need?" Hope gleamed in her eyes before I nodded.

"Yep, thanks." I winked again, and her cheeks flushed before she turned around and went back to her friends, looking back at me every few seconds.

"Trying to make Madeline jealous?" Hayley asked, holding back a laugh.

"Something like that." More like making her come to her senses.

Christian's head popped forward. "Are you sure you wanna make her jealous? She seems like the kind to bash your headlights in when angry."

I scoffed. "She wouldn't dare." I sobered up for a moment. "You don't know her like I do."

He shrugged, pulling Hayley back into his neck and kissing her on the side of the head.

And me?

I sat back and waited for the show to begin.

If Madeline felt even a fraction of what I felt for her, she'd be here soon.

CHAPTER FORTY-ONE

MADELINE

MY HAND SHOOK like a leaf as I stared at the photo. I hated social media because I knew how fake it was, but I also knew it was like crack to teenagers—mainly because it used to be crack to me.

As soon as I got Eric's text, my heart dropped to the floor. It bled out all over the place, jealousy oozing from every open vessel.

Then, once I gained my composure again, realizing he was likely trying to get to me, I pulled up Missy's IG account, and that was when my entire body froze.

Eric's head was entirely too close to her stupid, perky boobs. He had a beer in one hand, and the other was wrapped around her waist as she sat on his lap.

Fire coated my skin, and heat stung my scalp. Jumping up from my bed, I began pacing my bedroom floor.

This was better.

He should be with someone else.

Someone who wasn't fucked up like me.

Someone who didn't have a diary-worth of drama at her back door.

Someone who the entire fucking school didn't hate.

Nope.

Didn't care.

I stomped over to my closet, briefly glancing at the glow-in-the-dark stars before pulling down my dusty-pink long-sleeve sweater and tight black mini. I threw on my Doc Martens, lacing them quickly, and slathered on some cherry lip gloss.

I was being driven by mad envy, and despite the rational part of my brain that knew very well if I showed up at the party, ripping Missy off Eric's lap, I'd be labeled as much more than the school leper, I still pushed my car into drive and headed to the cabin.

Eric knew what he was doing.

And I was falling right into his trap.

———

I parked at the very end of the gravel drive below the cabin, off to the side some, in case I needed to make a fast getaway.

My feet stopped for a second. *There will be no fast getaway.* If I was going to do this, I was going to do this right. For months, I'd been cowering. My mouth had stayed shut; my head had stayed down. I'd let everyone walk all over me. I'd let them call me a slut; ignored them when they threw garbage in my locker. My crown was crooked, and I didn't have the energy to straighten it.

Eric was pushing me into a territory that I didn't necessarily want to be in any longer, but I'd learned that, when it came to him, I had no say. I was going to walk into Piper's birthday party with confidence and look him and everyone else right in the eye.

And if Missy was on his lap, I'd tear her off. Not because I wanted to fall into that "mean girl" status again, but because I truly had no self-restraint. *Fucking me the night before and then cozying up with Missy. The audacity.*

The gravel crunched under my boots, my heart flying through my chest. I was nervous, but my need to show everyone that Eric was mine far outweighed the jitters.

I felt a small piece of the old Madeline shift back into place, and I liked it. I liked having a purpose again.

The door swung open, and I pushed my blonde hair behind my shoulder. My lips tasted like cherries as I ran my tongue over them, scanning the cabin as I walked into a full-fledged war.

Jaws dropped.

Eyes widened.

Not a single person spoke. The only voice was Juice Wrld as he rang out through the speakers.

I found Eric instantly, my eyes going right to the place we were in last night, naked and panting like rabid animals.

Of course that was where he chose to sit.

The smirk on his face widened the longer we stared at each other, and it made me hot. I was angry but also a little exhilarated.

I peeled my eyes away when I heard a feminine voice whisper, *"What is she doing here?"*

Missy was the source of the voice. She was halfway across the room, with one of the football player's arms draped over her shoulders.

Eric tricked me. He lured me here.

I sliced my gaze back to his, and he shrugged innocently.

Walking farther into the cabin, I kept my chin straight and my shoulders level. I'd have been lying if I said it wasn't intimidating to be standing in a room full of people I'd once bullied for my own benefit. It made my back sticky and my stomach knotty. But it felt right. Like it was a step in the right direction.

I moved into the kitchen area, with everyone still gazing at me as if I were in the spotlight on a stage all by myself. Someone had cut the music, and if there were a microphone, now would have been the time to tap it a few times before speaking.

Piper and Ollie were standing at the counter, each with a plate of cake in their hands. She was wearing a headband that had a birthday crown on it, looking like her adorable, sweet self. I hated myself for being mean to her.

"I'm sorry to crash your birthday party, Piper." I reached into my Doc Marten and pulled out a gift card that was stuffed between my sock and boot. I slid it over the counter, and it landed right below her levitating plate of cake. She moved the plate out of the way and glanced down. "Happy birthday. I know you like iced coffee, so..."

She looked up at me briefly before looking down again. I heard murmurs around us. "You got me a birthday present?"

I glanced around. I wasn't good at being nice. It made me squirm, but it was the least I could do with crashing a party I wasn't invited to. Piper was nice. If it were anyone else, I might not have cared.

"It's for one hundred dollars..."

I shifted nervously before I crossed my arms and shrugged. *Was that too much?*

She stared at me and then glanced at Hayley across the room who lifted a shoulder with her lips rising. Piper reached her hand down and slid the card toward her and placed it in her back pocket. "Okay...well, thanks."

I gave her a nod and said, "I'll be gone soon. I just need to go smack Eric, and then I'll leave. I'm sorry for crashing your birthday party."

No one laughed except Hayley. Piper smashed her lips closed with a faint chuckle. "Stay as long as you'd like."

"But no one wants her here," someone said from across the room. I didn't even want to know who said it.

Hayley's voice cut through the room. "It's Piper's party and Eric's cabin. If they say she can stay, then she can stay."

I silently thanked Hayley with my eyes, and she barely gave me a swift nod.

Then, I shifted my eyes to Eric, again, who was still doing that annoyingly attractive bad-boy smirk.

I narrowed my eyes, and he hitched an eyebrow as if asking me what I was going to do.

The room began to feel heavy, everyone watching our stare-off. My feet pulled me forward, stepping over a few empty cups, and before I knew it, I was standing right in front of him. Our knees brushed as he sat forward on the couch, peering up at me with his dark eyelashes fanning over his cheeks.

"Interesting place to sit," I said, looking down at him from above.

"Sure is," he answered lazily.

His hand wrapped around the back of my thigh, and a few people gasped. I hated that we were putting on a show for everyone, which was so surreal because, before Christian and I broke up, that was all we ever did. We put on a show for everyone to keep up our statuses.

"You're forcing me into being the person I wanted to bury, Eric."

"What do you mean?" he asked, tilting his head to get a better look at me.

Mostly everyone was staring at us, even Hayley and Christian.

"For a second there, I thought I was going to have to come in here and tear Missy off your lap by her hair." Someone gasped, likely her. "And that's not who I am anymore. I don't want to be that girl who inflicts pain and mortification on others. I don't want to be that version of myself anymore."

I said the last part quieter, because it was embarrassing to admit, especially in front of all these people.

Eric pulled himself to a standing position as he gripped me by the hips. My heart climbed to my throat as I looked up at him. A dense feeling of vulnerability clogged my senses, and I didn't like it. "I think I'd take a combo of the two. I like every version of you." His eyes softened around the edges, and suddenly, I didn't care about anything else, except him.

"Let's go," I whispered, grabbing onto his wrist.

"Where are we going?"

"I don't care. I just want everyone in this room to know you're mine."

He smirked as I glanced back at him. "Challenge accepted." Then, he pulled his wrist back, spun me around, and lifted me up by my butt and wrapped my legs around his waist. I kept the shock hidden from my face, but he grinned at me like he was going to devour me in front of every single person in this room. His head buried into the crook of my neck, my hair eclipsing him from the rest of the room. His breath was warm as it hit my sensitive skin. "Let's go fuck, and let's be as loud as possible. That's a sure way to let everyone know."

My core sparked, and I pushed myself into him. His hands dug even harder into my thighs, right under my butt.

"It's a sure way to be labeled a slut, too." I kept my gaze on his, too swept up in the moment to see the disgust on everyone's faces.

"No one will call you that." He pulled back and stared at me with a dark look in his eye. "Not now."

There was that protective boy I'd grown to crave. Who would have ever thought I would have a guy to protect me like this? So fierce and unyielding.

I licked my lips, the cherry taste coating my tongue. "Then let's go."

His eyes dipped to my mouth before he growled excitedly and carried me upstairs.

CHAPTER FORTY-TWO

ERIC

THE NEXT MORNING, Madeline and I both left the cabin at the same time to get back to our houses. I pulled into my driveway at the exact moment she pulled into hers, and I was out of the driver's seat so fast I was able to pull her door open and help her out of hers. I gripped her body and pulled her over to the side, slamming the door shut. Her back hit the black paint, and her legs widened, letting my thigh sneak in.

"You act like we didn't just have sex a few hours ago —*again*." The apples of her cheeks rose, a cute pink color painting the delicate skin. Her hair was still a mess from last night, her skirt wrinkled from being thrown on the floor.

"I can't help it," I mumbled as I smoothed her hair down. "I told you I have a hard time keeping my hands to myself. Do you know how long I punished myself for even looking in your direction? How long I refused to picture you as I beat off?"

She half-rolled her eyes, grinning. "You had plenty of girls to fuck. Why would you need to masturbate?"

A deep chuckle reverberated out of my chest. "You just have no idea, do you?"

"What?" Her fingers slid into my belt loops.

"It didn't matter how many girls I kissed, touched, or fucked. I was *always* left disappointed in the end."

She rolled her eyes again. "How is that possible?"

I tipped her chin back and brushed my mouth over hers. "Because they weren't you." I sighed. "It's always been you."

Madeline opened her mouth to say something. Her eyes ping-ponged between mine. Something shifted between us. I felt my chest sliding open. But we both snapped our attention away when Madeline's mom pulled into their driveway, parking right behind Madeline's BMW.

We pulled away instantly, the moment between us breaking. Guilt crumbled her features, the dazed and swoony gleam in her eye fading.

"I gotta go talk with my mom...about the other night with my dad." I glanced behind me to my house. "She's waiting to talk to me before she sleeps from her shift last night."

I couldn't bring myself to look at Madeline's mom. I didn't want to. So as soon as Madeline nodded, I turned on my heel and jogged up my porch steps without another glance back.

"Mom," I shouted as I walked through the front door, shoving my keys in my pocket. "I'm home."

"Hey, baby," she answered. "I'm in the kitchen."

The scent of coffee wafted throughout the foyer, dragging me to where she was with two steaming mugs sitting on the counter.

"Thanks." I reached out and grabbed one, wrapping my hand around the ceramic.

My mom was nervous, that much I could tell, and that didn't particularly sit well with me because that meant whatever she was about to say was going to be the wrong fucking thing.

"Did you have fun at the cabin?"

I drank a sip, locking onto her worried eyes. "I did. Surprised Dad hasn't banned me from it yet. He's taken everything else."

She placed her mug down, the clank an unwelcome sound to my ears. "We need to talk about your father."

I strode over to the kitchen table, placing my mug down on top. I was pretty sure I needed something to ground me with the increasing look of apprehension in her eyes. "That's why I'm here at 8 am on a Saturday, Mom." My eyebrow lifted as I leaned back in the chair and crossed my arms over my chest. I could feel the beating of my heart behind my rib cage.

"Your father and I have decided to work on things."

What I imagined in my head was shooting up from the table and freaking the fuck out, stomping back and forth while reminding her that I had to listen to her cry in her bedroom for months and months, and how I watched her work herself to death at the hospital just so she had something to do other than deal with his bullshit.

"I know you're upset," she said, her voice wobbly.

"Damn right, I am." I pierced her with a look. "He hurt you."

Her gaze shifted to her mug. "And he hurt you."

Yeah, he fucking did.

"But you have to understand. I've known your father for many, many years, Eric. We've been through a lot of ups and downs." She sighed, and I couldn't even look at her.

It wasn't my decision to make. I was their son, not their fucking marriage counselor. But the thought of him coming back into our lives like he hadn't done a single thing wrong made my blood run hot. "It's just..." She paused, surely waiting for me to look at her, but I wouldn't.

I stood up quickly, the chair scraping the floor beneath my feet. "You don't need to explain." The breath I inhaled felt like breathing in a million little shards of glass as I reeled in my anger. "I need to know if he's moving back in, because if he is..." I glanced through the kitchen window above our sink, peering at Madeline's house.

"No!" she rushed out. "We're working on things, but that doesn't mean he gets a free pass. He's still going to live in the city, and we will live here—well, I will, because come fall, you're going to college."

"Maybe."

She gave me a look. "What does that mean?"

"Dad said he wouldn't pay for my college if I didn't stop ignoring him."

She shook her head. "That's not true, but I do think you need to talk to him, Eric." My mom tiptoed over to me on her quiet feet and gave me a hug from behind. "He wants to apologize."

He probably only told her that to make her happy, because so far, my father hadn't even recognized that he fucked up. He'd only sent angry, threatening texts since the day my mom threw him out.

When my mom pulled back, I finally turned and looked at her. I was antsy on the inside, annoyed and frustrated, but I didn't show her that. "As long as you're happy, I'm good, Mom." I began pulling away and started down the hall. "But just because you forgive him, doesn't mean I do."

Because how can you forgive someone who doesn't even have the decency to admit they're wrong?

CHAPTER FORTY-THREE

MADELINE

Eric- No Netflix and chill tonight with my mom. She got called into work.

My heart jumped. *Finally.* I'd been waiting for Eric to text me since he bolted to his house this morning when my mom pulled up from "a night with a friend". Which really meant she'd stayed at some man's house instead of bringing him home.

I couldn't really be mad about that, because at least she wasn't bringing them near me anymore, but at the same time, I wanted to shake her and ask why we hadn't just *left*. But every time I'd bring up my father or ask about him in any way whatsoever, she'd leave the room while mumbling about not wanting to talk about it.

She didn't even ask about Eric and me this morning. She brushed right past it, as if she hadn't slept with his father.

Pushing the thought of my mom away, I texted Eric back.

Me: So does this mean we can't Netflix and chill, or...?

Eric: I'm already walking over. Unlock your bedroom door.

I instantly got giddy. Last night was a crazy whirlwind between us. From me walking into the cabin, reinstating myself with everyone, claiming Eric without caring who saw. After the high wore off this morning, I panicked a little. I wasn't sure how school would look on Monday, but what was done was done.

I was in this. Selfish or not.

After unlocking my bedroom door, I ran over to my window and peered down at Eric walking through the dewy grass. He was wearing dark-gray joggers, his Nikes, and a dark hoodie with the hood pulled up. He didn't glance at my window, but before long, I heard him climbing the steps.

My door swung open, and happiness started to make my skin tickle, but then he made eye contact with me, and my happiness faded.

"What's wrong?" I slowly crept toward him as he glanced to the floor. He sighed loudly, his fists clenched by his sides. "Is it about your dad? What did your mom say this morning?"

I wanted to text him and ask how things went, but I didn't want to seem clingy. I'd never been a *real* girlfriend before, which sounded so pathetic, but Christian and I were never like that. We never pried into each other's lives— precisely why we stayed in our fake, apathetic relationship for so long.

Eric's jawline was sharp as he looked past me, his temples rocking back and forth, his high cheekbones as sturdy as stone. "Eric?" I asked again, gripping onto his flexing fists.

"She's taking him back."

No way.

"Even after..." I stopped myself from bringing up the one act that tore us apart.

He slanted his head, looking to the ceiling as if the

thought was inconceivable. "Yes," he bit out. "Even after fucking your mom—and whoever else he fucked."

I flinched, that annoying bout of guilt hitting me.

A loud growl escaped him as he tore his fists from my hands. He brought one hand to the bridge of his nose as his eyes closed. "I'm sorry."

"You have no reason to be sorry," I whispered, grabbing his hand again and pulling it away from his face.

His eyes opened. "I didn't mean to get angry. Your father is so much worse than mine. I'm just..." His head shook back and forth, and I pushed his hood back. The dark strands of his hair were damp from a shower, and the smell of his shampoo filled my bedroom.

"Hey, it's okay." I shushed him, pulling him into me. Eric's arms wrapped around my body, and his head came and rested on mine. He nodded a few times before pulling back and taking my lips in his.

It was always an instant attraction between us. The second our lips touched, the lights glowed, the floor swayed beneath our feet, my back arched to press against his hard chest. Eric gripped me tighter, spinning me around and shoving me down onto my bed. He was on top of me, pulling my shirt up and my pants down with a look of pure, wild desire in his eye. There was a gleam there and I took complete hold of it.

Except...

"Eric." His mouth hovered over the hem of my pants as he peered up at me from below. "I..." I looked away, unable to watch his reaction. "I, um...it's just..."

"What's wrong, Maddie? Am I going too fast? I thought after last night..." He immediately pulled up, and I clenched my legs around him.

"That's not it." *That was really not it.*

I pushed the words out before I could stop the vulnerability. "I just wanted to warn you that I haven't done anything... in my bed...ever. Except when..." *Why was this so hard to get out?* My stomach grew queasy.

"Except when you were taken advantage of?"

This took vulnerability to an entirely new level. I wanted to be back at that party last night as I wore my confidence like a steel mask.

Eric tried getting out of my thigh grasp, his hand gently touching my knee. "Let's stop for the night."

"No!" I urged. "I just wanted to warn you, in case I freaked out."

He gave me a stern look, searching my entire face. "Are you sure?" I nodded quickly, spreading my legs. His hand caressed my thigh slowly, getting higher and higher to the spot I wanted him to find. "How can we make this work for you, then? Tell me what you need, baby."

I decided that I loved when he called me that. It did something wicked to me, like a button he could push that immediately made me wet.

"Why don't you let me be in charge?" I asked, reaching my hand down between us to touch his hardness. I skimmed my hand over it, feeling him jump behind my touch.

Eric's eyes immediately turned dark, his plump lips spreading. "Let you be in charge?" He smiled slyly. "If that's what you need..."

I think it's what we both need.

"It is," I replied, sitting up and sliding out from his grasp. Eric pulled his hoodie from his back and dropped it to the ground, lying on the bed, displaying his steely abs.

I straddled him, rubbing my sex over his hard length before taking my fingers and tracing each, perfect abdominal muscle with a light touch. My lips grazed his ear as I lifted up a little, teasing him with small nips at his skin before slinking down to my favorite spot.

His hips flexed as my fingers dove into his pants, pulling down his joggers and boxers in one swift movement. He sprang free with a hiss as I blew a quick breath over his length.

"Fuck, Madeline," he hissed. Watching Eric wither underneath me from need was the biggest turn-on of all. He was so hot with his eyes clenched and splotchy cheeks. His jaw was clenched, his abs tight. "I've dreamed of this," he forced out as I ran my tongue over him.

"Of what?" I asked, gripping him hard with my hand.

His eyes flew open with his answer. "Of fucking that pretty little mouth of yours."

Desire pushed me over the edge, and I took him in and sucked long and hard. His gasps were ragged as his hips thrusted to meet me halfway. I usually started off slow, but something about the way his words hit me had me moving my head as fast as I could. I wanted him to feel the pull. I wanted to be the one to make Eric come so fast and hard that he'd never ever be able to forget it.

"Madeline, *fuck*. Slow down before I come."

"Nuhuh," I mumbled, sucking and pulling. I felt him get wider and harder, as if that were even possible. Eric's hand went to the back of my head, pushing down once before pulling me back and flipping me over onto my back.

"Let me fuck you," he panted, pulling my pants down my legs. "*Please*."

I could never say no to him. It didn't matter that, on this very bed, I had been taken advantage of. It didn't matter that I was broken beyond belief one night in the dark underneath these covers, because Eric was taking that awful memory and destroying it little by little. He made me feel strong again. He made me feel whole. With each kiss on my lips, I felt my ashes coming back to life. That broken, vulnerable girl was being reborn.

I nodded as Eric waited for my answer, and when he got it, he thrusted into me fast and hard. I was wet and ready, already moving my hips to find that sweet spot that made me forget everything in the world except him.

Eric's tongue thrusted into my mouth, and we kissed roughly. Lips were being pulled; teeth were clanking.

"That's it, baby." His hand found its way underneath my bra, and he squeezed. "Find that spot you like. Let me take care of you."

He was everywhere. He clouded every single one of my senses. His lips and hands touched every part of my body.

"God, Eric," I moaned, feeling myself tip over the edge. "I think I might love you." Then I exploded. My toes curled, and I was done for. Bliss took over, and my body shook as he pounded into me one more time.

"Good," he said in between kisses. "Because I think I love you too. And I don't give a fuck what anyone has to say about it."

Neither do I.

CHAPTER FORTY-FOUR

ERIC

"HEY, PRETTY." I smirked, slinking up beside Madeline as she dug inside her locker. I scanned my gaze down the back-side of her as I rested my shoulder along the metal lockers. Her sun-colored hair tumbled down her back in voluminous waves. Her plaid skirt all but begged me to lift it up so I could see what color panties she was wearing.

"Eyes up here, Eric," she chided as she slammed her locker shut. "I thought you said you weren't gonna lay it on heavy today."

I laughed under my breath. "No. You asked me to take things slow at school today. I never agreed to that." I glanced around the hall. Nearly everyone was gaping except my tight group of friends. "Why would I? I want everyone to know you're mine."

Madeline rolled her eyes. "No one wants me, Eric. Remember? I'm the school loser. There's no need to show your possession." She glanced away and bit her lip.

My thumb pulled it from her teeth, and a little popping sound filled our close quarters. "But you like that, don't you?"

Her blue eyes widened. "What? No."

"Oh, really? I recall you walking into the cabin two days ago, reclaiming yourself, wanting to tell everyone that I was *yours*."

She sighed as she began to walk to her next class, trying her hardest not to look anyone in the eye. "That's because everyone wants you. No one wants me."

I snorted as I grabbed her hand and intertwined our fingers together. "School loser or not, guys still look at you."

"No, they don't."

We stopped walking, and I jerked her back a little. She tipped her head, giving me a look. "Do you recall me choking Taylor a few weeks back?" She nodded, glancing past my shoulder. I hated to see her cower. My girl was strong. She needed to show it. "That's because he made a comment about you sucking his cock. A few other guys, too." I pulled her in close, her breath hitching. "Don't go back to that scared girl, Maddie. You can be both strong and nice. Selfless and confident. Who cares what they think? If I want to kiss you, I'm going to kiss you."

She was breathing a little heavier, glancing down at my mouth as I said the word kiss. "And you're sitting with me at lunch. I won't take no for an answer. We can't only be *us* hidden away in your bedroom. I love you too much to hide you."

She blushed, looking away. "You don't love me."

"Always have. Always will." The bell rung above our heads, and I gave her a quick kiss on the lips before backing away and smacking her on the butt. "Now get to class. I'll see you in the cafeteria."

Her face flamed, and it was surreal to see her get flustered like that. She had a damn good poker face at school; not many people could break it.

When I turned around to follow Christian and Ollie, they both shook their heads. Ollie was holding back a grin as he adjusted his tie, and Christian was stone-faced, as always, while holding Hayley's hand.

"You ever gonna give us the details on her? Tell us what you were so bent on hiding the other night? Explain why she's always been a bi—" Hayley tugged on Christian before he could finish his sentence, and it was a good thing, because I was about to put him through a locker.

I cracked my neck instead. "Didn't realize you cared so much."

Christian stared at me. And I stared right back. He dropped his head and shook it.

"He cares about you," Hayley answered for him. "We all do." She smiled and patted my chest as we walked into class. "I'm just happy to see you happy."

I winked at her before going and sitting at my desk, only to count the hours until lunch.

———

It only took ten seconds of being in the cafeteria before I noticed just about every single student at English Prep giving me the side-eye, trying to figure out what my game was. Missy was brave enough to ask as I stood in the lunch line, scanning the room for Madeline so I could make sure she actually sat at my table.

"I thought you hated Madeline like the rest of us." She placed a hand on her hip in typical mean-girl fashion. *Why did I fuck her again?*

"Things change, Missy," I forced out, moving past her to

grab a soda. "Much like your ever-changing hair color. What even is your natural color?"

"You should know. You've been downstairs a time or two." She winked as her friends giggled behind her.

I arched an eyebrow, ready to retaliate. "Hmm," I thought out loud, appearing bored. "It's a shame I can't remember much from when I fucked you. I guess you're not all that memorable. Same ol, same ol. Just another boring lay."

She gasped, her cheeks turning red as she glanced around the moving line. "Oh, whatever. That's not true. If it was, why did you come back for seconds?"

I simply stated the truth. "Because you were easy, that's why."

Ollie's loud laugh came from behind me, but I brushed it off.

Missy's face blanched as she tried to come up with something good to say, but she couldn't, because she *was* easy, and she knew it. "Look," I started, grabbing a slice of pizza and placing it on my tray. "I don't mean to be a dick. I don't enjoy putting girls down. But"—I gave her a look that had her wavering—"keep Madeline's name out of your mouth and we'll be good, all right?"

Her eyebrows shot up. "Wow."

"What?"

"I never thought I'd see the day where you stuck up for her. Makes me wonder what changed."

She did. That's what.

Missy must have been finished with the conversation, because she flipped her hair behind her shoulder and began chatting with her friends.

"Makes me wonder, too," Ollie said from behind my shoulder. When I turned around, he was avoiding eye contact with me. He even began whistling, as if he wasn't the one who had said it.

I wasn't sure if I'd ever be able to tell my friends the truth. It was Madeline's business. The abuse, the sexual assault. Those were two very personal subjects, and Madeline didn't trust people easily.

"You're just going to have to trust me, Ol. I would tell you if I could."

Ollie ran a hand through his blonde hair before nodding. "I got you. Just know we're here for you, Madeline or not. I've already talked to Christian. He's gonna lay off."

I tipped my chin and threw up a fist. He pounded it, and we gathered the rest of our lunches. Once I got back to our table, Piper and Hayley were already chowing down and talking adamantly in between bites about something that I didn't care about. Christian was talking to Kyle, and Ollie was already halfway done with his food even though we had grabbed our lunches at the same time.

I stayed standing until I caught a swirl of blonde hair in the lunch line. Madeline was holding a cup in her hand, teetering back and forth on her feet, trying to decide what she wanted to drink. She was so fucking hot in her schoolgirl uniform. I understood why she thought no one wanted her anymore, because she was publicly shut down and her friends had turned their backs on her, but she was truly dense if she thought the guys in this school didn't long to be in between her legs.

I chuckled under my breath as I took a step backwards away from the table, ready to remind her that she wasn't getting out of sitting with me. But as soon as I went to step away, I heard the crash of something up ahead. The lunchroom quieted for a moment, or maybe it was just in my head, because the look of panic on Madeline's face tore through me like a fucking jackhammer. Her drink was splayed on the floor around her feet, her blue eyes big and round.

"Is she paralyzed?" Piper asked honestly. "What's wrong with her? Did someone knock her drink out of her hand?"

"Eric." Hayley's voice was a warning of sorts, but I continued to stare at Madeline and her mannerisms. *What was going on?* "Do you recognize that man?"

My eyes scanned past Madeline, and I locked onto an older man standing beside Headmaster Walton near the two cafeteria oak doors. He was tall and clearly very wealthy by the look of his suit. His dark hair didn't move an inch, likely full of expensive gel, as he nodded to something the headmaster had said. The man had no interest is whatever the conversation was about because his lip curved upward as he stared back at Madeline. He winked, and my vision blurred.

I glanced back at Madeline who was slowly stepping backwards, away from her spilled drink. Her naturally pink cheeks lacked color, matching the whiteness of her school blouse.

Who the fuck was—

My head tilted in a predatory way as I sliced my attention back to the man. Headmaster Walton was urging him to take a look at something across the room, nodding and slowly striding to whatever it was.

"Ollie," I barked, not letting my gaze waver from the man. "Go look out the window. Tell me if you see a cherry-red Porsche parked up front." *It fucking couldn't be.*

Ollie must have recognized the vileness in my voice because he was up and out of his seat before the words even piled out of my mouth. "On it," he shouted back.

The longer I stared at the man, the more my heart pounded. My skin itched as blood came rushing to the surface. I wanted so badly to look at Madeline, but I was too afraid to take my eyes off of the man, too afraid he'd slip from my grasp before I could get to him.

"Yeah." Ollie came rushing back. "There's a red Porsche. What's going on?"

The cafeteria doors opened and closed, and I saw the tail end of Madeline's hair as she bolted. I snarled as I watched the man stare after her while still pretending to listen to Headmaster Walton.

"Hayley and Piper, go check on Madeline. I know you don't like her"—I gave them both a brief pleading glance—"but it's important."

They both got up right away.

"Eric," Christian warned, coming into my vision. "Whatever you're about to do, stop. I see that look. I know that feeling. Reel it back. I cannot get you out of whatever you're about to do. Headmaster Walton is right over there."

I pushed past him and set my eye on the target.

"Eric." Christian's hand clamped on my arm, and I tore it away, ready to deck him.

"If someone raped Hayley, what would you do?" My question came out full throttle. It was like I'd metaphorically smashed a blunt object on his head.

"I'd kill him."

I was only a couple of yards away from the duo of men when I turned and looked at Ollie and Christian. "Stop me before I do. I don't want to go to prison."

Both of their jaws went slack.

Ollie shook his head. "Dude. Are you sure he...?"

"Yes," I snapped. "You both wanted to know what I was hiding. Here's your fucking answer." *Part of it.*

Rage was beginning to blind me as I tapped the man on the shoulder. He and the headmaster both turned around, their eyebrows furrowed.

"Eric..." Headmaster Walton looked behind my shoulder to address Ollie and Christian. "Boys. What is it?"

"Sir," I calmly started, ignoring the headmaster. "Do you drive a red Porsche?"

He was confused at first. "I do, why?"

"Then," I laughed menacingly. "You know who Madeline is, correct? The blonde you just winked at?"

The man's chin jutted forward, his eyes giving me a warning that I snatched and threw behind my shoulder.

"I'll take that as a yes."

I wound my arm back and pounded him in the face so hard my hand went numb.

That rage that was beginning to blind me before? Well, it completely took over, and everything went dark.

CHAPTER FORTY-FIVE

MADELINE

THIS IS KARMA. I should have known that karma wasn't finished with me. She was a sneaky bitch, and the very second I had let my guard down, she came back around like a black cat in an abandoned alleyway.

Why was he here?

Sweat trickled down past my forehead, leaving a streak of wetness all the way to my chin.

Did he come here on purpose?

My body trembled in the empty stall, my hands resting on the navy tiled wall above the toilet.

Was it a coincidence?

I couldn't breathe. Oxygen was nonexistent. Images and ugly feelings of fear and guilt and weakness were coming down on me hard, and there was no way to protect myself.

None at all.

My eyes watered as I bent over the toilet and threw up. I coughed and sputtered, clawing at my lungs to let air in.

What if he was still out there?

I shook my head. He couldn't get to me. This wasn't my dark bedroom in the middle of the night. There were lights and a wide-open room with lots of eyes.

Suddenly, the stall began to feel very claustrophobic. My hand messed with the lock a few times before it finally swung open, and I fell to my knees on the hard tile, trying to get away from the small space.

"Madeline!"

"Oh my God. Are you okay?"

I flew to my butt, my palms landing on the floor behind me. My body shook again, trembling in a way that I couldn't seem to get a handle on.

Oh my God. Why can't I stop shaking?

Piper's face was a mix between worry and pity as she glanced at Hayley. "She's as white as a ghost."

"Get a wet paper towel." Hayley bent down and grabbed my chin gently. "Hey, take a breath, Madeline. It's okay."

I shook my head. *I can't breathe.*

Bile coated my tongue, and my hands went around my throat as I rubbed up and down. I gasped as more tears clouded my vision.

"Look at me." I locked onto Hayley's face as something cold hit my forehead. Piper shushed me, and I realized right then how lucky they were to have each other. To have a best friend. "Tell me what you see, Madeline. What do you see?"

You...being too nice to me.

"Nice," I choked out.

Her brow furrowed as she brushed her dark hair away. "What do you feel? Touch something. Bring yourself back down to the ground."

I shot my hand up and touched the coldness on my forehead. It was the wet paper towel from Piper. It was comforting. "Cold. Wet."

"Good," Hayley encouraged. "That's good. What do you smell?"

"Puke."

Hayley smiled behind a laugh as Piper went behind her and flushed the toilet.

"There you go," she said, putting her hands on mine. "Just take deep breaths."

I nodded, feeling comforted that my chest was rising and falling again. Breathing was getting easier. My state of panic was lessening.

"You're good at that," Piper whispered, coming behind Hayley.

"Christian and Ollie helped me through a panic attack once. I remembered what they did."

All three of us stayed huddled for a few minutes, breathing together like we were taking a meditation class. Deep breaths in, deep breaths out.

I couldn't even wrap my head around the situation I was in. Hayley and Piper were in the bathroom with me, helping me, being nice to me, and I didn't even have the energy to care that they were seeing me like this.

In fact, I almost wanted to cling onto them.

Wait.

"Where's Eric?" I asked, getting to my feet with the help of Piper.

Hayley paused. Her lips rubbed together as she looked to Piper for help.

There was a zip of panic that tore down my spine. *Wait*.

"He sent us in here to help you."

"What do you mean?"

Piper leaned back onto the sink, crossing her arms over her navy blazer. I couldn't bring myself to look at my reflection in the mirror behind her. "Well…" She looked uncomfortable. "He saw you kind of...freak out. The entire cafeteria did, actually."

Oh, no. No. No. No.

"Tell me he didn't..." My hand flung to my mouth as I tried to calm my breathing.

Hayley's phone pinged, and she pulled it out of the pocket on her blazer. Piper and I both ran behind her shoulder to read the text. She didn't even bother hiding it.

Christian: Eric's in deep shit. Pretty sure the guy is gonna press charges. Eric fucked him up. Is Madeline okay? Eric won't settle the fuck down until I answer him, and Headmaster Walton is likely to die of a heart attack if he doesn't.

"Oh my God." I covered my face with the palms of my hands. "This is bad. This is really bad."

"Madeline." Hayley pulled my hands down. "What happened?"

I stared into her emerald eyes. "This is bad, Hayley. This is so bad. What am I going to do?" I shut my eyes, wanting to disappear. "This is exactly why I told him to stay away from me! What if the headmaster tells my dad?!"

"Who was that guy?" Hayley asked again. "What did he do to you?"

I snapped my attention to hers. "He fucking raped me, okay? He raped me."

Her shoulders dropped, but she kept her hands wrapped around my wrists. Piper gasped.

"I know what you're thinking." My voice shook as I tried to keep myself steady. "I deserved it...after I made up that rumor."

Silent tears rolled down my cheeks and fell onto our joined hands.

"It's karma," I said. "I know."

Hayley and Piper didn't say anything, and it made me feel

even worse. I didn't necessarily want them to say I was wrong; I actually think I would have felt better if they said I was right. But their silence ate away at me.

The bell rang out above our heads, but none of us moved.

Hayley finally dropped my hands, and I kept my gaze on our joined shoes.

"What do I do?" I asked the question to no one in particular. Was I supposed to go to the office? Should I make sure Eric was okay? *That stupid fucking protective boy!* Look at what I got him into.

All three of our heads swayed to the intercom speaker just above the bathroom door when it echoed, "Madeline Haynes to Headmaster Walton's office."

Oh, shit.

Hayley placed her hands on my shoulders. Her gaze was steely and determined. "Keep your chin up. Don't you dare show that piece of shit that he made you weak. That's not you, Madeline."

Piper shot me a reassuring nod, and she came over to run her fingers down my hair, smoothing out the wild mess that I was sure it was.

I nodded once Hayley's hands dropped. A shaky breath left my chest, and I turned around.

"Madeline," Hayley said as I stood with my hand on the door. I glanced over my shoulder, and she and Piper were staring at me. "No one deserves that. We're here for you, okay?" Piper nodded, and I hoped they could tell how much their words meant to me before I turned around and trudged up to the office.

Here we fucking go.

CHAPTER FORTY-SIX

ERIC

"HAYLEY SAID SHE'S OKAY, so calm the fuck down so I can talk Headmaster Walton down a few notches." Christian's voice was a low rumble, only loud enough for me and Ollie to hear.

"It's not fucking Headmaster Walton you need to calm down. It's that fucker who's *hopefully* bleeding out in his office right now."

His blood was still on my knuckles, dried now, but it was still there. I smeared it on my shirt again, trying to wipe the evidence off, which was no use because everyone in the lunchroom saw the fight. My eye was swelling shut, but I didn't care. He was worse off than me.

Was he bigger than me?

Not by much, but he was.

Was he stronger?

Maybe.

But when someone you love was threatened, you gained undeniable strength.

"Eric." I swung my gaze forward when my father's voice boomed through the small office. Mrs. Boyd, the receptionist, paged Headmaster Walton the second she saw my father walk in.

"What the fuck are you doing here?" I asked, standing up.

His eyes immediately went to my eye, and he clenched his jaw tight, putting his hands in his pockets. "They couldn't get a hold of your mother, so they called me. What the hell happened?" He was angry, but I was angrier. "Is this about me? Are you fighting now to get my attention?"

I scoffed, slamming myself back in the seat. "Yeah, Dad. That's exactly why I beat a grown man's face in. Because I wanted my daddy to come save me." *Fucking idiot.*

"A grown man? What?" The muscles holding his tight expression fell. "For fuck's sake. Did you beat a teacher up?"

Ollie laughed under his breath.

Mrs. Boyd spoke up from her desk. "He assaulted one of our board members."

My father's face blanched. "Are you—" Just then, the door swung open, and Madeline's mom walked in.

Just fucking perfect. My father took a step back. "What are you doing here?"

Madeline's mom took in the scene quickly, noting my swollen face and bloody shirt. Her eyes ran over my father, searching his face with a frantic look, and then down to his knuckles.

"Who?" she asked me, ignoring my dad.

In a stone-cold manner, I answered her vague question. "He drives a red Porsche. Didn't quite catch his name. You should know that he was one of your boyfriends, though."

The headmaster must have given her a run-down, because she knew what I was referring to when she asked the question.

"What is going on?" my father demanded, standing up

even taller, looking from me to Madeline's mom. Before anyone could answer him, the door to Headmaster Walton's office opened, and he stood there, cherry-faced, glaring at me. "Your son assaulted one of the board members, that's what's going on."

I stood up quickly, angry all over again. "Did you catch the reason?" I shouted. "Did you ask him *why* I attacked him?"

Madeline's mom's dainty voice squeaked from beside me. "Where is my daughter?"

"I'd like to know the same," I said as I crossed my arms over my chest before sending Headmaster Walton a glare. "Where is the actual *victim* in this situation? Has anyone even fucking checked on her?"

"Victim?" my father asked.

This time, I turned to my dad and answered, "Yeah, Dad. That board member in there? The one threatening charges? He raped Madeline. So I retaliated."

He held my stare, and I expected him to glower at me or look disappointed, but instead, his shoulders dropped slightly. There was a dip in his cool expression for a single, fleeting second before he turned and looked back at Headmaster Walton.

"I suggest you find my daughter." Madeline's mom was on the smaller side, a Tinker Bell look-alike except with longer hair, but even I could feel her anger from across the room.

We all turned when the office door opened again, and in walked Madeline.

It felt like I'd been shot in the chest. Her mascara was skewed, no sign of life in her eyes at all.

Her mom choked on a cry as she wrapped her arms around her slender torso. "I'm so sorry. I'm so sorry." She kept repeating herself, over and over again, getting more and more worked up, and everyone in the room was uncomfortable.

Headmaster Walton cleared his throat, but Madeline's mom didn't even acknowledge it. She pulled back, holding onto Madeline's tear-streaked face.

Look at me, babe. I needed Madeline to look at me.

Her mom's voice shook. "You do not have to go into that office, Madeline. We can leave right now."

Headmaster Walton cleared his throat again, this time louder. My father stood in front of Madeline and her mom, almost blocking them from him. I wasn't sure if he was protecting them from him or the other way around.

I switched my gaze back to Madeline, but she still wouldn't look at me. *Why won't you look at me?*

"Is he pressing charges?" Madeline directed her question to Headmaster Walton, brushing her mother away.

Headmaster Walton nodded. "That's what he's stating, yes."

"Madeline," I warned.

She ignored me. "Tell him I won't go to the police if he drops the charges."

"You have no proof." The man came out from behind Headmaster Walton's half-opened door like a scheming snake, and I snarled.

"Don't fucking talk to her. Don't even fucking look at her." My voice shook the room. My father stood in front of me as Christian grabbed onto my forearm. He was standing now, along with Ollie.

Madeline took a step toward the man, everyone watching her command the room with bated breath. "How do you know?" she asked. I could hear the fear in her voice, but I could hear the strength too. "Do you really want to take a gamble on whether I have proof or not? How do you know I didn't go to the hospital after you left?"

The fucker was still sporting a busted nose and lip. Blood was dried on his crisp white dress shirt, just like mine. *I should have broken his fucking arms.* He scowled, knowing that the entire room would know what a piece of shit he was if he took her bait. But did he have a choice? Would he take a gamble on her threat?

"Drop the charges," she urged. "Or I swear to God I will go down to the police station right now and tell them all about you sneaking into my room, whispering in my ear that I wanted you even when I said no. And how you put your hand over my mouth and pulled my pants down, all while my mother was asleep in the next *fucking* room."

My father's shoulders tensed, and his fists clenched. "I'd take her offer, and if I were you, I'd leave this room immediately."

Headmaster Walton shifted his attention from Madeline to the board member, waiting. Everyone was waiting.

The man finally grunted, walking back into Headmaster Walton's office for a moment before coming back out with his jacket clenched in his busted knuckles. Madeline shifted on her feet as she made way for him to walk through. Her head turned to the side with disgust, or fear, maybe both, as he breezed by. She grabbed onto her mom's wrist, pulling her back, as she was about to follow him out with her quaking anger.

"Don't, Mom," she whispered. "Let's just go home. Please."

Her mom's eyes watered as she took in Madeline's request. Her lips trembled, and a brief gasp of air left her as she tried to gather herself. Then she nodded once, and as soon as we heard squealing tires sound out, they both turned to leave.

"Madeline." I rushed forward, but she pulled her mom even faster, trying to get away from me. "Madeline, look at me."

Her head barely turned, and we caught eyes. *Fear.* She was

battling something behind those blue eyes; I could see it plain as day. *What are you afraid of, baby?*

"Don't you dare," I whispered. Don't you fucking dare shut me out. Not now.

She licked her trembling bottom lip, shifting her gaze to everyone else in the room. Her light locks swayed in front of her face when she continued to turn, walking through the office door with her mom without a single word to anyone.

"Give her some space, Eric." My father came into view as I stood, staring at the spot she was just in like a lost puppy. *What was she still afraid of?* Was she afraid he'd come back? Was she afraid he'd somehow sneak back into her room?

I said nothing as Headmaster Walton called my father and me into his office to discuss what needed to be done about my impulsive act of violence, even given the circumstances. Mrs. Boyd gave me an ice pack for my eye and a wet rag for the blood all over my knuckles. My mom eventually showed up, and it was an entire family ordeal. I stayed silent the entire time, too stuck in my head.

The final bell rung for the day and my mom, dad, and I were all headed out of the office before it hit me.

Wait.

I ran back into Headmaster Walton's office with my mom yelling after me.

"Eric?" he asked, dropping his hand from his face. "What is it?"

"Did you call her dad?" Something I hadn't felt since I was five gripped me by the throat.

"Madeline's?"

I nodded, the fear only getting worse.

"Yes, I called him before I managed to get a hold of her mother. He said he was on his way, but he must have met them at home. Why?"

Madeline.

That was why she was afraid.

Fuck. What did I do?

I bolted out of the office doors, pulling my keys out of my pants as I bypassed both of my parents.

"Eric! Where are you going?"

I pushed past my peers leaving to go home for the day, some even falling to the ground in my dust. My father echoed in the background as he chased after me.

What the fuck did I do?

My hand shook as I shoved my key into the ignition and tore out of the parking lot, beeping at anyone in my way. Ollie and Christian were pushing people back, holding traffic for me to get through. They had no fucking idea what was going on, but they had my back regardless.

All I knew was that I had to get to Madeline's house before her father got home.

CHAPTER FORTY-SEVEN

MADELINE

MY MOM DROVE us both home; my car was still parked at school. The entire drive to our house, she cried. Her shoulders shook as quiet tears fell. I didn't know what to say. I didn't think she did either.

Right when we pulled into the drive, she shut her car off and wiped her eyes gingerly. Her hand wandered over to mine, and she squeezed it a few times, and we sat in silence for a very, very long time. Eventually, we both got out and began walking up the steps.

"I'm okay, Mom. It's not a big deal," I finally said, needing to say something so the echoing hurt didn't blind me. "And it can stay between us."

"It's not okay. And you father will find out, Madeline."

"No." I shook my head agitatedly, crossing my arms over my blazer. "Who's going to tell him? Surely not you or me." I gave her a pointed look. "If he finds out, knowing that it was one of your..." The words died on my tongue.

Squealing tires flew down the road, and my mom and I

both stood paralyzed. I wished it was Eric running after me, or maybe even just a random car who swerved to miss a squirrel in the road. But somehow, we both knew who it was.

"Go to your room and don't come out."

My stomach dropped. "How does he already know?" My father's Jaguar came into sight as it flew into the driveway. "Madeline." My mom grabbed my arms and shoved me inside the house. "Go. Lock your door."

Her blue eyes, the same vivid color as mine, struck me. "I have given you no reason to trust me. But I need you to trust me now. Go. Don't come out until I tell you to. No matter what."

The fear and submission my mother always wore on her face like a fine layer of makeup was no longer visible to me. They had somehow morphed into something I didn't recognize.

She took a deep breath as my father's door slammed. "*Go.*"

Her tone vibrated the fear in my chest, and I quickly made a run for it, skipping steps in three to rush into my bedroom. I slammed the door, fiddled with the lock until it was secure, and sunk down onto the plush carpet, hugging my knees to my chest.

My phone dinged a few times, and when I pulled it out, hoping it was Eric—even though I had left without saying a single word to him—I felt sick.

Unknown: Did that guy really rape u?

Unknown: Hi. It's Hayley, are you okay? I just wanted to check on you.

Unknown: Wow. Heard you got raped. That explains why you stopped putting out.

Cara: Hey. I know we don't talk anymore, but I'm sorry about what happened. If the rumors are true, I mean. Sure looked like it when Eric flipped out.

I ignored every message and clutched the phone to my chest as I heard the front door slam.

Maybe I should call 911?

He hadn't even hit her yet, but I knew he would. He always did.

Their voices climbed up the stairs, and I wanted to cover my ears.

"Do you know how embarrassing it is to get a call from the head-master, saying my daughter had been raped by a man who was fucking my wife? Is that even true?"

"That's all you care about? You should be concerned about our daughter! Who cares how embarrassing that is! Your daughter was sexually violated."

Something slammed; a shriek from my mom was next. My heart started to skip beats; my head started to pound from rising stress.

"You should have been the one to get raped. You always were trash! A dirty fucking slut. I can't even stand to look at you. Where is she? I want to know every last detail, and I want you to sit there and listen, too. Maybe then you'll feel so bad for bringing a man like that into this house that you'll kill yourself. Madeline is better off without you."

I slapped my hand over my mouth to keep myself from screaming.

"Well, I let you in here, and you're just as bad! Hitting me when you feel like it, fucking me like I was made for your own personal pleasure and nothing else. You're no more a man than he is."

"Are you fucking sticking up for the man who raped your daughter?"

No, Dad. She's trying to get you to see that you're fucked up, too.

There was another loud bang, and I jumped to my feet.

"Do you like that? Huh?" There it was. That psycho-like tone in his voice that had my hair standing up straight. I threw my

blazer off my shoulders and glanced at my window. Half of me wanted Eric to come to my rescue again, but the other half wanted him nowhere near my father.

"Do you enjoy getting raped? Maybe I'll just fuck you right now so you know how it feels!" My father's laugh made me sick. *"Oh, wait. I forgot. You're such a slut you'll probably enjoy it anyway."*

My mother cried out, and something broke. A plate? A picture frame?

I walked closer to my door, something pulling me forward. I was so fucking sick of being afraid. I was so sick of hearing this over and over again. There were big gaps in time where my father would disappear before he came back again, but when he showed up, it was like no time had passed at all.

A shuffling of feet and rushed footsteps sounded from below. I opened my door just a crack, and instead of my father's voice, it was my mom's.

"Leave."

"Are you fucking nuts? You won't fucking shoot me. You'll have nothing if you kill me. You'll go to prison. Madeline will be on her own. Put the gun down."

My eyes grew wide.

I rushed through the hall and leaned over the banister, peering down at my mother who was holding a black pistol in her shaky hands. Her shirt was ripped by the collar, and her hair looked as if it had been pulled. Her jeans were undone at the top. My father prowled the room in a predatory way, which made sense because that was exactly what he was: a predator. Someone who stood by and waited until prey walked by and then destroyed them over and over again. And I hated to say it, but my mother was the worst kind of prey—walking into the trap time and time again.

I crept down the stairs slowly on my tiptoes. I wasn't sure what possessed me other than the fact that something had to give. We were in a never-ending, fucked-up cycle of fear, hurt, and betrayal. It was time my father faced the truth, and what better person to spit it out than his ruined princess.

My mom caught my eye first, and she shook her head, her mouth set in a firm line. My father was too busy staring at the gun in her hands, trying to find a way to put her down before she put him down. His hands were in fists by his sides, his broad shoulders wide as he paced.

"I'll kill you before you kill me," he seethed, taking a step toward her.

I saw the flicker of fear on her face, that small show that she wasn't as confident as she wanted to be.

As soon as I said, "Dad," he jumped on her, and they both fell to the ground. I screamed, my hand rushing to cover my mouth as my mom tumbled to the floor, hitting her head on the table. Blood instantly seeped out from the wound, but she didn't give up. She withered underneath him as he laid on top of her, reaching for the gun.

My father was much bigger than her; he would win in the end.

Adrenaline flew through me, possessing me with the strength to run over to intervene, but my front door flung open, and Eric came rushing inside. His hair was messy, his face etched with worry. His shirt was bloody, and although his eye was bruised, he still appeared strong and ready.

"Who the fuck are you?" My father stood up as he snatched the gun away from my mom at the last second. *No!* She whimpered, holding her head while in the fetal position on the floor behind him. I think she was in and out of consciousness, too weak to stay fully present but too strong to fully let go. The gun was directed at Eric, and I stood in between the two of them as a barrier. His arms flew up as he shifted his gaze from me to my father.

"Put the gun down," Eric said calmly.

My father's eyes were wild with his rising temper. "I asked

who the fuck you are. Are you the one that raped my daughter? And fucked my wife, too?"

Eric still stood with his hands up while taking baby steps toward me. "I said put the gun down, sir. I didn't rape your daughter."

My heart was stuck in my throat. I stared at my father, focusing on how red his face was getting. "Daddy, stop."

He swung toward me, pointing the gun in my direction with his finger on the trigger. I yelped.

"Did he fucking rape you?"

"No!" I shouted, hearing car doors outside.

"This is all your mother's fault!" he yelled with more anger. The longer we stood in the room together, the angrier he got. Maybe he was embarrassed I was seeing him like this. Or maybe he was just so blinded by his own personal rage that he couldn't make sense of what he was doing.

The gun left me and was pointed at my mother. The way the nozzle pointed directly at her head was premeditated, and my father's eyes lit up like he was the happiest, with every ounce of control. "You deserve to die," he whispered as the door popped open. I didn't get a chance to see who it was because, instead, I ran and dove in front of my mom, and then the gun went off.

Turned out I was selfless, after all.

CHAPTER FORTY-EIGHT

ERIC

"MADELINE!" I yelled so loud my voice was hoarse. My heart flew out of my chest, and the pain was so severe that I looked down to see if I was the one who had gotten shot.

"Eric!" My father came into view as I began running forward.

Red. All I could see was red. Red blood coming from Madeline and her mother. Everything moved in slow motion. My father's face waving back and forth in front of mine, him pushing me backwards with all his might, sweat falling over his forehead. My mom slid into view, already on her knees in front of Madeline, putting her hands on her stomach to stop the bleeding.

Another gunshot sounded, and suddenly, the chaos was back. My mother screamed, dipping her head as she kept her hands steady on Madeline.

Madeline's father slowly fell to the ground, tumbling over like the twin towers, crumbling to his knees then hitting face first.

"Madeline!" I screamed, gaining the ability to push past my father. I landed on my knees in a pool of blood.

"Push down on her stomach, now. Keep the pressure." My mom was trying to stay calm, but she was panicked. She checked Madeline's mom's breathing because, at some point, she had checked out.

"Keep your eyes open, Madeline. Okay?" My mom was hovering over her face, smiling. "It's going to be okay."

Madeline was shaking underneath me; her blouse was soaked with blood. My hand was wet and sticky.

"Mom," I managed to choke out, feeling my soul rip in two.

"We gotta go to the hospital. We can't wait for an ambulance. Pick her up, and you run to the car as fast as you can. Put your hand back on her belly the second you get inside. I'm right behind you."

I did exactly as she said, flying through the house past my father who was on the phone with 911.

"Stay until the cops come," my mom yelled back to my father.

"Go!" he yelled.

This wasn't happening. This wasn't fucking happening.

"Eric, it hurts." Madeline's hand clenched onto my shirt, and I shushed her.

"I know, baby. I know. Don't talk. I'm right here."

My mom glanced back with blood all over her shirt and hands as she gripped the wheel. "Don't let her close her eyes, Eric. It's life or death."

An emptiness that I'd never experienced before clung to my bones like a deep cold as I pressed harder onto her stomach.

I stared down at Madeline's cold, clammy face. Her eyes were getting heavy, her breathing shallow. "Madeline," I barked. "Look at me, baby."

Her eyes fluttered as if she were trying to focus. She finally locked eyes on me, and I pressed harder onto her stomach. Her hand gripped my shirt again, which was good. That meant she still had some strength.

"Do you remember that time we watched a movie together through our bedroom windows?" I asked, trying so fucking hard to keep my composure.

Madeline swallowed roughly, her pretty, pale face wincing.

"We wrote notes back and forth and held them up during the commercials, commenting on everything we had watched so far." Her belly tightened underneath me, and she began gasping. *I will not fucking lose her.*

She was still staying locked on me, her hand still bundled in my shirt.

"Once you're better, we're gonna watch it again. I can't remember the name of it, but we'll watch it again."

I glanced ahead, and we were pulling up to the hospital. My mom was flying through the emergency area, our flashers indicating that *we* were the emergency.

"*Brink.*" Madeline's voice sounded far away. Weak. Too weak. "It was *Brink.*"

The car door opened, and I pushed us out, running after my mom who was already through the doors.

Things happened quickly. Madeline was torn out of my arms and thrusted into a stretcher. Her head fell to the side, rolling slightly as her eyes began to close. Blood was everywhere. They'd ripped her blouse in two, the buttons popping all over the floor. My mom was pressing on her wound now, running with the on-duty nurses.

"Gunshot to the abdomen. I haven't looked too much, afraid she'd bleed out, but I'm thinking pneumothorax. She'll need a thoracotomy with a chest tube placement."

Then, they all disappeared behind the swinging doors, and

I stood there, all alone, with Madeline's blood all over my hands.

"Eric!" Ollie and Christian came into view as I stood against a wall in the emergency area. A few nurses had recognized me as *Heather's son,* and soon, word got around about what had happened. They offered to help me clean up, giving encouraging words about Madeline. *Heather is the best trauma nurse we have. Everything will be okay. Do you need anything?*

What I fucking needed was to know what was going on.

"Dude, are you okay?" Ollie gripped the sides of my face, pulling my chin up to meet his gaze. "We followed you home. There are cops and ambulances everywhere. Your dad told us to come here to check on you. He said he'll be here soon."

I shook my head back and forth slowly. I was in a daze, like I was high but not the good kind of high. This was the kind of high that made you paranoid but also frozen in time.

"Eric," Christian came into view. "Talk to us. Is Madeline okay?"

"I don't know," I answered, my bloody hands hanging down by my side. I wasn't even sure how much time had passed since they took her from my arms.

"Talk to us," Ollie urged. "What can we do?"

I shook my head again. "I...I don't know."

"Eric," Christian's voice deepened. "What happened?"

I blinked once, trying to focus on anything other than my bloody hands. "Her father shot her."

"What?" Ollie yelled.

Even though my hands were dirty, I still brought them up and ran them through my hair, pulling on the ends. "He went to shoot her mom, but Madeline blocked her." I looked them both in the face. "He was abusive. Had been for a very long time. Whenever he'd come home, he'd hit Madeline's mom for stupid shit. But..." I could barely get the words out. This was partly my fault, and it was difficult to accept. "When everything at school went down, Headmaster Walton had called Madeline's dad and told him what was going on with Madeline. He must have shown up at their house, ready to fight, because when I walked in, Madeline's mom was already bleeding. There was broken glass on the floor, and Madeline was scared to fucking death. There was a gun. It happened so fast. She was too quick." Something tore inside my chest, and I quickly turned around and punched the wall behind me, my knuckles crumbling in agony.

I didn't care, though. Not a single bit.

Pure anguish went through me. It was maddening. I was lost. There was something tormenting about wanting to fix something that was completely out of your hands.

Arms wrapped around me; I wasn't sure whose until Christian said, "Your knuckles have had enough, Eric."

"If she fucking dies, Christian," I bit out, resting my head against the cool wall with his arms still around me. "I will never be able to look at myself in the mirror again. I should have protected her better."

"She's not going to die, Eric. It's fucking Madeline. She's too much of a fighter to die."

I fucking hoped so.

"Your dad is here," Ollie said.

Christian's arms dropped, and the moment I swung around, my father's frantic eyes found me, and he rushed forward. I stood back, unable to do anything but just keep myself standing. I wanted to fall onto the ground.

"Eric." His hands went around my biceps, and he squeezed hard. His eyes watered as he cupped the back of my head and brought it toward him in a hug. "It's going to be okay."

A soul-wrenching sob clawed out of my chest and ripped through the room like an earthquake. My father's hand tightened on my head as he kept my face down. *Fuck.*

"I'm here, son. It's okay."

It was funny how something so pressing in my life didn't seem all that big anymore. My hatred for my father was overshadowed by the fact that Madeline's life was hanging in the balance because of a mistake I made.

"What if she dies?" I asked, pulling myself back. I felt the moisture on my cheeks, but I made no move to wipe it.

"She won't." He was confident with his answer.

"How do you know?"

He gave me a look. "Because your mother is the best goddamn nurse there is. She won't let her die."

The sound of swinging doors tore us away from each other as my mom came tumbling out. She was still covered in blood, but she looked relieved to see us standing there. Her mask was pulled down as she gave me a sad smile. She wrapped her arms around me quickly before backing up and peering up into my face. "She's okay." She pushed my hair off my sweaty forehead. "The bullet missed the important stuff. Her lung did collapse, but we got the bullet out and fixed her up. She's in the ICU for now, but I think she's going to be okay, baby."

She was okay?

"God," I croaked, almost bending over to steady myself. "Are you sure?"

Her hazel eyes shined. "I'm sure." Then she looked over to my dad. "How is her mom?"

"They brought her in shortly after the police showed up. She was incoherent. They think she has a concussion. I stayed and gave them a run-down of what happened." He glanced away before shaking his head, coming to terms with something. He reached his hands out and pulled my mom into his chest, wrapping his arms around her small frame. His cheek rested over her hair, and he whispered, "I thought the second gunshot was headed for you."

"I did, too."

"Put things into perspective pretty fast for me."

She pulled away for a moment, a single tear rolling down her cheek and landing on the floor. "Me too."

He leaned in and kissed her forehead, and she closed her eyes.

In all my eighteen years of life, I didn't think I'd seen them express that much emotion in such few words. Something began to heal between them, and that was okay with me.

"Now"—my mother pushed away and gave me a look —"you need to go get cleaned up."

"I'm not leaving."

She came over and wiped my face free of something. "Do you really want Madeline to wake up and see you looking like that?" I glanced down to my blood-stained uniform and crusty hands. Her voice was hushed. "You look like a crime scene, Eric. Go shower. Then you can come right back. I'm not leaving her, okay?"

"You're staying?" I confirmed.

She nodded. "I'm going to stay and check in with her. It's not my shift, but I can pull some strings. I'm going to check on her mom too. I don't even know if anyone has filled her in."

My brow furrowed as my father began pulling me by the arm.

"Where is her dad?"

She glanced at my dad, confused, then back to me. "He's dead, Eric."

"Oh, shit," Ollie muttered.

"So..."

My father spoke this time. "The second gunshot was him shooting himself. He shot himself after he shot Madeline."

Oh, damn.

CHAPTER FORTY-NINE

MADELINE

I WAS FREEZING. So incredibly cold. My eyes stayed closed as I pulled the blanket up higher, but I was still cold. My eyes fluttered; the room was dark. Not pitch black, but it wasn't the normal glow of my bedroom light that I was used to. When I adjusted my eyes a few more times, I scanned the room and started to sit up before I felt a pain in my side.

A low whimper left me as I looked down and saw a white cotton blanket that I didn't recognize. I had on a blue...shirt? Gown?

I was in a hospital gown, and there was something hanging out of the side of my rib. My fingers found a tube that led to somewhere below.

Panic started to surface, a nearby monitor beeping loudly. The door swung open, and when I saw Heather's face, I was even more confused.

Was I dreaming?

"Madeline?" I swung my attention over to a chair tucked away in the corner of the room.

"Mom? What's wrong with your head?" My mom had a bandage wrapped around her forehead, sending her blonde locks in several different directions.

Then it hit me.

Eric fighting.

My dad.

Yelling.

The gun.

"Oh my God!" I gasped before I yelled out in pain.

"Lie back, sweetie." Heather was dressed in scrubs, looking her always-cheerful self. "Your lung collapsed, so you need to take it easy, okay?"

I lay back slowly, trying to take in everything that was being thrown around in my head. I couldn't remember what was real and what I'd dreamt. Too many nightmares had occurred in my head over the last few months that I wasn't sure what was reality anymore.

"What happened?" I whispered, bouncing my gaze back and forth from my mom to Heather who was looking at monitors and writing something down.

"What do you remember?" my mom asked, coming to stand by the side of my bed. Her hand rested on mine, but it wasn't comforting. She was shaking.

"The gun," I answered quickly. The faster I knew the truth, the quicker the panic would be gone.

She nodded.

My stomach felt empty, but not in the way that told me I was hungry. It felt empty because there was something eating away at it. "Did he...?" *That couldn't be possible.* "Did he...?" I cleared my throat as I tried pulling my shoulders back to appear strong. "Did Dad shoot me?"

"Yes." Her head dropped. "Well, he was aiming for me, I was told, and you got in the way."

I shut my eyes before willing myself to ask the next question. My voice broke as I rushed the words out. "Did he kill himself?" I pushed away the visual, unable to truly come to terms with it.

"Yes."

Silence encased the room. Heather had slipped out at some point, leaving me alone with my mom. I wanted her back in here as a buffer. As a sort of comfort.

"Say something," she whispered. "Talk to me."

I shook my head, annoyed that my eyes were watering and irritated that I didn't know what exactly I was crying about. My father shooting me? Or himself? "I...I don't know how I feel."

She nodded as I blinked away the blurriness. "Me either."

I squeezed her hand back, unable to say anything because I was at a loss for words. There was too much to sort through and too much to take in. I was good at shoving things away, and I would likely be shoving this away, along with the visual of my father's face after he'd shot me, for quite a while.

"*Mom,*" Eric's voice sounded from behind the door, and I tried sitting up again. "*Please let me go in.*"

"Eric. She's talking with her mom; give her a second."

My mom caught my eye, and she gave me a sad smile. "That is one determined boy."

The door opened, and my mom backed away, giving my hand another squeeze. "We can talk later."

"Maddie." It was like he was reaching out and putting my heart back into my chest with one little nudge.

Eric ran in, bypassing my mom. He was wearing jeans and a t-shirt that was wrinkly. He was distraught, his dark eyes shadowed by whatever was going through his mind, which changed instantly when he got closer to me.

My lip was wobbly, and everything suddenly hurt. The second I locked onto him, I really let myself feel it all. Every-thing came rushing back to me, especially the look of agony on his face when he kept me from bleeding out in his mother's car. I remembered it all.

"Hey, hey, hey," he shushed, bending down and grabbing my face. His hands swiped my tears. "You're okay. You're fine."

I closed my eyes, holding back a cry.

"I'm here," he hushed, bending down and kissing the top of my head. "Tell me what you need."

"You," I barely managed to say.

He cupped my face and brought his forehead down to mine. "You've always had me, baby. Even when I pretended you didn't."

I hiccupped, and it burned my chest, but I stayed still, not wanting to leave his embrace. "Eric?"

"What?" he asked, still gazing down at me. I glanced away for a second before he brought my face back to his. "What is it? Do you need more pain medicine? Do you want me to get my mom?"

I winced, resting my head back on the pillow. "No." I let out a very shaky breath. "Do you know what I thought of right after..." I inhaled, ignoring the pain. "Right after I was...raped?"

His brow furrowed as he stayed silent, his hand still wrapped around my chin.

I answered quickly. "You."

"Me?"

I nodded again. "All I could think was how badly I wanted you to break down my front door and come to my room and save me from..." I looked away, unable to look him in the eye. "Everything. My dad. The man who snuck into my room. Myself. All I wanted was you." I began to ramble nervously. "Which is so stupid because we hadn't talked in years, not really, and it sounds so obsessive and pathetic."

Eric's finger reached up, and he placed it over my lips to

silence me. He traced his thumb around them before bending down and kissing me softly on the forehead again. "I will *always* be here to save you. I will always protect you, even though you are strong enough to protect yourself." His gray eyes deepened. "Do you hear me?"

I nodded, a single tear wetting my cheek. Eric swiped it before going over and grabbing the chair that my mom was sitting in and pulling it up to the edge of the bed. He sat down, grabbed a hold of my hand, and said, "Sleep, baby. I'll even protect you from the nightmares, okay?"

"I know you will," I whispered, squeezing his hand before drifting back asleep.

"Okay, one more step," Eric whispered into my ear. I smiled as I took one final step, and I felt him pushing me to my bedroom from behind.

"I can open my eyes now," I sighed. "I just didn't want to see where..." I couldn't finish my sentence, not wanting to bring up anything dealing with what had happened a week prior in my dining room.

He nipped my ear, his hand still covering my eyes. "Nope. I have a surprise."

My palm touched his wrist. "A surprise?"

"Mmhm."

I heard the opening of my bedroom door, and the carpet was soft underneath my feet.

"Okay, you can open them." Eric's hands were gone, and my eyes flew open.

"Oh my God." I giggled as my jaw fell. "When did you do this? When did you have time?"

Eric hasn't left my side. Right after I was discharged from

the hospital, I had my first therapy session. Eric sat in the waiting room the entire time as I awkwardly got to know my therapist and as we just barely touched base on everything that had occurred with my father and the rape.

Eric walked farther into my room, smacking one of the balloons—that took up my entire bedroom—out of the way before he smirked. "I didn't do this."

"Okay..." I said hesitantly. "Then who did? My mom?"

"Read the note." He angled his head over to my desk. I slowly padded over, still trying to take it easy.

If Eric tries to take credit for this, he's lying. This was all us. Welcome home, Madeline. We hope you feel better soon. We will save a seat at the lunch table for you.

Xo. Hayley & Piper

(Christian and Ollie helped too, but they won't sign their names.)

"Don't move," Eric whispered. "Stay just like that."

"What?" I half-laughed before I heard a snapping sound from his phone.

Placing the note back on the desk, I placed my hand on my hip. "Did you just take my picture?"

"I did." He winked, his cheeks rising to show me a smile that I hadn't seen in a while. "You looked pretty, all smiley. It's very unlike you to smile."

I thought for a moment before he came up in front of me, tipping my head back with a single finger under my chin. "Don't do that. Don't go to that dark place. You're allowed to be happy, Madeline. It wasn't your fault."

I took the familiar feeling of guilt and shoved it in my pocket for later and looked out the window toward the driveway in between our houses. One thing my therapist said was that, in time, I would start to feel better. That I'd be able to come to terms with everything that happened, probably making my nightmares disappear too. But for now, I still felt...stuck. I just kept replaying my father taking the gun and shooting himself in the chest after he realized what he had done.

"My therapist said it was normal for me to feel guilty, but eventually, I would have to learn that it wasn't my fault." I looked into Eric's eyes, and I could tell he saw right through me. I *did* think it was my fault.

"We will never know why he did it. Maybe he knew it was the only way he would keep you safe. Or maybe he just wasn't in his right state of mind. Or maybe it was *him* who felt guilty."

I shrugged, putting my attention back to the window. "Maybe." I hated that I kept bringing it up. That I couldn't stop feeling so overwhelmed.

"Hey," he urged, gripping my shoulders lightly. "I love you."

The coldness was washed away by warmth. I smiled, just barely, but I did. My hands wrapped around the sides of Eric's face, and I brought his mouth down to mine. "I know. I love you, too."

His tongue tangled with mine, and he gently pushed my body up to his. A slight moan left my lips, and his stormy eyes narrowed as he pulled back. "Don't tempt me. We're not allowed to have sex. Not with a fresh wound."

I grinned. "I know. I just like teasing you." It was strange how easily I could go from feeling heavy to light in a matter of seconds.

Eric grunted, gently pulling me over to his side and wrapping an arm around me. We both gazed down to the driveway where his parents were standing, ironically, exactly like us. His dad had an arm draped over Heather's shoulder, and my mom was standing back with her arms crossed over her chest. They'd seemed to put the drama of the affair behind them. It was surprising, but Eric and I decided we weren't going to let ourselves get in the middle of it any longer.

I glanced over to the For Sale sign in my yard. "As happy as I am to be leaving this house and all the bad that's associated with it, I'm not really okay that we're not going to be neighbors anymore."

Eric glanced down at me, grinning. "Don't worry. You can't keep me away from you."

I smiled coyly. "What if I go to college in..." I thought for a moment. "Alaska?"

He turned back to look out the window. "Then I'll buy us matching parkas."

I laughed, picturing him in a parka, and he did too before walking us over to my bed and turning on the TV. "What are we watching?" I asked, trying to accept the fact that, although everything else in my life was crazy and unsettled, things with Eric were the opposite. He was my safe place. My normal.

Eric sat down, leaning back onto the pillows as I tried to get comfortable. He pushed the rest of the floating balloons out of the way before smiling coyly. "*Brink*."

And with that, I snuggled up beside him as best as I could with stitches plastered on my side, and we lay in my bed for the rest of the night.

EPILOGUE

MADELINE

"This is weird, right?" I ran my fingers through my hair, smoothing the ends underneath my graduation cap. "I feel nervous."

Hayley and Piper were standing just up ahead underneath one of the evergreen trees that lined the entrance of English Prep, with Ollie and Christian close by. They were waiting for me, and I was stalling.

"Baby." Eric swatted my hands out of the way. "Relax. You've been sitting at our lunch table for the last few months. Why is this any different?"

I glanced at the girls again. "Because now I'm about to be alone with them while you, Christian, and Ollie go to your side of the line." I pouted. "I don't have you as my anchor. My buffer."

Eric chuckled as he put his navy graduation cap on. His dark, unruly hair was sticking out from the sides. I reached up and pushed a dark lock away from his eye.

I sighed as my hand fell. "I just wish things were different.

I want to go in the past and take it all away. I don't even know how they can stand me after being so...bitchy."

Eric grew serious, his brows crowding his forehead, his thick mass of eyelashes blinking. "No regrets, Maddie." He cupped my waist, pulling me toward him by the scratchy material of my graduation gown. The sun was above our heads, the warm, near-summer glow shining down through the limbs of the trees surrounding us. "Our experiences mold us into who we're meant to be, baby. Even the bad."

A small smile crept on my lips before I reached up and kissed him feverishly. He squeezed my hips, swiping his tongue into my mouth. Happiness bloomed within, and butterflies rubbed their wings and sparked me into a state of bliss.

When he pulled away, breathless, and shook his head, he said, "Am I ever going to get tired of kissing you?"

God, I hoped not.

"Madeline! Get over here!" Piper called out, throwing her hands up. Her copper hair was sleek and straight as it laid over her shoulders. Hayley smiled from beside her, waving at us. The apples of her cheeks were bright with happiness.

Eric grabbed onto my hand, and we walked over to his—my?—group of friends. Eric and Ollie fist bumped, and he and Christian nodded.

"Group photo?" Piper beamed, pulling out her phone.

Our classmates were scattered around, the seniors with caps and gowns, the juniors and the rest of the underclassmen in their school uniforms.

Ollie whined. "I can't fucking believe I'm going to be here alone next year. I hate that you are in a grade above me."

Christian chuckled. "Sucks to be the stupid brother, huh?"

I smashed my lips as he glared. "That's not why I'm a year below, and you know it."

"There, there, baby." Piper patted his chest gently. "He's

just teasing. Just think, you're gonna be the king of English Prep next year."

Ollie rolled his eyes. "Can't wait. While you five are away at college, I'll be twiddling my thumbs with these losers."

We all laughed before Christian grabbed Piper's phone, and we huddled in for a picture. Eric kissed the side of my cheek before it was snapped, and I couldn't help my cheese.

"Okay, we gotta go get seated!" Hayley gave Christian a peck on his cheek, and she dragged Piper and me with her toward our section of the graduation ceremony.

Once we were seated, we all leaned forward and looked down the aisle, smiling at the boys. Ollie somehow managed to sit with the graduating class. How? I had no idea. He stuck out with his school uniform on next to Eric and Christian who were sporting their navy gowns.

Once I got settled into my seat, I crossed my legs and glanced to the stage. Headmaster Walton was at the podium, the sun high above his head with clouds dancing behind. My stomach twisted as I shifted my attention to the five chairs lined beside him. My hand came down onto Hayley's leg as I gulped.

The board members were here?

"He's not here," she whispered as Headmaster Walton began to speak about the year.

"He's not?" I asked before letting out a held breath.

She shook her head, her short brown hair grazing her shoulders. "Christian's dad had a word with Headmaster Walton."

My mouth fell open.

"And Eric's dad was there too." She paused as everyone applauded for something the headmaster had said. "And Ann."

"Who's Ann?"

Piper pulled herself forward so she could look past Hayley

at me. "Hayley's ex social worker slash adoptive—but not really—mom."

I sunk back into my seat, feeling completely surprised and overwhelmed with gratitude.

Hayley patted my hand before giving it a squeeze, and Piper dipped forward to smile again.

The rest of the ceremony passed quickly, and soon, my aisle was lining up to get our diplomas. Hayley turned around before her name was called. "It's funny," she laughed. "I honestly wasn't sure I'd make it out of this school alive."

Piper laughed from beside me.

"You know what?" I said, ready to be real with them for the first time in my entire life. "Neither did I."

Hayley's name was called, but before she shook the headmaster's hand, she ran down the steps and gave Piper and me a hug. We all laughed and somehow formed a bond that I didn't think was possible.

"Here's to the next stage of our lives, babes," Piper said before letting Hayley go.

I glanced to Eric, and all three boys were beaming. Eric gave me a wink, and I knew right then that high school may not have been the best time of my life like everyone said, but it *did* have some of the best moments, and that was good enough.

The End

AFTERWORD

Wow. I can't believe the English Prep series is over. These books mean a lot to me. There is a big part of me in each and every book and I can honestly say this series has changed my career (in a good way)! This series clicked with me. These stories came from my soul, each and every word flowed out of me (almost) effortlessly. That doesn't mean they were easy to write, not even a little bit, *but* they felt right. I have found my *home* in this series and I just want to say an extra thank you to everyone who has read the English Prep series and who has also fallen in love with these characters. I appreciate all of your support so SO much.

xoxo.

SJ

ALSO BY SJ SYLVIS

English Prep Series
All the Little Lies

All the Little Secrets

All the Little Truths

St. Mary's Series
Good Girls Never Rise

Bad Boys Never Fall

Standalones
Three Summers

Yours Truly, Cammie

Chasing Ivy

Falling for Fallon

Truth

ACKNOWLEDGMENTS

Joe & our two sweet babes, you three will always be the first people I mention here because I love you more than anything in the world. Thanks for being my happiness. <3

To the rest of my family, thank you for always supporting me and buying my books, even if you don't read them (please do not read these, or I will never ever look you in the face again). I love you!

My girl gang (Tay & Kristen), I'd be lost without you and your (almost) daily tiktok dances. You two are my besties and I'm pretty sure we knew each other in a different life. Ilysm!

Laura, thank you for always sending me comforting words and for being the best friend ever! I am SO thankful we are in this together. Love you!

To my betas (Megan, Andrea, & Becca), thank you for beta reading Eric and Madeline and helping me make this story perfect!! You are gems.

To my editor, Jenn. Thank you for always making my work shine! I am SO thankful for you!

Dana, where would I be without our daily voice messages?

Thank you for being such a good friend and for helping me work through any plot holes! Love you!

Cass, you're pretty much my sister too since Tay and I are twins but anyway, thanks for proofing for me. <3

Emily—one of the smartest people I know—thank you for teaching me what a pneumothorax/thoracotomy is. Love you forever!

To my readers, bloggers, etc. THANK YOU for sticking with me through this journey. Thank you for supporting me, for reading my stories, and for loving my English Prep gang as much as I do. I love you!!

Xoxo,

SJ

ABOUT THE AUTHOR

S.J. Sylvis is a romance author who is best known for her angsty new adult romances and romantic comedies. She currently resides in North Carolina with her husband, two small kiddos, and dog. She is obsessed with coffee, becomes easily attached to fictional characters, and spends most of her evenings buried in a book!

www.sjsylvis.com

Printed in Great Britain
by Amazon